THE LOVE OF THREE GIRLS

A LOST NOVEL OF NELLIE BLY

The Love of Three Girls
by Nellie Bly

Originally published in the New York Family Story Paper

1893

Transcribed and edited by David Blixt

Cover by Cathy Hunter

ISBN-13: 978-1944540784

Published by Sordelet Ink
www.sordeletink.com

THE LOVE OF THREE GIRLS

THE RIVALRY BETWEEN AN HEIRESS, A BEAUTY, AND A FACTORY GIRL.

A FASCINATING STORY OF HIGH AND LOW LIFE.

A LOST NOVEL OF
NELLIE BLY

INTRODUCTION BY DAVID BLIXT

Books by Nellie Bly

Ten Days in a Mad-House
Six Months In Mexico
Nellie Bly's Book: Around the World in 72 Days

the Lost Novels

the Mystery of Central Park
Eva the Adventuress
New York by Night
Alta Lynn, M.D.
Wayne's Faithful Sweetheart
Little Luckie
Dolly the Coquette
In Love With a Stranger
the Love of Three Girls
Little Penny, Child of the Streets
Pretty Merribelle
Twins & Rivals

David Blixt's Bly Novels

What Girls Are Good For
Charity Girl
Clever Girl

VISIT WWW.SORDELETINK.COM

FOR ANNA

CONTENTS

THE LOST NOVELS OF NELLIE BLY
INTRODUCTION BY DAVID BLIXT

It was the first day of December, 2019, and like Alice, I was down a rabbit hole.

I was working on a short-story follow-up to *What Girls Are Good For*, my 2018 novel following the early career of groundbreaking undercover reporter Nellie Bly. My new story took place immediately after the exposé that made her a household name, her ten days spent as an inmate in the insane asylum on Blackwell's Island.

That experience had been turned into a book, *Ten Days In A Mad-House*, a terrific and horrifying read that remains hugely influential to this day (the nurses she describes were evidently the basis for Nurse Ratched in Ken Kesey's *One Flew Over The Cuckoo's Nest*). In order to catch up my readers on where the events of the story fell, I wanted to kick off with Bly receiving an offer from a publisher for that very book.

Trouble was, I had no idea how much money she was offered.

Fortunately, I knew the name of the original publisher, as well as the date of publication. But lacking a *Publisher's Weekly* to report book deals in 1887, I started following the paper trail of the publisher himself. I thought I might find a contract with another author, or perhaps some old balance sheets.

Instead I found something unexpected.

The lost novels of Nellie Bly.

Bly's publisher was Norman L. Munro, brother of famed publisher George Munro. George was one of the pioneers of the Victorian-era wave of cheap books for the masses. Ten, fifteen, and twenty-five cent novels were gobbled up by a hungry audience, most of them women, and George Munro made a fortune feeding their appetite for every kind of story.

The brothers Munro were born and raised in Nova Scotia. After college, George moved to New York City and worked at the American News Company until he amassed enough capital to launch his own weekly publication, *The Fireside Companion*, in 1867. It was a smash, and the foundation of an international publishing empire.

Tagging along, Norman worked for his older brother until 1873, when he decided to go it alone and launched his own rival weekly, the *New York Family Story Paper*. Direct competition caused a rift between the siblings, who are said to have never spoken to each other again except through lawyers (when George began publishing cheap versions of classic books, Norman followed suit, naming his imprint, "Munro's Library." George filed a lawsuit over use of the family name, but the courts ruled for Norman, claiming he had as much right to the name Munro as George did).

While Norman never had the literary heft of his brother's imprint, he found success publishing "Irish" novels, "Indian" novels, romance novels, what have you. He published the Allan Quatermain adventures, and 25 short novels based on the life of French highwayman Claude Duval. In 1883 he launched another weekly, *Old Cap. Collier Library*, featuring detective stories with a rotating roster of main characters.

Then, in 1888, Norman had an instant bestseller in Nellie Bly's *Ten Days In A Mad-House*. He immediately asked her for another, and released *Six Months In Mexico* that same year, reprinting the articles Bly had written as the *Pittsburg Dispatch*'s foreign correspondent in Mexico. He clearly was making a fortune on Nellie Bly, reporter.

But Bly had other ambitions. She viewed reporting as a temporary job, a launching point for a broader literary career.

She wanted to be a novelist.

Bly spent the three years after her cannon-blast debut in the pages of the *New York World* trying to top herself. She exposed the 'King of the Lobby' in Albany, outed a serial procurer of girls in Central Park, and interviewed the most notorious would-be murderess of the day. She kept putting herself in more and more peril in order to get a story. Why? Because the titillation of 'a girl in danger' sold papers—especially during the height of Ripper hysteria in London.

She reached the zenith of her fame by racing around the world in an attempt to best the fictional record of Jules Verne's character Phileas Fogg from *Around The World In Eighty Days*. She even got to meet Verne during her trip.

Bly was not alone in the phenomenon of "stunt girls," but thanks to that three-month race around the globe, she was by far the most famous. There were board games and trading cards based on her trip. Her face was known everywhere, and her ulster coat and cap were iconic.

But for Bly, stunt reporting had taken a toll. She'd begun to suffer terrible headaches. Stories that once would have fired her heart now left her cold. Celebrated and famous after her seventy-two-day girdling of the globe, she felt she had reached the peak of what newspaper reporting could offer her.

So when Norman Munro offered Bly a job writing for the *New York Family Story Paper*, she leapt at it. It's easy to understand why. Munro was offering her $40,000 over three years. Even for a star reporter, the most she could have been earning at the *World* was $5,000 a year. Munro's offer must have seemed a fortune.

Yet before signing she cleverly insisted her contract allow her to return to reporting without giving up her new career. As she wrote to her friend Erasmus Wilson in August, 1890:

> *I sent you a newspaper the other day containing a notice of the very good contract I have made with Mr. Munro. It allows me to do reporting work. I had made up my mind never to work for a newspaper again but I can do serial stories for Mr. Munro and never go out of my own home. I am busy on one now entitled "New York by Night." You know all the great English novelists began in this way, so I hope. The woman who wrote "Bootles Baby" which has sold more than 500,000 copies and has been dramatized and played in every city in Europe and America has always been a writer for such story papers. And then Mrs. Burnett wrote for The Ledger until she made a hit as a novelist, so I feel encouraged.*

Clearly Bly had high hopes for her literary career. Sadly, to that point, her record for fiction did not seem so very bright. Her first novel, *The Mystery of Central Park*, had been published a year earlier, first serially in the pages of the *World*, then in book form. The story was a murder-mystery loosely based on her 1888 exposé "Infamy of the Park."

While not nearly at the level of, say, Conan Doyle's recently-published *A Study In Scarlet*, Bly's short novel made use of her intimate knowledge of New York, and contained the same massive end-of-novel confession that Conan Doyle employed in his first two Sherlock Holmes novels. What's most fascinating about it are the links to both her own reporting and her own life (she berates a thinly-veiled version of her former beau, James Stetson Metcalfe, for being "brutal and unkind").

If Bly had been hoping to make a splash in this new career, alas, it was not to be. Of the four books released in Bly's name between 1888 and 1890, her one work of fiction was her least regarded. At the time, reviews of the novel were more reviews of Bly herself. A typical example:

> As a reporter, Bly has done much of the cleverest and most enterprising work known to the modern newspaper, and has a world-wide fame for sagacity, courage and spirited description of adventure. Her novel, we need not say, is bright, sparkling, and entertaining. (*Rochester Democrat and Chronicle, October 21, 1889*)

> "The Mystery of Central Park" is a well-written story, with a finely conceived plot. The story is told in "Nellie Bly's" own versatile way, and from the first to the last page holds the reader's attention. As a picture of the inside life of the great Metropolis, it should rank high. (*Indiana Democrat, October 31, 1889*)

Another contemporary review describes the novel as being "written in that sprightly style that characterizes her reporting and is rather better than the ordinary novel of this class." (*Philadelphia Enquirer, October 26, 1889*).

Talk about damning with faint praise.

Today *The Mystery of Central Park* is ridiculed for its stilted style, thin characters, and rather haphazard plot. Talking to Bly historians, I find everyone tends to shrug off her novels as an ill-fated endeavor, a bump on the road of her true career, reporting. Fair enough.

What strikes me about that first novel, though, is the story of the murder itself: an innocent girl becomes the kept woman of an unscrupulous and ambitious man. When he tires of her, rather than marry her as he promised, he murders her and leaves her body propped on a bench in Central Park.

While Bly did not yet have mastery of the art form, she was still Nellie Bly. She was still motivated by injustices against women.

She was still angry.

It was Bly's anger that first appealed to the writer in me. Oh, I'd heard about her madhouse stay, and her race around the world. But it was only when I discovered how she got her first reporting job that I became captivated by her.

Reading an article entitled "What Girls Are Good For," twenty-year-old Elizabeth Cochrane was so angry at the premise—that women belonged at home, not in the workplace—that she penned a letter of protest to the *Pittsburg Dispatch*. We don't know what was in that letter, but it got her an interview, and eventually a job as a reporter. As women did not, as a rule, write under their own names, she was saddled with the *nom-de-plume* "Nellie Bly."

The day I read that story, I put aside all my other writing and for two years focused on Bly, getting to know her writing, her character, her contradictions, her charm, and her passion. It resulted in a novel, but I was well aware that Ms. Bly had not finished with me. So I pressed on to write the next part of her story.

Which brings us back to the Munro rabbit hole, hunting for what Bly was paid for her madhouse book.

I discovered that there was only one known issue of Munro's *New York Family Story Paper* containing part of a Nellie Bly novel—two chapters of something called *Eva The Adventuress*. That was one of only two titles Bly was known to have written. The other title, gleaned from that 1890 letter to Wilson, was *New York By Night*. Outside of those two, we knew nothing about Bly's fiction career writing for Munro's paper.

On my hunt for her remuneration, I followed links and read extracts about both brothers. In one biography I found a reference to another of Norman's publications, the *London Story Paper*. Evidently the New York edition was such a success that Norman created a mirror version of the paper across the pond, literally reproducing the New York edition six months later with no changes to the typesetting (which is why you find Christmas poems published in July).

Idly, I started hunting. At once I found searchable records of the *London Story Paper* at NewspaperArchive.com. So, buying a subscription, I plugged in the name "Nellie Bly" and hit return.

The results generated within seconds. Disbelieving, I stared at the screen.

There they were. The lost novels of Nellie Bly.

It took me hours that first day, collecting all the titles and putting them in order. When I was finished, I found I had eleven novels in all. More novels than any Bly historian had ever imagined she'd written.

The trouble was, half of the pages were completely illegible. Were the scans bad? Or did the original microfilm contain bad copies? It was near impossible to find out, as I quickly discovered there were only three library copies of the original microfilm in the entire world. One in London, one in Sydney, and one in Toronto.

So, in the break between Christmas and New Year's 2019, I drove to Toronto and spent a frantic day at the University of Toronto library. Yes, it was the original microfilm that was so faded. I discovered, however, that by zooming in close on the microfilm, I could get better resolution. Good enough to decipher every word. I took screenshots of each close-up and loaded them on a jump drive.

I walked out of the library blinking and aching, but certain I now had every word of Bly's lost novels. But what to do with them?

I approached a few agents, a few publishers. I was repeatedly told there was no interest for my discovery. This agreed with my attempts to sell my Nellie Bly novel two years earlier. I was told my novel about her life lacked "a hook." It was suggested to me that I make her a detective, or a vampire, or secretly a man (I kid you not).

So I enlisted several friends to help me transcribe these novels and determined to release them myself. You hold the fruits of our labor.

☙❧

Thanks to this discovery, there's a small but significant change in our understanding of Bly's timeline. Before now, we only knew of four Bly books: three based on her reporting, and her lone novel. What we didn't know was that during 1889 she'd written another novel as well.

Eva The Adventuress is a bizarre yet gripping tale of a red-headed vixen wronged by everyone and eager for revenge. With her signature move of stabbing men in the chest but failing to kill them, Eva Scarlett is clearly based on the real-life, red-haired aspiring-murderess Eva Hamilton.

Nellie Bly interviewed Eva Hamilton in prison in early October, 1889. Bly must have been truly inspired, for she couldn't have had more than a month to finish her novel based on the fiery Eva. On November 14th Bly set off on her race around the world, and *Eva The Adventuress* had to have been complete before she left.

Since the race itself came as a surprise—she'd been pushing for over a year to make the trip, but the *World*'s editors only agreed a few days before she departed—Bly had probably been trying to shop the novel in the days before she left. But after the resounding thud *The Mystery Of Central Park* had created, Munro might've been wary of publishing it.

Things undoubtedly changed once the race had begun. Suddenly Bly's name was everywhere, blazoned across newspapers around the world. It was the kind of free advertising Munro would have been a fool not to utilize. Thus *Eva The Adventuress* started to run just before Christmas, on December 22, 1889, with the headline: *By Nellie Bly, Who is now attempting to make the circuit of the world in seventy-five days.*

We have no exact sales figures, but based on the huge jump in circulation of the *World*, and the incredible timeliness of both Nellie Bly and Eva Hamilton, the two most notorious women in New York, one can only imagine the bounty Munro reaped. Munro himself said that her story had increased circulation of the *Family Story Paper* by 50,000. He later claimed she had doubled his circulation. Munro's gambit had paid off.

It paid off for Bly, too. Finished, as she thought, with reporting, she parlayed her fame to gain a regular contract with Munro. Perhaps she told him she'd let him have the book about her trip if he put her on salary. However it happened, she had that amazing contract, being paid better than most men in either the reporting or the literary world. $40,000 over three years, to follow her dream.

Thus, from 1890 to 1895, Bly wrote serialized weekly novels in the pages of Munro's paper. Some are silly. Some are genuinely terrific. All of them are very much in line with the gothic pulp romances and mysteries of the era, filled with melodrama and cliffhanger endings.

Even more interesting are the number of themes and stories she resurrects, not just from her reporting days, but also from her own life. Again and again Blackwell's Island is referenced, and factory girls. Again and again, orphans figure prominently (though her mother still lived, Bly often referred to herself as an orphan. Her first published work for the *Dispatch* had been under the pen name "Lonely Orphan Girl").

And again and again she has a woman contemplate, or even attempt, suicide by throwing herself into the river. Because as she wrote these novels, Bly herself was in the midst of a severe depression, hardly able to leave her bed.

In 1889 she'd reported consulting seven doctors about her crippling headaches, to no avail. If she had hoped quitting the *World* would cure them, she was disappointed. Then in late 1890 she suffered a sprained or broken leg. Writing to Wilson in January, 1891, Bly reveals she is bedridden, and feeling hopeless:

> *I would have answered your letter at once but I was trying to catch up with my work and it's so tiresome writing in bed that I (am) soon played out.*

> *I am glad, dear Q, that you always hope for the best. Life cannot be entirely cheerless while hope remains. It is a year since I have entertained such a feeling and, strange to say, I have not the least conception why I am, or should be, thus.*

Two months later, in another letter to Wilson, she addresses her depression directly:

> *I received your kind note some time ago and meant to answer it at once but I suddenly became a victim of the most frightful*

depression that ever beset mortal (sic). *You can imagine how severe it is when I tell you that I have not done a stroke of work for four months. The doctor says it is my blood that is responsible for this languor and nervousness, still I am growing fat.*

Apparently reporting was her cure. After three years away, Bly returned to the pages of the *World* in November of 1893, picking up as if she'd never stopped. Munro would continue to publish her novels through June 1895, though he himself soon sold the business.

While her nonfiction books remained bestsellers, the eleven novels she'd written were never collected or reprinted. She seems to have given up on being a great novelist. After two more years as a reporter, she married a millionaire and settled into a life of leisure that would last nearly two decades, until lawsuits, poverty, and World War I forced her out of retirement and back to reporting. She died in 1922, writing and crusading to the very end.

Nellie Bly is rightly remembered for her reporting work, her early feminism, and her part in the rise of "stunt" journalism. She was also a canny industrialist, a generous employer, a devoted patron to many causes, a tireless fighter for the oppressed and dispossessed.

She was also a novelist.

Above all else, what I love about these books is the window they provide us into Bly's mind. Finding them has opened up a wealth of new insights into the clever, crusading, contradictory character that was Nellie Bly. I'm delighted to be able to share them.

I never did find out what she made from that first book, though.

I have made some editorial changes to Bly's work to ease modern reading, mostly consisting of removing extraneous commas before adverbs. I have occasionally merged paragraphs where the layout artist separated the same set of thoughts to fill space on the page. Sometimes I have changed an unharmonious verb tense—quite often when Bly is particularly excited about a scene she will lapse into present rather than past tense. If I thought this was conscious on her part, I would have left it as written. But it seems haphazard and accidental, the thing any editor would have picked up.

However, I have not altered a single particle of her stories themselves. Which leads to this caveat: these are products of their time. While certainly enlightened for her era, Bly engages in all the ethnic, cultural, and racial stereotypes of Victorian America. She pens descriptions and employs dialects for certain characters that are clearly offensive. Please read with care for yourself and forgiveness for her.

To that end, I have omitted one novel from this collection. In her seventh novel, *Dolly The Coquette*, Bly employed racial stereotypes all too common to her era. In particular she exploits at great length the racist trope of the Black "Mammy," a formerly enslaved woman devoted to a young white Southern girl (a trope Margaret Mitchell would make infamous in *Gone With The Wind*). In an age when we are still, as a culture, attempting to break free from exactly these hurtful and offensive racist tropes, I feel it would be irresponsible to publish it. While a possible curiosity to scholars, *Dolly* has no business being marketed as entertainment to the wider reading public. Like Disney's *Song Of The South*, it should remain in the vault as a product of a less progressive time.

It is important also to remember that these were serialized novels. I have left intact all of the insane cliffhangers Bly crafted for her readers, who normally got around three chapters per week. Therefore the melodrama is high to start, then lulls, then peaks, and so on. If it feels she's spinning her wheels, she's waiting for that next cliffhanger.

I want to draw attention to one of Bly's true talents—naming her characters. From Ruby Sharpe to Dimple Darlington, from Eva Scarlett to Amor Escandon, I truly love the names she invents.

For each volume I have added an afterword containing the articles from her time as a reporter that seemingly inspired part or all of each novel, from paper-box and shoe factories to Eva Hamilton and the "Infamy of the Park." The story is preceeded by a biography of Bly that ran in the *London Story Paper*. I have also included selections of the art that accompanied the early chapters of these stories.

I owe several people a world of thanks, most especially Judith West and Robert Kauzlaric, who are more involved in my writing career at times than they could ever have anticipated. Thanks, too, to Sarah Ann Leahy, Syed Asad Nawazish, Bharati Mohapatra, Eric Eilersen, Lauren Grace Thompson, Liz Wiley, Eryn O'Sullivan, Hope Newhouse, Tanya Dougherty, Barbara Figgins, Heidi Armbruster, Ian Geers, Wendy

Huber, Mikaila Publes, and my mother, Jill Blixt.

Huge gratitude as well to Brooke Kroeger and Matthew Goodman, whose books about Bly remain the gold standard.

As ever, I could not attack my keyboard each day without the love and support of Janice, Dash, and Eva. I love you.

That's enough from me. I hope you enjoy this, the eighth lost novel of Nellie Bly, starring Christmas Cherry, Amor Escandron, and Lillian Day, the heroines of *The Love Of Three Girls*.

— David Blixt
Chicago, 2021

Nellie Bly

NELLIE BLY

Nellie Bly is a descendant on her father's side of Lord Cochrane, the famous English admiral, and is closely connected with the present family, Lord and Lady Cochrane, at whose home Queen Victoria's daughter, the Princess Beatrice and her husband spent their honeymoon. In some characteristics Nellie Bly is said to closely resemble Lord Cochrane, who was noted for his deeds of daring, and who was never happy unless engaged in some exciting affair. Nellie Bly's great-grandfather Cochrane was one of a number of men who wrote a Declaration of Independence in Maryland near the South Mountains a long time before the historic Declaration of Independence was delivered to the world by our Revolutionary fathers. Her great-grandfather, on her mother's side, was a man of wealth, owning at one time almost all of Somerset Co., Pa. His name was Kennedy, and his wife was a nobleman's daughter. They eloped and fled to America. He was an officer, as were his two sons, in the Revolutionary War. Afterward he was sheriff of Somerset Co. repeatedly until old age compelled him to decline the office when then was considered one of power and importance. One of his sons, Thomas Kennedy, Nellie Bly's great-uncle, made a flying trip around the world, starting from and returning to New York, where his wife, a New York woman by birth, awaited his arrival. It took him three years to make the trip, and he returned in shattered health. He at once set about to write the history of his trip, but his health became so bad that he had to give up his task, and he was taken to his old home in Somerset, Pa., where he shortly died, a victim of consumption. He was buried there with the honors of war. Nellie Bly's father was a man of considerable wealth. He served for many years as judge of Armstrong Co., Pa. He lived on a large estate, where he raised cattle and had flour mills. The place took his name. It is called Cochrane's Mills. There Nellie Bly was born.

Being in reduced circumstances, owing to some family complications, after her father's death, and longing for excitement, she engaged to do special work for a Pittsburgh Sunday newspaper. She went for them to Mexico, where she remained six months, sending back weekly letters. After her return she longed for broader fields, and so came to New York. The story of her attempt to make a place for herself, or to find an opening, is a long one of disappointment, until at last she made a list of a number of daring and original ideas, which were submitted to a prominent editor. They were accepted, and she went to work.

Her first achievement was the exposure of the Blackwell's Island Insane Asylum, in which she spent ten days, and two days in the Bellevue Insane Asylum. The story created a great sensation, and she was called before the grand jury. An investigation was made, and her story proved true, so the grand jury recommended the changes she suggested, such as women physicians to superintend the bathing of the female insane inmates, better food and better clothing. On the strength of the story $3,000,000 a year increased appropriation was made for the benefit of the asylum.

Her next work of state interest was the story of her exposure of Ed Phelps, who was said to be the king of the Albany Lobby. For publishing this story she was summoned before an investigating committee, this time at Albany.

These two things alone made Nellie Bly's name known in other countries as well as this, and English and French journalists constantly noticed her work.

After three years' work on a New York paper she conceived the idea of making a trip around the world in less time than had been done by Phileas Fogg, the fictitious hero of Jules Verne's famous novel; but when she first planned the trip to do it in 58 days, it was not met with favor by her editor. When she did go, almost a year later, it was impossible to make close connections but she, however, was the first person to make an actual record, which was 72 days. On her return she was greeted by ovations all the way from San Francisco to New York such as were never granted the most illustrious persons of our country. Thousands of people fought for glimpses of her at the stations, and no President was ever greeted by as large crowds as welcomed her at Jersey City and New York.

Since then she has spent her time lecturing and writing a book describing her experience while flying around the world. Nellie Bly has received letters from all parts of the world, in all languages, congratulating her on her successful journey, and begging autographs. Papers in every country, even Japanese and Chinese, published accounts of her novel undertaking.

Nellie Bly at an early age already showed great literary ability in verse as well as in prose, and many poems were contributed by her to the Pittsburgh and New York papers. She has, so far, written two novels—"The Mystery of Central Park" and "Eva, the Adventuress"—the latter published some time ago in THE LONDON STORY PAPER. Her latest story—"New York By Night"—which will begin in two weeks, bids fair to be one of the greatest successes of her life. She has stopped all newspaper writing, and is under contract, at a large sum, to contribute exclusively to the columns of THE LONDON STORY PAPER.

Her portrait published herewith is an excellent likeness. Nellie Bly is unmarried, and resides with her mother.

London—March 28th, 1891

EDITOR'S NOTE: The description of Bly's professional career is basically accurate, though the refusal to name the paper that made her famous is perplexing.

As with much published about Bly's personal life, however, there is as much fiction as fact here. There is no evidence linking her family to British aristocracy, nor to any signers of any Declarations of Independence or Revolutionary War soldiers. This does not mean these facts should be entirely disregarded. The story about her great-uncle, for example, is entirely true.

The Love of Three Girls:
OR,
THE RIVALRY BETWEEN AN HEIRESS, A BEAUTY AND A FACTORY GIRL.

A Fascinating Story of High and Low Life.

By NELLIE BLY,

Author of "In Love With a Stranger," "Eva Lynn, M. D.," "Wagner's Faithful Sweetheart," "Little Luckie," "New York by Night," "Dolley Good, the Coquette," Etc., Etc.

[This Story will not be Published in Book Form.]

Two tiny white hands were thrown up helplessly, and, with a prayer for aid in his heart, the young man sprung to the girl's rescue.

THE LOVE OF THREE GIRLS

THE RIVALRY BETWEEN AN HEIRESS, A BEAUTY, AND A FACTORY GIRL.

A FASCINATING STORY OF HIGH AND LOW LIFE.

PRELUDE

ONE CHRISTMAS MORNING.

IT WAS STILL WITHIN AN hour of dawn on Christmas morning when an officer, covered with mantle of downy snow, entered police headquarters.

The few sleepy men that sat around, impatiently awaiting their hour of relief, looked lazily at the new-comer, who brought with him an air of freshness.

He carried a large basket on his arm.

"Some drunk lost his Christmas dinner," hazarded one of the men with drowsy humor.

"Somebody's been givin' him a Christmas gift," laughed another.

To these sallies the officer made no reply. He walked up to the desk, and placed the basket before the sergeant, who grumbled wearily:

"What have you there?"

The officer knocked the snow from his helmet, and with a tinge of pity in his rough voice, replied:

"A baby!"

"A baby, eh?" repeated the sergeant, placing his pen behind his ear, and leaning forward to look into the basket.

"Told you Tom had a Christmas present," laughed one of the officers, who, together with his companions, had come forward to have a look at the strange contents of the market-basket.

"Where did you get it?" inquired the sergeant.

"On a stoop in Cherry Street," was the grave answer. "There was no one in sight, so I brought it here without delay."

"Take it up to the matron and report if she finds any name or mark on it," was the careless command; and, unmindful of his co-workers' jokes, the officer picked up the basket and departed as suddenly as he had appeared.

The matron in the rooms at the top of the building answered the officer's ring almost directly.

"Bless my heart! Are you bringing me a Christmas gift?" she asked cheerily.

"One that nobody wanted!"—sorrowfully—"I found it in Cherry Street."

"Poor little unfortunate!"—with a sigh. "Give it to me and come right in, officer. May Heaven punish the heartless wretches who cast off innocent and helpless babes in this way."

In a few moments the sleeping babe was lifted from the basket, and examined minutely by the good-hearted matron.

"Bless its little heart," she said, as she sat before the open grate with the child across her knee. "It is a little girl, officer, more's the pity, and there is not a line or mark anywhere about it."

The officer stepped forward, and stood gazing down at the sleeping infant.

"It seems to be well dressed," he observed quietly.

"That it is," acknowledged the city's mother. "I have never had a baby with such costly clothes on before. Why, look at this cloak! It is as soft as down. Some rich girl's child, I suppose. Poor little dear! Better for it if you had left it out to die of the cold."

"But that is not lawful, matron."

"I know it's not!"—shortly. "But I know so well the fate of these poor little waifs, I always thank God when one dies, and small chance they get to live on the Island, I can tell you."

"This one looks healthy, don't you think?"

"My, yes! It's a beautiful big girl, only a few hours old, too. How can people be so heartless? It came like a Christmas gift from Heaven, and they cast it into the streets to die. Ah, bless my soul! I always grieve when a little girl is found. It's so much harder on girls, you know, to be nameless and homeless."

"So it is," agreed the officer, thinking of his own ewe lamb at home. "Let's give her a Christmas gift, the most valuable one in the world—a name."

"Bless your heart, of course she must have a name! You found her and you have the right to name her."

"And she was found on Christmas morning, born on Christmas, too, you say. Why not call her Christmas?"

"Lovely!" exclaimed the matron. "But she must have another name."

"I don't know what the other shall be unless we give her the name of the street I found her in—Cherry Street."

"Christmas Cherry!" laughed the matron softly. "I've never heard of such a thing."

"You see them in the fine shops on Broadway sometimes, and I tell you they cost money at Christmas time, they are so precious."

"And so is she, in the sight of Heaven," solemnly affirmed the matron. "Christmas Cherry she shall be, and may God in His mercy bless her."

The officer stooped and gently touched the tiny, clinched fist. A baby girl, nameless, forsaken. Alas, that such heartless monsters as her parents existed!

"Keep her as long as you can, matron," he said, as he rose to go.

"I must obey the rules and send her to the Island at the proper time," she replied, "but so long as she is here I shall give her the best of care."

"Good-bye, Christmas Cherry," he said; and then he tiptoed out of the room, leaving the matron sitting before the fire with the little waif on her knee.

At the same hour that this event was transpiring at police headquarters, one not unlike it was taking place in a mansion not many miles from Philadelphia.

It was the palace of the wealthy Cuban, Ricardo Escandon.

Any one passing would have wondered why there was such a hurrying to and fro within the elegant mansion, why lights gleamed from every window. Had they inquired the cause, the smiling servants would have said that a long wished-for and prayed-for heir to the Escandon millions had been born.

Ricardo Escandon had been married once before, but his wife left him childless. Then he met and fell madly in love with beautiful Inez, who was young enough to have been his daughter. With blind determination he wooed, and, despite her own wishes, the parents of Inez forced her to marry the wealthy Cuban.

For years they had lived together, the gentle Inez almost in fear of the worshipful love lavished upon her by her husband. There was only one thing needed to complete the perfect bliss of Ricardo Escandon's life, and that was the advent of an heir.

It almost seemed as if Heaven had intended to deny him this happiness, but after long years it came at last.

And in a delirium of bliss Ricardo Escandon was kneeling by the bedside of his beautiful, pale wife, devouring her and the bundle of priceless lace by her side with love-lit eyes.

"What shall we call the little angel, darling?" he whispered fondly.

"It shall be as you wish, Ricardo," the wife replied resignedly. "Heaven has granted your life-long prayer, and the little one shall be named by you alone."

"But I am sure I can never decide upon a name half sweet enough for her!"—tenderly. "I am sure she will have your lovely eyes. I want her to look like you, my precious wife."

"I am sure your eyes are handsomer than mine, Ricardo,"—wearily—"but if you wish her to favor me, I hope she may."

She was always obedient, always subjective, this little wife. Her husband's wish was her law, because she feared him, in no way so much as in his mad love for her. It oppressed her, and kept her in mortal terror of what it might drive him to do. She had experienced his jealous rage once, and she prayed to Heaven never to witness it again.

She welcomed the coming of her child in the hope that it might claim so much of its father's love as to relieve her, and then it would be something gentle and tender that she might love, for she stood too much in fear of her husband's wild and intense affection to love him.

"We shall live now for our daughter," continued her husband. "She shall be the richest, the most accomplished, the most envied of girls. And I know she will be beautiful, like you, my treasured wife."

"Gently, Ricardo, I pray you," pleadingly remonstrated the wife. "I fear Heaven will punish us, if we love our darling too greatly."

"Don't!" he cried in alarm. "How can you call down Heaven's wrath by such uncalled for prophesies. Never speak to me so again, and if harm ever comes to the little angel, I shall always feel that your careless words brought it!"

"I am sorry," murmured the gentle wife in great fear. "Forgive me."

Then looking down at the little bundle by her side, she added softly:

"My dear little love!"

"Ah!" cried her husband, forgetting his momentary anger. "You have named my daughter. She is the loveliest thing upon this earth, and Love shall be her name."

"As you wish, Ricardo, but Love is not soft and sweet as many a Spanish name you might choose."

"Then we shall call her Love in Spanish. Amor! How does that sound? Amor Escandon."

"Very sweetly. She shall be—Amor Escandon, the love and light of our home and life."

So one baby-girl was being christened by idolizing parents in a mansion, that Christmas morning, while another baby-girl was being christened at police headquarters by the officer, who found her deserted on the street.

I

CHRISTMAS CHERRY'S SIXTEENTH BIRTHDAY.

"FOR GRACIOUS SAKE, SHUT THAT youngster's mouth!" exclaimed the head nurse in a rough, threatening voice. "It's the crossest kid on the Island. Make it shut up, do you hear me?"

The speaker, clad in the habit of a nurse, stood in the door of the children's dormitory.

It was a long, cheerless room, this abode provided by the city for its nameless family. From one end of the room to the other, in prim rows, stood cribs, every one of which contained a little waif.

A glimpse of the white, pinched faces and blue-ringed eyes, within those cradles, would have wrung the heart of any but the attendants, whose hearts had long since lost all tenderness and pity. A helpless waif, more or less, a death more or less, it mattered not to them. It was only, "there's a new kid come," or "there's another kid gone." It did not affect them one way or the other, unless it was that they grumbled at the sight of a new one, and were loud in their thanks when pitying Death removed another from their charge.

The only attendant in the dormitory beside the head nurse was the person she addressed, a slender girl kneeling by the side of a crib, vainly trying to quiet the crying babe.

"Did you hear me? Make that child shut up," repeated the nurse angrily.

"I've been tryin',"—softly replied the girl, raising a pale, thin face toward the woman. "I guess she's sick, for she won't stop."

"Won't she? I'll see about that," exclaimed the nurse, and pushing the girl aside she grabbed the crying child from its crib, and holding it aloft proceeded to give it a rough and vigorous shaking.

"Don't! don't!" screamed the girl in terror, when she saw what the nurse was doing. "She's sick and you'll make her worse. Oh!"

The scream of horror burst from the girl who had been attending the baby. And well she might scream, for in her anger the nurse let the baby fall, and it lay in a little heap on the hard floor at her feet, quiet enough now to please her, even.

After one cry of pain the child was silent, and when the nurse, a little frightened by her own violence, stooped to pick up the fallen babe, the little attendant seemed transformed into a very fiend.

With a cry of maddened rage she snatched off the nurse's cap, and twisting her slender fingers in the heavy coils of hair, deftly flung the brutal woman to the floor. Then she pounced upon her, and like a savage scratched and bit and kicked, until she was dragged off by the nurses who had come running hither alarmed by the unusual turmoil.

"You little imp!" cried a nurse as the head nurse, bleeding and ragged, was led from the dormitory. "You'll pay dearly for this! Are you crazy?"

"She killed my baby!" hissed the girl, still panting.

"It isn't dead, you little idiot!" said another nurse as she lifted the babe and put it in its crib.

"You'll catch it for this!" threatened the first one, releasing her hold. "Miss Grady will have you sent to the insane asylum or to jail for this, and you'll have your temper cooled there."

As soon as she was released the girl sprung to the side of the crib, and dropping down on her knees cooed like a tender mother of the little child.

"Are you hurt, my little angel?" she whispered tenderly. "Did she hurt my poor sick baby? Never mind, little darling, sister won't let them hurt her baby."

"I'll bet you've seen the last of your precious 'sister,'" scornfully ejaculated a nurse. "Grady ain't a forgiving kind, and you'll get your walking papers as soon as she is patched up, mark my words. I wouldn't be in your shoes for a fortune."

The girl's thin face whitened perceptibly as these taunts were hurled at her, but she had been a charity waif for sixteen years and had learned to bear all insults in silence. In fact, she was noted for her cheerfulness and good humor in all circumstances.

The chief beauty of the girl's face was her sensitive, prettily curved lips, and her great, bright, expressive eyes. They were no particular color, a peculiar hazel, some said, but they could tell a tale if the lips were mute.

As she raised them now and looked appealingly at the nurse, they were filled with tears. Their troubled depths contained not the slightest trace of the anger which a moment ago had made them blaze with an insane light.

"Baby looks very sick," she said tearfully. "Can't you bring the house-physician to see her? I'm sure she's hurt; Miss Grady let her fall so hard."

"Catch me sending for the doctor," laughed the nurse carelessly. "I think he would laugh at me, if he didn't get mad."

"Let me go for him," pleaded the girl tremulously. "I sha'n't mind it if he is mad. Please let me go, Miss Rose, for I'm sure my sister's hurt. She won't smile at me, she doesn't seem to know me, and she breathes so heavy."

"Christmas, you're a little simpleton about that child. If she was really your sister or your own baby, you could not be any sillier about her. Ever since she was brought here, two years ago, and you heard that she had been found on Christmas morning, just as you were, you have been her slave. If she has an ache, you cry, and if she smiles, you laugh. You're awful foolish, that's all I can say."

"She is all I have in the whole world, Miss Rose," Christmas replied softly. "She is the only thing that ever belonged to me. I never had no father and mother, none of the babies on the Island have, and I have been here sixteen years, and yet Miss Grady tells me every day I'm only a charity girl and hain't got no home. Baby is the only thing I ever owned, I've nursed her since she came here, two years ago, and I can't tell you how much I love her."

"How you could like her, I can't see. She's always been sick and cross," nurse said.

"Christmas Cherry!" called a cold voice, and a new nurse appeared at the door. "You're to come 'long with me. I've got orders to lock you up in the receiving-room until Miss Grady can tend to you."

"You're going to get it," supplemented the nurse with her.

Christmas flushed painfully, and then her face grew whiter than before.

"My baby is sick. You ain't going to take me away from her?" she said anxiously.

"I guess I am! Come 'long now, and don't go trying to kick up such a fight with me as you did with Grady or you'll get a different dose."

"Good-bye, my precious baby," whispered the girl to the child in the crib. "Sister must leave you, but she'll come back as soon as she can."

Hastily brushing the tears from her eyes, she arose to follow the attendant. "Be good to my baby and please, please send the doctor to see her," she said to the nurse remaining.

"She's all right, Christmas," the nurse answered more gently. "Don't worry about her; I'll look after her."

Without another word Christmas walked through the endless, uncarpeted corridor after the nurse. Without the least remark she was pushed into a cheerless room and the door was locked behind her.

Hour after hour dragged on, and still Christmas was a prisoner. It grew dark, supper time passed, and still no one came to her.

Poor little Christmas! It was the worst punishment she ever endured, and her punishment these long years in a charity home had not been mild. Only her own good temper and cheerful obedience saved her from many a beating.

To-morrow it would be sixteen years since she was found deserted in Cherry Street and taken to police headquarters. All these years had been passed on the Island with a few interruptions, when she had been given out to families. But she always wandered back in a short while, and she was so handy and useful and patient in the care of the little waifs, that they had given her a home, such as it was, for her labor.

Christmas had grown up uncared for, untaught, knowing much of rough words and blows, but nothing of kindness. How the child hungered for love and for something to cling to was shown by her devotion to the little waif, who, like herself, had been found deserted on the streets one Christmas morning. Christmas declared the child was her sister, and the nurses laughingly humored her fancy. In fact the baby became known as Christmas' sister, and her idolizing devotion to it was known to every person on the Island.

And now as the long hours of the night crept on Christmas trembled with suspense. Her baby might be crying for her, and she could not hear it; the nurses might slap its pale, white face, as they were wont to do, and she was not there to shield it.

What if it were worse, dying, and she not near? Oh, the thought was terrible! It made Christmas shiver as if from the cold.

She heeded not her pangs of hunger, her heart was too sore to feel any pain but its own. If she were only near it, if she could only slip her arms around it and smile down into its little pleading eyes, how happy she would be.

Might she not make her escape and see her baby? All the nurses, except the night watch, would be in their beds. She might visit her baby and come back again, and none would be the wiser.

Christmas was young and impulsive, and she loved her adopted sister very passionately, so when the temptation came to escape and see for herself how the baby was resting, she never thought to consider it, but climbing up on the knob of the door she swung the transom open, and in a few moments was standing breathless on the outside of the door.

Taking off her shoes and carrying them in her hand, she crept along the dimly-lighted hall, holding her breath in fear someone would detect her.

She reached the long dormitory, where she had left her little charge. Cautiously she turned the knob, and softly pushed the door open.

It took a moment for her to see clearly, and then she saw a screen set between her and where her baby's crib had stood.

Her heart almost stopped its beating, she grew as cold as ice, and a regiment could not have taken her alive from the dormitory now.

Alas! How often she had seen that screen used before. And how well she knew the meaning of it.

It was the token of illness—the death of a baby. It was always placed around a dying child to shut it out from the other children.

With that dreadful agony convulsing her heart, Christmas rushed forward, unmindful of everything, and threw herself on her knees by the crib.

"She is worse, my poor baby," she gasped.

"Christmas! where did you come from?" cried the astonished nurse, who proved to be one of the kindest in the institution.

"I crawled out through the transom," Christmas said defiantly. "They kept me away from my darling, and she is worse."

"Yes, very much worse," assented the nurse.

"You don't think that she will die?" begged Christmas, with a pitiful quiver in her voice. "I can't bear that. You know she is all I have in the whole wide world."

"It is too bad, Christmas, and you're so fond of her, too. But then it will be easier for you to give her up now than after awhile, and you know you couldn't have her all your life."

"I would have worked for her," declared Christmas between her sobs. "I am only a charity child, and so is she; but we loved each other, and I meant to make a home for her. You don't think she's got to die, do you?"

"I am afraid there is no hope. In fact, the doctor said in the evening that it was only a matter of a few hours, and now it must be almost morning."

"Baby! Can't you see me, dear?" Christmas whispered. "Look at your poor sister. Don't go away and leave her all alone. Oh, baby! can't you hear me?"

The little pale face on the pillow never moved a muscle. The large, blue-ringed eyes, stared fixedly into space; the little thin hands on the outside of the counterpane were clasped rigidly; the spasmodic breath made the breast rise and fall unevenly.

"Oh, nurse!"—with a painful cry of distress—"she how strange her eyes look. She can't see me, she can't hear me."

"Hush, Christmas, you can't help her!" cautioned the nurse.

"I know I can't. It's dreadful, dreadful! I wish I was dying with her. I haven't anything to live for. I am only a charity child. I wish I could go with the only being that ever loved me."

The last sentence died away in a gasp on her white lips, and she leaned over the crib gazing with wild, frightened eyes into the little white face below her.

"Look!" she cried in a startled voice. "She isn't breathing. Oh, my baby is dead!"

The nurse pressed the lids over the staring eyes, touched a cheek and hand, and replied:

"Yes; she is gone."

With a low cry of agony, Christmas fell face downward upon the floor, where she sobbed with unrestrained grief.

The violence of her sorrow had a softening effect upon the nurse. Such evidence of love was something unusual to her, and it made her regard poor Christmas with some compassion.

"Poor Christmas!" she said kindly. "Don't cry so. It can't bring her back, and it's a bad way to begin your birthday."

"She's left me all alone!" Christmas moaned. "All alone in this hard world."

"And all your tears will not bring her back. She is better off, Christmas; there is no pain and sickness where she has gone. She doesn't need a home and parents there. Would you have wanted her to live and be alone and homeless like yourself? Did you know the matron was notified yesterday to send you away? No one was ever kept here so long before."

"Send me away?" Christmas gasped in abject terror, sitting up and looking at the nurse. "Why, I've no place to go!"

"Well, you'll have to make your own way in the world, and if I were you, Christmas, I wouldn't wait for anything, but I'd go away at once. You hurt Miss Grady pretty badly yesterday, and she deserved it, too, for she always was a brute to the babies. But nevertheless she'll be for punishing you, and it will be no easy punishment either. So if you take my advice you will go to New York at once."

"But how can I get there?" Christmas asked, wide-eyed with fright.

"The doctor is going over in the boat at seven o'clock. I'll get him to take you over if you want to go. You mustn't be discouraged, Christmas, there is always some way for a girl to get along."

"I'll go," said Christmas with sudden determination. "There is nothing to keep me here now since baby is gone, and if there is any chance in the world for a nameless charity girl, I'll find it!"

"IF THERE IS ANY CHANCE IN THE WORLD FOR
A NAMELESS CHARITY GIRL
I'LL FIND IT!"

II

FOR AMOR'S SAKE.

THE HAPPIEST GIRL IN ALL the world was Amor Escandon on Christmas Eve, the eve of her sixteenth birthday. For on that evening she was to be formally introduced to society, and for that purpose hundreds of invitations had been sent out, and the grand old mansion had been decorated in honor of the occasion.

For Ricardo Escandon, like all Spaniards, believed in girls being presented to society as soon as their schools-days permitted.

And on this night he had the proud knowledge that few fathers ever had a daughter to present who was so accomplished, so graceful, so bewitching, so fascinating, so sweet as Amor Escandon.

She had been all her fond parents pictured. Her nature had not been spoiled by the petting and indulgence that had ever been hers. None met her but spoke of her sweetness and became a victim to her various charms.

She had just returned from a long trip abroad, a polishing, as it were, to her splendid education, and before her return she had bought a Worth gown, in which her French maid was deftly arraying her.

When her toilet was completed, she stood before her mirror and critically viewed her sweet self from head to toe.

She could not have gazed upon a more beautiful sight. Her slender form, rounded to perfection, was clad in an elegant gown of soft pink. Her lovely shoulders, as smooth and white as marble, gleamed like ivory above the warm pink of her bodice. Her beautiful arms, that a sculptor would rave over, were bare from shoulder to wrist.

Diamonds gleamed everywhere, for Amor was fond of them, and her father always humored her every caprice. Around her neck and wrists, on her tapered fingers, even on her tiny pink slippers, and in her luxurious hair, gleamed the precious gems.

Amor had hair of raven blackness, and eyes as soft and rich as black velvet, fringed with wondrous curled lashes. Her lips formed a perfect curve, and her teeth were like pearls.

"I think I will do," she said to her maid, and then away she skipped to show herself in all her glory to her fond parents.

"My darling mamma," she cried gayly, rushing into her mother's dressing-room. "What do you think of your little girl?"

"My beautiful Amor!" cried her mother, with sparkling eyes. "How lovely you are."

"And how sweet you look, mamma!" Amor said enthusiastically. "I declare you look young enough to be my sister." She placed her dark head against her mother's and gazed into the long mirror before them. "I never say your cheeks so pink before. I am sure I have the loveliest mamma in the world."

"Little flatterer!" exclaimed her mother tenderly. "Run to your father, child, and let him see you. I have barely time to complete my dressing before the guests will begin to arrive."

Amor pressed a kiss upon her mother's brow, and then rushed from the room, a laughing, merry-hearted child. Well might she be happy and gay. No trouble or sorrow had ever passed her bright pathway, and she had never known a wish ungratified.

"Where are you flying, my lovely cousin?" demanded a soft voice, and Amor came to a sudden standstill.

Before her in the corridor stood a short, wiry man with piercing black eyes and black hair grown white on the temples. He was her father's cousin and the only person on earth Amor disliked. How bitterly she disliked him, she did not know, for she bravely tried to crush the feeling as unkind and unworthy of her. With all her sweetness, Amor was inclined to be imperious, and she never spoke to her relative but that her delicate nostrils dilated, and her little head became more proudly erect.

"I beg your pardon," she answered stiffly. "I am going to my father."

She made a move to pass, but the man with a passionate fire in his black eyes, stretched forth a detaining hand, and clasped her white wrist with burning fingers.

She drew herself up with the offended grace of a queen and released his detaining hand. "Mateo Blanco, even your relationship does not give you the right to touch me," she said, with scorn.

"Amor, you act as if you hated me," he said bitterly.

She shrugged her white shoulders daintily, and elevated her penciled brows.

"And I, poor fool, worship the ground you tread on," he added fiercely.

"I must ask you to excuse me"—icily—"I am anxious to see my father."

"Not until you hear me out, by Heaven. I love you, I want you for my wife—"

She did not wait to hear him finish. Drawing herself up to her full height, she observed cuttingly:

"My father's kindness to a relative does not give you the right to insult me." And she passed on, leaving him standing there, the picture of silent rage.

"My Amor, my precious daughter," exclaimed her father when she entered his room. "You will win all hearts to-night, and you will be the most envied woman on earth before your youth has passed, I always said it."

"I am glad you are pleased, father," she answered, letting him kiss her white brow.

"But you look angry, you are flushed, my Amor," he cried in distress, quick to notice the slightest change in her beloved countenance. "Has anything displeased you?"

"Yes, father."—frankly. "Your cousin, Mateo Blanco, has said words to me which have offended me."

"He *dared* to offend you?" demanded Ricardo Escandon in amazement.

"He dared to say that he has conceived a foolish fancy for me!"—haughtily. "I don't like him; I never did."

"There is no need to say more, my love. Mateo has outraged my hospitality and insulted you. I shall know him no longer."

That was the only unpleasant episode of the evening. Amor very readily forgot it in listening to the flattering speeches which greeted her on every side. Ah, it was a night that remained like a dream to her all her life; it was the happiest time of her life.

Well might she wish time would forget to move, and that she could laugh and dance and hear the sweet music and inhale the fragrance of countless roses and see the crush of beautiful women and handsome men forever.

It was the proudest moment in the lives of Ricardo Escandon and his submissive wife. Friends were congratulating them on every side on the beauty and grace of their sweet daughter.

That Christmas Eve was the happiest night of their lives—and the most wretched.

Straying off for a moment alone, Ricardo Escandon wandered into the conservatory, where he dropped on a bench to dream alone over his idolized child's triumph.

He had hardly seated himself when he heard subdued voices and the unmistakable sound of weeping. He would have gone away at once had he not feared that in going he would make his presence known to the couple, which would lead to endless embarrassments. So he remained still, hoping they would go.

He tried not to listen, but in spite of himself he heard a man's voice and it pronounced the name of—his wife!

Amazement, horror, mad, jealous fears held him still and silent then.

His wife crying! A strange man calling her Inez! My God, what could it mean?

"My dear Inez," the strange voice said tenderly, "after all these years, do you love me still? Ah, Inez, ours has been a sad fate! A little over sixteen years ago I left you because you prayed me, for the sake of the child soon to be born, to go from you. Loving you I went, and for sixteen years I have never set eyes upon your beautiful face, but hungering for the sight of you I have wandered back, loving you still the same."

"And this unexpected meeting has unnerved me," he heard his wife reply. "I forgot my duty to my husband and child and only remembered that I loved you. No, Richard, you must not plead, you must not remain. I am not strong enough to see you, and I fear my husband too much. For the sake of the honor of my daughter, my sweet Amor, you must go, and so long as we live, we two must never meet again. Maybe in Heaven, Richard, we may be happy at last and our severed hearts reunited."

"Tell me of your child, Love! A fitting name indeed. Does she favor you or—"

Ricardo Escandon felt as if a dagger had pierced his heart. His brain whirled, a mist came before his eyes. My God, was he going mad? This dreadful suspicion which had burst like a thunderclap within his brain. What could it mean?

Love! Amor! A fitting name! Favored her mother! Had gone for the sake of the child soon to be born! Whose child? Whose child? Whose child?

A million fiends seemed to be screaming it into his ears, a thousand different lights flashed before his failing sight, and without a cry, he fell senseless upon the floor.

When he regained consciousness he was still upon the floor, and his guests were rapidly thinning out. It was Christmas morning, just sixteen years, he remembered with a groan, since he had welcomed the birth of Amor Escandon.

Crawling wearily to his feet he made his way unsteadily and unnoticed to his room, where he sank upon a lounge listening to the carriages rolling away and planning, planning, planning!

At last he rose and went to work, strange work it was and laborious, but he performed it quickly and deftly. When it was completed he rung for his valet.

"Tell Mrs. Escandon to come to my room after the guests have gone; and, John, send me up a glass of wine. That is all."

The sound of his own voice surprised him, it was so calm and composed. After his man had gone he sat down to wait and not a throb of pity shot through his bleeding heart. Ricardo Escandon was mad. He knew neither pity nor mercy.

The last guest was gone, the lights were turned out, and the belle of the evening was in the hands of her clever French maid.

"Put me in a dressing gown, and then you may go," Amor said to the weary maid. "I intend to wait until my father and mother are sleeping, and then I am going to steal into their rooms and put their Christmas gifts just where their eyes will light upon them the first thing on waking."

Mrs. Escandon had not waited to change her elaborate ball-dress before going to her husband. She was not a little uneasy over his summons. There was a guilty feeling in her heart which increased her fear and her displeasure.

When she entered the room and saw how white and stern his face was, she almost fell upon her knees. But mastering her emotion, she said, as calmly as possible:

"You sent for me, Ricardo?"

She watched him with a strange fear as he locked the door and placed the key in his pocket.

"Inez Escandon," he said huskily, as he returned to her side and glared down in her frightened face, "I demand the truth from you."

He paused. He drew his breath in sharply. Then he continued, hoarsely:

"Is Amor Escandon my daughter?"

"My God, Ricardo, are you mad?" cried his wife in distress.

"No! I am not mad. I overheard your interview with your lover, madam, and now I demand you to speak the truth before your God and me. Is Amor the daughter of that man or is she mine?"

"Ricardo!"—in great terror—"you misjudge me. I swear to you that man is not my lover."

"False! False!" he muttered, angrily. "Madam, it is useless to lie. I heard him tell his love, I heard you, shameless woman, confess yours. Now, by Heaven, I must know whose child it is I have raised."

"She is yours, Ricardo; oh, believe me, she is yours, and I was guilty of no untruth to you," beseeched his wife.

"Madam, there is only one way for you to prove that Amor Escandon is my daughter," he said coldly, as he lifted a slender wine glass from the table. "I have put a deadly poison in this wine. If Amor is my child, take this glass and drink its contents."

"Ricardo!" she breathed in abject terror, her face blanching to a death-like whiteness. "Would you murder me?"

"Not if Amor Escandon is some one else's daughter," was the empathetic reply. "If she is, confess the truth and save your life, but from my house both of you go this very night. As dearly as I have loved her, just so bitterly shall I hate her if I find she is not my daughter. The very knowledge that I have been loving and idolizing another man's child all these years would almost make me kill her."

"Ricardo," gasped the woman piteously, "spare me, have mercy! I am not fit to die. I will tell you the truth, on my bended knees; before Heaven, I will confess the whole truth. Shortly after we were married my cousin, Richard Gray, who had been abroad, came home. Probably you remember him. How I came to love him I do not know. I used to meet him when I pretended to go to my drawing lessons. I loved him. Oh, pity me. I was afraid of you, and I wanted something to love, but when we found how dearly we cared for each other, and I knew that I was soon to become the mother of your child, I begged him to go away. He refused to leave me until I prayed, in the name of the innocent child I was to bear, for him to aid me in doing right, and then he obeyed. I never saw him again until to-night."

"Well, well, madam?"—impatiently.

"I swear Amor is your child. Oh, believe me!"

"There is only one way to prove it," he replied, holding out the glass.

"Mercy! Mercy!" she wept, clinging to his knees, her costly gown dragging on the floor.

"I know no mercy."—coldly. "I give you five minutes by the clock to drink the poisoned wine in proof that Amor is my daughter, or to take her and go out into the world nameless and penniless."

"I shall go, I shall never see her again, if you will believe me," she entreated, but he was marble.

"Drink the poison or she goes as well as you!"

"Be merciful, be merciful!"

"You have yet three minutes!" said the cold voice of her heartless judge.

"I cannot die, I am not fit to die!" she wept in anguish. "I pray, let me go out into the world alone. I'll be the same as dead to you both."

"There remains one and a half minutes. Will you drink the poison or do you and your daughter leave here at once?"

"But if you kill me you will be punished. Amor will know the truth," she pleaded.

He pointed grimly at the wall. His trembling wife turned and saw where he had made an opening in the bricks, leaving a long closet-shaped cavity.

That was to be her tomb!

"The time is up!" he announced, holding out the glass.

Her teeth chattered, her limbs knocked together, her eyes were wild with horror. She reached forth a trembling hand but hastily drew it back again.

"Then you leave at once," he said, making a move to set the glass upon the table.

"Give it to me!" she whispered faintly. "May God have mercy on you!"

She took the glass, she raised it to her white lips.

"For my daughter's sake I drink!" she said as she drained the glass.

She moved as if to set the empty glass upon the table, when she reeled and fell upon the floor—dead!

Calmly, deliberately, Ricardo Escandon picked up the lifeless body of his wife and placed it in a standing position in the opening in the wall. Without so much as a glance at the face of the woman he had loved so well, he carefully replaced the bricks, and when all was done he tacked the tapestry back in its place and calmly surveyed his handiwork.

"I would defy the cleverest person to tell that had been removed," he observed. "Amor is my daughter and none but Heaven knows my guilt."

"Oh, yes, my dear cousin, I have witnessed your crime," said a smooth voice at his elbow.

With a cry of fear he turned and faced his cousin, Mateo Blanco.

Just then, as fate willed it, Amor Escandon came stealing to her father's room to place her gift near him. She put her ear to the key-hole, to make sure that all was still within, when she heard his voice cry in alarm:

"You will not betray me, Mateo?"

She listened, trembling with great fear.

"There is one way you can buy my silence," was the response. "Give me your daughter's hand in marriage and half your fortune."

"You are mad!" she heard her father reply angrily. "Amor does not like you, and I will never compel her to marry you. No, you ask too much."

"Then, my dear cousin"—pleasantly—"I will be compelled to notify the police that the wealthy and respected Ricardo Escandon this night most brutally and heartlessly murdered—his wife!"

The words seemed to burn themselves in Amor's brain. She felt herself grow faint with horror.

"For god's sake, hush!" she heard her father beg. "I killed my wife because she merited it, but if you swear never to let my daughter know the truth, I promise to make her marry you. It will break her heart, I know."

"Not so quickly as the knowledge that her father killed her mother," was the taunting reply.

She must know the truth. Surely she had not heard rightly. She would find her dear mother safe in her bed, and away Amor flew, in breathless suspense, anxious to set her horrible fears at rest.

No, her mother was not in bed. The bed was untouched, and her tired maid was asleep in a chair. Amor shook her roughly, and demanded her mother's whereabouts. The maid could not tell. Doubtless madam was in monsieur's room. She had not come yet to have her dress removed.

Cold with horror, Amor rushed back to her father's door. She would enter, she would denounce him!

No, no, not that! She must have time to think. If she denounced her own father, he would be hanged. No, much as he deserved the punishment, she could not be the cause of his death.

And if she remained there, she would have to marry Mateo Blanco to save her father from death.

Young and unreasonable, unknown to sorrow, Amor's horrible affliction nearly drove her mad. Creeping away from her father's door, she returned to her own room, and hastily donning the plainest dress she owned, she stole noiselessly from the room and house.

"Farewell forever!" she said, pausing for one last look. "I am going away to die."

III

CHRISTMAS MAKES A PLACE
FOR HERSELF IN THE WORLD.

IT WAS STILL EARLY IN the morning when Christmas Cherry landed in New York, homeless, friendless and with but twenty-five cents in her pocket.

The feeling that possessed her was one of intense desolation and despair. All around her, as she strolled aimlessly along the street, she saw evidences of Christmas joy. Even in the poorest homes she saw some indication of celebrations, and her own unhappy position seemed only the more hopeless by comparison.

She had nowhere to go, so she wandered on, feeling like a mortal suddenly landed on a new planet and growing more miserable with every step.

All Christmas Day she walked the streets with no definite idea of what to do.

"I know where the river is," she thought despairingly, "and I suppose I'd be better off if I'd jump into it."

As bright and attractive as death appeared to her under the dreary aspects of her position, Christmas still felt that she would be sinful and cowardly to put an end to her existence.

"Why, this is a great big world," she thought bravely, dashing away the tears which gathered in her big eyes in spite of herself, "and there's some place for a poor charity girl in it, if she only tries. I mean to try, I won't give up, I'll make a place for myself somehow."

But how? That was what she could not tell.

The long day had passed at last, and as the shades of night began to gather, Christmas found herself before a gay window filled with eatables.

Within the room she saw people eating, and as the door opened and closed she caught strains of music.

It was only a cheap restaurant in gaudy holiday attire, but to the homeless waif it seemed like a glimpse of Heaven.

She had not realized how long she had fasted until she stood at that window, and the sight of the delicacies roused the pangs of hunger to their fiercest pitch.

How tempting everything looked, and how terribly empty she felt.

She thrust a little rough hand, innocent of glove, into the folds of her cheap dress and drew out a solitary quarter. It was the parting gift of the good-hearted nurse.

Christmas looked at it with tears in her eyes. It was all she had in the world and she was afraid to spend it.

With a sigh she put it out of sight again and turned away from the tempting window.

"Of course I'm not as hungry as I thought I was," she said bravely. "It was just looking at those good things that made me think I was hungry. I'll walk in dark streets where I won't see them, and then I won't be hungry any more."

So she sought the dark streets and wandered on tirelessly and aimlessly until she was in the midst of the manufacturing portion of the city.

The tall, gloomy buildings, closed for the holiday, towered threateningly above her. In her wandering eyes they seemed cold and cruel and heartless, and she despaired of ever finding work in any of them.

As she was gazing at them a light suddenly appeared in the lower window of a building that had looked the tallest and grimmest of them all.

Christmas gazed fascinated at the light. It gleamed forth like a ray of hope.

There was some one within that building—some one who lived and breathed.

Perhaps if she were to go in there she could get work.

No sooner did this thought suggest itself than Christmas hurried across the street. She tried the knob; it yielded to her touch, so, softly opening the door, she calmly stepped in.

She found herself in a small office, and its solitary occupant was seated before a desk, lost in the contents of a large ledger. He did not see the new-comer until, like a little dark spirit, she stood by his elbow.

"Great guns!" he exclaimed in surprise, "where did you come from?"

"From the Island," Christmas replied softly.

"From the Island!"—still in amazement. "Well, what do you want here?"

"A job," she answered trustingly, gazing at him with appealing eyes.

"I am sorry, but we don't need any more girls," he replied, as if that settled the question.

He was tall and broad-shouldered and wonderfully handsome, this man in the office. His hair was the color of gold and his blue eyes were so kind and noble that Christmas felt encouraged.

She remembered that she had said if there was no place in the world for her she would make one, so now she meant to persevere.

"Won't you make a place for me?" she pleaded simply. "I can't go back to the Island, they won't keep me any longer, so I must get a job."

"I am very sorry," he began.

"Oh, now you're not going to send me away,"—tremulously—"I'll do anything you want. Clean, carry wood and coal, and make the fires, and then sweep your room out and scrub the floor, indeed I can—I've done it lots of times."

The young man burst out laughing, but his laugh was so strong and good-natured that Christmas was not alarmed.

"What a queer little thing you are!"—laughing. "Where are you from—the workhouse, almshouse, or insane asylum? You say you are from the Island."

"I'm from the juvenile asylum; I'm too big to stay there any longer, so they sent me away."

"I am afraid"—gravely—"you can be of no use here. The work you offer to do is looked after by a man. This is a shoe factory, and the girls employed here know how to run a machine and make shoes."

Christmas' lips trembled suspiciously. "Can't I learn?" she faltered.

He hesitated. Her big, wistful eyes made his heart grow soft with pity.

"You ain't going to turn me out?" she faltered, seeing his hesitation. "Why, when I saw your light in the window, it seemed to warm my heart, and somehow made me feel as if I had a friend in the world. This morning I was miserable, and I thought of the river, and how easy it was to jump in and have it over. Then I wouldn't want no home and friends, and I wouldn't be lonely any more."

"And why did you not die then?" he inquired interestedly.

"Because I thought it didn't seem right. I felt ashamed to do it. It did not seem right. I just thought in this big world there must be room for even a charity girl, so I put all thoughts of the river right out of my head."

"Why, you little trump," he exclaimed, "you are plucky, at any rate."

"Then you won't send me away?"—rapturously.

"I will see."—evasively. "What is your name?"

"Christmas Cherry!"

"Christmas Cherry?" he repeated. "What a curious name. Why were you called Christmas?"

"I don't know what you'll think of it, but I couldn't help it," Christmas said bravely, although she was very sensitive on the subject. "I was a deserted child. A policeman found me in Cherry Street on Christmas morning, just sixteen years ago to-day, and he named me Christmas Cherry."

"Poor little Christmas!"—sympathetically—"and this is your birthday. I will make you a Christmas gift—it shall be a position."

Christmas bit her lips to keep from crying. It sounded too good to be true. She could not speak her thanks, she could only look at her benefactor with her big eyes swimming in happy tears.

"I suppose this is the first Christmas gift you have had?" he asked, to give her time to recover her composure, for he could not help seeing the quivering lips and tear-filled eyes.

"A few days ago the doctor gave me a bit of mistletoe for Christmas," she faltered, "but before I left I put it in the baby's little hand, for I think she'll have Christmas somewhere, don't you?"

"Who is baby?" he asked curiously.

"My little adopted sister."—tenderly. "She was found on Christmas morning, too, just two years ago, and—and—she died this morning."

The young man was strangely moved. He felt something rise in his throat and choke him.

"Do you think she will have Christmas where she's gone?" Christmas persisted anxiously.

"I am sure she will," he answered softly; and the girl was comforted.

"If you will come here in the morning," he said at last, "and ask for the foreman, if you don't see me, I will see what you can do. Come at seven o'clock prepared to work."

"I will; and you have made me the happiest girl in the world," she replied gratefully.

Her accent was illiterate, her language far from perfect, but the young man was impressed by the delicious sweetness of her voice, and the purity and honesty of soul he saw in her big eyes.

So Christmas Cherry went out into the night the happiest girl in the world, despite her being homeless. She had work, and she felt as if she could conquer worlds now.

All the night long she wandered in the vicinity of the place she had been promised work. She had no place to spend the night, and she feared if she wandered far away she would not be able to find the factory again, so she lingered near it, hiding in doorways when not walking to keep her chilled blood circulating.

She trusted herself, after awhile, to walk on to the river, which was not very far from the factory, and as the daylight began to dawn she heard whistles blowing, and saw people hurrying in all directions.

She was no longer afraid of being seen by the police, as she had been when the streets were deserted.

She had heard a bell, somewhere, toll out the hours all the night long, and she had heard it toll the hour of six when she walked down toward the river again, waiting until a half hour or so should pass before she would return to the shoe factory.

As she walked out on a pier she saw a young girl standing on the extreme edge of it, and gazing down into the dark, rushing waters below.

It was beautiful Amor Escandon!

Some thought of the brief temptation the river had offered her in her wretchedness made her walk rapidly toward Amor, who, hearing steps behind her, turned a beautiful, white, terrified face toward Christmas, and then throwing up her arms, sprung into the river.

Christmas turned and ran swiftly in the direction she had come, calling wildly to the man nearest her.

"A girl has fallen into the river!" she shouted. "Quick! Quick! Come, save her!"

The young man heard her cry and rushed toward Christmas.

"Where is she?" he exclaimed rapidly.

"There! In the river!" replied the girl, running along by his side.

The young man pulled off his coat and hat and Christmas gave a cry of dismay.

It was her benefactor! The young man who had given her employment.

"Not you! Not you!" she cried wretchedly.

He did not take time to answer. He had seen a dark head and pale face appear above the rushing water. Two tiny white hands were thrown up helplessly, and with a prayer for aid in his heart he sprung to the girl's rescue.

"I have lost him!" cried Christmas, with a pain as fierce as death at her heart, but how she had lost him she little realized at that moment.

Two tiny white hands were thrown up helplessly, and, with a prayer for aid in his heart, the young man sprung to the girl's rescue.

IV

LOVE AT FIRST SIGHT ON HIS PART,
AND ON HERS.

IN AN AGONY OF SUSPENSE Christmas Cherry watched handsome George Chesterland as he battled through the swiftly-moving waters.

He was her benefactor, her sole friend on earth. If he were drowned—ah, she could not face such a catastrophe.

He had been kind to her, he had spoken gently, and her loyal little heart had gone out to him forever.

She forgot that in losing him she lost employment; she forgot the pale, despairing face of unhappy Amor Escandon; she only remembered that he was handsome, and good, and young, and she had been the one to send him to his death.

For it did not seem possible to miserable Christmas that he would come up alive. Even when she saw him clutch the drowning girl, she clasped her hands in breathless agony, expecting the weight of his senseless burden to bear him down to his death.

George Chesterland's danger was seen by others besides Christmas Cherry, and two men had set out in a boat to give their assistance.

They were none too soon. Heroic George Chesterland was well-nigh exhausted when he was drawn into the boat, after his lovely burden.

"Pretty close call, mister!" remarked one of the men dryly.

"It was indeed," George replied, with a sigh of relief. "The water is running very swiftly this morning. I am afraid without your help I should not have been able to make the shore."

He bent over the senseless girl at his feet, and as he gazed into her beautiful, pale face, his heart beat with a strange rapture.

"How beautiful and refined she is?" he thought. "What dreadful sorrow could have come to one so lovely to drive her on to such a mad act?"

But even as he wondered what sad fate had brought her to this end, he thanked Heaven that it had brought her to him.

"It is fate!" he thought, with a passionate thrill. "I have saved her, she must be mine!"

By this time the boatmen succeeded in effecting a landing, and George Chesterland was helped upon the pier with his lovely charge.

Quite a crowd of persons had gathered and now pressed forward, curious to see the victim of death. It was only another case of a sudden hopelessness and flying to seek forgetfulness beneath the rushing waters.

They were too familiar with such stories to feel any sympathy for the poor unfortunate; they were only curious to catch a glimpse of her pale, drenched face, wearing the last expression of her death's agony.

Before they could sate their morbid desire, a policeman appeared, and pushing them roughly back, took his position beside poor, senseless Amor Escandon.

Alas! What a dreadful position for the beautiful petted heiress, the child of luxury! Had her idolizing father been there to gaze upon her in all her heart-broken misery, surely the sight would have driven him mad. The punishment for his terrible crime had fallen sure and swift.

"What's this?" demanded the officer, and Christmas crept protectingly to the side of George Chesterland, who took no notice of her.

"Another suicide?" the officer added.

"She is not dead!" George Chesterland observed defiantly.

"All the worse for her," replied the officer grimly. "The law's pretty tough on them that try suicide."

Christmas saw the painful start which George Chesterland gave and the flush that came into his cheeks and the fire into his eyes.

He had forgotten the penalty for attempting suicide. Ah, pitiful Heaven, would that beautiful unconscious girl be sent to prison, to associate with the wicked and the low?

"I'll call an ambulance and take her off to the hospital," remarked the officer calmly—adding: "What is your name and address, young man? You will be held as witness against the prisoner."

"I cannot appear against the young lady and I must refuse to give you my name," George said angrily.

"Then I must make you my prisoner," snapped the officer, laying his hand on the young man's wet shoulder, "and you will be detained as a witness unless you can furnish bail for your appearance."

What desperate measure George Chesterland would have adopted to save himself and his beautiful love from the hands of the law, it is impossible to say, but at that moment, Christmas Cherry planted herself resolutely before the officer and said defiantly:

"Don't be too fast, Mister Policeman. You ain't going to take that young lady away because she didn't jump into the river. I threw her in!"

The officer gazed with amused contempt down on the little rebel, and the crowd stirred with renewed interest. This was better than a plain ordinary suicide; it promised a sensation, possibly a murder!

"What do you know about the case, anyhow?" inquired the officer.

"I guess I know more than anybody else"—rebelliously—"seeing there wasn't anybody but us two here together. I was feeling as if I didn't want to live any longer, and while I was looking into the water, down comes this young lady. I guess she suspected what I was up to, for she grabbed me by the arm and tells me not to do it. Then I wanted to all the more, cause I thought I was going to be kept from it, so I tried to get away from her and in the struggle, she slipped and fell into the water. Then I yelled for help and this young man saved her, so how are you going to arrest her for something she never tried to do?"

The crowd gave a shout of delight, and even the policeman smiled indulgently upon his little defier.

"Well, if there is no case against her, I'll arrest you for attempting suicide," he observed dryly.

Christmas' heart gave a great throb, and then almost ceased beating. But she was in for it, and she felt she would have to brave it out.

"You can't arrest me," she said boldly, "for thinking about doing a thing."

The crowd roared with laughter. It was something new to see a girl so fearless of an officer.

"You have to wait till I try to do it, see?" she added brightly.

"Go 'long!" laughed the officer, "and don't let me catch you around here again or I'll run you in on suspicion."

"Will you help me to get a cab?" George Chesterland asked the officer. "The young lady is a friend of mine, and I want to take her home."

"Certainly!" the officer replied, and in a moment a cab came rattling down the pier to where the crowd stood around the still unconscious girl.

"Won't you take me along?" Christmas asked pleadingly.

She was close to George Chesterland's elbow, holding his discarded coat in her hands. He turned in amazement to reply, and for the first time recognized the girl as his strange visitor of the day before.

"Why, it is you?" he said, in surprise.

"Yes! Won't you please let me go with you?"—earnestly.

He saw signs of reviving consciousness in Amor, and he was anxious to take her away before she was able to speak, so he replied, nervously:

"Get into the cab."

Joyfully Christmas sprung into the cab, and George Chesterland followed with Amor in his arms. The policeman closed the door, the driver cracked his whip, and they were off.

And just in time, for Amor gave a gasp, and struggling into an upright position, came back to life and reason.

George Chesterland took the front seat as he noticed signs of returning consciousness, so that when Amor opened her big black eyes their bewildered gaze rested upon the handsome face of her preserver.

And their glance, wild and startled as it was, filled George's heart with a tumult of joy. His face flushed, his lips trembled, and only by a masterful effort did he smother the impulse to clasp the unhappy girl to his heart and assure her that his life and devotion were at her service.

Amor was greatly frightened at finding herself in a cab with a strange man. She did not notice the girl at her side, but staring anxiously at George Chesterland, she demanded imperiously:

"Who are you, sir, and how came I in your company?"

"You fell into the river," George replied gently, "and I am taking you where you can be cared for until you are able to return to your home."

He saw a spasm of pain dart across her lovely white face at the mention of home, and he sighed.

"I do not know you," she replied stiffly, "I cannot go with you. Please tell the driver to stop; I wish to get out."

"But you are soaking wet, you are faint," he urged. "I beg of you—"

She lifted a tiny white hand as if to stop further argument. "I insist on your stopping the carriage," she said, as haughtily as a queen.

"The young gentleman saved you from death at the risk of his own life," Christmas interrupted, indignantly. "And do you think he's going to do you any harm after that?"

A slight color swept for an instant over Amor's pallid face. For the first time she saw her preserver was as wet as herself.

"I cannot thank you for saving a life I no longer value," she cried wretchedly, as her eyes traveled from Christmas back to the young man.

"You are too young and beautiful to seek death," he observed simply.

"Young? Alas, too young!"—despairingly. "If I were old I might be able to endure my misery until a natural death would bring me rest. But I am too young, too young. Only sixteen years old yesterday, and I may live fifty years!"

He could not help but see how she shrunk, appalled by the idea, and how her lips trembled, and how the big tears flooded her eyes.

"Sixteen years old yesterday?" repeated Christmas to herself. "Then she was born on the same day as myself. I am so glad. She is a sister sent to take the place of the little one I lost yesterday, and as I intended to do by it, so shall I do my this new sister, as long as we two live."

Unconscious of the vow of friendship being registered in the loyal heart of the little waif by her side, Amor renewed her protestations.

"I am sufficiently recovered to go my way alone," she remarked icily, "ungrateful as it may seem; I can accept nothing more at your hands."

Alas! He knew she was not even grateful for the life he had saved.

"You must let me out here."

"Your wet garments will attract unpleasant attention on the street," he reminded her kindly.

She frowned angrily. "It matters not," she said.

"Yes, it does," blurted Christmas. "If you get out, you'll be arrested for trying to kill yourself, and they'll send you to jail."

"To jail?" gasped the unhappy girl, and then she resigned herself to her fate. Closing her eyes wearily, she neither moved nor spoke until the carriage pulled up before a shabby genteel house, and George Chesterland opened the door and stood ready to assist her to alight.

"It is not necessary to explain anything to my landlady," he said to both the girls.

Without touching his proffered hand, Amor stepped proudly upon the pavement, and waited for him to lead the way into the house.

V

"HE HAS BEEN A FRIEND TO US BOTH."

WHILE GEORGE CHESTERLAND WAS MAKING some kind of an excuse for their wet garments to his landlady and begging her to find a dry change for the young lady, Christmas suddenly made herself the center of interest by fainting and falling in a little heap upon the landlady's parlor floor.

Her long fast, in addition to a sudden transition from the cold to a warm room, made her brain reel, and as she felt herself grow dizzy she started for a chair, only to fall to the floor before she could reach it.

"Poor little thing! She is blue from cold," George Chesterland said sympathetically as he bent over the prostrate girl and forced between her lips some of the liquor the landlady had given him.

"She looks thin and starved," the boardinghouse mistress snapped shortly.

"Probably she is starved. She is a poor girl I have employed in the factory," the young man explained.

Amor Escandon looked on helplessly and offered no assistance.

"You go to your room and change your wet clothes or you'll be sick next," added the landlady to her boarder. "I'll take care of the young ladies until you return."

George Chesterland did as she advised just as Christmas, very much ashamed of herself, came back to consciousness.

"Follow me, young ladies, and after the wet clothes are removed, we'll have some breakfast," the mistress said cheerily.

She led them to her own room and from the wardrobe brought some badly made and cast-off garments, which had once been worn by her daughter.

"These are not very good," she said, "but they'll do until your own dry."

"They will do very well, I thank you, madam," Amor replied politely.

"There is some mystery here," was the landlady's verdict. "That girl speaks like a lady born and bred."

But she said nothing and in a few moments the girls were ready to follow her into the dining room, where a warmed-over breakfast was served them on the corner of the table because breakfast hour was over.

"I am hungry, aren't you?" Christmas said to Amor.

"Not in the least," replied the heiress, making a wry face over the coffee which tasted like nectar to the starving charity girl.

When George Chesterland joined them, Amor's white face did not change from its weary expression. Nothing mattered to her, it seemed; her heart had been broken by her father's awful crime, and these new people, so poor, so unlike those to whom she had been accustomed, could be of no interest to her one way or the other.

True, the young man was very handsome, and he had saved her life. But she was not grateful for that; in fact, if anything, she owed him a grudge for depriving her of the peace that was so near being hers.

"I am obliged to go to my office," he said, his eyes resting admiringly upon the pale, proud face. "I hope you will permit Mrs. Brown to make you comfortable here until my return. You seem to be alone in the world; I wish you would let me be your friend."

"I have already received too much from you," Amor replied icily. "I cannot promise even to be grateful for what you have done, but the greatest kindness you can do me now is to allow me to depart, quietly and alone."

"May I go with you? You know, you promised to give me work?" Christmas interrupted anxiously.

"I have not forgotten my promise. I must go at once, but you may follow as soon as you finish your breakfast," was the kind reply.

"If you haven't any home, why don't you work for Mr. Chesterland too?" Christmas inquired artlessly.

Amor looked at the bold questioner in silent amazement.

Work! She, the heiress, who had never even buttoned her own boots?

Alas! She had forgotten. She was no longer the petted heiress. Her father's unnatural crime had made her an outcast, a wanderer on the face of the earth! She would never return to him or the home that had sheltered her since her birth. She was as dead to them as if the rushing waters had indeed closed over her wretched head.

She had some money, a fortune, it would have seemed to poor Christmas. But if she lived, Amor was practical enough to know it would not keep her long.

Then why not work? She asked herself the question, she considered it with a faint interest, the first she had felt in anything since leaving her home.

"If I must live," she remarked aloud, "I suppose I might as well work."

"I am so glad!" cried impulsive Christmas, and George Chesterland echoed her approval mentally, but considered it wiser to say little. He knew by bitter experience what it was to be brought from affluence to poverty at a single blow, and how worthless life first appeared to him as a poor man.

"There is my card," he said kindly, although his heart was throbbing with rapture at the thought of having her near him, of being able to see her every day. "If you will follow me, I shall be pleased to offer you what poor employment is at my disposal."

"We'll come all right," Christmas replied joyfully, and Amor, with a slight inclination of the head, murmured, "Thank you!"

They heard him speak to Mrs. Brown in the hallway and then the front door close after him and he was gone.

"My dear young ladies, just wait a moment until I return," the landlady said, appearing at the dining-room door for an instant.

In a short time she came back carrying a good-sized bundle wrapped up in a newspaper.

"I thought maybe you would not have any luncheon ready to take with you to-day, so I put up one for you," she said, just as if Mr. Chesterland had not instructed her in the hall to do so.

Again Amor inclined her graceful dark head and murmured her thanks, while Christmas' heart swelled with gratitude.

"What a good, kind world this is, after all!" she thought.

"And you can wear my daughter's old dress today," continued the woman. "Yours will not be dry enough to put on until evening."

"I will be glad to buy these garments if you can spare them, madam," Amor said calmly.

"Oh, I didn't mean to make you buy them, I'm sure."

"Still, if you will kindly name a price I shall be glad to buy them."—stiffly.

Poor Amor! What a great change for her. The miserable garments she wore would have been despised by her meanest servant at home.

"If you don't think five dollars would be too much, considering that I didn't want to sell them?" hesitated the woman.

"If you are satisfied with five dollars I shall buy them at once," Amor said coldly.

"Just five dollars gained!" the landlady thought gleefully, as she pocketed the crisp bill which Amor gave her.

"I will send for my dress as soon as I can," Amor remarked, as Mrs. Brown opened the door to let the girls depart.

"Very well, my dear. I hope you girls will be lucky and keep your places," she said in parting, and then went back to her duties to wonder about Amor and how she came to be forced into such a friendless position.

"Yesterday in silks and diamonds, to-day in rags!" laughed Amor harshly, as she walked down the street with Christmas.

"And did you lose all them things in one day?" Christmas asked, her big eyes opened wide.

"Yes, in one day—Christmas day!"—wretchedly.

"I thought I'd lost everything on Christmas, too," Christmas continued confidentially. "I never had any such things as you speak about, but I had a little baby to care for that I called my sister, and I had a home in the asylum on the Island, and I lost both yesterday."

Her voice broke, her big soulful eyes filled with tears and Amor, gazing at her, wondered how she could grieve after such trifling things. A home in an asylum? Ugh! And a cross, crying baby! Why, the girl should consider herself a gainer instead of a loser.

"I was feeling pretty wretched too, and once I thought of the river, just as you did, and then I thought it was braver to live and so, at last, I saw a light in Mr. Chesterland's office, and I went in and asked him for work, and he gave it to me, and it made me the happiest girl in the world."

"Why didn't you go to your home when you left the asylum?" inquired Amor. She thought probably the asylum was a house of reformation or punishment.

"I never had any home."—sorrowfully.

"Why, are both your parents dead?"

"I never had any parents, neither"—shortly—"none as was ever known of. I was born on Christmas morning, sixteen years ago yesterday, and a policeman found me a few hours later in Cherry Street. That's how I got my name—Christmas Cherry!"

"Christmas Cherry! What a strange name? You are just my age and born on the same day, too. It seems a strange fate that we should come together."

"If you haven't any home or parents"—pleadingly—"let me stay with you? I love you very much, and I know you are finer than I am, but won't you let me be your friend?"

"That you shall be, Christmas Cherry," Amor said solemnly, turning and stretching forth a soft, white hand to clasp the rough, hard hand of her companion. "I have no friend on earth except you, and you have no friend but me."

They stood at the door of the factory. Christmas glanced up at the dingy windows and replied tenderly:

"We mustn't forget Mr. Chesterland! He has been a friend to us both."

VI

THE THREE RIVALS.

WHEN THE NOON HOUR ARRIVED, George Chesterland sent for Christmas and Amor to come to the office.

There was some trepidation on the part of Christmas as she obeyed, but not a trace of any emotion was visible in Amor.

They had been given over to an assistant foreman on their arrival, and he had taken them into a large room filled with busy girls and buzzing machines. They were each given a machine and instructed in the way work was to be done. Christmas learned much more readily than Amor, who became confused and dizzy from the noise, and the close air.

Neither of the girls had time to pay any attention to the older hands, who were already exchanging many remarks and sly whispers about the newcomers.

They watched with some surprise as the assistant foreman led the new girls from the room just as the steam was shut off for the luncheon hour.

George Chesterland was awaiting their arrival with a tender light in his bonny blue eyes. Life had assumed a new aspect to him, and the dingy old factory seemed like a paradise, because *she* was within its walls. How her presence sweetened his daily toil!

"I sent for you," he began without parley, "to see if you were suited with your lodgings or if I could offer any assistance in securing a suitable place for you."

He knew they were both without homes, and now he quickly thought of offering his assistance. But yesterday it had not entered his mind to as Christmas if she had any place to stay. It was different now. Love prompted his thoughtfulness.

"Neither of us have a home." It was Christmas that replied.

Amor was watching him with her proud black eyes. She was saying to herself that he was wondrously handsome, so tall and broad-shouldered and frank-eyed. She had never seen a man before with such golden hair and such a clear, perfect complexion.

"What a shame that he should be only a poor working man," was her mental conclusion.

At the same moment honest little Christmas was saying to herself:

"He is the handsomest and best man that ever lived."

"Do you want to live together?" he asked, a winning smile resting on his beautiful lips.

He was pleased that they should remain together, this strangely mated pair—heiress and factory girl! He recognized Christmas' honest and loyal heart, he had heard her brave defense of the unhappy girl when on the verge of being carried off to jail. He felt satisfied that no harm could come to his love whilst Christmas was near.

And then he recognized in the pale charity waif, the pluck and bravery necessary to young girls facing the world.

His love did not blind him to certain traits in Amor's disposition which would tend to lead her into trouble. Her arrogant pride, her abject hopelessness, her ignorance of poverty, of subjection, would be thorny obstacles in her path.

His question was answered by Amor. There was something like defiance in her proud eyes, as with haughtily-lifted head, she said slowly:

"She has no friend in the world but me, and I, none but her."

George Chesterland laughed inwardly. He felt the implied thrust and wondered if his passionate love had shown too plainly in his adoring eyes and if she took this way to warn him to keep his distance.

"Ah, my haughty love, I'll win you in spite of yourself," he vowed in his throbbing heart.

Christmas looked confusedly from one to the other of these new and dear friends. She felt that Amor had purposely excluded their benefactor, and her heart was divided between them.

"We intend to be sisters, you know," she added, "and you have been the best friend in the world to us."

"Thank you!" he said, still smiling, but Amor's cold face did not relax. "You know that working girls receive very low wages and that your salaries will necessitate your living very moderately. I should advise—if I might—getting a room and board with some private family."

"Do you know of any place?" asked Christmas.

"We have a very estimable young woman in our employ who may be able to help us," was the answer, and tapping the bell on the desk, he said to the boy who appeared:

"Tell Miss Lillian Day to step here, please."

In a moment the door opened to admit a girl as beautiful as a dream. Even Amor, with all her calmness, gave a gasp of astonishment.

The girl was above the average height, and most exquisitely proportioned. Her hands were small and showed no little care, her feet were daintily arched and coquettishly booted, showing their possessor was not lacking in appreciation of their beauty.

To say that her cheeks were like red, velvety rose-leafs against the driven snow, that her hair was like gold, burnished by the crimson rays of the setting sun, that her eyes were as blue as an Italian sky, that her form held the grace of Venus, was saying but little.

It was impossible to describe the witching beauty of her smile, which displayed her pearly teeth and two roguish dimples, the baby-like expression in her big, blue eyes.

"To think that beautiful creature is only a working girl!" was Amor's mental remark.

"Miss Day, I have sent for you to see if you could tell me of any private family that would possibly take in a couple of boarders," George said.

Lillian's big eyes were taking in the two girls from head to toe, while her employer was speaking. Her eyes rested longest on the beautiful, high-bred face of Amor Escandon, and her ambitious soul was fired with jealousy.

Lillian's big eyes were taking in the two girls from head to toe, while her employer was speaking. Her eyes rested the longest on the beautiful face of Amor Escandon, and her soul was fired with jealousy.

"She is a beautiful girl, and has come from a rich family," was her shrewd conjecture. "I will do well to keep her under my eye."

"I don't know."—hesitatingly. "I think mother would take them. Father is driving a night cab now, and I could sleep with mother, and they could have my room."

George looked questioningly at the girls.

"We would need at least two bedrooms," Amor said, proudly.

"We could not take them, then," Lillian responded coldly. "They would have to sleep together at our house."

"I've never slept in the same bed with any one in my life," Amor declared in amazement.

"But two rooms would cost a lot of money," Christmas said to her. "I could sleep on the floor."—coaxingly.

"Oh, yes, of course," Amor said, with a short laugh. "I had forgotten the expenses we must economize. The room will do"—then turning to Christmas—"will it not?"

"Yes, we will be glad to get it," Christmas replied.

"You can go home with me after the factory closes," Lillian said, and the whistle blowing, the girls filed out of the office and back to their work.

It was the longest day Amor Escandon had ever known, the shortest to Christmas. Long before the quitting hour Amor took a violent headache, and Christmas worked all the harder, piling the larger half of her work by the side of her new friend.

George Chesterland waited at the door of the factory to have a chance to bid the girls goodnight. The brief glance he caught of Amor's pale face, and dark, ringed eyes, haunted him. Out of the lot, Christmas was the only happy one. For the first time in her life she had a home, and in addition she had a friend, a sister, and work.

Lillian Day was the victim of bitter jealousy. She was an ambitious girl, she knew the value of her startling beauty, and she had sworn to capture George Chesterland's heart and hand.

Of course he was not rich, but he was the only real gentleman she knew. Her father, Peter Day, had once been a coachman for George Chesterland's father, and he had told his daughter how young George Chesterland use to have a fortune yearly, just for spending money, and that his father had been a very grand gentleman, living in a mansion when at home, but traveling most of his time.

Then something went wrong, Peter Day did not know exactly what. Mrs. Chesterland had died abroad and Mr. Chesterland did not long survive her loss.

After he was gone, there was some talk of wild speculations, big schemes, and the result was that a friend and partner of a minor interest got everything and young George had to go to work, which he did in the factory that had once belonged to his father.

Now he was head foreman and manager, the present proprietor was abroad, and everybody said the boy's chances were good to reclaim in a measure the fortune his father had lost.

Peter Day was a tall, weather-beaten, red-headed man, of rough speech and hearty manner. His wife was also fair and had once possessed considerable beauty, which had sadly faded.

They had been good and wise parents. They were fully aware of their daughter's beauty and she was the apple of their eye, but at the same time, they had been vigorous in their watchfulness. They knew the temptation at every turn in a great city for a beautiful girl, they knew of the wretches who would flatter her to her ruin, and their watchful eye was ever on guard.

Peter Day was very glad to admit the two girls to his family. That they were sent by George Chesterland was enough to insure them a welcome, and his own knowledge of faces convinced him that his daughter would not be injured by companionship with the strangers.

"It'll be company for our gal, mother," he said, when discussing the subject with his help-mate. "She ain't goin' to fret so much to get out now when she has company of her own age in the house."

"Now, gals," he said, when they sat down to their humble supper, "you ought all to be great friends an' have a nice time together, but no beaus, mind you, unless I know them, and no bein' out 'o nights. It ain't proper for young gals, specially pretty young gals like you all."

"What's the use of being pretty if one can't be seen?" pouted Lillian.

"You're pretty to please mother and me," he said fondly.

"Yes, but I can live here and die an old maid for all the good it will do me," was the pettish reply.

"There, there, now, my gal, plenty of time yet before you're an old maid. Do not worry your pretty head over that," her father laughed, patting her golden head with his great, rough hand. "I'll get you a good husband with the right time comes."

"If you're too long about it, I may look for one myself," she said, warningly.

The Days had but four rooms: the kitchen, general sitting and dining room, and two bedrooms. They were all very poorly furnished, their best room being the one that belonged to their only child. It now became the room of Amor and Christmas.

Peter Day took a great fancy to Christmas at once. He treated Amor with more formality, for she was more like Mrs. Chesterland had been, he told his wife in confidence.

And how happy his easy friendliness made Christmas! She watched the parents fondling over their daughter and she thought she would be the happiest girl in the world if she had a father and mother.

When supper was over, Peter Day bade them good-night, and with a luncheon hidden in his coat pocket, went forth to his work.

"When the weather gets nice I'll take you all for a drive in the park some Sunday," he said in parting, and Amor was secretly amused at the picture of herself, the Escandon heiress, riding in a shabby night-cab with two factory girls.

"You mustn't mind father's talk about young men," Lillian remarked confidentially, as the three girls sat around the open fire, Mrs. Day having returned to the kitchen to wash up the dishes. "He has old fogy ideas and the only way to get along with him is to keep still. You can go out Sundays and when you want to go evenings, you can pretend you're going to see some girls, or if you join the Working Girls' Club, you can say you are going there, just as I do, and he won't be any wiser, and what he doesn't know won't hurt him."

"But you would not deceive him?" Amor said, indignantly.

"What are you going to do when you have a father like that?" Lillian retorted.

"I just wish I had a father like that," Christmas ejaculated, rapturously. "I'd never leave him, no, not for the best man in the world!"

"Not even for—Mr. Chesterland?" slyly asked Amor, not a muscle in her face changing.

"But I haven't a father," Christmas retorted brightly.

"No Mr. Chesterland either," Lillian added grimly, and then a strange silence fell upon them and remained unbroken until Amor and Christmas went to their room.

"Do you know?" Christmas whispered, wonderingly, "I believe she's in love with him."

"Him?" questioned Amor stiffly.

"I mean Mr. Chesterland."—softly.

Amor Escandon, or Gray, as she had given her name, threw herself across the bed.

"I don't believe"—she said after a moment's silence, raising her head and glancing rebelliously at Christmas—"I don't believe—he will ever love her."

For some reason unknown to her, poor little Christmas's heart contracted with sudden pain.

VII

A HOPELESS LOVE.

"IT IS IMPOSSIBLE. I CAN'T go to work to-day," Amor said, raising herself on her elbow only to fall back on the pillow again with a heavy sigh.

"Of course you can't, dearest. I seen at once you was too sick to get up," Christmas replied, in a tender, caressing voice.

It was two weeks since the two girls had found a home and work. They had become the closest friends and Amor really clung to patient, helpful Christmas, who adored the stricken girl.

For awhile Christmas was happier than she had ever been before; Amor was suffering intense mental torture.

Every day George Chesterland saw her grow paler and thinner, and his heart was wrung with pain. He knew she was too delicate to endure the mental torture which was hers. She remembered something, he knew not what, and that remembrance was slowly stealing her health away.

Every little thing in this new life grated upon Amor's sensitive nerves. The hearty sound of Peter Day's voice, the shrill, nasal tones of his good-hearted wife, made her shiver with pain.

She realized and appreciated Christmas' unfailing kindness, but still the ignorant speech of the poor girl annoyed her.

"Please, Christmas," she replied peevishly, "don't say, 'I seen,' and 'you was.' It is such bad English."

"I'm sorry," Christmas murmured. "I don't know no better. You know I never was—or were?—sent to school."

"'Was never!' And don't say 'seen' unless you say 'have' or 'had'. Always say, 'I saw,'" Amor added wearily.

"Do you think"—hesitatingly—"there is any place I can go to learn the things you know? I could go after working hours."

"That is a good idea," Amor said, brightening up a little. "There is the Young Women's Christian Association that you could attend evenings. My darling mamma used to be a director in one, and I know working girls were taught everything, free of expense."

"And you think they would take me?"—eagerly.

"I know they would, and I will help you all I can. There, go now, or you will be late. Make my excuses at the factory. If my head gets better, I shall come in at noon for a half day."

"I hope it will get better, dear Amor, but don't come until to-morrow. You will be stronger then," Christmas murmured fondly, passing her hand caressingly over the dark, silky hair, in mute farewell.

Days when Amor was unable to go to work had always been long and tiresome to Christmas, but this day passed like a dream.

Her mind was filled with the thoughts of getting an education and becoming more fitted to be the friend of her darling Amor.

Her thoughts wandered off into a pleasant dreamland. Many were the bright castles she built, as she stitched ceaselessly upon the machine. In every stitch, there went a hope of a better life, a determination to make something of herself.

"How surprised Mr. Chesterland will be when I learn something," Christmas pondered, a pleased flush on her brow. "I suppose he has noticed how ignorant I am. I won't be so any longer, if there is any way out of it, and I'll never, never say, 'I seen,' again."

She started violently when a caressing, manly voice, close by her said:

"Good-morning, Christmas. You seem to be working very rapidly this morning."

"Yes, Mr. Chesterland. I really hadn't noticed how rapidly the work was piling up."

He picked up a vamp and examined the stitching, as he added:

"You are a very faithful girl. There is not another in the factory who gives me more satisfaction."

Christmas raised her great shining eyes to his handsome face.

"You make me very happy," she said, simply.

"The foreman tells me that Miss Gray is unable to come to-day," George said, slowly.

"She is not well," Christmas replied, sadly. "She did not sleep all night, because her head ached so, and she couldn't get up this morning."

"She does not seem strong enough for the work," George said, anxious to prolong the conversation. Even to hear her dear name made him inexpressively happy.

"I hope, sir, you won't think of sending her away"—imploringly—"she is not strong, but it would break her heart to be sent away."

"You think she likes it here?"—joyously. The very suggestion that possibly she liked to be there, maybe, to be near him, set his heart beating wildly.

But it sunk again like lead when Christmas said, honestly:

"You know she can't like it, it is not natural that she should. But she must work, and I know we will never again get any one like you, Mr. Chesterland, to work for."

He sighed sadly. He did not heed Christmas' loyal appreciation, he only thought that Amor did not care. Ah, it was growing too bitter to bear. Every sign of weariness and pain on the loved face drove him to distraction. He knew she was slowly dying, but he feared to offer the only remedy in his power.

It might drive her from him. Oh, horrible thought! And then? Well, life would be an empty space too terrible to endure.

He walked away from Christmas, and Lillian Day stopped him to ask some trivial question. He replied, he stayed near her for a moment because she too had been near his loved one. He tried to turn the conversation toward Amor, but Lillian skillfully avoided the mention of her name.

At last he said bluntly:

"Miss Gray sends word that she is too ill to work to-day."

Lillian laughed softly, showing the two lovely dimples in her cheeks.

Her eyes were very innocent and baby-like as she raised them coquettishly to the handsome face above her, and said:

"She isn't sick, she was out late last night and was too sleepy to get up this morning—oh, my goodness, maybe I shouldn't have told you? Oh, I am so frightened, Mr. Chesterland. I hope you won't let her know I told, and don't discharge her or I'll never forgive myself."

George Chesterland's brow grew black and his heart chilled with sudden fear. He believed no wrong of the girl whose life he saved, and yet the words seared his heart and made him miserably unhappy.

Had Amor, his precious love, an unknown lover? He had never thought of it before. She seemed too young, too innocent.

And still, when he remembered her unceasing grief, her melancholy brooding, there seemed no other reason for it.

"She looks like one who would love once and forever," he thoughts, wretchedly. "It must be that. Any other grief a girl would outlive, but her sorrow is eating out her breaking heart."

The day dragged wearily to him. He watched for the hour of noon with feverish expectancy. She might be able to come then.

But noon came and passed and Amor did not make her appearance.

He longed for night and yet wondered how he could pass the long hours until morning when he would see her again.

Maybe she would not come with the morning. She might never come again.

He had meant to walk with Christmas a part of the way home, but she had gone at the first blowing of the whistle.

Lillian Day was lingering around and when she saw him she said, invitingly:

"Are you going my way, Mr. Chesterland? Christmas Cherry has run off without me."

No girl in the factory made so free and familiar with George Chesterland as did Lillian Day. All the other girls envied her boldness and looked upon their handsome young foreman as Lillian's especial property.

They did not doubt but that it would be a match, for Lillian's wonderful beauty elevated her as far above their level, as was George Chesterland.

George had a very warm admiration for Lillian, and her father had been a faithful servant to his parents, so the young man took more than an ordinary amount of interest in the exquisitely fair Lillian.

"I am going your way, Lillian. May I walk with you?" he asked politely.

"If you think father won't scold."—coquettishly.

"I will take my chances," he replied lightly, and Lillian's vain and ambitious heart beat high with hope.

"I'll win him yet," she thought joyously.

Purposefully she walked slowly along the poorly-lighted streets, grasping his arm at the sight of every slippery place, and turning her baby-like eyes toward him in a pretty, dependent way.

But the walk could not last forever, and George Chesterland had not said the words she longed to hear when they reached her home. She paused on the stoop and gave him her hand, holding on to his while she said, tremulously:

"It was so good of you to walk home with me. I get so frightened, now that it gets dark so early, because men stare at me and speak to me. Oh, I wish I did not have to go out from my home to work."

He felt sorry for her. He knew her beautiful face would bring her unpleasant attention. He felt his blood boil at the thought of low scoundrels insulting poor working girls, and, it must be confessed, he thought of Amor walking home at night with Lillian, whose artful words gave him a chance to offer his escort.

"I can come this way just as well as any other," he said, in reply to her last remark, "and if I am ready in the evenings when you are coming home, I shall walk with you and save you from the rough persons who molest you."

"How good of you!" she cried, impetuously pressing his hands. "I shall be thankful for your company. Good night!"

He lifted his hat, and as she watched him walk away in the darkness, she said joyously:

"He shall be mine, he shall be mine!"

Finding her headache somewhat better toward the evening, Amor got up and dressed. It was dark when she looked from the dingy little window, and Christmas had not yet come from work.

Ever since Christmas Day, when Amor deserted her home, she had feverishly watched the papers, hoping and yet dreading to read some news of her father. What did the world think and say? How had her father accounted for the absence of his wife and daughter? Had the crime been discovered? Were there detectives looking for her?

"I think I will go out for the evening papers," she said suddenly to Mrs. Day, who was busy in the kitchen. "I think the fresh air will help my head."

"Don't be long, then, for father will be getting up in a few moments, and the girls will be here for their dinner," Mrs. Day replied.

Amor walked to the corner newsstand a few blocks away, where she bought the evening papers. She paused in the gaslight to scan the printed pages, looking ever for the proud old name of Escandon.

This time her search was rewarded. With a sharp cry, she saw the name, and breathless read the brief notice. It was as follows:

> "Mr. Mateo Blanco, the wealthy Spaniard, is making New York his headquarters this winter. He is a great favorite, socially, and is much entertained in face of the fact that he is affianced to his beautiful cousin, Miss Amor Escandon, who is the sole heir to Señor Ricardo Escandon's millions. Señor Escandon is traveling about for the benefit of Mrs. Escandon's health. Miss Escandon is with her parents. The sudden failure of Mrs. Escandon's health makes the date of the wedding a matter of conjecture; but when it takes place it will be one of the most distinguished society events that has aroused interest in years."

"Oh, my God!" said Amor, in bitter anguish. "What frightful tales they tell to escape justice. My poor dead mother!"

The tears rolled down over her pale cheeks. Crushing the newspaper in her small, trembling hand, she started to go, when a firm hand grasped her shoulder, and a smooth, oily voice said, gloatingly:

"My dear Amor, I thought I would soon put an end to your romantic escapade."

With a sharp cry of distress, beautiful, helpless Amor turned and looked into the cunning black eyes of—Mateo Blanco, her deadly enemy!

VIII

PUT ALL TO THE TEST AND—LOST!

AMOR'S HEART STOOD STILL WITH terror.

She hated and feared Mateo Blanco with all the intensity of her being.

The sight of his triumphant face so near her own made her lose all presence of mind.

She forgot to run—forgot to try to escape, but stood there motionless, gazing fixedly into Mateo Blanco's gleaming eyes.

"My dear little beauty, I thought I would find you!" he continued, gloatingly, paying no heed to her frightened silence. "And now I do not mean to lose you again."

"What do you want?" Amor gasped indignantly.

He tightened his hold on her arm, and his eyes flashed with passionate love as they feasted on her pale, frightened face.

"I want you for my wife, my disdainful beauty, and I mean to have you," was the determined reply.

Amor shuddered, and with a gesture of supreme loathing, tried to free herself from his grasp.

"Let me go," she said, hoarsely. "How dare you profane me with your touch?"

"Those are not sweet words to hear from my betrothed bride," was the reproving response.

"Your bride!"—with passionate vehemence—"I would die first!"

"Not so fast, my pretty Amor—my love!" he replied calmly. "Your father consents to our union."

"Even his command could not make me wed you," Amor declared angrily.

"Not so fast again, my Amor; I have something better than your father's command—I hold your father's life in my hands! Do you hear?"—roughly. "If you refuse to become my wife, I will send him to the gallows for murder!"

Amor gave a cry of horror. Although she had known the worst, his words pierced her heart like a knife.

Her father's life depended upon her. Unless she consented to marry this man, her father would have to pay the penalty of his terrible crime upon the gallows.

He had murdered her precious mother, it was true; still, he was her father. Dying for his crime could not give back that gentle life.

Long ago had Amor consigned him to Heaven's mercy. "God rewards and God punishes; it is not for me to do either," she had thought.

And now she must sacrifice herself if she wished to spare her father the disgrace of dying the death of a loathsome murderer.

She might parley with Mateo Blanco, and gain enough time to make her escape, she thought, cunningly.

"If you are determined to sacrifice either my life or the life of my father, let it be mine. Return to my home, and I shall meet you there to-morrow."

He laughed in her face.

"Do you take me for a fool?" he demanded. "You are quite cunning, my beautiful love, but not cunning enough for me. You must go with me, and I shall see that you have no chance to indulge in your romantic escapades again. Come along; I will be able to find a cab on the next block, perhaps. There does not seem to be much of anything except darkness in this God-forsaken neighborhood."

"Let go of my arm!" Amor protested in a low, frightened voice, "or I shall call the police."

"Do, my dear," he retorted coolly, proceeding to drag her down the dark street. "Call all you please—and when they come, I shall tell them that you are my crazy wife, that ran away from home, and that I have just found you."

"You would not dare!" she cried, terrified, still struggling with all her strength to free herself.

"I would dare anything to make you mine," was the firm answer.

"Oh, Heaven! Is there no one to save me?" cried Amor, feeling her strength deserting her.

"Yes, there is!" answered a clear voice behind her, and Mateo Blanco caught but one glance of the stranger before a well-directed blow laid him senseless upon the hard pavement.

At the sound of that voice, a flood of great joy swept over Amor, and with a glad sense of being safe and secure, she turned and threw herself into the arms of her preserver.

"Save me!" she pleaded trustingly, gazing with big, beseeching eyes into the handsome face above her.

She could not help seeing how tender it grew, how passionate love beamed from the bonny blue eyes. She could not help noticing how his strong form trembled and how wildly his heart beat.

And for some reason unknown to herself, she thrilled with joy to think that her rescuer was none other than handsome George Chesterland.

For one sweet, brief second he pressed her to his heart, forgetting everything but that the girl he loved to madness was in his arms.

Then he remembered her danger, her enemy lying so still upon the pavement, and with a sigh he released her from his embrace.

Instinctively he knew that Amor would not want her annoyer arrested. George had seen the whole interview, and though he had not heard what had passed between them, he had seen enough to know that they were not strangers, and that Amor's only desire was to escape from this man.

"Come; let us go before he revives," he said, and drawing her arm through his, they walked rapidly down the street, carefully keeping in the shadows.

He took a roundabout way to her home, choosing the darkest streets, and wishing the journey might last forever.

For a long time they walked in silence, George too happy to think of anything to say. She was by his side, her little dimpled hand rested upon his arm, he could gaze to his heart's content upon her lovely white face.

Amor was the first to speak.

"You saved me from death, Mr. Chesterland, and I could not thank you for it," she said, tremulously. "To-night you have saved me from a fate too horrible to recall. Your kindness has put upon me a debt I can never repay."

"Please do not think of it," he begged quickly. "I thank God for His goodness in placing me near you at your time of need."

"I hope you may come to no trouble through your kindness to me," she continued, thoughtfully.

His heart gave a quick throb of joy. Could it be that she cared a little for him? Surely there was something more than relief in her manner when she cast herself into his arms.

Why should he not speak to her now? He could not bear the constant agony of thinking he might lose her, that she might go out of his life again.

If he were ever to speak, why not now? Surely she would never be in a gentler mood to listen to his love. And besides, he could not bear to think her unprotected, hourly exposed to the danger from which he had just saved her.

"I wish I might have the right to protect you from all danger," he said, huskily.

Amor caught her breath with a quick gasp, which George, in his excitement, did not notice.

"To see you growing paler and weaker and thinner, day by day, " he continued, hoarsely, "has been torture to me. It makes my heart ache to see your pale face bending over the heavy machine; and yet, if you were too ill to come to the factory, your absence would make me just as miserable. Not an hour since I saved you from the river have I known any peace."

She did not speak, and encouraged by her silence he continued, his voice thrilling with the wild love that throbbed in his heart:

"Amor, I love you! Will you be my wife, to cherish, to protect, to love, so long as we two may live?"

She felt herself turn cold. Little drops of perspiration stood on her marble brow, her curved lips trembled, and yet within her burned a resentment as unjust as it was cruel.

"Does my indebtedness to you give you the right to insult me?" she inquired icily.

"Insult you?" he repeated, wonderingly, a sharp pain cutting his heart.

"I think you would understand that for you, a working-man, to presume to address me, is an insult," she explained, as haughtily as a queen.

Had he been less the gentleman, George Chesterland might have retorted that as she, Amor, was his factory-girl, the honor was on his side. As it was, he strove manfully to hide his deeply wounded heart, and said softly:

"A working-man may also be a gentleman, Miss Gray. Money and position alone are not all that is necessary to make one."

They had arrived at her humble home. The sight of it recalled to proud Amor that she was no longer the Escandon heiress, but a poor little outcast, depending upon this man whom she had so scornfully refused for her daily bread.

"I hope," she began tremulously, "that you will not allow this unpleasant incident to affect Christmas Cherry's position in your factory."

"Rest assured," was the hasty reply, "that nothing can make me esteem the brave little Christmas less than I have done since her first appearance in the factory."

"You are very good!" Amor responded, much more humbly.

She turned to leave him, and a great fear at his heart made him forget his pride and her scorn. He could not let her go this way. Her anxiety for Christmas seemed to warn him of something more—a something he felt unable to endure.

"Miss Gray, one word more, I beg of you," he pleaded impetuously. "No, I shall not 'insult' you again"—seeing the expression of fear creep into her face—"I only wish to ask you not to allow my words to-night to drive you away from the factory. For the sake of Christmas, whose heart is wrapped up in you, do not go away. I promise never to annoy you again, and I think you may rely upon me to keep my word."

"You have made it impossible for me to continue any longer in your employ, Mr. Chesterland."—haughtily. "I am too much in your debt as it is."

"You can discharge the entire obligation," he cried with passionate eagerness, "by remaining in the factory. I implore you, for Christmas' sake, as well as your own, to remain."

She glanced quickly at his handsome face, and the pleading, anxious look if bore only made her heart grow colder.

"Let me again thank you for your kindness to me, Mr. Chesterland, and bid you good-night."

"You will come to the factory?"—pleadingly.

"I beg you will not compel me to reply again. I have delayed dinner long past the hour, and I must ask you to excuse me—"

"Amor!"—desperately—"I swear to Heaven I shall not be responsible for what I do if you drive me mad by your cruelty. Promise to return to the factory or—"

"You mean to threaten me? Is this the conduct of a gentleman?"

"You were the first to remind me that I was not a gentleman, that I am only a 'working-man,' far beneath you. Don't drive me to desperation, I say, or the result will be on your own head."

"Good-night, sir," Amor returned, freezingly, and before he could prevent her, she stepped into the house and closed the door in his face.

"My God!" he cried, despairingly, as he staggered blindly down the street. "What have I done? Driven her from her only means of livelihood, driven her to starvation and death. My God! What can I do?"

On he walked, not heeding what he was doing until he found himself on the corner where Amor had met her enemy. And the self-same man stood before him.

"You scoundrel!" he hissed in low, angry tones. "Where did you hide that young lady? Tell me at once, or by Heaven, you shall be made to pay for this!"

George Chesterland was in a fit mood for a quarrel. He felt as if it would be a relief to his over-wrought feelings to knock some one down, and when he glared down on the little, thin, under-sized Spaniard, he looked very formidable indeed.

"Be careful how you fling names, my little dude," he retorted mockingly. "The young lady you tried to carry off is doubtlessly safe by this time and if I know where she is, you may be sure I will never tell you."

"I'll have you arrested! You will be made to tell in court where you took her," spurted Mateo Blanco, but less courageously.

"That is right; have me arrested," George retorted, fearlessly. "We shall see whether the ruffian who tries to abduct a girl, or the man who saves her, fares the better before a judge."

Mateo Blanco had not the least idea of appealing to the law. In fact it was the last thing he would have done, for the least breath of suspicion in the Escandon quarter might cause an exposé, and his cousin's crime once known, Mateo Blanco's power would be over. To gain Amor and the Escandon millions, that crime must remain known to him alone.

"I know your face, young man," he cried angrily, shaking his fist at Chesterland. "We'll meet again, and then, beware! You shall be made to pay dearly for having helped a runaway wife to elude her husband."

He walked away and was soon lost to view, while George Chesterland leaned weakly against a lamp-post, gazing fixedly into the darkness, and repeating aimlessly:

"A runaway wife! Her husband!"

IX

THE ANGEL IN RAGS,
AND HER WORDS OF WISDOM.

"IT IS TIME TO GET up, my dear! Here is a cup of coffee. I made it for you myself," said Christmas Cherry the next morning to her dear friend and companion, Amor Gray.

The night before they had had no chance to exchange confidences, even if Amor had been so inclined. Christmas had gone to night school at the Young Women's Christian Association, taken there by Peter Day in his shabby old cab, and if Amor was awake when Christmas returned, she made no sign.

Poor Amor had slept but little. Toward the morning she had fallen into an uneasy slumber and Christmas, always bright and early, had slipped out of bed to prepare a cup of coffee for her.

Amor opened her eyes reluctantly at the sound of Christmas' voice. She was too miserable to come back to life and thought. There was a load on her heart and a nameless fear within it. She felt that in some way she had lost something that had left life a blank. What it was she did not know.

"How early you always are, Christmas," she replied, resting on her elbow and gazing wonderingly at her friend.

"That is because I am so very healthy," Christmas explained, perching herself on the edge of the bed and holding the saucer while Amor daintily sipped the steaming coffee. "When you are strong and can sleep dreamless from the moment your head touches the pillow until day-break, you'll be able to get up early, too. I'm afraid you didn't sleep well last night, dear; you look so weary."

Amor sighed heavily, and handing the cup back, sunk down upon her pillow, her luxurious black hair forming an ebony setting for her pale face, lit up by great melancholy, midnight eyes.

"I did not pass a restful night; but talk to me about yourself, Christmas! Did you like the school?"

"I like it!"—rapturously. "Oh, dearest, I am the happiest girl on earth."

A bitter self-reproach cut Amor. To see the joy of this poor street waif over her meager blessings made Amor feel ungrateful and undeserving for the advantages she had enjoyed.

"I'm sure I'm the luckiest girl alive," continued Christmas. "I've you, the sweetest friend; I've work, and the noblest employer;"—(Amor winced)— "I've a comfortable home, and the kindness of friends; I've a chance to get an education just for the learning; what more do I need?"

"Contentment is the sweetest boon on earth," Amor remarked with a tinge of envy.

"And you'll be contented after awhile, dear Amor," Christmas said quickly, laying a loving hand upon the silken black hair.

"I am afraid not! You see, Christmas, it is all so different and so hard and so cheerless, after that which I have been accustomed to."—sorrowfully. "Life does not seem worth living when one has nothing."

"But, dearest, the remembrance of the past should help make the hard things easier!"—cheerfully. "Why, don't you think if I had a home and parents, and nice dresses to remember, I'd be happy in the thought they'd once been mine? I'm sure you are, too."

"Not a bit of it!" Amor replied stoutly. "It is the remembrance of what has been that poisons the present. If I had never known anything different to this!"—throwing her arms out with a despairing gesture—"and yet this must be my life so long as I live."

"Then why don't you make up your mind to forget the past and get all the happiness you can out of this?" sensibly inquired Christmas. "I'm sure everybody can find happiness if they only look for it. And it is all there is to live for, Amor. You may be in rags or silks, and if you ain't—I forgot— *are not* happy, what difference does it make? And if you are happy, what do you care whether it be in rags or silks? We've only got one life, and we don't know what's to come, and we should remember how short life is, and enjoy every moment of it."

"What a little philosopher you are!" laughed Amor, cheered in spite of herself.

"And you must be one, too. Come! Out of bed; I am going to help you dress," Christmas rattled on. "What was that pretty saying, or motto, or whatever you call it, that you repeated one night at the table? Tell it to me, for I intend to have it printed on the wall where you may read it every day. It was something about eating and drinking and laughing and dying!"

Amor laughed and jumped out of bed. Christmas Cherry was like a tonic to her melancholy spirits. "It was, 'Eat, drink, and be merry, for to-morrow ye may die!'" she replied softly.

Then laying her tiny white hands on Christmas' two shoulders, she looked into the charity girl's great, soulful eyes and added tremulously:

"You are an angel in rags, Christmas Cherry. I had intended to give up my work to-day and die, but your little sermon has given me new life and courage. I am going to work again, and I intend to try to be more contented."

"Girls, girls!" called a voice at the door. "Breakfast is ready, and father says he is as hungry as a bear."

There was no time for further conversation. Christmas pressed her red lips to Amor's pale cheek, and Amor saw the big tears which filled her loyal friend's eyes.

A little later the girls, with Lillian Day, set out for the factory, each with her luncheon under her arm. Even factory girls had ceased to carry luncheons, but wise Mrs. Day insisted on her girl taking something substantial for noontime.

"A wee bit of pie or a sweet cake, like those silly girls buy at noon, just ruins their health," she declared. "My girl sha'n't be too proud to carry their luncheon."

So Lillian Day was forced to take what her mother provided, even if she did hate to be seen carrying it to the factory. Christmas and Amor having no such silly notions, took their luncheons as a matter of course.

Up to this time Christmas had always insisted on the right to carry Amor's luncheon as well as her own. Amor was weak and easily tired, she argued, and Christmas usually had her way.

"I intend to carry my own luncheon, Christmas," Amor declared stoutly this morning. "Hereafter I must bear my share of the burden and not permit you to take it all."

Christmas was wise enough to let her have her way.

"I hate to carry a luncheon worse than anything in the world," Lillian Day observed, with a little pout. "I was so thankful last night that I had taken mine in a paper, for Mr. Chesterland brought me home, and I should have died if I had to carry a basket when I was with him.

Amor drew in a long breath at the mention of George Chesterland's name, but never lifted her head.

"I don't believe Mr. Chesterland would think any less of a girl for carrying a lunch-basket," Christmas said mildly.

"You don't know men, Christmas," Lillian responded loftily, with a toss of her beautiful, golden-red head. "They may pretend to be very careless, but then they walk the streets with a girl they admire, they don't want anybody making remarks about her. Mr. Chesterland knows how much men look at me. He says it's because I have such an unusual face for a working girl, and he wanted to see me home every night to protect me from annoyance."

Christmas felt her face grow crimson at this information delivered so boastfully, and Amor turned colder and her heart grew heavier.

"Does Mr. Chesterland make a point of acting as protector to all his employees?" Amor inquired, cuttingly.

"Oh, no, indeed!" Lillian answered, decidedly. "He has never so much as looked at any girl in the factory except myself. You see, my father and his father were friends in better days, and that was the first bond between us."

Amor could not repress a shudder. To think that George Chesterland's father might have been a night cab-man, the friend of coarse Peter Day! And the son of such a person had dared to aspire to her hand!

If Amor had only known the truth, that George Chesterland had been as nobly born and reared as herself, it might have made some difference in her unhappy fate. But between her blindness and pride, she stumbled on to the bitter end.

Lillian Day was fond of talking about being "reduced" and "better days," and although the two girls knew she was given to boasting and exaggeration, they did not imagine she would go so far as to picture the employer of her father as his friend, and they both fell into the error of thinking George Chesterland had risen from the depths.

"Let him pay his attentions to one of his own kind," was Amor's indignant conclusion, mentally. "It is dreadful to think he would dare to presume to address me."

And yet when they encountered him, pale and woe-begone, at the door to his office, she saw with a thrill of satisfaction how his eyes rested hungrily upon her face, and how his broad chest rose and fell with almost a groan of relief.

He gravely inclined his head to her, spoke kindly to Christmas, and answered Lillian's light banter, and yet Amor passed on to her work with a lighter heart.

"He cares more for me than he does for Lillian Day," she thought exultingly, and then hated herself for caring what a plain, ordinary workman might think of her.

"If he were my footman, he could not be farther beneath me socially," she thought, with all the lofty pride of the Escandons.

And still she waited feverishly for him to make his daily rounds through the factory. What would he say to her? Would he dare to reproach her?'

She worked as she had never done before. Christmas lifted her head frequently to give her a smile or an encouraging word; and remembering her resolve to try to do better, Amor felt less miserable.

At last George Chesterland came. She knew he was present before she saw him by the way the girls ceased talking and increased their work. She knew when he stood by Lillian Day, although she did not raise her pretty dark head, and her blood ran more rapidly when she heard Lillian's low, soft laugh mingling with his manly tones.

He could laugh! It cut her to the heart. Then he had not cared so much after all!

He stood by Christmas at last, examining her work and watching the color come and go beneath his glance. She would never be a beauty, he thought, but there was the prettiness of innate purity and nobility in her expressive face. Her color was certainly improving, and he fancied she was not quite so thin as she used to be.

"No one could think her homely when they see those great, soulful eyes of hers," George thought, as some remark of his made Christmas raise her eyes for one timid, worshipful glance.

Then the foreman came up and took him away, and he never once looked in Amor's direction.

She felt her heart flutter clear up to her throat and then sink down like lead when he walked away. So deeply was she disappointed that the tears sprung to her eyes and fell upon the leather she was stitching. All the hope that had been in her heart died away, her buoyancy vanished, and luncheon hour found her listless, weary, and dispirited.

And that was not to be all the humiliation she was to bear that day.

When evening came and the three girls started for home, George Chesterland made his appearance, and, lifting his hat in silent recognition of Christmas and Amor, requested Lillian Day to permit him to walk home with her.

Lillian could scarcely restrain her happiness. Up to this time she had a suspicion that George Chesterland had taken a fancy to Amor Gray. But his choice this night left no doubt in her mind as to his preference.

"I must do my best to bring him to the point at once," Lillian thought gleefully. "I don't intend to spend many more days in the factory. Once George Chesterland's wife, I'll dress and have a grand house and fine jewels—if he has to steal to provide them!"

Unconscious of the vain thoughts in the beautiful girl's mind, George Chesterland walked beside her, answering her coquettish remarks with light sallies, and keeping his watchful eyes upon the two girls walking arm-in-arm in front of him.

As they hurried their pace, he increased his to keep up with them, in spite of Lillian's evident desire to lag behind.

"Shall we wait to say goodnight to Mr. Chesterland?" Christmas asked hesitatingly as they reached the Day abode.

"It is unnecessary," Amor replied coldly. "Our presence would only be unwelcome."

So they passed in, and George Chesterland hardly heard Lillian's sweetly spoken good-night, for the bitter cry which burst from his aching heart:

"My god! She hates me too much to even bid me good-night."

X

FORGIVEN.

IN A SMALL, DINGY ROOM, sitting by a window that took in a dismal vista of dirty back-yards and roofs and innumerable clotheslines, sat Amor Escandon.

She wore only her night-clothes, the clinging folds of which disclosed the painfully sharp angles that were rapidly replacing the curves of her once exquisite form. She had drawn her dress-skirt around her shoulders, and was sitting with her feet under her to keep them warm. Her heavy black hair was streaming carelessly over her shoulders and around her sad face, which gleamed like ivory against the black mass.

There was no fire in the dingy room, but unhappy Amor never thought about the cold. Her big, melancholy eyes wandered from the dreary window vista to the solitary bed and its slumbering occupant.

Once Amor was always the last to wake up in the morning. Now she never seemed able to sleep.

"Two months!" she sighed sadly. "It seems like years! Can I be the same Amor Escandon who rested on a bed of down beneath silken coverlets, whose slightest wish was law to an army of servants, whose meanest dress was worth more than I can earn in a whole year? Sometimes I think it is a nightmare, or that I died suddenly and this is the punishment they say comes hereafter. But I must not think so. In that way madness lies, if I am not already mad. I know Christmas is real and healthy, and flesh and blood. There is nothing unnatural about her, except her goodness.

"I have half a notion to go back," she continued—"back to the dear old life! And yet"—she stopped with a shudder—"it would not be the same—it could never be the same again. Mother is dead, by this time she is—Oh, God, have mercy upon me—teach me to forget."

She paused, her lips twitched with pain, but that was the only sign she gave of the agony in her heart. Tears did not come easily now.

"But why not give up the struggle and go back?" she resumed. "Surely it would be less miserable to live as Mateo Blanco's wife than to endure the privation and agony of this? I should have money enough to buy forgetfulness, I would have enough to send Mateo away. No one would care if I disappeared from this life, no one except Christmas. I could take her along, I could give her fine clothes, a luxurious home, and then—"

"Amor, do you mean to kill yourself?" cried Christmas, waking up suddenly. "Please come back to bed at once. I am sure it is not time by an hour for us to get up."

Amor roused herself and tried to smile. "I will come, Christmas," she replied obediently. "I could not sleep and I did not want to dress for fear of waking you."

"There, get into my place," Christmas said, moving to the other side of the bed, "you will get warm the quicker. Oh, dearest, how cold you are! Your feet are like ice and your teeth are chattering. Lie close to me until you get warm."

"I did not know I was cold until I moved," Amor said apologetically. "I am afraid I shall chill you."

Christmas' reply was to slide her warm arm around the half-frozen girl and draw her closer.

"Poor Amor!" she murmured fondly. "It breaks my heart to see you so sad and unhappy. Is there nothing we can do to help you?"

"Nothing!"—wearily. "Death is my only hope of rest.

"Have you forgotten the two suicides I read about last night?" asked Christmas reproachfully. "A man who committed suicide because he was out of work and he had not been dead who hours until a letter arrived from Germany announcing that a large fortune had been bequeathed him. The other, a poor woman whose husband had been reported lost at sea, had barely swallowed a large dose of poison when her husband rushed in to tell her of his rescue and return, only to have her die in his arms. Surely the darkest hour is just before the dawn. How many suicides do you think would willingly seek death if they knew what good would be theirs by the exercise of a little hope and patience? My dear, can't you think your hardships are blessings in disguise? Some day you will see how you could have lost everything worth living for, if it had not been for what now seems like your misfortunes?"

"Christmas, you always see some good in everything."

"And am I not right?"

"Not always. What good has resulted from my misery, pray?"

"Loads of good!"—vehemently. "In the first place, it gave me something to love, and then you suggested to me the way to get an education. You have helped me with my lessons, and by associating with you, I have learned to correct my faults of speech and manner. Why, only yesterday Mr. Chesterland said he could hardly believe I was the same girl who marched so boldly into his office on Christmas Day and demanded work. And that was only two short months ago!"

"Two short months!"—with a groan. "Two eternities!"

"Do you know, Amor, it pains me to hear you talk so. You are naturally brave, why have you given up so thoroughly?"

"It does seem foolish," agreed Amor, less sadly. "I try to remember to 'eat, drink, and be merry' for when I die, I'll be dead a long time, and the grave is not a cheerful place. But memory will not be still, and, and—well, I will try to do better!"

And she kept her word. After one of Christmas' little lectures, Amor always worked better for a few days, and then she gradually drifted back to her sad musings.

In all this time since Amor had scornfully refused George Chesterland, they had barely spoken. He always had a word for everybody else, but if he even noticed her work he talked to Christmas while he was doing so. And still, he did not look like a happy man.

Since the night he rescued Amor from Mateo Blanco, George had moved down-town, nearer to the Days. He wanted to be near Amor, for day and night the memory of the Spaniard's dark, evil face was ever before him. His heart was seared by the last speech the Spaniard had hurled at him:

"His runaway wife! Her husband!"

Many times he could barely restrain the impulse to go to her and cry out that he knew the truth, that she was a wife. And then the fear of driving her entirely out of his life kept him back.

He still walked home with Lillian Day. How was she, as well as Amor, to know he did it for the sake of his love? Had Amor even permitted it, he would not have walked with her, for every day he expected to meet Mateo Blanco, and he did not want Amor to be seen with him.

Amor was feverishly bright at her work that day; Christmas watched her with deep anxiety, for the girl had eaten no breakfast, and her face was as white as wax, while her hands burned like fire.

When George Chesterland made his rounds, instead of lowering her pretty black head over the machine, as was her custom, she looked up at him with a pleading smile upon her white lips.

His face flushed and his heart almost stopped beating when he saw the change in her demeanor. He dare not ask himself what it meant, he dare not even think about it.

"How is my work, to-day, Mr. Chesterland?" she inquired, her voice trembling in spite of herself.

He reached over, nervously, to examine her work; his hand touched hers and the contact set his blood on fire and made him tremble like a leaf.

His breath came in labored gasps. In vain he tried to master himself enough to reply. He straightened up, intending to give himself time, when he saw that her beautiful face had grown deathly pale.

She had mistaken his emotions. She thought he would not speak to her, and feeling herself growing strangely weak, she got up, only to fall into a dead faint in his outstretched arms.

Telling the foreman to quiet the fears of the girls, George Chesterland carried Amor out of the noisy room into his office, followed by Christmas, wild with alarm.

"She has only fainted, Christmas," he said, huskily. "Dip that sponge into the water and hand it to me, please."

Christmas quickly obeyed, but Amor rested a long time against George's heart before she came back to life.

"Amor?" he cried appealingly, fearing that she would never look at him again—"Amor! For God's sake, answer me?"

The sound of his voice brought her back, and she gazed fixedly up into his handsome face.

A look of relief crept into the dusky depths of her midnight eyes, and a burning blush spread gradually over her white face.

"Will you forgive me?" she whispered faintly.

He lifted her white hand to his lips, and, unmindful of Christmas, kissed it reverently.

"It is I who begs your forgiveness," he replied, brokenly.

"Then you will not be angry with me any longer?" she asked, gladly.

"I have never been angry"—sorrowfully—"I have only tried to act as I thought would please you best."

And then he remembered her husband and with a slight inclination, motioned for Christmas to take his place.

Although the silence between them was broken, Amor found on her recovery that she was still far from him.

While Amor would have as soon thought of cutting off her right hand as of marrying a workingman, still she was so human that it hurt her to know that another woman stood a fair chance to win him.

"He could not have loved me much, or he would not be so attentive to Lillian Day," she thought, with selfish resentment.

George and Christmas both insisted on Amor returning home for the day. She was not fit to work, they could see. Christmas took her home, and quit her work half an hour earlier so as to have some time to sit with Amor before the hour for school.

So it happened that George Chesterland walked home alone with Lillian Day. When within a square of Amor's abode, George came face-to-face with Mateo Blanco.

There was no doubt about the recognition, for the Spaniard paused, and a hateful smile crossed his dark face. His eyes rested on Lillian Day and a gleam of admiration came into them.

"Ah! Here is my chance for revenge!" he said to himself. "That fellow is in love with this beautiful girl. I'll take her from him! One good turn deserves another, and so does a bad turn. He stole Amor from me; I will steal his sweetheart from him."

Brave as George Chesterland was, his heart stood still at the sight of Mateo Blanco.

"Heaven help me! It is her husband!" he groaned. "He will find her—he will take her from me!"

"Did you speak, Mr. Chesterland?" inquired Lillian, noting with some anxiety the young man's pallor.

"No. I have a pain in my head. Would you mind giving me your company for a few blocks fathers? I think the air will do me good."

He did not want to take her home while Mateo Blanco was on their track.

"He wants a chance to propose," thought vain Lillian all in a flutter, and aloud she said:

"I shall be happy to go with you. Don't you think you could get something to help your head? I am afraid you do not take the proper care of yourself. You work so hard, and you have no one to look after you and—care for you!"—with a sigh.

"That is true!" he responded sadly. "I have no one to care for me."

"Oh, my dear Mr. Chesterland, don't say that."—with pretty wistfulness. "I did not mean that exactly; I meant that you had no home of your own. Of course there are a great many that care for you—care a very great deal, too."

George was too busy thinking about Mateo Blanco's movements to hear every pretty word which fell unceasingly from Lillian's pretty lips, so her last remark was received with silence. She had considered it a master stroke.

She bit her lips with vexation when he turned about and took her back home. The way was clear; Mateo Blanco had disappeared, and George rushed Lillian into the house, fearful lest the Spaniard should reappear before she had vanished.

"He is too provoking," Lillian thought tearfully. "How long, I wonder, does he expect to keep me on a string? If I only had some one else to play against him, I would soon bring him to terms."

Within the house Amor lay in bed, cuddling against her pale cheeks the flowers that George Chesterland had missed his lunch to buy her.

No name came with them, but as she caressed them fondly, she murmured:

"He still cares a little bit."

XI

CHRISTMAS HAS TWO ADVENTURES.

"CHRISTMAS! ARE YOU READY, GAL, to go to school?" called out a loud voice.

"I am coming, dear Mr. Day," replied Christmas, leaning over to press a farewell kiss upon Amor's soft cheek.

It was the day following Amor's fainting spell, and she had been too weak to leave her bed. Christmas had come home early, and Lillian came home alone, for some unusual business kept George Chesterland in his office after hours.

"Air ye ready, daughter? It's gittin' late," Peter Day continued, at the door of Lillian's room.

"I'm not half ready, father," Lillian replied. "You go on with Christmas, and I'll stop for one of the girls on my way."

"But I don't like yer goin' alone, gal," her father said anxiously. "The other gal might be gone 'fore ye git there."

"No; she promised to wait for me," was the reply.

"All right," was the half satisfied answer. "Come out and give yer old dad a good-night kiss."

"I can't, father; I told you I wasn't half dressed."—petulantly.

"All right, daughter. Take care of yourself. Remember ye're all mother and dad's got to live for," he said affectionately. Then, giving his wife a hearty kiss, he took Christmas by the hand, and when out, grumbling:

"I don't like these here girls' clubs. Better fer gals to stay at home nights with their mothers; but then, I can't deny my Lilly every pleasure. 'Twould break her dear little heart."

"I am sure the working girls' club must be a very nice affair, dear Mr. Day," Christmas murmured, consolingly. "And Lillian must have some amusement."

"Why ain't you hankerin' after amusement, gal?" he demanded shortly, "'stead o' goin' to school an' studyin' hard? I kin tell ye"—as he pulled at the door of his battered old cab—"it's 'cause ye ain't a beauty. If ye were, you'd have no notion fer anything but fixin' yerself up and gittin' people at admire ye."

"I am sure that is not true of Lillian, and she is certainly beautiful."—loyally. "Besides, you must remember that she is through her school days; mine have just begun."

"I'm thinkin', little Christmas, you've got something they don't larn in books."—softly. "And as ye say, Lillian's a good gal, but I'm afeared if we didn't watch her, her vanity would lead her into many slippery places. Ye see, Christmas, I ain't been a 'night-hawk' for all these years and not learned the evil of the world, and the plans that's laid for pretty gals. Jump into yer victoria, little lady, and yer driver will take ye to school."

Christmas saw Peter Day hastily wipe his eyes ere he mounted his box, and with a cheery word of "Sal," his bony, faithful old nag, drive down the street.

Next to his wife and daughter, Sal was the apple of Peter Day's eye. His dear old partner, he always called her, for she helped him make a living for the two at home. Sal got the best of care within his means, but in spite of it she was a bony old white horse, more miserable looking than the majority of her class.

"There's nothin' like a white horse fer night trade," Peter Day had confided to Christmas—a warm friendship had sprung up between these two. "My pard Sal brings me more customers than a red lantern. And a lot of sense the old gal has got, too. She knows a drunk soon as she sets eyes on him, an' she lifts up her head and grows uneasy like, just as much as to say: 'Partner Peter, here's a customer; yell "Cab,"' and I do, and she's mostly right."

These evenings passed all too rapidly for Christmas; she consumed everything she was taught with unslaked thirst, and she had become the wonder of the school. The teachers took a great pride and interest in her, and seeing that she was anxious to gain an education, spared no pains to help her on.

Peter Day drove her to school, because it was on the way to his stand, but Christmas always went home alone.

She did not mind this. Fear was unknown to her, and she was so engrossed with what she had been taught during the evening that she saw and heard nothing of what when on in the streets.

But this night she was forced to notice an occurrence that had an effect on the course of her whole after life.

In one of the prominent thoroughfares she saw a crowd of people gathered. She intended to cross to the other side of the street, and so avoid them, when she heard the voice of a woman.

There was something in her voice that made Christmas' heart stand still with horror, but at the same time some strange feeling urged her on until she had made her way into the midst of the crowd.

She saw wailing in the dirt within the gutter an old white-haired woman in a dreadful state of intoxication.

The crowd was jeering the pitiful creature, amusing themselves at her expense. The poor wretch had sense enough to know this, and in her rage had pulled and dug at the pavement, trying to get a stone to hurl at her tormentors, until her hands were torn and bleeding.

Christmas gazed on the sickening sight with disgust at first and then a gentle pity entered her soul. Without a moment's hesitation she stepped before the groveling creature, and turning her big, flashing eyes upon the laughing crowd, exclaimed:

"Stop! This poor degraded creature may be some one's mother!"

An intense silence fell upon the crowd at once. Several men drew back as if ashamed of their conduct.

The old woman ceased to yell and gazed with stupid wonder upon the girl that had placed herself between her and her foes. Then she began to utter in a maudlin way, most frightful words.

The crowd looked at her brave little defender and laughed uproariously.

"What if she were your mother?" Christmas asked, sadly.

"She's right!" a man declared, huskily. "I'll give fifty cents toward taking the old woman off somewhere until she gets a chance to come around."

"I will take charge of her, my friend," said a man, advancing from the outer edge of the crowd. "I am interested in a home for such poor mortals. If some one will call a cab, I shall take the woman there at once."

Christmas looked at the speaker. He was a tall, well built man, with a dark, handsome face that bore in every line of it the stamp of goodness and nobility.

He was dressed well, but plainly, and did not look to be over thirty-two years old.

"I arrived just in time to hear your noble defense of this poor woman, miss," he said to Christmas. "I thank you from the bottom of my heart for a very Christian act. Will you permit me to give you my card, and to invite you to visit my church?"

Christmas Cherry was covered with confusion. She accepted the card, thanking the minister, and quietly took her departure, not waiting to see the outcome of her adventure. But the memory of it was buried deeply in her heart.

It proved to be a night of surprises for her.

Hurrying to her humble home, and when very near it, she stumbled upon two persons standing at the corner. They were engaged in earnest conversation, and as she raised her head to apologize for her rudeness, she found herself looking into the beautiful face of Lillian Day.

Confused and surprised, Christmas gazed from the handsome girl to her companion, a slender, dark man who eyed Christmas with no amount of curiosity.

"Lillian—I beg your pardon!" Christmas murmured, brokenly.

Lillian was no less confused, only with her confusion was mingled a little anger.

"How awkward you are, Christmas! Will you wait for me at the door? I want to speak to you before you go in."

"Will you not introduce me to your little friend?" the stranger asked, carelessly.

There was no way out of it, so Lillian performed the introduction with bad grace.

"Mr. Matthew White, my friend, Miss Christmas Cherry!" she said shortly.

Christmas felt herself shudder when she looked into his little shining, beady eyes. Somehow her thoughts flew back to Peter Day, and her heart grew soft with pity.

"If you are not coming, I must go on, Lillian," she remarked stiffly.

"You will not forget, my beautiful friend?" murmured Matthew White, bending very low over Lillian's hand.

Lillian's foolish heart fluttered triumphantly as she assured him of her intention to remember.

"Good-night, Miss Christmas!" he added, holding out a hand, which the girl pretended not to see.

"Good-bye, sir!" she replied as haughtily as even Amor could have done.

He laughed softly as if amused, and stood twisting the ends of his black moustache, and watching the girls as they walked to their door.

"If it were not for my revenge," he mused slowly, "I'd rather have the ugly one. How those wonderful eyes of hers flashed! A girl with eyes like those would love to desperation. I'd like to bring the love-light into them; it would be some amusement. I wonder if I can't manage both?"

In the meantime, Christmas and Lillian had reached their door.

"I don't want you to tell any one about seeing me with a young man to-night," Lillian said, nervously.

"You mean to deceive your father and mother?" Christmas inquired indignantly.

"I don't mean to be tied down like an old maid."—angrily. "I mean to have some fun and see the world. What's the use of being good-looking if I can't be admired? You won't tell on me, Christmas, will you? What they don't know won't hurt them."

"Lillian, I don't like to be unfriendly, but you told your father that you were going to your club and instead you went out to meet a strange man. If you don't tell them what you have done, I must!"—decidedly.

"Tell them!"—desperately—"and I'll run away from home with him!"

"Now I shall most certainly tell them," Christmas said as she took out her key and unlocked the door.

XII

"A RICH MAN AND—A POOR MAN?"

LILLIAN DAY ALMOST FAINTED WHEN she heard Christmas Cherry's low, determined answer.

Tell her father and mother that she had deceived them? The very idea made her tremble with terror.

She must do something, it mattered not what, to alter Christmas' decision, and so save herself from exposure.

"Christmas, listen to me!" she pleaded nervously, laying a detaining hand on the girl's shoulder. "That is the brother of one of our club members. He came there to take his sister home, and then he walked on up with me. You won't tell, will you, Christmas? You see, I didn't exactly mean to deceive father and mother, but you know how they would scold, and they wouldn't let me go to the club any more."

"Why did you stop on the corner?" asked Christmas suspiciously.

"Because I was afraid to let him come to the door. I didn't want any one to see me with him," was the tearful reply.

"Then why did you let him come with you?"—sternly.

"I couldn't refuse. It seemed so silly to say, 'My father won't let me walk with a man because I'm pretty.'"

"I don't think that was necessary. You walk with Mr. Chesterland, and nothing is said about it."

"If my father didn't know him, you would hear me catch it!"—shortly.

"Then you shouldn't walk with a man your father does not know."

"The truth is, Christmas, that I was ashamed to say I wasn't allowed"—petulantly—"but if you don't tell on me this time, I'll never do it again. I vow I won't."

Christmas relented. It was not a pleasant task to tell the fond parents their daughter had deceived them, and Lillian seemed so repentant, and her story seemed so simple and straightforward, that Christmas decided the best thing to do was to put her on her honor for the future, and to keep secret her one mistake.

"If you promise me, on your honor, never to deceive your parents again, I will not tell this time," she said.

Lillian joyfully gave the required pledge, and the girls entered the house the best of friends.

Christmas was delighted to see how greatly improved Amor was the next morning. A little smile transfigured her pale, sad face, and a strange light of happiness beamed from her soft, black eyes. She seemed not only able to be up, but displayed a feverish eagerness to return to her uncongenial labors.

The decided change in the girl who had, previously resigned herself wholly to her unhappiness, was noticed by the whole household.

Christmas was delighted beyond measure; Peter Day and his good wife were pleased to see the improvement; Lillian Day alone looked upon the change with disfavor.

If Amor had attracted George Chesterland before, in spite of her chilly haughtiness, how much more attractive she would be to him now, in this new, soft, gentle mood.

So Lillian reasoned to herself, and found no happiness in the conclusion.

She had set her heart upon George Chesterland; she meant to win his love and become his wife. He was the only man she had ever known who came near to satisfying her worldly ambitions.

She wanted family, position, and wealth, and although George Chesterland had at his father's death been reduced from affluence to poverty, his name would still have given him admittance to the choicest circles had he wished to be in society.

And Lillian Day knew this. She was determined to become George's wife, and then she meant to find her way into the charmed circle of society, to be a member of which seemed the acme of bliss to her.

In her daydreams all this seemed possible. Her enrapturing beauty was to her the magic passport to success.

Lillian had never feared a rival until she met Amor Escandon, or Gray as the girl was known.

There was that something of innate delicacy and refinement that bespoke the lady, born and bred. Lillian was conscious of it, and although she counted herself much handsomer than Amor, still she feared her.

So Lillian Day watched George Chesterland with the keen eyes of jealousy when he made his rounds that day.

She saw how timidly he approached Amor, and she bit her lips with vexation because his back was toward her.

Some one else—Christmas—was near enough to see how quickly Amor raised her head to speak to her handsome employer, and how the delicate pink stained her white cheeks beneath the glance of his tender blue eyes.

Poor George Chesterland! Amor had never deigned to smile upon him before, and when she bestowed her sweetest smile upon him this morning, he could hardly overpower the impulse to clasp her to his heart and claim her as his own in spite of herself and grim fate.

"It was very kind of you to send those sweet flowers," she said in a low, thrilling voice. "I am afraid I held them in my arms until they died."

His face flushed with happiness, and Amor trembled when she heard the passionate ring of love in his voice as he replied:

"I am glad if I have done something to give you happiness."

"You have done a great deal," she answered lowly, her lips trembling.

"I wish I were not 'only a working man,' so that I might be your friend," he said longingly.

"I see; you have not forgiven me," she whispered reproachfully.

"If you committed the most unpardonable of sins against me, do you think I could refuse you forgiveness?" he asked quietly.

In after days they thought of this vow with tears and heartaches.

"I don't know," she murmured confusedly, looking down at her work.

"Amor"—masterfully—"look at me!"

Her heart fluttered wildly, a strange, new shyness made her fear to meet his eyes, and yet she could not disobey his quiet command.

Slowly her big black eyes were lifted, and for one instant the loving blue ones gazed into their midnight depths as if to read her very soul.

"Amor," he breathed, a passionate wistfulness in his voice. "You know I would give my life to serve you."

"Yes, I believe you," she said sadly.

He gave a sigh of relief. "Then, knowing that, you will let me warn you of your danger. Do not be frightened, but last night I saw—your husband again."

Amor looked at him wonderingly, her black brows meeting in a puzzled manner. "My husband?" she repeated. "You are certainly mistaken."

"I assure you, no."—earnestly. "I remember his face distinctly, for I saw him again that night after I left you."

"Oh!"—with a shudder—"is it possible you thought me married and that wretch my husband? Why, I am but a few months past my sixteenth birthday, and that man is my bitter enemy. How could you form such an idea?"

"Nothing was further from my thoughts until he made such a declaration to me," George explained, his face radiant with joy. "He said you were his runaway wife."

"Then you questioned him?"—haughtily.

"Amor!"—reproachfully.

"Pardon me. But did he tell you—everything?"—anxiously.

"We met, as I said, after I left you. He demanded your whereabouts, and when I refused to tell, he vowed he would take me to a police court, and we should see if I could keep a runaway wife from her husband. But as he did not seem inclined to carry his threat into execution, we parted."

Amor gave a great sigh of relief. "You are too kind to me," she said gratefully.

"You will be careful of yourself?" George whispered anxiously.

"Before I would be in that man's power, I will kill myself!"—passionately.

He was satisfied. He meant to shield her from harm; he vowed to win her for his own, and he was happier than he had ever been before in all his life.

She was free to be won, and all else was as nothing. What mattered her haughty pride, her bitter prejudices? He was a man, he meant to be master. All her opposition must melt before his love. In spite of herself, he would win her love.

His dream would not have been so roseate could he have glanced into Amor's heart at that moment. Removed from the sweet magnetism of his presence, she was frightened by her forgetfulness.

"How handsome and manly he is!" she thought with a sigh. "It is cruel that he should be a poor man, a mere nobody. If he were only rich! But he isn't, and I could never love a poor man. Imagine, marrying a foreman of a factory! Ugh! It makes me shudder! To live like the Days, and probably have a half dozen of sickly children to look after. Heaven defend me! If I loved George Chesterland with all my soul, I could not marry him."

"What are you thinking so seriously about, Amor?" called Christmas, looking up from her work.

Amor gave her friend a gentle smile, but a haughty curve was on her pouting lips as she replied, pensively:

"A rich man and—a poor man!"

XIII

CHRISTMAS CHERRY'S FIRST LOVER.

IT SEEMED AS IF A little cloud had come over the spirit of Christmas Cherry's bright dreams.

However dark and intense it was within her heart, it seemed but a fleeting shadow to her friends. They saw a suspicious nearness of tears in her soulful eyes, a sweet, pathetic droop of her sensitive lips, a weary languor of manner, and nothing more.

And they said among themselves: Christmas has worked and studied too hard, the strain is telling on her at last.

"You had better give up your study for awhile," Amor said, anxiously. "You have undertaken too much. I fear you will make yourself ill, and what should I do without my little ragged angel?"

Amor always tenderly called Christmas her angel in rags. Not that the tidy girl had the sign of a rag about her, but because she was such a poverty-stricken angel.

Christmas smiled sorrowfully. She said nothing, but if they could have known, instead of lessening her studies she increased them and feverishly demanded occupation for every spare moment.

"I must not think," she would say to herself with a sort of mild frenzy. "It is no use. It only increases my unhappiness and does not alter it. Nothing can change matters. I must learn to bear it."

Even George Chesterland, engrossed as he was in Amor, saw the change in his favorite, and was alarmed by it.

"You are unhappy, Christmas," he blurted forth. "Tell me what it is, little girl, and let me help you."

Her face grew pale as death at his words, and her heart felt as if it must split in twain, so bitter was its pain. But like the brave little heroine she was, she replied softly:

"It is nothing, Mr. Chesterland. Amor says I study too hard, and Mrs. Day says I don't eat enough, and Mr. Day says—"

She stopped in confusion, remembering what he had said.

George laughed. Amor had anxiously repeated honest Peter Day's words, as if she feared they might be true.

"What did Peter Day say?" George urged laughingly.

"I would rather not say," she replied, too honest to pretend she had forgotten.

"He said you were too good for this world," repeated George, watching the sweet, downcast face. "And Lillian—what did she say?"

"Now, please don't," murmured Christmas in deep confusion. "Lillian has been telling you."

"Lillian did not say a word to me. But what she said to you—is it true?"

What Lillian Day had said was that Christmas acted as if she were in love, and to have George Chesterland tease her about it was almost more than Christmas could endure.

"What if I should ask you such a question?" she replied defiantly.

"I should say, 'Yes, Christmas, I am in love.' And you?"—still laughing.

"Please, Mr. Chesterland!" she pleaded, so piteously that his heart ached because of his thoughtlessness.

He could not help seeing how white her face turned, not the big tears which fell on her work.

"Pardon me, my dear girl," he said humbly, and she managed to give him a pitiful smile in token of her forgiveness.

"Christmas is in love," he said to himself afterward. "Poor little girl! I am afraid her love has not brought her any more happiness than mine brought me."

Poor, blind man! If he had only known the bitter truth, he would have been the most wretched mortal on earth.

This interview gave Christmas a feeling of desperation such as she had never experienced before.

"I can't stand it!" she thought with a sob of anguish. "I thought I was strong enough, but I was mistaken. I will have to go away, leave Amor and my work and my school—and him! My heart will break if I stay here."

It was like death itself to think of giving up Amor, her friend, her sister. And yet, how could she remain with her? This torture day after day would drive her mad.

It was while she was in this despairing mood that her greatest temptation came to her.

As she was returning from her school one evening, she saw a gentleman take off his hat to her as he was passing, and then turn and come back.

"Miss Christmas, have you forgotten me?" he said at her elbow.

She turned and recognized Lillian's friend, Mr. Matthew White.

"You passed me without speaking," he continued, without waiting for a reply. "Have I unwittingly offended you or did you mean me to understand that you did not wish me to be honored by your acquaintance? However you put it, I consider that you were very cruel."

They had been walking on while he made this long speech, and the eyes he thought so entrancingly beautiful were gazing at him in surprise.

He did not mind that. So long as they were turned in his direction and he could feast his soul in their limpid depths, he was conscious of a certain happiness. And he hungered for more. He had longed to see those witching eyes again, and he felt himself more than repaid by the first glance she gave him.

"Don't you mean to speak to me?" he asked.

"Yes," she replied frankly. "I was wondering what to say."

He laughed so heartily that Christmas smiled in sympathy, without knowing in the least the cause of his mirth.

"You are a strange girl. Why shouldn't you know what to say to me?"—curiously.

"Because I cannot understand why you took so much trouble to speak to me."—simply. "If you expect me to tell you anything about Lillian, you will be very much disappointed. Her father does not permit her to know young men, and I would not help her to deceive him."

"Bother Lillian!"—carelessly. "I don't want to know anything about her. Now can you guess why I took so much trouble, as you call it?"

He looked boldly into her sweet, earnest face, and wicked as he undoubtedly was, his worldly heart throbbed as it had never done for woman before. And that for the sake of a nameless waif, when he could have had his pick and choice of any number of society's fairest flowers.

"I am sure I cannot imagine."—wonderingly.

"It was because I was hungry to gaze into the most beautiful eyes in the world, to listen to a voice that is the sweetest music to me," he explained breathlessly.

"You mean—!"—in amazed stupefaction.

"I mean"—tenderly—"Christmas Cherry!"

He took her hand and in spite of her silent resistance, drew it through his arm and with his warm, gloved hand, held it there. She could feel his heart throb fast, strongly, passionately, and a little sense of awe crept into her own.

"Don't try to draw away from me, Christmas," he said huskily, giving way to the love that throbbed in his breast. "You may think me mad, or what you please, but I have never loved a woman before as I love you, and

Heaven knows, it has not been for a lack of opportunity. I never believed in love, such love as I feel for you. I never thought I could experience it. But the first glance of those lovely eyes of yours, the other night, stole my senses away and I have thought of nothing else since. Are you going to let me love you, little girl?"

"I am sure you are jesting," Christmas faltered, piteously.

"Heaven above is witness of my truth."—solemnly. "Look into my face! Do I look like a man who is jesting?"

She turned her tender, shining eyes toward him. She could feel how his arm trembled beneath her light touch, she could see that unmistakable something in his eyes that shows the love in the heart—a something that cannot be feigned. She had seen it in George Chesterland's bonny blue eyes when he was looking at Amor. Though it had never shone for her before, she knew it well.

"You are convinced," he continued, huskily. "And what is to be my fate?"

"I do not care for you. I do not know you, you do not know me! Oh, it seems unnatural," she said in distress.

"It will seem natural enough, if you will let me teach you to love me," he replied, impetuously. "Let me see you sometimes, let us get acquainted, and then—"

To one disappointed in love, it is very comforting and soothing to find oneself the object of another's affection. Christmas was no less human than any one else in this respect, and she found herself listening to Matthew White's pleading with an eagerness that surprised her afterward.

"But I cannot see you," she said, not without a tinge of regret. "Mr. Day, with whom I board, does not permit his daughter to see gentlemen, and I could not think of disobeying his rules."

He looked at the slim, girlish figure at his side and the purity in her face made his heart grow gentle. For one moment a good impulse prompted him to go away and leave her happy in her sweet innocence. Then he thought, selfishly, if he left her, some other man, a worse one probably, would find the pearl, and his sacrifice would have been for nothing. Besides, he was more used to indulging himself than listening to good promptings.

He could have told her a different story about Lillian Day, and one that would have horrified Christmas, but it did not suit his purpose to do so.

Lillian and Christmas could have told him something, too, had not a strange fate kept their tongues silent. They could have told him where to find Amor Escandon. Lillian Day was silent because she feared to introduce a rival; Christmas, partly because it was not her habit to speak about absent ones, and partly because every thought of Amor opened her heart-wound anew, and she was trying to forget.

"But if you knew me better, you would not care for me—at least, not enough to marry me."

Matthew White gave a start at the mention of marriage.

"You see, I am very poor and friendless," she added, sadly.

He knew her entire history; he had it from Lillian, who, alarmed at his many questions concerning Christmas, was only too glad to expose her nameless condition.

Matthew White rejoiced that it was so. It suited his purposes better.

"I know your history," he said tenderly. "Don't ask me where I heard it; but you know a man in love is going to learn all he can about his sweetheart. I love you all the more because you are alone—I am, also; but, unlike you, I have money, plenty of it, little one, and if you will consent to love me you shall have a grand home and fine jewels, your own horses and carriages, servants by the score, and myself as your fond lover and slave."

The very possibility of such wealth and grandeur made Christmas grow breathless. Bright dreams flashed into her mind. If she accepted this man, she could give Amor all the luxuries for which she craved; she herself could satisfy her hunger for learning and travel. And dresses and horses and servants!

Why, she could give Peter Day a new and young horse, and Lillian should have some pretty dresses. And, oh, how much good she could do among the sick and destitute!

And yet—and yet—

They were within a couple of squares of her home. They were passing a saloon, and as the door swung open, the light fell upon a group near the curb.

A man stood holding a young by the hands. The boy was staggering, and yet he was bent upon entering the saloon, although there was a trace of shame in his face, brought there by the pleading words of the handsome man who held his hands.

Some magnetism in Christmas' gaze made the man lift his eyes, and Christmas saw it was the minister who had befriended the intoxicated woman.

A look of recognition flashed into the minister's eyes as they met Christmas', and the noble look on his handsome face sunk deep into her heart and remained there.

"What a noble life is his!" she thought enviously, "always trying to raise and better poor fellow mortals!"

"You will let me see you again?" Matthew White was pleading, and she roused herself to reply.

"I do not know."

"You must! I know you won't be cruel. How can you bear to give me such needless pain? Only let me see you once again, I ask nothing more now," he begged.

"If you meet me by chance again, I cannot prevent it," she replied. "But I shall never make any engagements with you."

Little she knew that Lillian Day had told him all about her ignorance, and how she went to school at the Young Women's Christian Association every night.

He did not enlighten her, but he smiled triumphantly as he said, fondly:

"Good night, cruel love! We shall meet soon."

Christmas thought of the expression on his face, and the expression on the face of the minister as he tried to reclaim the wayward youth, and, as she unlocked her door, she murmured:

"I wonder what Amor meant by: 'A rich man—a poor man?'"

XIV

UNKNOWN TO THOSE MOST CONCERNED, fair Lillian Day was having a struggle with herself.

Ever since the day she met Mateo Blanco, or Matthew White, as he had given his name to her, she had been the victim of a thousand fears and doubts.

Time after time she had, on one pretext or another, gone to meet him, and her ambitious little soul had listened greedily to his talk of wealth and position.

She knew he was preparing the way for something; she had a faint idea of what, and she waited the end divided between her worldly ambition and her fears.

Often she grew reckless when thinking of what might be. She was tired of her dreary life, she hated to work, she was ashamed of her honest old father and mother, she longed for ease and luxury and fine raiment.

With all her weaknesses and faults, she cherished a sincere affection for George Chesterland, as deep at least as she was capable of feeling. He was strikingly handsome, he was masterful and withal so tender that almost any woman was bound to feel a certain regard for him. Even Amor, with all her pride and disdain, could not withstand the charm of his manner.

Lillian knew, all too well, that Amor had given up the struggle against her heart, and had allowed herself to drift—drift toward the haven of George Chesterland's love.

And it was this knowledge that was helping to drive Lillian Day on to an unhappy fate.

"If I must give up George Chesterland, where am I to find another that will satisfy my demands?" she had questioned herself. "I will not stay here to see another girl take him from me, and yet I am afraid to listen to Matthew White."

Heaven knows she did not love Mateo Blanco, her Matthew White. His dash and fine clothes and gay talk dazzled her, and made her more discontented with her humble lot, but she did not imagine she loved him.

Without a doubt the man's flattery pleased her foolish vanity. She remembered every light speech of his, flattering words that he said to pass the time and forgot as soon as they were uttered.

If it had been little Christmas, or any one less vain than beautiful Lillian, she would have detected Matthew White's insincerity at once. There was no ring of passionate love in his voice when he addressed Lillian, as there undoubtedly was when he talked to Christmas.

And yet he admired Lillian Day. It would have been impossible to have done otherwise. She was undoubtedly beautiful. He had seen many beautiful women, as he told her, but none so beautiful as herself.

If she had but known, he added to himself:

"And I have never yet met a superbly handsome woman who possessed any soul."

The night following the one on which Matthew White had walked home with Christmas, he was engaged to meet Lillian.

It was just as well, he said to himself, to stay away from Christmas for awhile. Besides, he had not forgotten his revenge in his new-found love.

More ambitious than Lillian, even, was Mateo Blanco. His heart was set on marrying his cousin's daughter, to gratify his greed for wealth, for position, and for the name of having the most beautiful wife in all their grand circle.

George Chesterland had been instrumental in depriving him of all this.

Mateo Blanco had Ricardo Escandon in a position where he must sacrifice his daughter or his life, and it needed but the presence of Amor to give Mateo Blanco the desire of his life.

There were not many hours in which Mateo Blanco did not remind himself of what he had lost through George Chesterland, and never once did the vengeful Spaniard waver in his plan of revenge.

Had honest little Christmas seen him greeting Lillian Day, she would have been thunderstruck. No fond lover could have been more tender, more attentive.

"You have made me so happy," he breathed tenderly, when his hands clasped Lillian's. "I almost feared you were not coming, and I was wretched beyond compare."

"Father stayed home so much later to-night, and then I had to work to quiet mother's fears," Lillian pouted, looking very sweet. "I know mother is growing suspicious, and I will soon see you no more."

"You mean to harden your heart against me—to shut me out of your life forever," he said, very like a fond lover.

Lillian's heart bounded with pleased vanity.

"He loves me very dearly," she thought. "He'll be wretched if I do not see him. I wish George Chesterland could see how other men love me. I have half a mind to let them see that I can marry a finer and wealthier one than George Chesterland will ever be.

And then her heart would sink like lead. The plain, honest words of her poor old father came back to her in solemn warning.

"Never have anything to do with a man," he had often said, "who won't come out and above regarding his intentions to ye. If he wants to be sly and stealthy, make up yer mind he isn't honest and means ye harm."

"I don't care," she once thought recklessly. "Anything is better than this dreary life. I've decided to go with him, if I suffer for it."

"I am sure you have some other lover you care for more than you do for me," Matthew White said to her. "That is why you mean to stay away from me. But perhaps that lover has another girl. How can you know? And would he give you all the luxuries that should be yours? Can he give you diamonds to wear around your exquisite white throat? Can he give you independence, servants, carriages, and dresses fit for a princess? I can—I will! I only ask one thing in return—your love!"

"But you don't say anything about marriage," she suggested frankly. "I can only accept such gifts from my husband."

"My beautiful Lillian"—tenderly—"have I not explained to you that I am a man of impulses, of romantic notions? If I wanted a wife in the ordinary every-day way, would I not have been married long ago? But instead, I have been searching for my ideal, and"—softly—"I have found her. But I demand a test on her part. Must I give her everything, wealth, position, love, and get nothing in return?"

"Ah, no!" he continued with a sigh. "I must know she loves me—not for what I can bestow upon her, but for myself. You may say I am wrong"—sadly—"nevertheless, it is my belief, my hobby, and I will never take a wife that refuses to accept that test!"

"And that is?" Lillian inquired lowly.

"That she must resign herself to me without fear, without a question; that she must love and trust me enough to go with me without a word to father, mother, or friend, that she must love me enough to make my life her life, my people her people, my ways her ways. Will you give me this proof, oh, my beautiful lady, the most lovely of all women? If you intend to open those perfect rosebud lips to say me nay, it would be kinder to take my dagger and run it through my heart!"

Lillian shuddered. Her father's face rose before her, and she could hear his wise advice:

"Beware of a man that's sly and sneaking! He means you harm!"

"I can't give you an answer to-night," she replied faintly.

He smiled. The old saying, that the woman who hesitates is lost, came to his mind. He felt sure he had won—and his revenge would soon be complete.

"You are not sure of your love."—with soft reproach.

"It is not that."—evasively. "But it is the thought of the pain I shall cause my parents. It makes me hesitate. Give me a day or two."

"I will give you two days. Meet me two nights from to-night, and if you will not do as I ask then, I shall never see you again. Until then, my beautiful dear, farewell."

Poor, foolish Lillian Day! She walked back to her humble home thinking only of what she could gain by submitting to his odd request.

Strange to say, the very idea that had come to Amor and Christmas came to her. And still stranger was it, that they were all thinking about the same man when the thought came to them.

"George is poor," Lillian thought reproachfully. "Of course I love him best, but Matthew White is rich, and what I lack in love, I can gain in luxury. Which shall I take, the rich man or the poor man?"

XV

THE GREED FOR WEALTH,
THE FEAR OF POVERTY.

THE THREE GIRLS, THE HEIRESS, the beauty, and the charity waif, did mighty battle with their hearts the next day.

Rich man—poor man? They asked themselves the question a thousand times, and each time were no nearer a decision.

It would have been very easy for Christmas Cherry to decide had there been the least hope for her where her love was given. There was no vanity in her to mislead her with false hopes.

She loved George Chesterland with all the intensity of her honest little heart. She regarded him with a kind of worship. He had been her first friend, her benefactor, her deliverer. No one could ever be to her again quite what he had been.

Why she had been so foolish as to let herself love him, she could not tell.

Many times, during the first dark days of her pain, she had recalled the morning she had sent him to save Amor from death, and so had lost him. In spite of her sincere love for Amor, the unhappy girl drifted into dreams of what might have been had she not called handsome George Chesterland to Amor's rescue. How would that have changed their fates?

Had George not known Amor, he would not have suffered the pangs of unrequited love. Had he never known and loved Amor, he might have learned in time to care for friendless Christmas. Had she not called George, Amor certainly would have been spared much suffering.

It might have been! By her own volition she had lost him.

Poor Christmas! Her face burned when such thoughts came to her, and her loyal heart rebelled.

"How wicked and mean I am!" she cried in horror. "It is almost as if I were planning dearest Amor's death. I deserve to lose her and her love for being able to harbor such thoughts. Heaven knows I am glad that I have her! I am glad that it is as it is. I have them both now, where otherwise I could only have one, and perhaps even then he would not have cared any more for me than he does under the present circumstances."

So, with tears in her eyes and a fierce pain in her heart, Christmas tried to think everything was for the best.

Unlike Lillian Day, who could see no good in all her trouble. Lillian grew more fretful and peevish the longer she brooded over her position.

She hated the very sight of Amor's pale face; she shuddered at the sound of her mother's high, sharp voice; she felt ashamed of her father's coarse garments, and despised the broken-down old Sal and the shabby cab, by which Peter Day gained his livelihood; she felt an impatient resentment against Christmas, and as for her humble home, she could have set fire to it with the greatest pleasure in the world.

Everything about her only served to remind her of what could be hers.

In place of old, shabby dresses, there would be Paris gowns "fit for a princess." Instead of the barren old home of four rooms, she could be a mistress of a brownstone residence large enough for a hotel.

Instead of seeing her father's old cab at the door, she would have her handsome brougham and victoria, drawn by a high-stepping team, gay with clinking, silver-mounted harness. Instead of working in the factory, she would have an army of servants to wait upon her.

Heaven help her! It seemed impossible to resist, to throw away all the grandeur, and yet she feared. She feared for the safety of her good name. It almost seemed as if she knew Matthew White did not mean to act honorably toward her.

She was not blinded or deceived by his talk about finding an ideal and testing her love. She knew if he were honest and meant to do what was right he would ask no test.

"It means that I give up this life forever," she said to herself, with a pale, frightened face. "It will be a terrible risk, but maybe I can make him love me well enough to fear some one's taking me away from him. Then I could frighten him into making me his wife, and the world would never be any the wiser."

The more she thought of it, the more it seemed worth the terrible risk.

There was only one thing to prevent her taking that risk, the terrible risk of her soul and reputation for a few worldly luxuries. And that was the faint home that George Chesterland would eventually ask her to be his wife.

She would take George Chesterland and his prospective wealth a thousand times sooner than Matthew White and his present fortune. The one she knew would be above reproach, the other, she felt, beneath it.

"I must have a little more time," she thought despairingly. "I must have time to see if I can win George Chesterland in spite of that white-faced mystery."

If she could have read the battle that was going on within the trouble dmind of sweet Amor Escandon, she would have shouted with joy.

For Amor felt herself drifting farther and farther from handsome George Chesterland. The more she thought of him and his love, the colder grew her heart.

He was only a poor man, and a working-man at that. She might have possibly forgiven his poverty, possibly, she was not sure, but she could not forget his being the manager of a factory and the son of a cab driver, or something like that.

She found herself when in the company of Peter Day, which happened only at breakfast and at seven o'clock dinner, picturing that George Chesterland's father must have looked so coarse and weather-beaten, must have spoken such frightful English, and, horror of horrors, may also have eaten with his knife and drank his coffee from a saucer!

It was impossible for her to appreciate the goodness that underlay all this uncouthness.

Christmas could forget the little faults of breeding in the knowledge of the true heart beating under the coarse old coat. But that was because Christmas had once possessed almost the same faults herself, Amor remembered pityingly. It was only natural, she said to herself, that Christmas should not feel shocked at such exhibitions of ignorance.

As for herself, she had never seen the like before. From her birth she had been surrounded by cultured and polished people.

Never once did Amor's heart soften toward her handsome young lover, but that some unpleasant thought of his lowly parentage hardened her again.

Once, when she felt a little pity for George, believing his father to have been so coarse and vulgar, she felt a thrill of disgust sweep over her when she remembered that she had never seen George eat. She had taken his refinement for granted.

It seemed impossible to think him like Peter Day. And yet, perhaps he ate with his knife and in his shirtsleeves.

"Imagine if I were so crazy as to listen to his love," she thought with tears in her big black eyes. "Why, he might sit before the fire without his shoes just as Mr. Days does, and come to the table in his under-shirt and trousers. Heavenly Father, I must be mad to think of him for a single moment. Poor, lowly born, ill-bred, a laborer!"

She sighed. She could not help it; it seemed so wrong that one so handsome, so winning, so noble, should have been so unfortunate as to have been born the child of poor parents.

"It almost reconciles me to the thought of going back home and marrying Mateo Blanco," she thought, with a pitiful quiver of her rose-bud lips. "There at least I would find no ill-bred persons to shock me, and poverty would never haunt my dreams again."

Often Amor thought there was nothing else left for her but to return to her home and the man she hated the worst on earth. This miserable existence could not last forever. There must be a change or she would go mad.

The only thing that had bound her to life at first was loving Christmas Cherry. Amor returned the sincere affection Christmas had given her. She had found strength and courage and hope in Christmas' simple honesty and sensible way of looking at things; and Christmas had found Amor of inestimable service to her in her studies.

Christmas created no little sensation one morning while at breakfast by saying to Peter Day:

"I feel that I have been acting underhandedly to you by letting you believe that I have always come home alone from school."

Everybody looked at her in amazement. Christmas saw the sorrowful surprise depicted upon Peter Day's face, and her own flushed rosily, but she continued bravely:

"I do not feel, while I am under your roof, that I have a right to do anything that you would not permit Lillian to do, and that is why I tell you that a young man walked home with me the night before last."

"What a fool the girl is!" was Lillian's mental comment.

"My noble little angel in rags," Amor thought, a suspicious tightness in her throat.

"I don't know as I have any right over ye, Christmas, gal," Peter Day replied frankly. "Long as ye are well behaved, an' I know ye be that, I ain't got no right to say what ye shall so an' what ye sha'n't do in regard to young men. I ain't got no fears of ye doin' wrong, but be careful, gal, for your own sake. You be very young, an' ye don't know the wickedness of men, so be careful fer your own sake."

"I am sure Christmas will be careful, Mr. Day," interposed Amor, giving her friend a fond look.

Christmas had told Amor as much about her experience as she deemed loyal to Lillian Day, and now she told the same thing to Peter Day. That she did not tell the entire story was because she had promised to shield Lillian, not that she had any desire to deceive any one.

"I met a gentleman on my way home from school," she continued in her sweet, brave voice. "He had been introduced to me before by a girl friend of mine."—they all, even Lillian, supposed she referred to some school-friend. "Although the young man is still a stranger to me, I am sure he is honest and good, for he asked me to be his wife."

Poor honest Christmas! Mateo Blanco's words had no other meaning to her. She thought his offer of love and wealth an offer of marriage.

"And if ye consent, gal, I know Heaven above will pour its blessin's on ye," was Peter Day's hearty reply, as he hastily brushed his eyes.

Christmas' confession created a sensation. They all began to look upon her as if she had acquired a new interest for them.

Lillian thought, with a pang of jealousy, that even Christmas, who had no good looks to speak of, was likely to marry before her, with all her beauty.

"I have not accepted him," Christmas answered Peter Day with a little smile, "but I wished you to know, because I may see him again."

"And be good to the lad when you do, for a man that comes straight out an' asks a gal to be his wife is honest and trustworthy. It's the kind that fills your ears with pretty speeches an' don't say a word about marriage that ye've got to beware of," Peter Day observed.

Lillian shivered, as if a chill had struck her heart.

XVI

THE FIRST TRUE LOVE OF HIS LIFE.

"YOU SEE, LITTLE SWEETHEART, I have found you again," laughed Mateo Blanco at Christmas Cherry's look of surprise when she found him after school hours waiting for her upon the first corner.

"I see you have," she replied, not without a thrill of gladness.

It was very sweet to have some one care so much for her. And now, since she had told Mr. Day all about it, she felt she might indulge herself, and enjoy the pleasure of this new experience without doing wrong.

"Won't you say that you are just a little bit pleased to see me?" he pleaded, hungrily, taking her warm hand and holding it close in his.

How her big eyes glistened! They were like two bright stars as she raised them to his face and let him feel the magnetism of their intoxicating depths.

"I am glad to see you"—earnestly—"I never thought I should be so glad."

"My darling!" he murmured rapturously, and his heart bounded with joy, for he thought the prize he longed for was almost within his grasp.

"I don't mean to let my little love walk any more if I can help it," he said, drawing her arm within his. "I have a carriage here and I mean to drive home with you."

Christmas laughed happily. It seemed so kind and thoughtful of him, and under the circumstances she had no more hesitation in accepting his kindness than she had in letting Peter Day drive her to school every evening.

"Isn't this better than walking, darling Christmas?" he asked joyously as he took his place beside her, "and you would never need to walk again if you would only listen to my prayer."

"Please don't begin on that subject," Christmas pleaded pointedly. "Let us just be happy, and after we are better acquainted we can talk about love and marriage."

"So we can," he affirmed. "But you will bear in mind, in the meantime, that I am a very impatient and jealous lover. I want you for my own at once."

"If you get me at all, you will have to bide my time," she said spiritedly.

He laughed, as if highly amused, and took her hand.

"What are you laughing at?" Christmas demanded, trying to draw her hand away.

He pressed her hand to his lips and then released it, as he replied:

"I am laughing at my independent little sweetheart. I wonder if any of the beautiful young ladies I know would be so indifferent to the offer of my heart and home?"

"I am not exactly indifferent."—smiling a little. "I am lost in amazement just yet because you care for me at all. I can't see why one so wealthy and all that could care for a poor little nobody like me and wish to marry her."

"Can't you?" he repeated evasively. "And do you also doubt my love? Do you think it all pretense, little Wisdom?"

"Oh, no"—stoutly—"I know you love me honestly and—very, very much. If you did not, you would not want me to be your wife."

"What a wise little girl you are."—tenderly. "Ah, my sweetheart, I never thought I could love a woman as much as I love you."

For an instant a wish entered his soul that he might be innocent of all worldly ambitions. Then would he have clasped pure Christmas Cherry to his heart and defied fate to take her from him.

But the love of gold, and of the luxuries and vanities of this life, was stronger to him even than it was in Lillian Day. He knew if he gave up Amor and her millions and married Christmas, that he would soon forget his love in the face of poverty.

Nor could he give up Christmas. The very thought of never seeing her again was as bitter as death. To leave her, to know she would be won by some one else, to feel that those soulful eyes would beam with love upon another man, was like trying to pull his heart, warm and throbbing, from his breast.

"I will die before I give her up," he swore to himself, and yet he never once thought of giving up all hopes of Amor, nor even his revenge on George Chesterland through Lillian Day.

"Tell me that I may come for you to-morrow night," he pleaded, as they stopped at Christmas' door. "You will let me bring you home if I wait on the same corner for you?"

"I cannot tell you not to come, if coming pleases you," she replied softly.

"My sweetheart!" he exclaimed with passionate tenderness, kissing her hands, because he feared to kiss her tempting lips. "Until to-morrow night, then?"

"Until to-morrow night."—softly.

"Confound Lillian Day!" Mateo Blanco exclaimed as he rode away. "I had forgotten entirely my engagement with her for to-morrow night. Well, she will have to wait, that's all there is about it. I mean to see Christmas to-morrow night. I'll send Lillian a note, saying business prevents my keeping the engagement. When she consents to go with me it will keep me away from Christmas for some time. I don't like that, but I must have my revenge on that scoundrel, who cheated me of Amor Escandon."

If he had known the truth, nothing could have suited Lillian Day better than his absence. She gave a great sigh of relief when a ragged street boy accosted her on the way home from work and gave her Mateo Blanco's note. It seemed like another day of life for her.

That morning she had experienced the first serious quarrel with her mother.

Mrs. Day was becoming greatly alarmed by Lillian's frequent visits to her club, as she said. A strange change in her daughter—a feverishness, a restlessness, and uneasy sleep had worried the fond mother.

She knew Peter Day would not permit Lillian to go, as she was doing, almost every night to her club if he knew it. She had weakly allowed Lillian to have her own way. Now she feared to tell her husband and arouse his anger. It were better to remonstrate with Lillian, and to tell her she must remain more at home.

At the first word, almost, Lillian flew into a great rage. She had no fear of her fond mother, as she had of her father. Her mother might threaten anything, she knew, but she would relent before doing it. It was not so with Peter Day. When he said a thing, he meant it.

Many a time had Mrs. Day threatened to punish Lillian when she was a child, only to forget her promise at the first sight of temper or tears. And, child as she was, she soon learned her power over her mother, and she exercised it until it came to such a pass that, instead of fearing to hurt her child, Mrs. Day was afraid even to offer to punish her.

All this rebellious Lillian remembered when her mother said, mildly, that there must not be so much club going at night.

"Do you mean to deprive me of everything worth living for?" Lillian had demanded angrily.

"You know it ain't right for you to be gaddin' about every night."—reproachfully.

"What else is there for a girl like me to do?"—scornfully. "I have no friends. I never go anywhere or get to see anything. I'm tired of living, and I wish I was dead."

"Oh, my darling child! how can you say such awful things?" cried her frightened mother.

"Well"—shortly—"what have I got to make me want to live?"

"Just remember how many girls have less than you. You should be ashamed to talk this way. It ain't right."

Lillian tossed her beautiful head scornfully and gave an impatient cry. "For Heaven's sake, don't be preaching this is right and everything else is wrong to me all the time. I am sick of it all, and I wish I had never been born!"

"Oh, Lillian!" cried her mother, weeping, "I don't see how you can go on in this sinful way. You are in the world, and you should make the best of it."

"Is it my fault that I am here?" snapped Lillian irritably. "Is it my fault that I am a poor nobody? I don't see why some people should be born with everything that life can give, and others with nothing. It isn't fair! And it's no wonder poor girls like me sell their souls for a little pleasure."

"Lillian!" exclaimed her horrified mother, gazing with fear at the passion-white face of her beautiful daughter. Then she added quietly:

"Now I shall tell your father when he comes home."

"Listen to me, mother," Lillian said hoarsely. "If you breathe a word to father about my being out, or in any way try to keep me in, I shall run away from home."

Without another word she marched away, leaving her mother in tears and agony of mind.

So Peter Day was not told about his daughter's wicked disobedience.

And Lillian Day—vain, weak, headstrong, envious and mercenary—drifted on to the bitter end of all such worldly ambitions.

XVII

AMOR MUST TAKE HER CHOICE
BETWEEN WEALTH AND POVERTY.

"CHRISTMAS! DO YOU THINK I can ever kill my disgust and dislike for uncultured and ill-bred persons?" Amor inquired, thoughtfully, as the two girls sat in a corner eating their cold luncheon.

Lillian Day was not with them. She preferred the livelier and louder company of the other factory girls, who unanimously entertained a bitter hatred for Amor, because of her proud, cold manners, and a spite against Christmas because she was so "thick" with one who looked down on her betters.

"There are some persons you must like, even if they are not well-bred," Christmas replied seriously. "Take dear, good Peter Day, for example. It seems wrong even to mention him as being unrefined, because he is so noble and honest. When he told us this morning about the girl who had come up to his stand and asked him if he knew where she could find a place to stay all night, and how he had questioned her, and finding that she had run away from home to join a man she thought she loved, and that she had regretted her action and had not gone to the man, as she had intended, but was ashamed to go back home, I could only think how noble he was to talk to the poor girl, and to persuade her to let him drive her to the station and buy a ticket for her to return home on. Don't you think some old farmer and his wife will always remember good Peter Day for sending their wayward daughter back to them?"

"That was very good, I confess," Amor admitted, frankly. "A man in his business, who does a deed of that kind, deserves the highest praise; but still that does not answer my question."

"Surely you forgot his faults while you were listening to his story?"—earnestly.

"I could see that he ate with his knife, at the same time"—dryly.

"Is that fair?" Christmas demanded, simply. "You are blaming Peter Day for what is not his fault. You might as well say that you could not appreciate his noble conduct because his nose is crooked! He is not to blame for his nose."

"But manners are not quite the same!" laughed Amor.

"Not in your case, or mine, perhaps," Christmas retorted quickly. "You were blessed by advantages of every kind; you were taught what was right and proper and refined. If, under such circumstances, you still had been rough and rude, then most certainly would you have deserved reproach and blame."

"I think I begin to understand," Amor replied.

"If you will take Christmas Cherry for example"—laughingly—"you will see what I mean. If you had seen me in the foundling asylum, eating with my knife, you would have said: 'Poor girl! She is not to blame, for she has never been taught any better.' You could not say that now. So I remember when I see faults in people—faults of ignorance, I mean—I forgive them, because they have never been taught any better. I even pity them; and if you look at it in the same way, you will never be disgusted."

"I am convinced, my ragged angel! I wonder where you got all your wisdom? I am sure in some other world you have been a philosopher, beloved by all mankind," Amor replied with tender jesting.

With all the affection these two girls cherished for each other, a sense of delicacy and refinement forbade their inquiring into each other's personal secrets. Christmas never asked Amor one question about her former life and Amor did not question Christmas about her declared lover. She was deeply interested and thought a great deal about it, praying that it might only result in Christmas' happiness.

And still the knowledge that she was going to lose Christmas made Amor's courage vanish. A panic, a fear, possessed her at the very thought. Christmas gone, what would become of her? How blank her life would be?

One thing was certain: she could not live on in this miserable way without Christmas. She would die, or worse, go mad.

There was only one other way open to her. She could consent to marry Mateo Blanco and return to her father.

When they had returned to their work after luncheon, Christmas saw how deathly white and wan Amor became.

"Are you ill, dear?" she asked anxiously, leaving her work to lean over and speak to Amor, who was leaning weakly on the machine.

"Not ill, Christmas," was the piteous answer. "But I feel as if every bit of strength had left my body. My head is dizzy and I am so weak that I can hardly sit up."

"You had better go home, dearest," was the alarmed reply. "Stop your work and I will take you home"

"No, Christmas, I can't listen to such a thing," with a pitifully weak defiance. "If I give up the struggle, I don't' mean to drag you down with me."

"You don't mean that you are going to die?" faltered Christmas with a sharp cry of agony.

Such had been Amor's thought. This deathly faintness and utter weakness must mean death. And, oh, how gladly she welcomed the thought! To be dead, to be free from the agony of mind, the weariness, that was hers, seemed like the bliss of paradise.

"Don't distress yourself, my little angel," she told the trembling girl. "Those who long for death are always the last to die. I know I shall live to be very old and very miserable and—"

The sentence died away in a gasp on her white lips and Amor sunk back senseless into Christmas Cherry's arms.

The assistant foreman carried the fainting girl into the manager's office and laid her down on the old shabby lounge before the frightened eyes of George Chesterland.

Christmas had followed. She was more alarmed this time than she had been before. It seemed as if Amor must be dead or dying.

"Oh, Mr. Chesterland!" she cried piteously, wringing her hands. "I am afraid she is dying. She looked so ill, and she said all her strength had suddenly vanished and she was longing so much for death! You won't let her die, will you? You saved her once, oh, save her again!"

"She shall not die," George replied hoarsely between his clenched teeth.

When Amor opened her black eyes to them again, she did not rally back to strength. She was very weak and spent, and lay listlessly upon the old battered lounge, not caring to move or speak.

She smiled faintly at their frightened faces. "I am sorry to worry you," she murmured penitently.

"May I take her home?" Christmas asked, turning her tearful eyes on George Chesterland's handsome face.

"Return to your work, Christmas, and I shall send for a carriage and take her home myself," he replied with sudden determination. Then, turning to his assistant, he added:

"You can take full charge of the factory. It is only one hour of quitting time and I shall not return this evening."

"Very well, sir," the assistant replied.

Christmas remained by Amor's side until the carriage had arrived and

George Chesterland was ready to take the sick girl home.

"Do not worry," he repeated to Christmas. "I mean to take her for a breath of air, and then home."

Christmas brought Amor's wraps and watched them depart, and then, with tears in her eyes and the most dreadful pain in her heart she had ever felt, she returned to her work.

"I have lost him and I have lost her," she said bitterly to herself.

The fresh air did revive Amor. She brightened up wonderfully, and though she rested weakly against the cushions, her eyes gleamed more happily than they had done all day.

She did not ask George one question. She resigned herself wholly to his care, and found a strange, sweet peace by doing so.

She was too weak, too tired, to struggle any longer with herself. What did she care if his father was a driver? He was handsome as a god and he loved her. That's all she seemed to care for now.

He drove to a quiet restaurant in perfect silence.

"We are going to have a little luncheon, Amor," he said as he helped her to alight.

He ordered a bird and a glass of wine and insisted on her eating.

"You must eat every particle of that bird," he said in his tender, masterful way; and Amor smiled and did as he bade her.

When she drank her wine her glass was filled again, and at his word she drank its contents.

That was all that passed between them until, luncheon finished, he led her back to the carriage.

They drove to the park. It was getting dark, and all the carriages were being driven homeward, except theirs.

Amor breathed the fresh air, and new life seemed to flow in her veins.

George saw the change, and then he spoke.

Putting his arms around her slender waist, he drew her toward him until her dark head rested on his broad shoulder. Amor would have drawn away, but he held her firmly, saying:

"No, Amor, you must resign your will to mine."

She ceased to struggle, and a happy thrill crept along her veins clear to her heart.

"Amor!" he added with passionate intensity, lifting her cold face and pressing his lips to hers in one long kiss of deathless love. "Amor, when are you going to become my wife?"

Her heart fluttered wildly, and then she trembled from head to foot. She knew that he felt it, for he held her closer in his arms.

She wondered whether it would be easier to forget her hatred for Mateo Blanco and return to her luxurious home and become his bride than to forget her pride and George Chesterland's humble parentage and accept his love and devotion.

She looked wistfully up into his handsome face. She could feel how passionately and stormily his strong heart throbbed beneath the faint pressure of her lovely dark head.

She felt a strange cruelty stir her blood. Why did he insist on marrying her when he knew she despised him? Why did he love her so much when she treated him so badly?

"You know that I do not love you," she said slowly, distinctly and cuttingly. "You know that I despise poverty and consider a working-man beneath my notice. You know I consider your impudence in addressing me little less than an insult."

She paused. He made no reply, but he still held her clasped to his heart.

She could not see his face now, because he had removed her hat and his cheek rested lightly against her dark hair.

"Have you anything to say in reply to this?" she demanded haughtily, impatient at his silence.

"Yes, Amor," he replied coolly and calmly. "I have something to say."

She waited anxiously for him to continue.

XVIII

AMOR FINDS HER MASTER.

"WELL?" AMOR EJACULATED IMPATIENTLY. "SAY it and let us have done with this miserable business."

"I mean to say"—George Chesterland spoke calmly, without the least trace of ill-humor in his voice—"that you are a very foolish girl and that such narrow prejudices are an insult to your education and intellect. That you do not love me, I firmly believe, but that does not alter my feeling toward you."

"You will, at least, not offend me by repeating your recent declarations."— haughtily.

He laughed joyously. Her bitter words sounded as if she was determined to consider herself right in spite of the promptings of her better self.

He was so confident of winning her love in the end, it did not seem possible to him that she would never learn to love him.

"Amor, I have watched you fading away before my eyes until I can endure the agony of it no longer. When you were carried into my office this afternoon, looking so white and lifeless, a sudden resolution came to me. I mean to take you away from the factory and—make you my wife!"

His wife! The wife of a mere working-man! He must be mad! She would never endure such humiliation. She would rather die, or go back to Mateo Blanco.

"You must understand that nothing can alter my determination," he went on coolly. "Your bitter words I do not heed. They are unworthy of you, so you need not think to alter my decision by hurling all those unwomanly sentiments at me."

"If my sentiments are unwomanly and my words bitter, why do you have anything to do with me?" she cried indignantly.

"Because I love you."—softly. "When will you marry me, Amor?"

"Never, sir!"—emphatically.

"Does that mean to-morrow, or the next day?"

"You are mad!" Amor cried in a startled voice.

"With love of you—yes!" He released Amor, and opening the door, called to the driver and gave him orders.

"Where are you going?" inquired Amor, with a feeling of fear.

"To the minister, dear, to be married," was the astounding reply.

Amor gasped for breath. Her brain reeled dizzily, and she felt as if she were going to faint.

Handsome George Chesterland saw how deeply she was affected. "Poor little girl!' he whispered, tenderly, taking her in his arms.

All Amor's strength deserted her. She felt that she was conquered. She had met her master, and as her weary head touched his broad shoulder she burst into tears.

George let her cry on until her tears were exhausted, and she rested, weak and breathless, against his heart. A passive feeling had come over her. She did not know whether she felt most relieved or hopeless by having things decided for her.

His tender masterfulness was comforting in a way. Whatever the outcome might be of this strange marriage, she would be free of all blame. On his head solely rested the consequences of his rashness.

"You know that I do not love you?" she observed, with a tinge of spitefulness.

"Yes!"

"That I never shall?"

"No?"

"If I make you the most unhappy man on earth, you must not blame me."

"You shall be free from all blame," was the confident reply.

Amor glanced shyly up at George when she thought he was not looking.

He was certainly very handsome, she thought, with a thrill of tenderness, and his masterful way of carrying the thing off was quite winning. Yes, it was a relief to have her choice decided for her. And then he loved her so much! But she would show him that she could never so far forget herself as to love a poor man.

He might force her to marry him. That was his affair. He could not force her to love him. And—the thought already entered her mind—if anything came up to make her freedom desirable, she could easily obtain a divorce.

After that they did not seem to have much to say, and went through the long drive to Jersey City almost in silence.

To have her in his arms, to know that he had won her, was happiness enough for George Chesterland. He was filled with pleasant dreams of the life he would enjoy with beautiful Amor by his side.

Little cared he what pain life held for him what privations, what labor, so long as the girl he loved to madness belonged to him forever.

"You are taking me without knowing who or what I have been," Amor remarked, as they crossed on the ferry. "You must not cheat yourself with false hopes of ever knowing. My past is the same as if it had never been. My life dates from the day you cheated me of death."

"It is not your past I love, but your self," he replied loyally. "And I know some day you will say to me, 'George, I never lived before the day we met,' and then life can give me no more."

"The name you know me by," she continued, not replying to his fond speech, "is not my entire name. Will it have any effect legally?"

"It is better to give the proper name, but if you do not wish to do so, the name cannot make the slightest difference in regard to the legality of the ceremony."

So in a few moments Amor Gray became the wife of George Chesterland.

It was all done so quickly, so quietly, and in such a matter-of-fact way, that Amor could not realize the change. It did not seem possible that she was no longer Amor Escandon, the beautiful heiress, but Amor Chesterland, the working man's wife.

She never once asked George what plans he intended to make. She was passive and indifferent. She allowed him to lead her to the carriage after the ceremony, and asked no questions as to his future movements.

And George said nothing to her. He did not even hold her in his arms, as he had done when they were coming over. He merely took her hand and held it closely until they arrived at a restaurant, and then he said simply:

"It is too late for you to get dinner at home, and so we will dine together before I take you back."

She flushed rosily, and wondered nervously if he meant to leave her with the Days. She had meant to be angry if he tried to take her with him at once, and now, when he so calmly disposed of her, she was conscious of a feeling of resentment.

When he had been determined to marry her, why did he not keep her with him? She wondered about it, but she would not have asked him for the world.

Amor was so far recovered that she could see how daintily he ate, and with what graceful ease he looked after all her wants.

It was wonderful that one, whose father had been a friend to Peter Day, should possess so many charms and graces of person and manner. But she dismissed it with the thought that doubtless George had been educated above his station.

"Do you wish to remain with the Days until I can secure a place for us, or would you rather come to my boarding-house?" George asked Amor, as they were driving homeward.

"I would rather remain with Christmas."

"It will only be for a day or so," he added. "I shall come to see you every evening until I take you away with me. I intend to go in and tell Mrs. Day to-night, unless you object."

"It does not make the least difference to me," she coldly replied.

"Let me kiss you good-night now, my darling," he said tenderly, allowing his passionate love to master him for a moment as he clasped her to his heart.

"I trust that you will not expect too much from my submissiveness and force me to endure your embraces," Amor said, hoping to stab him.

She succeeded. He released her, chilled and disappointed.

"If my embraces are a matter of indifference to you," he said kindly, striving to hide his pain, "why not submit to them with as good grace as possible?"

"I warned you in advance what to expect," she reminded him.

"And I told you that you must love me!" he responded firmly. "But I cannot expect everything from a tired little girl. Good-night, my darling; may Heaven watch over and protect you."

Mrs. Day was alone. Christmas had gone to school, Peter Day was off attending to his work, and Lillian had gone to her club, the lonely woman explained.

She was not surprised to see George Chesterland. Christmas had quieted their fears at supper by explaining that George had taken Amor for a drive. But when George told her that he and Amor were married, Mrs. Day's astonishment knew no bounds.

"I want to leave my wife in your care, Mrs. Day," the young man said, "until I can find suitable apartments for us. I know you will take good care of her, and I especially desire that she shall not go out of the house unless I am with her."

"You may trust her to me, Mr. George," Mrs. Day replied. "My husband would tell me to care for any one that belonged to you as I would for my own child. He hasn't forgotten your father and what he was to him."

"Thank you, Mrs. Day," George replied.

And saying good-night to both, he went away.

"My heavens!" Amor thought miserably, staring fixedly after him. "To think that I have married the son of Peter Day's old friend! Can I ever forget it?"

XIX

AS PURE AS GOLD.

THE NIGHT OF AMOR'S MARRIAGE proved to be the most unhappy of Christmas Cherry's life.

She had gone home from work miserable and uneasy about Amor's illness. She knew the girl was failing very rapidly, and that she was even then too ill to work.

But she knew, also, that without earning something it would be impossible for her to live.

Gladly would tender-hearted Christmas have worked for both, had it been possible for her to make enough to support her dearly-loved friend. But work as rapidly and unceasingly as she could, from morning until night, she could not earn enough to pay the board for two.

What was to become of poor Amor?

Christmas knew only too well what was in the heart of George Chesterland. She knew that his life and love and devotion were at the proud girl's service.

It would have helped to resign Christmas to her loneliness had she known that Amor returned George Chesterland's love and would unite her fate with his.

But she knew George loved in vain. Amor was too haughty and proud to marry a poor man. Christmas was not blind. She had seen the drift of Amor's scornful comments of the poor and ignorant.

If Amor would not marry George Chesterland, and Christmas was positive that she would not, she must be taken care of in some other way.

That way Christmas had decided upon. She would sacrifice herself, her dreams of love, to provide a home for Amor.

There was only one way she could do it, and that way she must take.

What mattered her life, her dreams, her poor ambitions? Amor must have a home, Amor must be made happy, Amor must be saved from work, and to be able to do this, Christmas meant to marry Mateo Blanco.

Why should she hesitate? she asked herself. Why should she selfishly consult her own wishes? Her sacrifice would make Amor happy, and how could she doubt but that it meant the happiness of her declared lover, Matthew White.

Poor little heroine! Poor little Christmas!

Her tears would well up into her big eyes while she was in school. She did not regret the step she was about to take, but it was hard to become the wife of one man when her mind was filled with the image of another.

Besides this, she had no wish for a life of indolent luxury. She had dreamed of a life spent in doing good, and she only wished for money enough to be able to help life's unfortunate ones.

All this was lost to her. She must make up her mind to spend her life uselessly and to no purpose. She knew her lover well enough to see that deeds of charity and work among the poor would prove obnoxious to him. All his talk and thought was of the vanities of the world, all his aims and ambition pointed in that direction.

Mrs. Matthew White must be a woman of fashion, not a woman of charity.

It was a very doleful, pathetic face that Christmas raised to the adoring eyes of Mateo Blanco, who, true to his promise, waited for her on the nearest corner.

No lover had ever waited more impatiently for his sweetheart than Mateo Blanco did for Christmas. A wild love for her had taken full possession of him. He thought about her awake and dreamed of her asleep.

He had not thought to find her in a mood so wistfully sad and gentle. He had expected to have to plead and coax a cold, willful girl, and when instead he saw how she seemed to lean on him, as if for help and love and guidance, his brain whirled with the madness of as passionate and intense a love as ever man experienced.

"My darling!" he cried, lovingly, "we can't go home at once. I must have a little of your sweet society. You can't imagine how the long hours have tortured me since I left you. I almost thought some one had told the earth to stand still and that night would never come to us again. And now I have you again and I mean to keep you as long as I can."

Christmas gave him a pathetic little smile that tempted him to clasp her to his heart and cover her pure, sweet face with hungry kisses.

"My God!" he breathed, huskily, almost crushing her hand in his. "I never knew a man could love as I love you. Do you know, you sweet little angel, your eyes could drive a man mad?"

Christmas felt comforted by his love. It made it so much easier for her to face her martyrdom.

They went to a restaurant and Mateo Blanco ordered a supper fit for a queen.

Christmas had never before experienced the sweet sensation of dining, surrounded by all the elegancies of a well-set table, and served by a waiter as noiseless and efficient as he was polite. It was like a glimpse of paradise to her.

Mateo Blanco read her delight in her expressive eyes. He noticed with pride how graceful and easy she was. What would he have thought had he known her teacher was none other than beautiful Amor Escandon, the girl he had sworn to wed?

He wondered curiously where Christmas had learned all her pretty, graceful ways, and he thought how a little experience and training would transform her into the very picture of refinement.

"True refinement is born in one," he said to himself. "And good blood always tells. I would wager my life, if the truth could be known, that Christmas Cherry's parents belonged to the aristocracy." And the evidences of her refinement made him love her all the more.

He talked to her, while they ate, about different things—his fine home, his fast horses, the fragrant flowers that daily graced his rooms, the beautiful women he met; their fine jewels he described to her in glowing terms.

Very cunningly and craftily he remarked, with apparent carelessness, how he would like to see Christmas as the graceful mistress of a lovely home.

Then he went on to say what color he thought would be the most becoming to her style of beauty—what shade would bring out the splendor of her glorious eyes, and how he would like to see a diamond necklace of his possession around her slender throat. Its sparkle would pale beside the brilliancy of her eyes, he knew.

Easier and easier became the idea of martyrdom, until it vanished completely in the ecstasy of the thought of accepting all this greatness and tasting of its bliss.

Between the brightness of her eyes, the hesitancy of his love, and the elation caused by the wine he drank, Mateo Blanco was determined and reckless. Why should he wait longer? Surely she loved him already.

They had not been in the carriage on the way home very long until he took his little love's hand, and said, with trembling huskiness:

"My darling, do you never intend to love me?"

"I care a great deal for you now," Christmas replied, determined to accept him at once. "You are so kind that I cannot help caring for you, and

I have made up my mind to marry you as soon as you wish me to."

Mateo Blanco felt as if he had been dealt a heavy blow. He gasped faintly as if his heart had ceased to beat.

Marry him! Great heavens! How was he to tell her the truth?

Once again a wild, eager desire came to him to take her at her word and marry her. A faint, sweet dream of a modest little home, away from the worry and noise of the selfish world, with only himself and her there, happy, alone, content!

What bliss! What rapture!

He shook himself and hastily brushed his eyes, as if he wished to remove some illusion. He remembered his cravings for wealth, for social distinction; the proud, haughty face of Amor Escandon flitted before his troubled eyes.

No, no, he could not do it! He was mad to think of it for a moment.

Love never yet lasted forever, and the Escandon millions and social power would solace him for his lost love. Besides, he did not mean to lose her entirely.

He must be brave and let her understand his intentions.

She would be shocked at first, it was the way with women, he argued, and it was also their way to find the offer of wealth and ease too tempting to resist.

"You have misunderstood me, my sweetheart," he said, recklessly. "I want you for my wife, my own dear little wife, but I am too advanced, too broad, to believe in the old slavery idea of matrimony. I only want our love to bind us together. It must be the only tie between us."

Christmas felt her heart turn cold with horror. She remembered what Peter Day had said about wicked men of the world, and she shuddered to think she had almost been entangled by one, as black in heart as Satan.

The blindness fell from her eyes in an instant. She saw his purpose, understood his motives, and she even gave him credit for shaming the love he bore her.

An outraged sense of injury rushed in a fever heat to her head.

"And you have thought me so low and base and contemptible as to accept your insulting offer?" she demanded, indignantly. "If I had not been too simple to understand your evil intentions, I should never have spoken the second word to you. You have made me despise you, and I pray to Heaven I may never set eyes upon your false face again."

Before Mateo Blanco could recover from the speechless surprise to which her burning scorn had reduced him, Christmas opened the door of the carriage, and by a sharp command made the driver bring his horses to a standstill.

Mateo Blanco saw she was leaving him. He felt his blood run cold at the thought of never seeing her again, and clinching his teeth he grasped her by the arm.

Her foot was already on the pavement, but holding to her he tried to draw her back into the carriage.

"You shall not leave me!" he hissed between his closed teeth. "I swear to Heaven I'll kill you before I give you up!"

"Let go my arm!" Christmas replied, undaunted, "or I shall call for help."

Paying no heed to her threat, Mateo Blanco, with a low imprecation, tried by main force to draw the angry girl back into the carriage.

Christmas felt his strength overpowering her own. He had her almost into the carriage again, and the night cabman, not unused to similar scenes, was waiting the result, offering neither word of remonstrance nor help.

"Help! Help!" Christmas cried frightenedly. "Driver! Help me to get away from this man."

"Better get in the carriage and settle your fight there, miss," was the driver's reply.

"Help! Help!" Christmas cried appealingly.

And help appeared just in time to prevent Mateo Blanco from lifting her bodily into the carriage.

An arm was thrown around her, and an indignant voice said authoritatively:

"Release this young girl, you scoundrel!"

Mateo Blanco gave a cry of rage.

"Oh, save me from him!" cried Christmas, clinging desperately to her protector.

"Do not fear, child, you are safe. As for you, scoundrel, the moment I see a policeman I shall have you arrested."

"You shall be sorry for this!" Mateo Blanco cried hoarsely to the terrified girl.

And then, with a terrible oath, he commanded the driver to drive away as quickly as possible.

In a second the carriage was lost to sight, and Christmas turned to thank her preserver.

She looked up into his handsome, noble face, and with a cry of surprise recognized the minister who had praised her defense of the drunken woman.

And he recognized Christmas. He grew very grave and sad, and Christmas, with a burning blush of shame, readily divined the cause.

He thought her silly and weak, like many poor girls, and doubtless considered her fitly punished for an act of foolishness.

"If you will tell me where you live, I shall see you safely home," he said gravely.

Christmas told him her address, and they walked along together in silence until they reached her door.

"I wish you would come to visit my church," he said to her, his earnest eyes trying to read her burning, downcast face. "I have not forgotten your noble defense of the poor old woman, and I should like you to see the work we are trying to do."

"I have never been to church in my life," Christmas replied honestly. "I know nothing about religion and feel no need of it."

"I am sorry," he said gently. "I don't mean to preach religion to you, but it would make me very happy to have you visit my church once."

"If I ever feel the need of religion, I shall go," Christmas said willfully.

"Thank you! I will remember your promise and—you will come before long."

With these prophetic words upon his lips, he lifted his hat and walked away.

XX

A HOUSE OF MOURNING.

AMOR WAS STILL AWAKE WHEN Christmas returned. She watched her, through half-closed eyes, tiptoe around the room, trying to undress quietly.

She wondered lazily what Christmas would say about it all. Would she be pleased? She must go with them and form one of their little household. There would be no living without her "angel in rags."

Amor would have rather stayed at the Days' forever than to give up Christmas, the only person on earth she loved.

Softly Christmas blew out the ill-smelling oil-lamp and crept into bed.

Amor turned and slipped her arm around her.

"Did I wake you, dear?" Christmas asked, sorrowfully.

"No, my angel; I could not go to sleep until you returned," was the reply.

"Are you ill?"—anxiously.

"I am very much better. Christmas"—pleadingly—"if some one asked me to marry him, what would you tell me to do?"

A chill crept over Christmas and her heart beat with labored throbs.

"I would tell you to marry if you loved the man."

"But I don't love any one on this earth but you."—poutingly.

"You may learn to love some one else, dearest."

Amor sighed. "I hardly think that possible," she said.

"I knew a girl once who loved no one except a girl-friend just as I love you," Amor continued after a slight pause. "There was a man who seemed to care very much for her, but she hated him. Yes, I am sure she hated him, but he was determined to marry her; so one day when they were together he told her it was useless to oppose him, that he intended to marry her whether she liked it or not. He marched her off to a minister's without so much as 'by your leave,' and they were married. What do you think of such a man as that?"

"I think he was honest, and I admire his courage," Christmas cried vehemently.

"And the girl? Don't you think she was crazy?" persisted Amor.

"I think"—slowly—"she would never have submitted had she not really, in her heart, loved the man!"

"But I don't! I declare upon my honor I don't!" exclaimed the indignant girl.

"Amor!" cried Christmas. "Oh, Amor!"

"I did not mean to break it to you that way, my darling," cried repentant Amor, detecting the wild pain in Christmas' voice. "But it's true; I could not help myself, and that horrid man took me off and married me." She laid her head close against Christmas' and burst into tears.

Christmas let her cry on, but her own eyes were dry and burning. She was so thankful the room was in darkness. If Amor could have seen her pale face, distorted by her heart's agony, she might have suspected the truth—that Christmas loved George Chesterland!

She began to tell Christmas that she would never be parted from her, but Christmas refused to listen.

"You must talk no more to-night or you will be ill again," Christmas said positively. "Wait until to-morrow, and then tell me all your sweet plans for the future."

Pressing a light kiss upon Christmas' cold lips, Amor sunk back upon her pillow and was soon asleep.

Morning found Christmas with unclosed eyes. It was impossible to sleep. It seemed as if her brain was on fire and her heart turned to ice.

A strange feeling toward Amor took possession of her. She had lost her only friend, and she loved her only friend's husband. It was dreadful, unnatural, wicked.

She felt that if she touched the sleeping girl she must gain some knowledge of her weakness, so when Amor awoke she was surprised to find Christmas lying on the extreme outer edge of the bed.

Lillian Day did not hear the news until during breakfast. She was glad no one noticed her emotion. For a few moments she thought she would faint.

After the first shock, her heart grew hard and bitter. "I have lost the only man I will ever love; now I care for nothing but wealth, and that I will have if it takes all my life and soul and hope of heaven!"

She went to work with Christmas. She would have gone without kissing her father good-bye had he not called her back.

Christmas saw how his daughter's indifference pained good Peter Day, and as she walked to the factory she said to Lillian:

"I don't see how you can forget to kiss your dear old father, Lillian. It pains him so."

Lillian Day turned on her with flashing eyes. "Please don't meddle with my affairs," she said insultingly. "It's none of your business if I hate my parents."

"I did not mean to offend you!" Christmas responded with tears in her eyes. "The sight of your father's pain made my heart ache, and I spoke before I thought. I hope you will forgive me?"

"Do you know, Christmas Cherry!" hissed Lillian, turning savagely upon her. "Your pretended goodness makes me sick! Don't ask me to forgive you! I hate you and your fine lady friend! I believe you are both hypocrites!"

Christmas was too shocked and pained to reply to this torrent of undeserved abuse. She wiped away her fast-falling tears and walked on alone to the factory, for Lillian had paused and refused to walk another step with her.

Lillian worked until noon, and then she quit.

Of course Christmas would have asked no questions had she even known Lillian was going.

She was surprised to find on reaching home that Lillian was not there, and her surprise changed to fear when Mrs. Day asked anxiously why Lillian had not returned with her.

"I thought she was home by this time," Christmas said hesitatingly.

And a hasty thumping on the front door cut short her explanation.

"That's Lillian now," Peter Day said happily, and went to unlock the door.

It was not Lillian, but a messenger boy, who handed him a note and disappeared.

"Wonder who's writin' to me?" he said, curiously tearing open the envelope.

"Would I not better read it to you?" Christmas offered.

"Do you want to make the old man think he hain't got no learnin' at all?" he laughed loudly. "I'll show you what the old man can do."

For some reason they all waited breathless as he slowly scanned the pages of the letter. He paused at last and a death-like whiteness crept around his compressed lips and into his bronzed cheeks.

"Mother!" he whispered hoarsely. "We have no daughter!"

With a heart-broken cry he buried his pallid face in his arm, and burst into wild, agonized sobs.

XXI

A HEARTLESS DAUGHTER.

"READ IT TO ME," BEGGED Mrs. Day, picking up the crumpled letter which had fallen from her husband's hand and giving it to Christmas. "Let me know the worst."

Christmas would rather have bitten off her tongue than read that note to the heart-broken mother, but there was no escape for her. The sight of terrible anguish on the poor woman's face was more than she could bear.

"Better let her know the worst at once," Amor whispered sadly. "It will do them no kindness to hide the truth."

So, nerving herself to bear the pain, Christmas read softly Lillian Day's heartless farewell.

It was as follows:

> "It is no use to waste any time searching for me. I could not stand the old life any longer, so I have gone away with a man who can give me the fine gowns and easy life I have always wanted. Do not blame me, but blame yourself for bringing a beautiful girl into the world when you could not provide for her any better than you have done. I have nothing to be sorry for, nothing to regret.
>
> "Again I tell you not to waste time searching for me. I would rather die a thousand times than return to you. If you think of me at all, picture me as the happiest girl alive, with jewels and fine dresses and the idol of a handsome man's heart. For the last time I sign myself Lillian Day."

Several times did Christmas break down before she could finish the heartless letter. Even Amor was horrified beyond description. It seemed impossible to her that a daughter could be so wantonly cruel, and her cheeks burned with righteous indignation against the beautiful Lillian.

Mrs. Day's grief was terrible to behold. For awhile it seemed as if the blow had deprived her of all reason. It was only by pleading with her to calm herself for the sake of her heart-broken husband that Christmas finally induced the unhappy woman to try to control her feelings.

"Oh, Father in Heaven, have pity on me!" she wept wildly. "Once when she was a wee little baby that only knew how to hold to my finger and smile like a little angel up into my face, she was sick. The doctors said that she couldn't live, and it almost drove me crazy. I thought I couldn't give her up, and I prayed night and day to Heaven to let me keep her. I said I would curse God if He took her from me. In my prayers, I wildly asked Him to take a child from some large family and spare my only one. I said I would bear all my trials, every one He wished to send upon me, without a murmur, if He only spared my daughter. This is my punishment now. I was given her life only to wreck her soul. Then she was innocent and pure, now—Oh, God, if I had only let her die then!"

How many unhappy mothers have thus reproached themselves in after years. Mrs. Day was not the first, nor will she be the last, to regret that she had begged Heaven to let her baby live.

The two girls finally persuaded Mrs. Day to lie down, and Amor bathed her head until, exhausted by her grief, she cried herself to sleep.

Christmas endeavored by kind and gentle words to rouse Peter Day from the stupor of despair into which he had fallen.

"You have not eaten any supper," she reminded him kindly. "Come, let me help you; you will feel better if you eat something."

"Ah, gal!" he groaned. "Every mouthful would choke me. 'Tain't no use tryin' to do anything any more."

"You must not give way to hopelessness like that," Christmas remonstrated. "You must remember your poor wife. She needs you to lean on and to comfort her."

"Neither of us care no more."—wearily. "There is nothing left for us but to die."

"There is much left for you. Remember the good you have done to your fellow creatures. There is more for you to do. How many poor repentant souls are blessing you for saving them from ruin?"

"But who saved my daughter?"—bitterly. "How can I believe in a Heaven that lets me save other men's daughters, and lets my own go to ruin? It's wrong. There can't be no Heaven. I'll never believe again."

"Is Sal to go back to the stable?" Christmas asked, to change his thoughts.

He started up awkwardly. "I must work. 'Tain't no use to sit down."

Christmas knew by experience that the best medicine ever made for heartache was work, and plenty of it.

"That is true," she replied with forced cheerfulness. "Come on into the kitchen and eat a bite while I put up your luncheon."

He followed her obediently, and she pressed him to eat a few mouthfuls, though the tears were wetting his weather-beaten cheeks.

He had just gone when George Chesterland arrived.

Christmas invited him to sit down and called Amor away from the side of Mrs. Day, who was sleeping soundly.

"I will put the supper on the table if you and Mr. Chesterland will eat," Christmas said, shyly, and Amor looked at her handsome young husband inquiringly.

"Thank you, Christmas, I have just dined," he replied. "But please do not let me keep you from your dinner. I shall read the evening newspapers until you return."

The two girls ate their supper in silence. Once or twice they made some whispered remark, but that was all.

"If you think I should remain at home to wash the dishes, I will not go to school to-night," Christmas said.

"It is no use to miss your school, if you can think of studying to-night," Amor replied. So Christmas put on her hat and coat and, kissing Amor and wishing George Chesterland good-night, went away, leaving husband and wife alone.

George pushed a rocking-chair up to the fire for Amor, and when she was seated, drew his chair alongside of her. He quietly studied her pale face as she looked into the blazing fire.

She felt his gaze and did not raise her eyes, but when the silence became painful she said, in a low, sad voice:

"The Days have met with a severe affliction. Their daughter, Lillian, has run away from home."

"Poor foolish Lillian!" sighed George, feeling nothing but pity for the wayward girl.

Very softly, so as not to disturb the sleeping woman, Amor told all there was in the sad story, and George was truly sorry for all but for none more than for the vain Lillian herself.

"The poor old people will be very lonely when you go away," George said. "I rented a little flat for us to-day. It is furnished, and I think we can be very cozy and comfortable. What hour will you be ready to go there to-morrow?"

"To-morrow? Must I go so soon?" gasped Amor in a startled way.

"I cannot bear to have you away from my care any longer," the young husband said, as if that settled the matter.

Amor felt the old rebellion stirring her blood. She liked him to be masterful, and still she liked to oppose his will.

"I cannot leave Christmas."—resentfully. "She is the only one I love on earth, and I will not be separated from her."

"You need not."—kindly. "I am sure we should both be happier if she were with us."

"How good you are!" Amor cried delightedly. "You have made me very happy."

"That is my sole desire in life, my darling," was the tender reply.

She talked with him quite freely after that, carefully avoiding all tender subjects, and devoting the most of her conversation to Christmas and her goodness and aims and ambitions.

"I call her my angel in rags," she said with friendly confidence. "She is the noblest girl that ever lived, so pure and true and straightforward. I wish I had money to devote to her education, although now she has gathered a fund of information more varied and useful than most girls gain by a course at college."

So she rattled on and George listened to her, happy in her artless prattle, and fondly imagining she was learning to like him better.

He remained until Christmas returned and she was immediately told of their plans for her to make one of the members of their household.

Christmas felt as if they had asked her to pull out her bleeding heart for them to gaze upon. To live with them and witness day after day George's love for Amor, to see him caress her, to see Amor indifferent to the caresses that would have turned earth into a paradise for herself, was more than Christmas could endure.

But she must not let them know why she could not go with them; they must never suspect the secret of her hopeless love.

"You are very kind," Christmas said, trying to command her voice, "but I cannot go with you. I am sure it is better for you to live alone."

"But we do not think so! You must come with us!" Amor cried anxiously.

"I am sure, dear, you would not ask me to go away and leave these poor, stricken people. They have no one now, they need me, and you have— your husband."

"If you will not go, neither shall I," Amor declared stubbornly.

"You see, Christmas," George urged earnestly, "if you do not come with us, you will cheat me of my wife."

His words stabbed Christmas. She could endure her torture no longer.

"Let me stay here for awhile," she pleaded with trembling lips. "The Days need me, and when they recover from their trouble, then, if you cannot get along without me"—playfully—"I shall go to your home to live."

"How grudgingly you say that," Amor murmured reproachfully. "I can't doubt your love for me, but you must have taken a dislike to Mr.

Chesterland, that you are so reluctant to live with us."

Christmas wildly pressed her hands to her heart and George Chesterland wondered why she grew so pale.

"Something has reminded her of her love," he thought, remembering how some careless remark of his about her acting like a girl in love had, not long ago, made her burst into bitter tears.

"Poor little girl!" he said to himself. "She has met with some disappointment."

If he had only known!

XXII

IN THE DEPTHS OF DESPAIR.

IT WAS THREE MONTHS SINCE Amor had married George Chesterland—three months since Christmas had discovered Mateo Blanco's unworthiness—three months since Lillian Day had deserted her parents.

And the three months had brought but very few changes.

Christmas Cherry still labored all day and studied all evening. She had never left the Days, and they had learned to lean more and more upon her.

Poor little waif! She had more than taken the place left vacant by their unfeeling daughter. She was so helpful and thoughtful and affectionate. She mended Peter Day's shabby clothes, and she bought from her scanty earnings enough linen to cover the cushions of the dirty old carriage, and made it look clean enough to delight the hearts of Peter Day and his partner, Sal.

Sal had a good warm blanket, too, that Christmas bought, and doubtless she was as grateful to the kind girl as her old master when she stood under it, cooling from a speed much too rapid for her age, or when it shielded her bony old frame from the night winds as she dozed and dreamed of happier days until the voice of her master reminded her that she was the junior partner of Peter Day, night-hawk.

In all this time the Days had had no line or word from their absent daughter. Peter Day had forbidden her name to be spoken.

"She's dead to us," he had said, "and the only way to forget her is not to hear her name."

But when Christmas heard him sigh as she helped him on with his coat, or ran to get his hat, she knew he was thinking of Lillian.

Mrs. Day was also silent about her daughter, but she had never recovered from the shock of her desertion. When her husband was absent, she spent much time in tears, and her hair had turned a snowy white from constant grieving.

George and Amor still occupied the little flat they had first moved into. They had never ceased trying to induce Christmas to come to them and Amor was very unhappy without her.

But Christmas would not go. She insisted that the Days needed her the most and she remained with them.

As often as she could, or rather, when she could not avoid it, Christmas shared their Sunday dinner. There was not much to distress her at these meetings, for before her, Amor and George treated each other with the calm courtesy of ordinary acquaintances.

No one ever suspected what was in Christmas' heart. She always pretended to be very busy now when George made his daily rounds of the factory, and when he told her frankly that she no longer treated him in a friendly way, she gave him an evasive answer.

"I would rather not have you talk to me in here," she said. "The girls, knowing what near friends your wife and I were, might imagine you favored me, and it would make them discontented and dissatisfied."

After that George talked less to Christmas than to any girl in his employ.

These three months had altered him somewhat. He was older and graver, and his winning smile did not appear as frequently as of yore.

If he had acknowledged it to himself, his was gradually becoming hopeless. Day after day he had hoped Amor would grow a little kinder, a little less cold, a little less disdainful. But she did not.

She always treated him with the studied politeness of a stranger. She was that and nothing more to him.

He had given her a separate room at first, and she retained it still. He would no more have dared to enter it than he would have dared to sign his employer's name to a check.

At first he had insisted on kissing her good-night, and good-bye when he left in the morning; but she received his little tokens of love with such displeasure that gradually it became distasteful to him, and he no longer offered her the hated kiss.

She used to get up to breakfast with him; but gradually she stopped that, and now he never saw her except at dinner and in the evening.

He could only afford to provide one housemaid, who did all the work. Amor would not have known how to work had she even felt so inclined.

But time grew heavy on her hands after awhile. It was easy to be indolent when one was wealthy. She could drive or shop or visit or do a hundred things to pass the time.

Now she could do nothing but fold her hands and think. If she had even possessed a piano she could have managed to make many a lonely hour pleasant, but she had nothing except the newspaper and a few books which he bought for her with every spare penny, and which she read over and over again until she knew every word in them.

One day she walked aimlessly into her kitchen and saw her maid of all work studying a book.

"What have you there, Bridget?" she inquired with idle curiosity.

"Sure an' it's a cook-book, mum!" the maid replied.

"I wonder if I could make any of those things?" she asked interestedly.

"Sure, an' ye could, mum! I niver cooked a thing in me loife till me sister give me that same book."

After that, Amor found something to do. She experimented with one thing after another until she became a perfect marvel.

She had the advantage of knowing when a thing was right, and she took a delight in making things look as she had seen them in her palatial home.

"Our maid is a perfect treasure," George remarked one night at dinner. "Some of her dished are as fine as Delmonico's."

And Amor flushed with pleasure, but kept her little secret.

For some unexplainable reason, she wanted her husband to think as poorly of her as he could. All her better self and nobler impulses she kept carefully hidden from him.

In the same way she began to take care of his clothes, putting on missing buttons, daintily darning holes and mending rents, and always letting him think it was the work of his housemaid.

Such was the state of affairs when George's employer, Mr. Hill, suddenly returned from abroad.

He had once been an employee of George's father, and by faithful service and industry was promoted until he became a partner, and then when Mr. Chesterland, Sr., died, it was discovered that he had borrowed so much money from his partner, and lost it in wild speculation, that his son was left penniless.

Hill was many times a millionaire. People had often spoken of his kindness to his late partner's son, and had thought that the boy's rapid promotion meant that he was one day to be taken into the firm.

But George learned, much to his sorrow, that this was not to be.

Joseph Hill assumed control of the factory immediately upon his return. His manner was, from the first, very pompous and offensive to George.

"All salaries must be cut down ten per cent," he observed roughly the first day he looked over the books.

"That is impossible, sir!" George replied sternly. "The poor souls can scarcely live now on the prices they are getting, and our dividends are unusually large."

"Our dividends?" his employer repeated. "Since when were you made a member of this firm?"

"I had no intention of giving offense," said George, trying to restrain his temper.

"That comes of my giving an upstart too much power. If I had stayed away much longer, you would have owned the factory next," snorted Hill savagely. "I want you to notify the employees that I am boss here, and that I have cut down their wages ten per cent. I am going to present a library to my native town, and I've got to save enough money on their wages to do it."

George Chesterland turned very pale. He knew that this reduction meant to the poor, struggling souls dependent upon their labor for their daily bread.

"I hope you will think over this reduction," George pleaded humbly. "I am sure the employees cannot stand it, and it will surely result in a strike."

"Who is boss here? Will you or won't you obey my orders?" snapped the wealthy manufacturer.

"Send a book-keeper here," he continued roughly. "I'll have a list of prices made at once."

George did as he was bidden, and Amor was silently distressed by his unhappy looks that night. She longed to know what was wrong with him, but she was afraid to ask.

She was to know only too soon.

The next day all the workmen, on being told of the terrible reduction, walked out of the factory. A strike was declared, and Joseph Hill, wild with rage, shook his fist at his handsome young manager, George Chesterland.

"Get out of here as quick as you can," he shouted savagely. "You are to blame for this strike. You threatened me with it, and I know you advised the men to go out. They shall stay out till they starve, and you go too!"

"You wrong me, sir," George cried, alarmed at the thought of being deprived of work. "I had not a word to say to your men besides that which you ordered."

"Get out of here!" was the only reply he received.

With a look of despair on his handsome face, George put on his hat, ready to go.

"There is a bundle of old papers in that desk," he said quietly, "which belonged to my father. I found them among a lot of discarded papers. I wish I might take them with me."

Joseph Hill jerked the desk open and flung the yellow package disdainfully at George's feet.

If he had known what that package contained, he would have murdered George Chesterland before he would have let him have it. He threw the package away, and with it went all his good luck and wealth.

But George did not know that. Picking up the despised parcel, he walked sadly out into the street.

It seemed as if he must have air and time to think, so he walked on and on, never heeding his weariness, until he came to Central Park.

There he sunk despondently upon a bench, and unmindful of all around him, gave himself up to bitter thoughts.

What could he do? Where should he turn? What would Amor say?

Had he been alone, he would not have felt the blow so keenly. But Amor, his beautiful, heartless wife, how could he break the terrible news to her?

She had always despised him because he worked; what would she think now when he was without work, without the means to support her?

Would she leave him? he wondered. Would she disappear from his life and leave him but the dream of her presence?

How bitterly she hated him! He remembered once how she had turned from him in disgust after noticing the stain of leather on his hands.

He laughed aloud, a cold and mirthless laugh, when he thought of it, and people passing turned round to look at him curiously.

Utter darkness of night reminded him to go home at last.

He did not see the pale, frightened face of his wife, he did not hear her sigh of relief at his return. He could see and hear nothing but the misery in his own soul.

He could not eat, and he did not notice how wistfully Amor watched him, and how her own plate went away untouched.

When she asked him, very softly, if he was ill, if his head ached, he answered roughly to keep from breaking down, but Amor thought it was because he no longer loved her.

He went off to bed immediately after dinner, never once saying good-night, and Amor's heart sunk like lead when she heard him close and lock his door.

"He has ceased to love me," she sobbed, as she threw herself upon her bed.

XXIII

DID SHE LEARN TOO LATE TO LOVE HIM?

AMOR HEARD THE TRUTH FROM Christmas.
She was horrified when the young girl came in the next day and told her about the strike. Christmas was looking for work, and Amor knew, since George had been absent from early morning, that he was engaged in a similar quest.

She waited anxiously and impatiently for his return, and when he came, late in the evening, footsore and heartsore and hopeless, her heart overflowed with pity for him.

She paid him a thousand little attentions that once would have given him the greatest happiness, but he did not seem to notice them.

She tried to force herself into a cheerful mood and to induce him to talk, but she saw, with a great fear, that he seemed to shrink from her.

She did not tell him of Christmas Cherry's visit, she did not want to introduce the painful subject of the strike.

And George said nothing to her. As soon as he could, he went to his room and she was left alone again.

Several days passed in this way, and every morning George Chesterland went away, and every night he returned, more hopeless and wretched.

Amor watched him with fear and anguish. She longed to share his trouble. She felt that she would give the world if she could press his poor, pale face against her breast and tell him to cease his worry and to hope for the best.

She would have told him that and more, had she possessed the courage.

The love he had longed for and prayed for, was his. His affliction, his grief, his sadness, had opened her eyes to the truth.

She loved her husband. Poor man! Poor workman! Whatever he was, she loved him with her whole heart, with a passion as intense as he had given her.

A hundred times she wished he might know the truth; but the fear that he no longer cared made her too timid to show her love.

She knew they could afford a servant no longer, so she dismissed the maid and bravely did the work herself.

But George did not notice the girl's absence or the burned face of his wife.

Christmas had not been near Amor since the morning she had told her about the strike, and at last Amor decided to go down to see her, to get wise counsel.

She found Christmas at home, busily engaged at some copying that had been given to her by an acquaintance of one of her teachers.

Laying her work aside, she greeted Amor lovingly, and inquired anxiously after George.

"I have come down to talk with you about him," Amor said sorrowfully. "I have been so wretched for days, and I knew no one could set me straight but my little angel.

"George has not found work," she continued. "I know by his manner, although he has never even told me yet about the strike. He is so unhappy, Christmas, and he never pays the slightest attention to me. Do you think he has learned to hate me?"

The pitiful appeal in Amor's voice stirred gentle Christmas. She took the little hand that bore the blisters of unaccustomed toil, and gazed lovingly into the troubled black eyes.

"My dearest!" she replied fondly. "What notions you get. I know he loves you better than his life."

"Then why does he treat me so badly?" Amor demanded indignantly, her eyes filling with tears. "He never offers to kiss me, he never notices one thing that I do for him."

"Did you ever encourage him to confide in you, to share his sorrows and his joys with you?" Christmas replied with tender reproach.

"I do not suppose that I ever did. But it is different now."

"Yes; and worse. If you repulsed and scorned his little troubles, would he dare to come to you now? No, Amor dear. He may be dying for a kind word from you, but he does not dare ask it."

"I am sure I am trying to be kind to him. He might see that I am not angry or hateful as I used to be."—tearfully.

"He would not believe it if he did see a change. He would be afraid to trust it. Oh, Amor, you have been dearly loved by one of the most noble men on earth. Now in his hour of trouble, can you not repay his kindness by being brave?"

"I am trying!"—piteously. "I have dismissed the servant and I am doing all my own work. What more can I do?"

Christmas smiled thoughtfully. The sting of her love was past, she thought.

"Go to your husband," she said, kindly. "Tell him you have been unkind and that you are sorry. Beg him to share his troubles with you, and he will forget all his wretchedness and be happy in spite of grim fate."

"But I am afraid."—hesitatingly. "He looks so stern and unforgiving."

"Did you not once look so at him? Oh, my dearest Amor, if you loved your noble husband, you would still find the way to his breaking heart."

"I do love him," sobbed Amor, falling on her knees and burying her crimson face against Christmas' heart. "I was afraid to tell you before, but his unhappiness has opened my eyes, and I know that I love him, my darling husband, better than my life."

Christmas was also weeping. She pressed Amor close to her heart and silently thanked Heaven that happiness had come at last to those two she loved so madly.

"Dear, dear Amor!" she whispered tenderly. "How happy this will make poor George."

Then she aroused herself. It was drawing near dinner-time, and George might be even then waiting sad and lonely at home. He must know of his new-found happiness at once.

"You must go home, Amor, at once," she said, with a pretty little show of authority. "It is not right to cheat George out of one instant of happiness. Go to him at once, darling, and in his arms, against his loving heart, tell him that which will make him the happiest man on earth."

Amor started home quite eagerly. Since she had decided to tell her husband that she loved him, she became impatient to see him.

Her heart throbbed madly when she thought how the lovelight would return to his bonny blue eyes. And their lips would meet in a long kiss of love and reconciliation.

She did not realize it before, but she was hungry for a kiss, hungry for the return of his old, fond, masterful ways, hungry to rest in his arms and listen to his tender, thrilling voice whispering fond words to her.

So lost was she in her happy dream of love that she heeded no one, saw nothing, and was oblivious to all the world.

Breathlessly she ran up the long flight of stairs to her flat, never once pausing.

He might have returned before her; she fondly hoped he had.

A chill of disappointment crept over her when she found the flat still empty. George had not returned.

Never waiting to change her street dress, she tied on a large apron and started to the kitchen to prepare dinner.

A knock at the door called her back, and her heart stood still with a sudden tumult of joy.

It must be her love, her husband, her king!

Should she tell him at once? Yes; she would open the door and greet him with a kiss, and then she would tell him she loved him with all the strength of her soul.

On wings of love she flew to the door, scarcely breathing in her excitement. She turned the key, she opened the door, and—

Found herself face to face with Mateo Blanco!

With a sharp cry of fear, her hand pressing her heart and her face blanched to a deadly pallor, she gazed with unspeakable horror upon her bitter enemy.

He stepped into the room and closed the door behind him.

"Did you think you could escape me forever?" he demanded insolently.

"What do you want?" she gasped hoarsely.

"You, my dear girl, you and your father's millions!" he answered with cool candor.

"How dare you come here, you scoundrel!" Amor breathed indignantly. "Go! Leave me this instant, or I shall call my husband to put you out!"

"Your husband?" he repeated with a cry of hatred. "Your husband!"

He grasped her hands with cruel force and, pushing her back against the side-board, hissed between his clinched teeth into her frightened, upturned face:

"Tell me the truth! Are you married? By Heaven, if you are, your father shall hang for murder!"

XXIV

"YOUR FATHER'S LIFE OR—YOUR HAND."

AMOR GAVE A LOOK OF agonized fear at Mateo Blanco's wicked, revengeful, swarthy face.

She could not answer him. It seemed as if his dreadful threat had robbed her of speech.

The sight of her white, woe-begone face upturned so helplessly to him only served to increase the revengeful Spaniard's fury.

She had scorned and insulted him in the days of her prosperity, she had eluded him and cheated him of the wealth for which he was willing to give his soul, and now she was in his power, at his mercy, shrinking pale and trembling before the demon blazing from his eyes.

The knowledge of this made him happy. As she had insulted and scorned him in the old days, he would repay her with harshness and cruelty now. She should yet sue on bended knees for the favors she had once scorned.

As he was a living, breathing man, so surely was the beautiful girl in his power. Mateo Blanco knew she would endure a thousand maddening shames before she would see her father die the death of a common felon.

"Tell me the truth!" he repeated, giving her an impatient shake. "Are you married?"

"What difference can it make to you?" Amor demanded with a flash of her old defiance.

"It makes some difference to the length of your father's life, and the manner of his death," was the sarcastic reply.

"Do you think you can frighten me by your empty threats?" was the fearless reply.

"Are my threats empty ones?"—coolly. "Why did you run away from home, my dear?"

"That had nothing to do with you or my father!" she answered stiffly, gaining more courage and determined to brave it out to the bitter end.

"You do you not mention your mother?"—with a cutting laugh.

Amor gasped, and his keen eyes saw the pain that came into her beautiful face.

"Why should I mention her when all your vile, contemptible threats are directed solely against my father?" she retorted evasively.

"You are trifling with me!"—angrily. "What would make you give up home, luxury, wealth, for this"—with a contemptuous glance around the humble flat—"if you were ignorant of your father's secret?"

She breathed quickly. What answer could she make? Why would she have given up all the luxuries of life, unless driven to it by a knowledge of her father's crime?

"You cannot answer me—you know what my threat means despite your pretended ignorance," he gloatingly declared.

"I hesitated because I did not wish to give my reason for running away. Many girls before me have given up as much as I have, and for the same reason?"

"You mean?"

"That I left home for—love's sweet sake!"

"And you are in love?"—curiously.

"With all my heart and soul."

"It is lucky for your father that you are only in love—not married. For if you were, I swear upon my life, I should send him to the gallows!"

Amor could hardly endure her torture. She longed to cry out to him that she was a wife—the wife of the noblest man that ever lived. She longed to hurl her hatred at his head and drive him from her presence—but her father!

Oh, the agony of that thought! If she spoke, her father's blood would be upon her head.

Heaven pity her! She must not speak the truth, she must brand herself as an object unworthy the name of woman—to save her father!

She opened her lips to speak, but the words died away in a gasp. What could she do?

"I wonder what my angel mother would advise?" she thought wretchedly. "Would she tell me to debase myself to save my father? Oh, I know she would save him, if she were in my position; she would count any sacrifice very small that would spare his life. And I must do as she would advise, I must try to be brave enough. It cannot matter much what he thinks of me, and it will save my father."

"Put on your coat and hat, and come with me," Mateo Blanco said suddenly, pointing to her wraps which lay upon the chair where she had thrown them aside.

"Go with you?" Amor repeated tremblingly.

"Yes; come with me. We shall be married at once, and then, if you play any more tricks, I shall be solaced by your millions," was the cool answer.

"I will not go with you. You must be mad! Have you not heard what I have said, that I love a man, that I am living here as—a wife?" she cried in alarm.

"That does not alter my plans."—indifferently.

"Surely"—pleadingly—"after what I have told you, you would not want me for your wife?"

"Bah"—scornfully—"what do I care? It's not you I want, my beautiful Amor; I have long since recovered from my brief infatuation of your pale, cold beauty. It is your money I am after, and mean to have."

"Take it, then, and welcome. I shall never claim it!" she eagerly cried.

"And do you think your father is going to hand his millions over to me unless you are my wife? He isn't such a fool. I make him give me a royal income now, but in case of his death, unless I marry you, I shall be left without a penny."

"Do you suppose when I tell my father what you so frankly tell me, that he will permit his only child to become the wife of such a heartless villain?"

"I have told you, proud Amor, that your precious father can't help himself."—with a bitter laugh. "If it were in his power, I know he would kill me, so much does he hate me, but I have made myself proof against his wrath by telling him of a confession which I have written and intrusted to the care of a friend, to be opened and made public in the event of my death. Since that Ricardo Escandon has been more than solicitous about my health. Of course you know what are the contents of that confession?"

"How should I know?"—disdainfully.

"Then it is time you did. That confession tells how your father murdered—your mother!"

A sharp cry of distress escaped Amor's white lips in spite of her forced composure.

She knew the truth. What moment since she left home had she ceased to remember it? But to have it spoken to her so brutally was like thrusting a knife into her heart.

That little cry, so full of shame and agony, convinced Mateo Blanco that the girl had spoken the truth, that she was ignorant of her father's crime, and that she had deserted home and friends for love's sweet sake.

"Now you know what power I hold over your father! You can see why he readily gave his consent to my proposal for your hand. He is fully as anxious as I am to see you my wife. Quite a change, isn't it, my haughty

Amor, to ordering me from his home because I dared to admire his beautiful heiress? It is my day now, and I mean to feather my nest."

Amor stood motionless and pallid before him. She was asking herself, miserably, how she was to elude him, how she was to compel him to go away and leave her.

It did not seem possible that she would have to go with him. She would rather have him strike her dead where she stood than to give up her husband, her handsome young husband whom she had learned to love so madly.

"Come!" he commanded impatiently, "we must be off."

"I cannot go!" she cried, with dreadful fear. "I will not go."

"You wish to see your father hang!"—angrily.

"No, no. In mercy's name, not that!"

"Then come!"

"I cannot! I shall die if you take me away."

He laughed harshly. "If it pleases you to pine away and die for love's sweet sake, after we are married, I shall have no objections. But before— that is another matter."

Was there no way to move him? No way to soften his heart?

She looked at his swarthy, wicked face, with the low brow and hanging jaw. There was not a line of pity, of generosity, of mercy, in that face.

And if she went with him? Might she not escape?

Yes, that might be possible, but she knew she would never get the chance until he had made her his wife. She could not do that—never that. She must escape him now.

"Are you trying to wait until your lover returns?" he inquired scornfully.

"Heaven help me!" cried Amor, with new terror. "Above all things, he must never know the truth."

"Then come at once. I am weary of this delay."

"I do not intend to go," she said, with sudden boldness. "I intend to remain here."

"By the heavens above, I shall waste no more time with you," he vowed, with terrible anger. "This night your father shall sleep in jail, and he shall know that it was you who sent him there."

"You could not—you dare not!" she panted, her eyes flashing dangerously.

"You shall see what I dare."—determinedly. "You shall taste my daring when your father's body hangs in the air."

He dropped her trembling hands, now red-marked from his cruel grasp, and started to the door.

Guessing his intention, and knowing he would carry out his threat, Amor sprung madly after him. Catching him firmly by the arm, she cried wildly:

"You shall not go! You cruel wretch, you shall not go!"

He tried to shake her off. "Do you think that you can detain me?" he asked.

"I will do anything—promise anything," she continued wildly, sinking on her knees, "if you spare him. Have mercy! In God's name, have mercy!"

"I only ask you to come along, and marry me," was the impassive reply.

"Have you no heart?" Amor wailed piteously. "Are you made of stone, and will nothing but my father's life or mine satisfy your cruelty?"

"Your father's life or—your hand!"—carelessly.

"Is there no other way?"—piteously.

"None! I am weary of scenes. Come; it is time we were away from here."

As he spoke the door opened and George Chesterland, pale and weary from his vain search, stood before them.

His eyes fell upon his kneeling wife and the swarthy man before her. He recognized the Spaniard at once, and with a cry of rage, sprung forward, seizing him roughly by the collar.

"You villain!" he said hoarsely. "What has brought you here?"

Mateo Blanco smiled triumphantly as he replied:

"I have come—for my wife!"

XXV

"IF SHE WERE THE LOWEST WOMAN ON EARTH, I SHOULD STILL PROTECT HER."

"YOU SCOUNDREL! YOU SHALL SUFFER for this outrage," cried George, enraged by Mateo Blanco's insolence.

"I think the outrage is on the other side, sir," exclaimed Mateo Blanco, trying to free himself. "You have been harboring my wife."

"If you say that again," cried George savagely, "I will choke the life out of your miserable body."

"Oh, let him go, pray let him go!" Amor pleaded tremblingly.

"No, by Heaven! He shall suffer for daring to enter my house."

"I came for my wife," cried Mateo defiantly.

"If you dare breathe that word again," George began in fury, but Mateo Blanco interrupted him, saying quietly:

"If you doubt it, ask the lady herself!"

Something in his manner, the persistency and audacity, made George Chesterland suddenly release his hold and turn his blazing eyes upon his frightened wife.

"You heard what he has said," he cried imperiously. "Why do you not tell him he lies?"

"She dare not!" sneered Blanco.

"Speak, I command you!" cried George, never removing his burning eyes from Amor's terrified face.

"I will explain—I am—" she hesitated, brokenly.

"Speak! At once, so that I may give this scoundrel the treatment he deserves. Let me hear your lips declare him a liar."

"For your *father's* sake," Mateo Blanco interposed with emphatic significance, "tell this man that—I am your husband."

For her father's sake! Oh, Heaven! Must she tell that frightful lie? Was there no hope, no escape for her?"

None! None! Before her stood her judge, her husband, with the love light gone from his bonny blue eyes and a fury of rage burning there instead.

Beside him stood the man who held her father's life in his hand, with a face of merciless warning.

"Are you going to tell me this man lies?" repeated George savagely.

Her head bowed in shame, her breast heaved with emotion.

"I—cannot!" she faltered in a broken whisper.

George Chesterland staggered back as if he had received a heavy blow.

"You *cannot?*" repeated George hoarsely. "Then you were married to this man?"

"I told you so," Mateo Blanco answered for her.

George took no notice of him. His eyes were still fixed on Amor, who could not bear the frightful agony they held.

"Forgive me! For God's sake, forgive me!" she cried, sinking to her knees and raising her clasped hands supplicatingly to him.

He laughed mirthlessly. There was such a ring of agony in the sound that Amor shuddered.

"If the angels in heaven had told me this thing, I could have sworn they lied. But your own lips confirm it, those proud, cold lips! My God!"

She could endure the sight of his agony no longer. She felt that she would go mad if that wild, heartbroken look remained on his handsome face.

"I spoke falsely when I said that," she cried frantically. "I am not his wife! It is a lie! Oh, I swear to you, it is a lie!"

"How easily you change from one side to the other," was the weary retort. "First you declare yourself this man's wife, then you swear you are not. Why do you take the trouble to deny the truth? What can you gain by it? Do you think you can ever blind me again? Why should you care to try?"

"Before God and Heaven, I tell the truth!" the unhappy girl cried despairingly.

"Amor," Mateo Blanco interrupted warningly, "for your father's sake, let this man know you are my wife. I don't ask it for my sake, but for the sake of your old father."

"I cannot wreck my life, even for my father's sake," she cried wildly. "Do what you will, I shall swear I lied when I said I was your wife."

"You have spoken your father's doom."—threateningly. "Those words have killed him as surely as if you ran a knife through his heart."

"If you have no shame in you, woman," George said hoarsely, "at least spare your father."

Poor, blind man! He thought Mateo Blanco meant that Amor's disgrace and untruth would kill her father. Had he only known the true meaning of those words, how different life might have been for them both!

His bitter reproach cut Amor to the heart. It seemed like a voice from Heaven, that even he should tell her to spare her father. That was the least she could do.

She had lost her husband's love, and now the only service she could do for any one was to shield her poor, sinful father.

"Don't be angry," she said weakly, almost prayerfully, to Mateo Blanco, "I shall acknowledge anything—for my father's sake! Fate is too strong for me. I am your wife—anything, anything!"

"I am glad that you have decided to act wisely," he replied in tones of forgiveness. "I shall forget your past misdoings, and together we shall share the declining years of your father's life. Come with me, for it is time we left this house."

"I have acknowledged all you wished," she replied desperately. "Now leave me in peace."

"No, indeed; you have already been absent too long. You must go with me now."

George Chesterland had fallen heavily into a chair. With blood-shot eyes he watched Amor but made no move to speak or interfere between her and her evil-faced companion.

Mateo Blanco saw that Amor would not accompany him without the use of a little force, so picking up her hat and jacket, he caught her by the arm and drew her unwillingly toward the door.

"I will not go with you! I would rather die!" Amor cried desperately.

But the Spaniard paid no heed to her words. Perfectly unconcerned, as if he were deaf and blind, he dragged her forcibly after him.

Amor's strength was giving out. The long strain had taken effect and she was becoming as weak as a child. She knew her strength could not withstand his, she knew he was carrying her away from her unforgiving husband, she knew if she went then she would never see George again, so with a voice filled with agony she cried:

"Save me, for God's sake, save me from this man! I cannot go with him! Save me!"

George Chesterland started up as if the wounds in his heart had burst out afresh. He could not withstand her prayerful pleading. He could not bear to have her, the girl he had loved with all his soul, the girl he had believed as pure as the angels, dragged away unwillingly.

That she was unworthy, he did not attempt to deny. Her own lips had confessed it. But if she was the lowest creature on earth, he could not stand by and see her dragged off by a man she hated so deeply.

And of her hatred for this man George could not doubt.

"Stand back and release her!" he commanded imperiously, springing to his feet. "If she is your wife a thousand times, you shall not drag her away in this manner."

"If you dare to interfere between husband and wife a second time, I shall have you arrested," Mateo Blanco declared emphatically.

"You threatened me once before. I told you then, as I tell you now, to go ahead and do it," was the cool reply.

Mateo Blanco was a small, undersized man, and as he glanced up at George Chesterland, tall and strong, powerful and determined, he thought it better to at least release his hold on Amor.

"I cannot consent to have my wife remain another night under this roof," he said quietly. "I do not think you can blame me for that."

"I know she is your wife and has proven herself unworthy of all consideration," was the indifferent reply. "But she is still a woman. She cries for help, she refuses to accompany you, and if she were the worst creature on earth, I should still protect her against your brute strength. For my own part, I hope never to set eyes on her after to-night; but so long as she chooses to remain here, the flat is hers."

"Then I remain also," was the sour reply.

"I beg your pardon. I pay for this flat and you are not welcome here. If you do not like this you can, to use your favorite threat, appeal to the law and have us both arrested. Then do as you please, but it pleases me for you to leave this house within the next second, and if you don't, I mean to throw you head first down the stairs."

"I shall go!" Mateo Blanco retorted, black with rage. "But mark my words, you will regret this night's work before long. I shall never rest until I have revenge!"

George Chesterland pointed silently toward the door, and with a savage oath, Mateo Blanco went out, leaving husband and wife alone together.

Amor gave a sigh of relief. She looked at her husband's stern, unrelenting and unforgiving face, and with clasped hands cried pitifully:

"Oh, my husband, hear me and forgive your unhappy wife!"

XXVI

ALONE IN HIS MISERY.

AMOR'S PITIFUL APPEAL FELL UPON indifferent ears. The heart of the man who had loved her to madness had been turned to stone by her startling confession.

She was worse than nothing in his eyes. She had proven herself to be worse than false.

She had lied to him, and while the lawful wife of another man, had wedded him.

Her own confession had proven her to be unworthy and unreliable.

The truth had been no sooner wrung from her unwilling lips than she tried to lie out of it again.

This was George Chesterland's mental attitude toward unhappy Amor.

It is not surprising, then, that her prayers were unheeded—that her agony ceased to touch him.

She had betrayed him—she had broken his heart, and he could never forgive it.

"I pray you to listen to me," Amor continued, seeing he was as cold as ice. "I swear to you I am not married to that man! On my soul, I never married any one but yourself!"

He gave her a look that cut to her heart. She shuddered as if she had felt the full force of his hatred and scorn.

"Are you marble?" she cried in tones of anguish. "Can you not see I am suffering the bitterest agony? Oh, I pray you to say you believe me, or my heart will break!"

"There is nothing to say," he replied wearily, as if forced by her vehemence to say something. "Why torture yourself trying to give the lie to your own confession?"

"But it was not true! It was forced from me by that man," she moaned.

"How could that man, if he were nothing to you, force you to tell a lie in my presence?"—incredulously.

"He holds a power over me," she said with a tinge of hope in her voice. "I dare not deny what he says, I am helpless—helpless!"

"What is this power, this secret?"—suspiciously.

If she could only tell him! If it were anything but the story of her father's crime!

But to tell the history of that frightful murder was too much. Might George not look on it in a different light and insist on her father paying the penalty?

And in any case, would he not shrink as much from the daughter of a murderer as from the supposed wife of Mateo Blanco?

It was not to be thought of for a moment. She must bear the secret alone, if it cost her life, happiness, and love.

"I cannot tell you," she murmured helplessly. "But you must believe me, and know that it is a secret of frightful importance, since it made me confess to the blackest lie that was ever invented by an evil man."

"Please say no more."—wearily. "Your evasions only increase my belief in your forced confession. Let us say no more about it."

"Then you will not forgive me?"—with a cry of anguish.

"There can be no forgiveness or anything else between us."—coldly. "This house is at your disposal. You may remain here as long as you wish."

"And you?" she asked faintly.

He looked at her. Her eyes fell beneath the quiet scorn of his, and the hot blood rushed into her pale face.

"At least I shall not remain here," he replied haughtily.

"You will not desert me and leave me alone?" she cried in alarm, although she had understood his scornful glance only too well.

"Have you lost all shame?" he said angrily. "I have not, and as soon as I can gather together my few belongings, I shall go away where I will never see you again."

He had no more to say, and no more was necessary. His cruel words deprived the beautiful suffering girl of all power of speech.

George walked away from her, and shut himself up in his room. His brain was whirling strangely, he seemed unable to think, to reason.

He thought he would not begin to pack at once. He would sit down until he became more composed, and then he would take what things he needed and go away from the place where he had been so unhappy, where he had received the severest blow ever dealt to man.

The sound of heartbroken weeping came to him, and it worried him without creating any pitying feeling for the one in distress.

It was Amor weeping, he knew, and he wondered why she wept so long and so bitterly. It bothered him—he wished she would not sob so loud.

Then his thoughts wandered. He thought of the factory and the poor souls who had struck for their rights. Would any of them starve? he wondered. Curious, that so many trials should fall on those least prepared to bear it.

Probably he should starve to death also. A miserable death he had heard it was. The frightful pangs of hunger added to the agony of mind until at last the reason became unbalanced, and then—death.

Strange that he should die such a death, born as he was amid wealth and luxury.

Death seemed sweet and peaceful to his mind. He had not known before how weary he was and how he longed for rest. It would be bliss to die, to know no more, to cease to worry, to give up the struggle of life—to forget!

It seemed quite plain to him now why so many persons committed suicide. And what a sin it was to try to prevent them from seeking the blissful unconsciousness of death!

He had prevented one weary mortal from taking her own life. How wrong it was, she had longed so much for death. If he had not saved her—

George Chesterland laughed loudly—a wild, insane laugh. He listened quite curiously until the last sound of that unnatural laugh died away, and then it struck him that everything had grown strangely still and silent.

What did he miss? Something, and yet he could not tell what.

Ah, yes; he remembered! It was the sound of Amor's violent weeping he missed. He remembered now that her crying had grown calmer; he had not noticed when it ceased entirely.

George rose from his chair. He was surprised to find himself weak and dizzy. The blood rushed wildly to his head, blinding him and creating a deafening noise in his ears.

Staggering weakly, he opened the door and walked out into the dining-room where he had left Amor.

She was not there. Her chair stood just where it had been hastily pushed back.

George felt a strange repulsion against being alone. He was tired and faint; he wanted company, even the company of the woman who had broken his heart.

He would find her, he would ask her to remain with him until this strange feeling passed away.

From one room to another he went, looking in every conceivable nook where even a cat could not have hidden, but finding no sign of Amor.

He remembered Mateo Blanco had offered her her coat and hat, and he walked out into the dining-room where they had been.

One glance was sufficient. They were gone. He knew the truth—Amor had gone away.

It was cruel, he thought, cruel to leave him when he needed company. This silent house would drive him mad. It was like a house in which death had entered.

Why should he stay there and be oppressed by it any longer? Amor was gone, why should he remain? He would go, too.

Wearily and with terrible effort he returned to his room. Gathering up his clothing in his arms, he carried them aimlessly into the dining-room and laid them on the table. He might as well take them along, and yet it seemed such a trouble.

There was the yellow package which had belonged to his father, and which Joseph Hill had scornfully hurled at him when he gave George his dismissal.

He did not care to take them along, and yet they bore the handwriting of his father, and for that reason they were dear to him.

There was no hurry to leave. He might look the papers over, and select a few to take with him in his wanderings.

Still in that strange, dazed, unfeeling way, George Chesterland opened the bundle and read one paper after another. Despite the dizziness of his head, he understood every word he read.

And what he read proved Joseph Hill's villainy, proved the heartless millionaire a thief, a forger. Line after line, note after note, columns of figures stood out in indisputable evidence.

Instead of George's father, at the time of his death, being indebted to Joseph Hill, Joseph Hill was indebted to his father. Not one stone did he own in the factory, not one farthing of the millions he had stolen.

The millions belonged to George Chesterland, and to no one but George Chesterland. All these weary years he had labored as a hireling in his own factory. Joseph Hill had no right, not so much as the lowliest working-man!

Ah, those poor down-trodden workers! They should have their rights now. He was their master, their employer, their friend. They should suffer no longer, for instead of being a poor, helpless wretch like them, he was—a millionaire!

A millionaire? What joy that thought should have brought him once. But now?

Of what use would be those millions? Could they bring him happiness, forgetfulness?

No! They could not restore his love for Amor! They could not bring back the happiness of his unreserved confidence. They could not restore his belief in her purity.

A millionaire, but his wealth had come too late!

George Chesterland's head dropped forward on the precious papers which had restored to him millions of dollars. He forgot the wealth, forgot everything. He seemed to be drifting peacefully away and then came the blackness—the bliss—of utter unconsciousness.

Some good angel took Christmas to see Amor that evening. She was on her way to school and a feeling of disquiet, of unrest, turned her face in the direction of Amor's home.

Obeying the impulses that urged her on, Christmas Cherry walked up the long stairs to the door of Amor's flat.

She knocked. No one heeded it, but the sound of wild, incoherent words made her open the door and enter.

George Chesterland raised his head and gazed with wild, unrecognizing, blood-shot eyes upon the frightened girl.

"You must go!" he said wildly. "I cannot keep another man's wife in my house!"

"Oh, Heaven!" cried the frightened girl, shrinking back with horror. "He does not know me. He is mad!"

XXVII

"TEN CHANCES TO ONE HE WILL
NEVER BE SANE AGAIN."

AT CHRISTMAS CHERRY'S FRIGHTENED CRY, George Chesterland was aroused to greater frenzy.

"Oh, God!" he cried wildly. "Those lips I hardly dared to kiss have confessed that the woman I thought as pure as the angels was another man's wife when she married me!"

"He's mad!" Christmas cried again, and then hoping to rouse him to some knowledge of his surroundings, she cried loudly:

"George! George! Arouse yourself. Tell me, where is Amor, your wife?"

The blood-shot eyes gleamed fiercely into hers for a moment, and then a loud, mirthless laugh fell from his dry lips.

"Amor! Amor!" he repeated bitterly. "Another man's wife! Go at once! You cannot stay here—go with your husband. Don't you hear him calling you?"

"Something terrible has happened and it has turned poor George Chesterland into a raving lunatic," Christmas thought, her face as pale as death.

She understood his words, she understood their terrible import, she seemed to understand the significance of the deserted flat, the lonely, raving man.

Amor was gone. The beautiful girl she had loved so dearly, the girl who had won the heart of the man Christmas worshipped.

Amor was gone. The mad words of the deserted man told why, and yet, loyal little Christmas could believe no evil of her friend, her sister!

"There is a mistake somewhere," she decided instantly. "Amor was too good and pure to commit this terrible wrong. She will come back and explain it all."

Encouraged by her belief in Amor's purity, Christmas closed the door and walked over to George's side. His head had fallen helpless again upon the table, while he muttered on in a wild, incoherent manner that wrung Christmas' tender heart.

"George!" she said, very softly and tenderly, laying a hand on his shoulder. "Come into your room and lie down. You are weary and ill."

Poor George Chesterland paid no attention to the sweet, pleading voice.

"What am I to do?" Christmas wondered anxiously. "I cannot go for help and leave him alone in this condition, and I cannot do anything with him myself."

"George," she pleaded, taking him by the hand, "come into your room and lie down until you feel better."

He heard her voice, and some inkling of her meaning forced its way in upon his clouded brain.

With an unsteady movement he arose to a standing position, but his poor maddened senses were unable to direct the motion of his feet, and, much to Christmas' alarm, George Chesterland fell in a helpless heap upon the floor.

Wild with fear, the trembling girl flew into the hall and cry after cry escaped her white lips. The startled tenants left their dinners and rushed out to learn the cause of the turmoil.

When they understood the cause of Christmas' fright they kindly gave her their assistance, and in a few moments two men had put George Chesterland in bed, while another had gone to bring the nearest physician.

All thought of attending school had been given up, and, after sending a messenger to bring Mrs. Day, Christmas calmly installed herself as nurse.

George Chesterland raved on incessantly. He paid no attention to the curious and sympathetic neighbors who had come to his assistance, and Christmas, feeling a delicacy about their overhearing the delirious man's heartbroken cries, thanked them kindly for their help and begged them to leave her alone with the sick man. Their presence seemed to increase his ravings, she said, and so they returned to their apartments to discuss the sick man among themselves.

It was not very long until Mrs. Day arrived. The messenger had conveyed to her the news of George Chesterland's illness, and that was all. But it was enough to make her lose no time in coming to him. The love Peter Day bore for this lost, unfortunate member of his dear old master's family was sufficient inducement to Mrs. Day to do what she could for George Chesterland.

"That baby-wife of his ain't good for tending a sick man, and Christmas can't be left to do it all herself," she argued on her way up to the house over which the shadow of a great tragedy and death hovered.

Very wisely, Mrs. Day stopped at her husband's stand to impart to him her meager information.

She arrived just as he was about to depart with a patron. "Peter! Peter!" she called to him excitedly.

The kind old man's face turned white beneath its ruddy, weather-beaten glow at the unusual sight of his tall, loosely-built wife at his stand.

To his broken heart, her coming had but one meaning. She was bringing him news of their lost one—the one who had been the joy and delight of their fond hearts, the one whose name was never more mentioned at home.

His hands trembled so that the reins dropped from them. Mrs. Day saw the agony upon his face, and knowing what brought it there, continued quickly:

"It's news I've got 'bout Master George Chesterland. Christmas sent a telegraph-boy down to tell me to come up as Master George were very sick and I was needed."

Peter Day drew a long, labored breath. He picked up the reins again. The news he dreaded had not come. But it would some day, some day! There was only one ending to the foolish frail ones of her kind—death!

Ever since Lillian ran away, he had been training himself to bear the blow when it came. They would never find their daughter again, until after her fate grew too hard and she found rest in death!

The river most likely would be her end, he thought, and often he pictured to himself the sight of that dear form dragged from the dark river, the water dripping from the long, tangle, golden-red hair, the beautiful blue eyes forever closed to all crime and misery, the restless, rebellious heart forever at rest.

But it had not come yet. He gave a deep sigh of relief.

"Master George is sick!" he repeated slowly. "That's bad—that's bad. Go right along up, Sarah, and when I come back I'll drive up his way and see how he's gettin' on."

So Mrs. Day went on without him. Christmas met her at the door and in a soft whisper told her how seriously ill George was, and knowing it was useless to try to hide Amor's flight, she added that he was all alone, with no one to take care of him.

"Where is his wife?" asked Mrs. Day in surprise.

"I think she has had a disagreement with Mr. Chesterland and has gone away," Christmas replied evasively. "Of course she left before she knew he was ill. Doubtless she did not know that his brain was affected and took offense at some wild thing he did or said.

Mrs. Day shook her gray head sadly. She imagined there was more than a slight disagreement back of such a serious illness, but if she learned the truth from George Chesterland's incessant ravings, she never broached the subject to Christmas.

Christmas put away Mrs. Day's bonnet, and then led her into the sick-chamber.

George Chesterland was tossing restlessly on his pillow. "Go away, go away!" he shouted frantically. "You belong to another man!"

Christmas bent over him sorrowfully. "There is no one here, George," she said soothingly, "except Mrs. Day and myself—Christmas! Don't you know me?"

Once again her words seemed to pierce the fever of his brain.

"Christmas! Little ragged angel," he repeated wearily. "Stay with me, for I am all alone."

Tears sprung into Christmas' soulful eyes; but forcing them back she replied huskily:

"I will stay with you."

And she kept her promise to the end.

The doctor came at his leisure and took a survey of the surroundings before he examined the patient, which he did at last in a very careless and unsympathetic manner.

"Have you a family physician?" he inquired.

Christmas told him they had not. Then he asked who was to nurse the invalid, and if they had any means of support.

"Mrs. Day and myself shall nurse him," Christmas replied stiffly, "and shall also furnish whatever money is required."

"You have a long siege before you," the physician continued. "The man is suffering from an attack of brain-fever, and it will be a long time before he recovers, if, indeed, he has strength to live through his illness."

"As long as he is ill we'll stay with him," Mrs. Day declared stoutly.

"And if care and attention can save his life, he shall live!" Christmas added as solemnly as if registering a vow before Heaven.

"My God, another man's wife—not mine!" cried the raving man.

The doctor smiled coldly.

"If he loves it will be a miracle," he said, "and it may be better if he dies, for ten chances to one, after this attack, he will never be sane again."

XXVIII

CHRISTMAS MAKES A SACRIFICE
FOR GEORGE'S SAKE.

SEVERAL WEEKS HAD GONE BY and George Chesterland lingered on in the same condition.

Mrs. Day and Christmas Cherry were still his patient nurses, and kind old Peter Day looked in twice a day with tearful eyes upon the unconscious young man. Peter slept at his lonely old home, but he always had his breakfast with his wife, and drove up in time to get his dinner before leaving for his night's work.

These loyal friends had found it very hard work to make both ends meet since they took upon their shoulders the responsible and expensive burden of helpless George Chesterland.

Bravely did Christmas try to retain the copying that had been given to her by the Young Women's Christian Association, but it was not long until they said there was no more copying to do.

Christmas pleaded very hard for something else that she could do at home, and at last succeeded in getting envelopes to address.

It was slow work and difficult. After being up all night, she found it was impossible to write smoothly or in a straight line, and she was frightened at the number of envelopes she destroyed by misdirecting.

In spite of her bitter disappointment, she was not surprised on returning the work to be told there was no more to do at present.

And this left the entire family dependent upon the little earnings of Peter Day. He struggled nobly beneath the heavy load, and if he complained at all, it was because the weather was so fine, and so few persons cared to ride.

At last came a day that they never forgot. The patient seemed, if anything, worse, and with a sinking heart Christmas watched the doctor write out another prescription.

Oh, those daily prescriptions! They were a constant drain upon the family's slender resources, and in the end they seemed to do no good.

How on earth was she to have this one filled, Christmas did not know, unless Peter Day had the luck to find a customer on his way to supper.

"I have brought my bill, and I should like if you would settle it at once," the doctor said, after handing her the prescription.

His words were like a sudden thunder-clap to Christmas. She turned white as a lily, and sunk trembling into a chair.

"Your bill?" she echoed faintly.

The physician nodded and handed it to her. Christmas glanced at its contents, and her heart sunk lower than before.

"I shall be obliged for the amount at once," he said coldly.

"I did not know that it was customary for doctors to collect their bills before the patient recovered," she protested nervously.

"It is the custom to collect for every visit from patients we do not know."—icily.

"I am very sorry," faltered the poor girl, "but really I cannot pay you to-day. You need have no fear; we are honest people, and whether the young man gets well or dies, we shall pay you some time."

"Some time, miss, does not pay daily expenses. I cannot live on promises. If you cannot pay me for my services, I must resign from the case."

"You would not leave him in his dangerous condition without a doctor?" cried Christmas appealingly.

"If you have no money to pay a doctor"—impatiently—"the only place for the man is in a hospital."

"In a hospital!" she repeated in a tone of alarm. "You know that he would never get well if we sent him there."

"He would take his chances with the rest. But I have no time to lose. I shall call again to-morrow about noon, and if you cannot pay me then, my only course will be to give up the case and report it to the poor board or police," said the physician, as he took up his hat and departed.

Christmas' nerves were completely shattered, and with sobs and tears she confided the dreadful truth to Mrs. Day.

"The hard-hearted old scoundrel! I never did like him, and I don't believe he knows anything about doctoring, or the dear young gentleman would be on the mend by this time," Mrs. Day exclaimed angrily.

"What can we do?" cried Christmas helplessly. "We must pay his bill or he will have them take poor George to the hospital. And they will let him die there, I know they will."

"If they take him to the hospital, it will be over my dead body!" Mrs. Day declared fiercely.

"Oh, you know if we do not pay that cruel man, we cannot stop the police from taking George away."

"Peter will show them, never you fear," Mrs. Day replied firmly.

"But they will come when he is not here, and what can we two women do?" urged Christmas anxiously.

That was too much for Mrs. Day, so she sat down, looking greatly disturbed and a trifle frightened.

"I don't know where the money is to come from," she whispered slowly.

"I spent my very last penny yesterday for the medicine," Christmas said dolefully.

"And I had to take the last money Peter had in his pockets this morning to buy the ice," added Mrs. Day sorrowfully.

"And I am sure we could not live with any more saving than we do."

"I know we couldn't," Mrs. Day affirmed stoutly, with a little suspicious tremble in her voice. "We haven't had a smell of meat for two weeks, and the last bit of bacon you told me to save for Peter was finished last night, and when I set him down nothin' but bread and tea this mornin', I saw him look around to see if there was anything left for us. He hardly ate anything, and then he pretended he was so full and had no appetite-like."

Mrs. Day wiped her eyes with her apron and tried to keep her lips from quivering.

"I feel as if I brought all this suffering on you," Christmas said sadly. "I should never have sent for you."

"Do you suppose if we had never known you, Christmas Cherry, that my dear old man would ever have let his old master's son go to the hospital?" Mrs. Day asked indignantly. "Indeed, we a proud to care for him. We are only sorry 'cause we can't do more for him."

"Do you suppose Mr. Day can fix it up with the doctor?" inquired Christmas anxiously.

"I think he can. Anyway, don't let's worry any more till Peter comes, and I know he'll find some way out of it."

But Peter Day did not know the way out of their new trouble. He was more alarmed than the women at the thought of George Chesterland being taken to the hospital.

"It'ud kill the lad sure," he declared angrily. "That rascal of a doctor! I wish I could thrash him for this. I'll pay his old bill if I have to sell my business."

"Not Sal, father?" cried Mrs. Day, dropping back to the dear old name she had never used since Lillian left. Peter Day noticed it, and though he made no remark, his heart felt lighter than it had this many a day. Wonderful how sweet and familiar the name sounded! After awhile he very timidly called her "mother," and never again did they drop those tender terms.

"Yes, even dear old Sal," he said huskily. "Master George shan't be took to a hospital."

"But if you sell Sal, dear Mr. Day, you will have no way to earn a living," Christmas gently reminded him, "and then Mr. George would have to go to a hospital."

"That's right, Christmas, gal," he answered. "I must keep Sal. But I'll sell the carriage, that's what I'll do."

"And do you expect to make a living by hiring poor old Sal out as a saddle-horse?" laughed Christmas in spite of her troubles.

Peter Day laughed, too. "You're right, my gal, you're right. Guess I've got to keep 'em both. But I hain't got anything else to sell," and he glanced critically down over his shabby clothes.

"And I haven't anything left to sell," added Christmas regretfully. "I sold my jacket and my only good dress last week. I can't sell this dress, because it is all I have to wear."

"You might sell your hair," Mrs. Day said half in fun as she touched the heavy braids hanging almost to the girl's heels.

"Now, mother, don't put foolish notions in the girl's head," protested Peter Day, noticing the flush which crept into Christmas' thin cheeks. "Her purty hair is the only beauty she's got, and she ain't goin' to sell it."

"If you will remain with Mrs. Day a little while, I will go out and see if I can't find a doctor who will attend Mr. George until he gets well," Christmas said hopefully; and Peter Day took her place at the young man's bedside as she departed on her painful errand.

She returned a couple of hours later, very pale and weary and disheartened. The kind old couple saw by her wan face that she had been unsuccessful, and they asked her no questions as she sunk faintly into a chair.

"It is no use," she said hopelessly when she found the strength to speak. "No one will come. I explained the whole case to every one I saw, and I told them that we would pay them some day, but they gave one excuse or another and always refused to come. It was not professional etiquette to take another physician's patient, or they were overworked with their own patients, or they could not interfere where another physician had been attending. It was always the same, and the only thing they would say, when I asked what we were to do, was: Send him to the hospital."

"Blast them all!" exclaimed Peter Day hoarsely. "We'll keep Master George in spite of 'em. Now don't you women folks worry any more; I know I'll have luck to-night and make enough to stave that cold-blooded doctor off for a few days."

Alas, for his bright hopes! He returned in the morning as weary and hapless as even Christmas had returned from her search for a doctor.

"'Tain't no use, mother," he groaned, sinking heavily into the chair she pushed forward. "I hain't had no luck."

"You couldn't get any money?" gasped his wife.

"There's all I have in the world," he replied, throwing a little bit of silver upon the table. "About five dollars 'tis. And I nearly made a thief out o' myself too!"

"Oh, father, father, do you know what you're sayin'?" Mrs. Day cried, and Christmas, hearing their excited voices, hurried out to them.

"Has anything gone wrong?" she asked, all in a tremble.

"I nearly went wrong, gal!" was the sad reply. "It was just like this, Christmas. I didn't have no customers till late in the night, and then a rather poor dressed young man, very much excited, come runnin' down the street, and jumpin' into my cab, said: 'I'll give you three dollars, old chap, if you get me to the Central Station in twenty minutes.' Sal seemed to understand it just as well as I did, an' she jist went lickety-split all the way there. The young man never said a word, but openin' the door and handin' me three paper bills, rushed into the station. I turned Sal's head in the direction of my stand, foldin' up the money as I did so, an' thankin' Heaven even for the three dollars."

He sighed deeply and his listeners waited impatiently for him to continue.

"Just then one of the bills caught my eye. It didn't look exactly like a one-dollar bill, so I turned it over and found it was—a fifty-dollar bill!"

"Oh, father!" shouted Mrs. Day gleefully.

"Oh, dear Mr. Day!" Christmas gasped, clapping her hands.

"That's just how I felt at first. I would pay that cussed doctor, and I thought Heaven had not forgotten us. I was goin' to drive straight home to tell you the good news, when I stopped all of a sudden like. 'That man only intended to give you three dollars, Peter Day,' says I to myself. 'If you keep this, you are no better than a thief.'

"'But there is Master George. I wouldn't keep it if it warn't for him,' says I back to myself, but myself says back to me: 'Look here, Peter, you've always been honest afore this. Maybe if you steal to pay the doctor, Heaven will punish you by makin' Master George die.' 'You're right,' says I to myself, "tain't my money, an' I'll take it back.'"

"Oh, father!" wept Mrs. Day softly, and Christmas laid a sympathetic hand on his shoulder and said not a word.

"I knowed you'd both tell me I was doin' right, an' so would Master George, if he knew; so I drove as fast as I could back to the station an' I found the train just ready to go an' the young man I took there acting like a madman before the ticket office.

"He was beggin' an' pleadin' and threatenin', but all to no account. He hadn't enough money an' they wouldn't give him a ticket. I went up to him, an' I says, 'Here, young man, you gave me fifty dollars instead of one.'

"And would you think it, mother, he burst into tears, an' throwin' his arms around my neck, kissed me on the cheek.

"'God forever bless you!' he cried. 'That was all I had in the world to take me home, and if I had missed this train, I'd never seen my dear old mother again, because—she's dying! But for you I'd never heard her last farewell. God bless you—God bless you!'

"Then the train was movin', and he ran out, and I saw him jump aboard, waving his hand to me the last thing."

"Father, I always said I had the best man on earth," wept Mrs. Day hysterically as she hugged him. "The poor young man! Just think if it had been any other cabman!"

"Or if Mr. Day had listened to the promptings of his heart instead of the promptings of Heaven!" added Christmas.

"But this doesn't pay the doctor's bill, eh, gal?" the kind old man said with assumed lightness.

"Well, I think I know where I can get a little money," Christmas said cheerfully, "and added to what you have, it may satisfy the doctor for a little while."

She slipped away while Peter Day was trying to make a breakfast on dry toast and tea, and when she came back he had gone away to give Sal her much-needed oats and to take his own rest.

He left all his money lying in a little pile upon the table, and with a strained laugh Christmas walked straight up to it and laid a little handful of silver upon it.

"Oh, Christmas!" cried Mrs. Day. "Where on earth did you get so much money?"

Christmas took off her hat and pointed to her head. It was closely shaven. Not a trace remained of the luxurious hair which had been her chief beauty.

"I sold it," she whispered softly, "for his sake!"

"Poor child!" thought Mrs. Day sorrowfully. "She loves him better than her life. And he will never forget the beautiful girl who has broken his heart."

XXIX

CHRISTMAS THINKS SHE HAS A CLEW
TO AMOR'S WHEREABOUTS AT LAST.

CHRISTMAS' SACRIFICE OF HER BEAUTIFUL hair was all in vain. The doctor came and took the little pile of odd coins she tendered him. It was all she had to give, but it was not enough to pay his bill.

"It is rank folly for penniless people to try to keep a man as sick as this one is from the hospital where he would get proper care and attention," growled the physician, "and I shall not encourage the foolish prejudices of poor people against city hospitals by attending the patient."

"Maybe if the rich were compelled to see their dear ones dragged off to hospitals, where young physicians learn their profession by practicing on the helpless patients, they would be just as prejudiced as we are against them," Christmas replied stiffly.

The physician did not stop to argue the case but took his departure at once, never waiting to look at his patient who was weakly fighting a battle between life and death.

Christmas sat down and gave way to despair too deep for tears.

All her money was gone, all Peter Day's money was gone, and they were without a physician and without the means to hire one.

"I wish I had not given him a cent," she moaned.

"Never mind, my dear, we'll manage some how," Mrs. Day said cheerfully. "It's too bad about your pretty hair, but you know you used always to say that everything happens for the best."

"I know I did," replied Christmas dolefully. "But there doesn't seem to be any best any more. Amor gone and never a trace of her; George on the verge of death, and not a penny to buy medicine. Really, I feel almost hopeless."

"If you give up, I don't see what we'll do."

"Then I will not give up."—lightly. "I mean to try again; I am going down to the association and I intend to ask some of the teachers to help us get a doctor; I know they will not refuse."

With a new hope stirring her sad heart, Christmas almost ran to the building of the Charity Association which had befriended her, and without any hesitancy presented herself before the secretary.

"Why, Christmas Cherry!" exclaimed the young lady coldly, not at all pleased by the girl's shabby appearance. "I am sorry that after doing so well, and we taking such an interest in you, you should have quit us in this way."

"I could not help it," Christmas replied with tears in her soulful eyes. "A very dear friend of mine is ill unto death, and I have had to nurse him. I haven't been able to earn much and the good people who are helping me have given everything, but now we are all penniless. There is not money enough in the house to buy a pound of ice to cool the poor sick man's feverish lips. The physician we had left us to-day because we could not pay his bill, and we must have another or the young man will die."

"What is the young man to you?" inquired the secretary when Christmas had finished her wild, passionate outburst.

"He is my benefactor. He gave me work when I was friendless and penniless. He is the husband of my dearest friend," she replied eagerly.

"Why don't you call in another physician, then?"

"Because they won't come. I have been to a number of them, and when I tell them we are penniless they find some excuse for not coming and tell me to send him to the hospital."

"Probably that would be the better way," the woman replied uneasily.

"You tell me that, too!"—indignantly. "We love him, we want him to live. Do you think, then, we will send him to such places? Oh, in Mercy's name, tell me of some doctor that has a heart that will attend him and wait until we can pay him!"

"I am sorry, Christmas, but I do not know of any physician. If you call again to-morrow, I will make inquiries and—"

"To-morrow!" Christmas gasped with a sharp cry of despair. "To-morrow—may be forever too late!"

A woman, dressed quietly but elegantly, entered the office, and the secretary turned from Christmas to her.

Christmas saw that the lady's face was not only beautiful but gentle and kind, and in her desperation she did not pause to weigh the consequences of her rashness.

Approaching the lady, and raising to her beautiful face those soulful eyes in which lingered a prayer for mercy, she spoke in an incoherent, feverish manner:

"Madam, I hope you will pardon me, but you look happy and prosperous. In Heaven's name, will you not help me to save a life that will be lost for the want of a few paltry dollars?"

"What is wrong with the poor child?" asked the lady kindly but in some surprise.

"You must excuse her, madam," exclaimed the frightened secretary. Then turning to Christmas she added: "Go out into the reception room; I will see you after awhile."

But Christmas was desperate. She must have help or George Chesterland would die. She would have help; George Chesterland should not die because she was afraid to speak.

"Madam," she pleaded huskily, falling on her knees and grasping hold of the elegant gown, "I have a friend who is dying for the need of a physician. The doctor we had will not attend him any more because we had not enough money to pay his bill. We gave him all we had, Peter Day and I. See!"—jerking off her old hat—"I sold my hair this morning to pay the doctor, but still it did not satisfy him and he will not come again, and we are penniless, madam, penniless! I am not begging, I only ask for help which I shall repay as soon as I can."

"What is wrong with the patient, my poor child?" the lady inquired, her kind eyes overflowing with tears.

"Brain-fever, and, oh, he has been sick for weeks!" Christmas responded with a cry of unhappiness.

"Give me your address, my dear child, and cheer up and go home, for I am going to drive directly to my family physician, and inside of an hour he will be at your home."

Christmas tried to thank the kind stranger, but her sobs choked all speech. She could barely write the name and address upon the little tablet the lady handed to her.

"I will see you again, my brave child," she said as she hurried away.

With a heart overflowing with happiness, Christmas did not linger long, but hastened out after the kind stranger, and flew like one possessed toward her home.

What good news she would have for Mrs. Day. She could hardly wait to tell it.

Truly everything happens for the best, and the darkest hour is before the dawn.

She had just placed her foot upon the step to enter the street door when a strong hand grasped her shoulder and a voice said in her ear:

"Amor!"

With a start of surprise at hearing that beloved name spoken, Christmas turned and found herself face to face with—Mateo Blanco!

"Christmas Cherry!" he exclaimed, releasing his hold and stepping backward, more surprised even than the girl at this unexpected meeting.

"Matthew White, what brings you here, and why did you call me by my friend's name?" Christmas demanded haughtily.

"Your friend's name?" he echoed curiously.

"Yes, my friend, Amor!"

"It was a mere slip of the tongue, I assure you," he replied easily.

"But you know Amor?" Christmas persisted, turning quickly upon him. "Had you any hand in her strange absence?"

"Why should you accuse me of having anything to do with the young lady?" he retorted curiously.

"Because I think you capable of all that is wicked and bad," was the blunt reply.

"Indeed."—indifferently, though his face flushed hotly. "And what if I confessed that I do know the young lady's whereabouts, my dear Christmas?"

"Christmas Cherry, if you please, without the 'dear'."—sternly. "But to answer your question: If I thought you had taken Amor away, I would follow you to the ends of the earth until I would find her and save her and—punish you!"

"Charming plan, I am sure," he laughed, but she did not see the cunning gleam which came into his small, sharp eyes.

"I am afraid, my dear, clever as you are, you would find it no easy plan to track me, even if I confessed that your friend, Amor, was an inmate of my house," he said wilily.

"Do you mean to tell me that Amor is in your house?" Christmas demanded indignantly.

"Do you think, after hearing your threats, I would tell you anything?" he retorted teasingly. "Of course not, my dear, and since you are in such an unpleasant humor, allow me to bid you good-afternoon."

He lifted his hat gracefully and walked away, a passionate throbbing in his heart that poor Christmas knew nothing of.

She looked wistfully after him and then wistfully up to the windows of the little flat where George Chesterland lay struggling with death.

"The doctor would soon be with him," she thought, "and if I go up now I may never find Amor. The only thing to do is to follow Matthew White to his home and rescue Amor from him."

Without another thought, she started after him, never pausing until she saw Matthew White take out a key and unlock the door of a tall brownstone house.

Her heart fluttered up to her lips when he entered, closing the door after him. Within those walls was Amor, her darling Amor, George Chesterland's beautiful wife! She would find her, she would save her, she would restore her to her heart-broken husband.

Breathlessly Christmas flew up the stoop, and catching the door-knob, turned it gently, hoping to prevent the door from being latched on the inside.

She waited long enough for Mateo Blanco to have gotten up-stairs, and then she pushed the door, and, to her delight, found it open.

Very softly she entered the large hall, and closing the door after her, started on tip-toe down the corridor.

Seeing a small reception-room to the left of the door, she darted into it and found herself separated from another room only by heavy velvet curtains.

She heard voices within the room—one the voice of Matthew White, the other a feminine voice, and one that sounded familiar.

"It is Amor!" she thought with a thrill of joy so intense that she turned dizzy. She had found Amor at last!

With a cry of happiness, she swept the rich curtains aside and stepped fearlessly into the other room.

XXX

WHAT CHRISTMAS FOUND.

AS CHRISTMAS CHERRY FLUNG THE velvet curtains aside and stepped into the adjoining room, she heard a woman give a loud, frightened cry.

Believing it was Amor, the beautiful girl for whom she searched, Christmas ran fearlessly forward, crying encouragingly:

"Amor! Amor! It is I, Christmas, come to save you!"

Mateo Blanco stood between the brave girl and the woman who seemed to be sheltering herself behind him. A satisfied smile rested upon his lips, and a gleam of passionate, triumphant love burned in his black eyes as they rested upon little Christmas Cherry.

"This is an unexpected surprise, Miss Christmas," he said with a laugh. "If you will kindly step into the other room, I will be pleased to see you alone."

"I will not!" Christmas flashed forth indignantly. "I came here to save Amor, and I shall save her in spite of you." Turning to the girl who cowered down behind the Spaniard, she said appealingly:

"Amor, my darling, speak to me! Do not fear."

"You'll have to show yourself, my beauty!" laughed Mateo Blanco.

He stepped aside, and Christmas Cherry ran forward when the wavering girl raised herself, and throwing back her head defiantly, faced the bold intruder.

Christmas fell back as if she had been struck a heavy blow. "Lillian Day!" she moaned sorrowfully.

"Yes—Lillian Day," replied the girl coldly.

She felt no longer the shame which made her hide her face at the sound of Christmas Cherry's honest voice. She was angry now, and indignant.

Why had this little beggar, who had always made a pretense of being so good, tracked her and found her out? Why did she not mind her own affairs? What right had she to look so shocked and sad now?

Lillian Day's big blue eyes flashed dangerously, and all the pretty color left her cheeks, making her very white and wan.

"What do you want?" she inquired contemptuously.

"Oh, Lillian!" cried Christmas gently, unmindful of the girl's manner. "Don't you know you are breaking the hearts of your dear old father and mother?"

Christmas help up her hands appealingly, but Lillian Day only looked angrier.

Mateo Blanco had watched this meeting curiously. Now he laughed and said cuttingly:

"You hear, my beauty? Why don't you return to your dear old parents, eh?"

"Dear Lillian, they are waiting to take you back into their hearts," Christmas pleaded softly.

"Mind your own affairs, Christmas Cherry!" Lillian snapped shortly, though she was trembling visibly. "I left home to please myself, and I'd rather die than return!"

"That is only because you did not know how your dear father and mother would mourn for their only child," Christmas continued pleadingly. "Dear Lillian, they are very unhappy. I know you will go back to them with me!"

"I give you my hearty consent," Mateo Blanco laughed insolently.

Lillian flushed painfully under his scorn, but it only seemed to make her angrier with Christmas Cherry.

"You always were a little meddler," she cried hatefully. "I never wish to speak to you again, but if you go away from here and make me trouble, I'll have revenge!"

With those scornful words upon her lips, Lillian Day swept from the room as haughtily as an angry princess.

"Lillian, Lillian, listen to me, I beg!" cried Christmas, who started to run after the departing girl, when Mateo Blanco caught her by the wrist.

"It is no use, Christmas," he said indifferently. "She will not go away. I wish to Heaven she would!"

Like a flash Christmas turned upon him. "You brought her to this. This is some more of your evil work. Oh, you coward, to betray poor, weak girls!"

The Spaniard felt her scorn in spite of the almost insane happiness which invaded him at the knowledge of the presence of the only being he had ever loved.

"Don't use harsh words, Christmas," he advised. "They do not mend matters, and I cannot see that I am any more to blame in this than Lillian Day herself. It was not what I said or did that brought her here, but her vanity and love of dress."

"You need not have made a place for her," Christmas protested.

"If I had not, some one else would, so there you are," was the short answer.

"That does not excuse you," retorted Christmas bitterly. "You have brought the severest trouble in the world to the kindest old couple that ever lived. Oh, it was heartless, shameful in you, in her!"

Mateo Blanco still held her forcibly by the hands, feasting his hungry heart on the sound of her dear voice, and steeping his soul into blissful intoxication by the glances of her great big brilliant eyes. What mattered it if those eyes spoke enmity or friendship, love or hatred, so long as she was with him? Her very presence was joy unspeakable to him.

"You drove me to it, my darling," he said passionately. "If you had not cast me off, I should have had nothing to do with this woman. I swear to you."

"Heaven forgive me if I brought this terrible affliction upon those poor people," Christmas cried heartbrokenly. "I would rather have had any ill befall me than to have caused them all that shame and grief."

"Is there any way to undo what is done?" he asked.

Christmas clung to him eagerly, her happiness shining from her big eyes.

"Do you mean it?" she asked joyously. "Would you help undo the terrible wrong you have done?"

"Gladly, my darling, if it pleases you," he replied tenderly.

Not heeding the tenderness of his manner, Christmas Cherry grasped the hope of restoring Lillian Day to her fond parents.

"Send Lillian away, then. Refuse to keep her and she will return to her parents. I shall take her back to them. You can tell her how you see now the wrong you have done and that you have resolved to undo it by restoring her to her home. Oh, do this, and I shall forever bless you."

"It shall be as you wish, my darling," was the humble reply. "Is there any other command you wish to lay upon me?"

Christmas looked at him with glistening eyes. Poor, innocent child! She did not doubt that he regretted his sins and was ready to do right. She had not the faintest inkling of the truth.

"I want you to bring Amor to me," she said trustingly.

He did not laugh at her, though there was a smile in his dark eyes. He only patted the little hands he held so closely in an encouraging way.

"My child, you friend, Amor, is not here," he said kindly.

"Not here?" Christmas echoed faintly.

"No, she is not here, I swear to you!" he repeated solemnly.

"But I thought you said she was?"—wonderingly.

"You misunderstood me."—kindly.

"But"—persistently—"you said you would not tell me if she were in your house?"

"I said *if* she was, I would not be liable to tell you after such terrible threats as you had hurled at me," he explained with a smile.

Wild-eyed, Christmas looked at him, the knowledge that she had been duped dawning upon her. But still she was far from realizing the truth.

She sunk, weak and helpless, into a chair unmindful of Mateo Blanco, who knelt before her. It was a keen blow to her to feel that she was not to find Amor. She had been so confident of success, so positive that she would be able to take the missing bride back to her afflicted husband.

"I thought I had found her," Christmas said pitifully, putting her little hands to her forehead and brushing back the short-cut hair as if it worried her.

"I have no more idea than you where Amor is," Mateo Blanco said earnestly.

"But you know her," Christmas said suddenly. "How did you know her? How did you know where she lived?"

"I did know Amor," he replied frankly; "but let me ask how *you* knew her, and you never told me?"

"There was no reason why I should tell you about my friends."—stiffly. "Did Lillian Day introduce you to Amor?"

Mateo Blanco laughed. "Upon my soul, I never knew until this moment that Lillian Day and Amor were acquaintances. It is as great a surprise to me as to know you and Amor were acquainted. How did it happen?"

Christmas felt that the man was speaking truthfully, but at the same time she had no intention of confiding in him the truth about her meeting with beautiful Amor.

"If what you say is true," she said evasively, "how did you meet her?"

"My dear child, I knew the girl many years before I ever saw you," he said easily.

"Have you seen her lately?" persisted Christmas anxiously.

"Not for some time, my darling."

"When did you see her last? Were you the cause of the trouble between her and her husband?" she demanded sharply.

"Her husband?" laughed Mateo Blanco meaningly, elevating his eyebrows.

"Yes, her husband," reiterated Christmas emphatically.

"Amor is not married to that fellow, my dear," Mateo Blanco said positively.

"That fellow?" she repeated warningly. "Do you mean Mr. George Chesterland, Amor's husband? If you do, I wish to tell you that you are speaking of the noblest and best man in the world and the husband of my dearest friend."

Mateo Blanco grew almost as white as the girl. He began to see his hopes of possessing Amor's millions fading away before the truth. There seemed but little doubt that Amor was really married.

"She has lied to me to save her father," he said to himself, then turning to Christmas, he asked:

"Have you any proof of their marriage?"

"I have seen the marriage certificate," was the simple reply.

Mateo Blanco muttered a fierce oath behind his closed lips. "I shall murder that jade, if I ever meet her," he swore to himself.

"If you will bring Lillian now, as you have promised, I shall be going," Christmas added anxiously. "I have been gone too long already from Mr. Chesterland."

Mateo Blanco consigned George Chesterland to the lower regions, and then demanded what he was to Christmas, and why she should return to him.

"He is my benefactor, and he is dangerously ill, and I am nursing him," she explained.

"Well, he can lie there and die before you nurse him again," was the savage reply.

"What do you mean?" cried Christmas angrily.

"I mean that you shall not care for any other man!" was the emphatic reply. "You seem to bear this man more than gratitude. Tell me, do you dare to love him?" The frenzied Spaniard hissed the last words into her face.

"What is it to you if I do?" Christmas inquired coolly.

"It is only this much, that I would kill him and kill you if it were true!" he cried in a great rage.

And in his heart he thanked Heaven that Amor was really married to George Chesterland. If she had not married George, Christmas might, and the passionate Spaniard felt that he never could have endured that.

"Call Lillian, for I must go," Christmas said again impatiently.

"Content yourself in patience, my love," he said affectionately. "Lillian shall go as I have promised, but when I led you here, as I did purposefully, my darling, I had no intention of ever giving you up again."

"What do you mean?" Christmas faltered.

"I mean, my darling, that you have walked into my net, and that you are—my dearly loved prisoner!"

XXXI

A FRIEND IN NEED.

GEORGE CHESTERLAND HAD GAINED ANOTHER friend, and one who would be most useful to him.

The physician, who, at the request of the kind woman to whom Christmas had appealed so beseechingly, had gone immediately to visit the sick man.

Giving one glance at the fever-flushed face, he bent with renewed interest over the delirious patient.

"What is the young man's name?" he asked Mrs. Day, to whom he had explained briefly how he had been interested in the case.

"He is Mr. George Chesterland, sir," Mrs. Day replied.

"I thought as much," the physician continued sadly. "Poor lad! Poor lad! He will have a hard fight of it, but if any power on earth can save his life, he shall live."

"Do you know the young gentleman, sir, may I ask?" Mrs. Day inquired anxiously, as the doctor bent over his patient again.

"Know him? I should say I do," was the reply, with suspicious huskiness. "I was his father's family physician, and was the first to tell the old millionaire of the birth of his son and heir. And to see the lad brought to this! Well, well, we are up to-day and down to-morrow! I suppose the boy hasn't a dollar in the world?"

"He hasn't, sir, though he isn't to blame for that," Mrs. Day said simply. "Master George has worked very hard, sir, and very steady, but since the strike at the factory he couldn't find any work, and then he was took down helpless just as you see him."

"And strangers have had to provide for him, so my good friend, Mrs. Neilson, tells me," muttered the doctor.

"We ain't exactly strangers, sir; you see, my husband was coachman for Master George's father many and many a year, and he's never forgot those who were kind to him," the woman explained modestly.

"Ah, indeed! You don't mean to say that you are the wife of Day? Why, I remember the man as well as I remember George's father. A good man he was, too, as good as gold! You don't mean to say you are really Day's wife?" the physician exclaimed cordially.

"I am Peter Day's wife, sir, and he's the same man," replied the delighted woman.

"Then I know young George is in kind hands," he said with some satisfaction.

"We've done the best we could for him, but to tell the truth, we are very poor."—with some confusion.

"I have heard the whole story from Mrs. Neilson," the doctor said sympathetically. "She was very much affected by the account of your afflictions, as told her by a young girl whom she encountered in the office of the charitable organization. By the bye, where is the girl? I am quite anxious to meet her."

"I don't know where she can be so long," was the anxious reply. "I'd think when she knew you were coming she'd been here."

"I'll see her when I come in again this afternoon. Now I am going to stop at the drug-store and send in what things we need," said the affable doctor, who soon afterward took his departure.

On his return, later in the day, he found Mrs. Day in a state of nervous apprehension. Christmas Cherry had not returned, she tearfully told him, and Mrs. Day feared something dreadful had befallen the girl.

Little by little the kind doctor learned Christmas Cherry's history from the frightened woman, and the story of the girl's uprightness and devotion to George Chesterland awoke a deep interest in him for her.

"Do not worry, my good woman," he said encouragingly. "The girl may be detained somewhere. Knowing your immediate need for money, she may be searching for work."

"'Tain't like Christmas at all, to make us uneasy about her," wept Mrs. Day.

"She'll turn up all right, never fear."—brightly. "Now I am going to send a trained nurse here to help you take care of this young man, and if our girl, Christmas, has not returned when I come back in the morning, we will send some one out to look for her, for she is too good to lose."

Mrs. Day, partially comforted, dried her tears and smilingly bade the jovial physician good-bye.

Peter Day was delighted when he came to his supper to find a trained nurse installed in the humble little flat, and to hear of the kind friend who had appeared in their direst hour of need.

Still he went to his work with a heart very heavy and sore. The unexplained absence of Christmas, the girl who was like a second daughter to him oppressed him with sad misgivings.

Was there a curse on him and those around him? First his own daughter, the apple of his eye, the pride of his home, the treasure of his heart, disappears, and he is left desolate. Then young George Chesterland's beautiful bride! Like a spirit she disappeared in the night, and is heard of no more.

And now Christmas! The ugly one with the heart of gold—the pure, honest, faithful one! What harm could have befallen her? She was not one, he knew, to be led astray by vanity, nor was she one to desert her friends under any circumstances. He could only account for the loyal girl's absence by thinking some harm had come to her.

So Peter Day was not disappointed when his wife told him at breakfast that Christmas Cherry had not returned.

Upon the advice of the physician, they waited several days before doing anything, and at last the doctor went himself to the police-station and engaged detectives to search for the missing girl.

Even George Chesterland seemed to feel Christmas Cherry's absence. His pitiful cries for Amor were now mingled with cries for Christmas.

So time slipped by until it was three weeks since Christmas had disappeared, and still there was no trace of her.

Even the detectives had resigned the case as hopeless. There was absolutely no clew for them to work upon. They could find no reason why she should have gone away unless, as they at last concluded, she had become so despondent that morning that she had committed suicide. Such being the case, they could only wait to see if the river would ever give up its dead, for only the river, they wisely argued, could have held the secret of her death so long.

"'Tain's no use hopin', mother," Peter Day said mournfully one evening as he sat for a few moments by the sick-bed. "The gal's gone fer good an' all, an' we've seen the last of her."

"'Twasn't like Christmas to treat us so," wept Mrs. Day, reluctant to give up all hope.

The sick man caught the name, and tossing his shaven head from side to side, he moaned wearily:

"Christmas! Christmas! Little ragged angel, let me see the tears in your soft eyes. They will cool my aching, burning heart!"

"She's dead, mother, she's dead," groaned Peter Day. "Nothin' else would keep her from him."

And bowing his head upon the bed, he burst into tears.

XXXII

AT THE MERCY OF A DESPERATE LOVER.

CHRISTMAS CHERRY WAS FAR FROM being dead.
Instead of lying cold and lifeless beneath the dark waters, as her friends sadly imagined, she was living amid luxury such as she had never dreamed of in all her life before.

If Peter Day could have looked upon the "little ragged angel," he would have imagined her transformed by some magic power into a princess.

The walls of her rooms were hung with priceless tapestries, the floors were covered with the softest of velvet, the cozy chairs and divans were as soft as down.

A reckless profusion of hot-house roses piled in priceless vases ladened the air with their rare, sweet perfume, while a tall, elaborate clock played lazy, dreamy airs between the tolling of the hours.

Upon one of the luxurious divans, snug in a nest of downy pillows, lay Christmas Cherry. She was clad in a gown of the richest and softest silk. There was not a trace lingering about her of the cheap, shabby apparel she had worn when she followed Mateo Blanco to his home.

By stretching out her little hand, whiter and daintier now than it had ever been before, she could touch a low inlaid table, upon which was carelessly strewn jewels worth thousands of dollars.

Christmas did reach forth and lift up a diamond necklace, which she ran lazily through her fingers, watching the fire and sparkle with weary eyes.

She soon tired of looking at them, and with a heavy sigh, replaced them on the table.

Hardly had she done so when a smart French maid, who spoke no word of English, entered the room and announced:

"Monsieur Blanco, mademoiselle!"

Christmas Cherry understood no French, but she had learned long since the meaning of this announcement, and so was not surprised to see Mateo Blanco enter the room as the maid departed.

Giving him one swift glance of bitter scorn, Christmas dropped her big eyes, and did not deign to look at him again. Nor did she speak to him, although he fell on his knees beside her and, forcibly possessing himself of one on her white hands, pressed it passionately to his lips.

"Christmas, my darling!" he murmured with a thrill of tenderness in his voice.

Christmas gave a shrug of disgust, but made no reply.

Mateo Blanco had never been so happy in his life as since Christmas Cherry, his love, had been his prisoner. He lavished the best of everything upon her; nothing was too good or too costly for her, and yet all his devotion had not won him one smile, one kindly word. Even the priceless jewels he thought to please her with remained unnoticed and unappreciated.

She was not like other women, he told himself—she could not be won by the glitter and vanities which appealed to the majority of her kind. And he loved her all the deeper for her pure worth. She was a jewel above price, he often said.

Regardless of the fact that he could win no tenderness from her, Mateo Blanco was wildly happy. He was like a man intoxicated with some magic wine which made him live within a halo of bliss and happiness. His love was near. He could be with her, and feast his hungry eyes upon her downcast face; he could touch her hand, and feel the exquisite thrill of love convulse his heart; he could sleep with the knowledge that the same roof covered them.

What mattered it then if she turned her eyes away, or refused to speak? Was she not his, and his alone? Was she not in his power, to keep forever? Let her be obstinate and angry! It only added spice to his wooing. He would win her yet—he never thought of failing—and then she would be all the dearer for having been hard to gain.

So long as she was with him, he could be patient. She would love him after awhile.

"You have not worn my poor offering yet," he said chidingly, glancing at the jewels spread upon the low table.

Christmas maintained absolute silence.

"Have you noticed these pretty rings, my love?" he continued, without heeding her silence. "Let me see how well they will look on these pretty fingers. How white and soft they are growing!"

He turned them over gazing at them admiringly, but with an impatient gesture, Christmas drew her hand away.

"Please let me put the rings on, my darling? I shall take them off, if you do not like them," he pleaded longingly.

He drew her hand to him again, and in a moment had her fingers decked with beautiful rings.

"Don't they look beautiful?" he inquired gayly, holding the hand up for her to admire.

Much to his delight, Christmas turned her big eyes and gazed earnestly at the hand which before this moment had never worn a ring.

"Do you like them, sweetheart?" he asked tenderly. "Tell me, love, what you think about them. They shall be changed to suit your sweet pleasure."

Much to his surprise and delight, Christmas answered him.

"I was thinking," she said, with slow deliberation, "how much happiness the money they cost would bring to some poor souls."

"But will you not say that they are pretty?" begged he, evading a reply.

"I can see nothing but the sinful waste of money."—stubbornly. "If I had what they cost, I could have hired a doctor for George Chesterland; I could have bought ice to cool his fever-parched lips. Oh, cruel, heartless man! I have looked at your jewels, but the only thought they bring to me is what joy the money that bought them would bring to those I love. Take them away! The sight of them only makes me hate you!"

With frantic haste she pulled the rings from off her slender fingers and hurled them at his feet.

"Always thinking of that man!" Mateo Blanco cried angrily. "You have no thought for any one else. It is always George Chesterland, George Chesterland. A man who loves another woman, who married another woman! You cry for him, you think of him, while for me, who loves you more than life, who would do anything to win one smile, you have not even a gentle word."

"I do love George Chesterland," Christmas replied with cruel calmness. "I have always told you so, and every hour you keep me from him only makes me hate you the more."

"I shall keep you from him forever, curse him!" was the bitter reply. "I never thought I would see the time when I was happy to know of Amor's marriage, but you have made me thank Heaven a thousand times that she is married and a barrier forever between you and that man."

"Why do you keep me here?" demanded Christmas fretfully. "It can do you no good and—and—"

"Well? Well? Say it all! Do not spare me!"—angrily.

"I only intended to say that he may die."—huskily. "We are very poor and I do not know even if he has the medicine and attention he needs. Mrs. Day could not nurse him all alone. Oh, won't you let me go? Can I do nothing to soften your heart? I am sorry for the mean, bitter things I have said to you, but it almost drives me mad to be kept a prisoner here, not knowing whether he is living or dead."

"Can you expect me, the man who loves you to madness, to care whether my rival lives or dies?" he asked harshly.

"I only know if you loved me as you say you do, you would not keep me in this terrible suspense," Christmas wept softly.

Mateo Blanco moved around impatiently. It cut him to the heart to see her cry and to know that he caused the tears.

"If I brought you news of him, would you be happier?" he inquired at last.

"Would you?" she asked eagerly, rising to a sitting position and gazing at him with big, wistful eyes. "Would you be so kind?"

"I would do anything to make you happy."—gloomily.

"Except release me?"—regretfully.

"Except release you."—determinedly.

"Then bring me news of them."—hungrily. "Tell me if he is better, if the Days are getting money enough to keep them. When will you go? At once?"

"It is half-past six," he said, consulting his watch. "If you will consent to dine with me, I will promise to go myself and find out how they are."

"You are very good," Christmas replied gratefully.

She was truly grateful for his little kindness, and she was very pleasant and friendly during the dinner, which was served in her rooms.

So it happened that Mateo Blanco left her—the happiest man in the world. He felt he had gained a great deal when the mere promise of news would make Christmas so agreeable.

"I will let you know before you sleep, if you will await my return," he said as he stood ready to depart.

"I shall wait for you," she responded, smiling brightly, and they parted happier than either of them had been in the last three weeks.

Parted, yes! Parted they little knew for what time.

During all these days Christmas had been a guarded prisoner in Mateo Blanco's house, she had not seen or heard anything about Lillian Day. Christmas inquired once of Mateo Blanco, but he assured her that he had promised Lillian should go, and that he had kept his word.

Christmas had good reason to know that Mateo Blanco had deceived her before he had left her a half an hour.

Hearing her door unlock, she expected to see the French maid, when, to her astonishment, Lillian Day entered the room.

The poor, wayward girl was clad in an elegant robe, and many jewels glistened on her breast and fingers. There was no trace of shame or repentance on her beautiful face; instead, she seemed aroused to the very highest pitch of anger and determination.

"Christmas Cherry!" she began, leaning threateningly over the little prisoner. "I have taken the first opportunity to tell you what I think of you. I wonder that I do not kill you while I have it in my power."

"I have done you no wrong, dear Lillian," Christmas said sorrowfully.

"No wrong!" repeated the girl with a harsh laugh. "No wrong, you little hypocrite! You creep in here and with your wiles steal away my lover, the man who should be my husband. You beg him to cast me into the street so that you can fill my place, and you all but succeed, for while I am alone and neglected in my rooms, he lavishes upon you all the love and attention and devotion that belong to me. Oh, you meek-faced hypocrite, you sly fiend, I call down the curses of Heaven upon you."

"Lillian—Lillian!" Christmas pleaded sadly. "You wrong me. I am not here of my own desire, you know that I am a prisoner."

"Bah! Another of your little pretenses. To make him want you all the more. Bah! You disgust me!" was the bitter reply. "You mean to keep up this sham indifference until he marries you, as he declares he intends to do. I tell you, it will drive me mad, and if you marry him, as sure as there is a Heaven above, I shall kill you."

"And I would rather be killed by you than to marry Matthew White," Christmas declared earnestly when the frenzied girl paused to catch her breath.

"Matthew White."—scornfully. "Don't you know his real name yet? He is Mateo Blanco."

Christmas sighed heavily. The Spaniard had done nothing but deceive her all along.

"It doesn't matter what his name is. I swear I would rather die than be his wife," she said solemnly.

"Do you mean it?" Lillian gasped, joy and suspicion struggling for the mastery.

"Help me to escape, Lillian, and you will see if I mean it."

Lillian Day shuddered convulsively, and her beautiful face whitened.

"I dare not!" she whispered tremulously. "He would kill me if I did."

"Then you will keep me here until he forces me to marry him?" suggested Christmas.

With a sharp cry of agony Lillian Day fell on her knees and, covering her pale face with her trembling hands, rocked to and fro, moaning:

"Not that, oh, Heaven, not that!"

"Then help me to escape. Unlock the door and let me go!"—persuasively.

"I cannot! I dare not! Mateo Blanco would kill me."

"Very well, Lillian Day, I will have to resign myself to this marriage, since you are determined not to help me," Christmas concluded with assumed resignation.

With a terrible cry that Christmas never forgot, Lillian Day sprung wildly to her feet, and with blood-shot, burning eyes, cast herself upon Christmas Cherry, clutching her by the throat and forcing her down among the pillows.

"You shall never marry him," she hissed, drawing a silver-mounted revolver from the folds of her gown, "for I intend to kill you!"

XXXIII

THE INEVITABLE END COMES TO LILLIAN'S WICKED LIFE.

CHRISTMAS CHERRY LAY PERFECTLY STILL without a struggle, while the frenzied girl pressed the cold steel of the revolver against her brow.

She knew, when she heard those terrible words, "I intend to kill you!" that Lillian Day was on the verge of madness, and that her life depended upon her coolness.

"I told you, Lillian, I would rather die than marry Mateo Blanco," Christmas quietly remarked. "But for the sake of your dear old mother and father, let not yours be the hand to cause my death."

The calm words seemed to quiet the madness in Lillian's brain. With a low moan she released her hold, and flinging the revolver far from her, sunk weeping and moaning upon the floor.

"For God's sake, go, before you drive me to some frightful crime," she begged hysterically. "I cannot control myself if you remain."

"Open the door and I shall go at once," was the quick reply.

"I shall set you free, let the consequence be what it may," Lillian cried with new-found courage. "But first, before you go, swear to me, on your hope of Heaven, never to tell them—my parents—where you were or that you saw me. Swear this, and you shall go, if I die for it."

"Are you not coming with me?" asked Christmas. "Dear Lillian, think how happy your return would make them. For their sake, come away with me."

"It is too late—too late!" the wretched girl moaned. "I have chosen my fate, and I must abide by it."

"It is never too late to turn back from the wrong way," Christmas whispered gently, taking the weeping girl's hand.

"It is too late for me. You do not know all," was the hopeless reply. "But if you would escape, it must be at once. Mateo Blanco may soon return, and then it will be forever too late. Will you swear never to tell where you were, or that you have seen me?"

"I will swear, since you wish it."—sadly.

"Then come with me. I have locked your French maid in her room, and there is no one to fear but the man at the door. I shall call him into the drawing-room, and while I have him engaged, you must open the front door and escape."

"But I cannot go on the street this way," Christmas said, glancing down at her elegant silk house-robe.

"Here is enough money to hire a cab. The night will protect you from the curious gaze of people. It is the best we can do, for Mateo Blanco ordered your old clothes to be burned, and there is not time to look for any of mine that would do. But wait! I have a cloak with you can throw around you. My rooms are in the other end of the house. You will have to wait here until I return."

"I would rather go as I am," Christmas replied nervously. "He might return before you get back."

"Then follow me to the bend in the stairs, from where you can watch down in the lower hall until you see the way is clear, then go as quickly as you can."

"You will not come with me?" urged Christmas sorrowfully.

"I cannot. And on your life, remember the oath of silence you have taken."

Without another word, Lillian Day rose and, unlocking the door, silently motioned Christmas to follow her, and without so much as a farewell glance around the luxurious rooms she had occupied all these weary weeks, Christmas tip-toed out into the hall.

With her heart in her throat she watched Lillian Day and the liveried servant step into the drawing-room, and then on winged feet, as noiseless as a fairy's, she flew down the wide oak stairs, through the broad hall to the door.

It was the work of an instant to turn the spring-lock and the next moment she was on the outside—free!

Without pausing to glance to the right or the left, and with a prayer of thankfulness on her lips, Christmas sped down the dimly-lighted street.

Hardly had she gone when Mateo Blanco returned. He went at once to Christmas Cherry's room, only to find his prisoner gone.

A terrible imprecation escaped his lips as he glanced around the deserted rooms. His face grew as pale as death and a wild expression of anger came into it. He seemed to divine at once who had helped his prisoner to escape from him, and with a hoarse cry of rage he rung the bell violently, calling aloud at the same time to the hurrying servants to bring the French maid and Lillian Day to him.

Lillian needed no one to bring her. With the dignity of a queen, she swept into his presence. She tried to be very brave, but her eyes fell before the threatening anger of his.

"Is this your work, madam?" he demanded hoarsely.

"Why should you suspect me?" she asked haughtily.

Just then the French maid entered. She was weeping hysterically, and without waiting to be questioned, explained that she had been made a prisoner in her own room, by whom, she did not know.

With a calmness terrible to see, Mateo Blanco turned upon Lillian Day. "Denials are useless. You have been the cause of all this," he said.

"Had I not a right?" Lillian ejaculated defiantly. "Do you think I would let her take my place?"

"Your place!" he hissed insultingly. "Don't you know your place? I intend to make that lady my wife!"

"Thank God, then I foiled you!" she cried desperately.

"You Jezebel! I have a mind to murder you!" he declared. And grasping her with cruel force by the hands, he brought her to her knees.

With frightened cries the servants scattered, not staying to witness what they expected would be a tragedy.

"Remember, Mateo, my condition," Lillian pleaded pitifully.

"I remember nothing but that I hate you, and that you have tried to wreck my happiness," he cried hoarsely. "I had intended to kill you, but I save you for a worse fate. I cast you off, to live or die, I care not."

"You will not desert me, Mateo?" she prayed piteously.

"No!" he laughed terribly. "You desert me. This hour and minute I throw you into the streets. Go now, just as you are, and never let me gaze upon your hateful face again unless you want me to kill you."

"Mateo! Mateo!" she whispered frightenedly. "You cannot mean this. You forget that I am alone, that I have no place to go."

"I care nothing about all that. Go to the dogs, anything you will, only go!"

"I cannot! I will not!" she moaned desperately, trying to cling to him.

With a fierce cry of rage he caught her by the arms and half pulled, half dragged her down the stairs and through the wide corridor.

"What would you do?" she cried in mortal fear.

He made no reply. Dragging her to the door, he opened it, and pushing her down the cold stone steps, went into the house and slammed the door in her face.

Crying aloud in her fear, Lillian ran up the steps, and beating upon the door, prayed and begged to be admitted.

But the door did not open at her call.

Realizing at last that she was cast out forever, she gave a moan of despair and sunk in a dead faint in the street.

XXXIV

LIGHT AND REASON AT LAST.

CHRISTMAS CHERRY FLEW BREATHLESSLY DOWN the dimly lighted street.

Fortunately she had not gone far when she heard the wheels of a carriage come rattling over the cobblestones.

Christmas was aware that she would attract unwelcome attention on the streets, clad as she was in a light house-dress and without hat or gloves.

So she paused upon the pavement and waved frantically to the driver, who, seeing the young girl was alone, and bareheaded, curiously drove to the curb and stopped.

Before he could understand what it all meant, Christmas had given him her address, adding:

"Please drive there as rapidly as you can."

Her hand was on the door, when with a cry of alarm she sprung back. The carriage was occupied, and she had not known it until she saw a gentleman thrust his head out of the door to inquire of his driver the cause for the delay.

Before he spoke the man saw Christmas Cherry and heard what she said to the driver. He divined at once that she was in some trouble, so, removing his hat, he said courteously:

"Can I be of any assistance to you, miss?"

"Oh, no, I thank you," she replied in some confusion. "I beg your pardon for stopping your carriage, but I thought it was unoccupied."

She was about to move on when the stranger opened the door and stepped out upon the pavement.

"May I place my carriage at your disposal, miss? I have plenty of time, and can wait for another," he said.

Christmas had recognized in the stranger the minister who had crossed her path so curiously before. She felt her face, that a moment before had been as pale as death, grow crimson with an embarrassed blush.

What would this noble man think of her? she wondered. Would he remember the night that he had rescued her from Mateo Blanco, and would he think she had not profited from that experience?

"I cannot think of inconveniencing you," she said hesitatingly.

"You are not properly clad to roam the streets in search of a vehicle," he said somewhat sternly, and she saw how sad a look came across his handsome, noble countenance.

"I am not an entire stranger to you," he continued gently, "and I claim the right of serving you. Will you permit me to help you into the carriage?"

In spite of her feeling of embarrassment, she felt a warm glow suffuse her aching heart when he assumed charge of her in that masterful way. How good and kind he was.

"If you will go with me, I will accept your offer to set me down at the door of my home, and be very grateful to you for it," she said softly, with downcast eyes.

He took her trembling hand, by way of answer, and helped her in.

"Drive to the place the lady directed," he said to the coachman, and then took his place by Christmas' side.

Poor little Christmas! She grew warm and cold by turns. Slyly she eyed the silent man by her side, as they drove on. She longed to tell him that she had been guilty of no wrong; she hungered to confide the whole story to him, and to beg his sympathy, and yet she feared he would count her overbold for a stranger.

She let the blessed opportunity pass, and when he helped her to alight at the door of George Chesterland's flat, she felt it was too late to set herself right in this man's eyes.

"Why should I care what he thinks?" she curtly asked herself, even as her hand touched his in farewell; and yet she knew she did care.

"I had hoped you would come to my church some time," he said a little wistfully as they stood for an instant at her door.

"I told you that I had never felt the need of religion," she responded quickly.

"Everybody experiences that need at some time or another," was the grave response. "When that hour comes to you, I would like to feel that you will come to me."

"I promise you that," she said with quickening pulse; and thus they parted.

He returned with a heavy heart and sad face to his carriage, sighing as he did so, and Christmas, with winged feet, flew up the long stairs to the flat where she had left George Chesterland three weeks before.

She knocked softly on the door, and when Mrs. Day opened it and saw the strangely missing girl, standing like a white spirit on the threshold, she gave a wild cry of fear.

"Do not be alarmed," Christmas begged gently. "It is really myself, come back again after all these weary, maddening days."

Mrs. Day caught the trembling girl in her arms and hugged her to her breast, crying fitfully over her.

"We'd given you up for dead," she wept. "Even father said only death could keep you away. This will be good news for us all. I wish you'd come back a bit sooner, so father could have known before he went to work. Where have you been, Christmas, and why didn't you send us word, and where'd you get such a lovely dress?"

Christmas shuddered.

It all came back to her now, her oath of secrecy, and she was not sorry that she had taken it. Could she have pierced these gentle hearts by telling them whose hand had set her free? Could she have bowed their white heads farther in the dust by telling them of their wayward daughter, who refused to return to her home?

No, no, a thousand times, no! She silently thanked Heaven it had been taken from her power to tell the secret of her absence.

"Tell me of Master George," adopting their term, she asked evasively. "Did that kind woman send a doctor? Is Master George better? And good Mr. Day and yourself. How did you get along with all the work?"

In a few words Mrs. Day told her how the new doctor had proved to be an old friend of the Chesterland family, and that two nurses had been provided for Master George, and medicine and delicacies were sent regardless of cost, and that the kind lady had called many times and had gone away very much disappointed by Christmas' unexplained absence.

If Christmas liked, she could go in and see Master George. He called for her quite as often as he called for his missing bride.

Quick tears filled Christmas' big eyes when Mrs. Day told her all this. Poor George! She had thought to restore his bride to his heart and home, but she had failed.

"Has he changed much and does he know any one yet?" she inquired with a little break in her voice.

"He is frightfully thin, poor fellow, and he doesn't know a soul yet. He's been kind of stupid for the last two days, but the doctor says he's doin' as well as can be expected," was the reply.

On tip-toe Christmas went to the bedside of George Chesterland and, leaning over him, scanned wistfully the wasted face.

He was woefully thin and ghastly pale, now the fever had died away, but

Christmas thought the wide-open eyes, gazing so fixedly up into her face, were less glassy and wild than they had been when she last saw him.

She noticed his white, helpless hand move nervously on the counterpane, and she placed her little cool one soothingly upon it.

Then his lips moved, his eyes still intently fixed on the pure, innocent face above him, and to the surprise of every one, he spoke.

"Christmas!" he whispered contentedly. "You have come back to me."

"Yes, George, and I will not leave you again," she replied reassuringly, her heart beating so rapidly that it almost smothered her.

With an almost inaudible sigh, he closed his eyes and fell asleep, and Christmas, lifting her face, now stained with tears, saw the physician viewing the scene from the doorway.

A happy look illuminated the doctor's genial countenance.

"Thank God!" he whispered huskily. "He has awakened to life and reason."

XXXV

THE RESULT OF DISOBEDIENCE AND VANITY.

LILLIAN DAY NEVER QUITE FORGOT the horror she experienced on coming back to life.

She was rudely pulled and shaken, and on wearily opening her big, tear-dimmed blue eyes, saw she was in the hands of a policeman.

"Come on now, wake up and move off or I'll have to run you in," he said threateningly, shaking her rudely to make her understand the better.

Poor Lillian struggled dizzily to her feet, terrified beyond measure.

"I will go," she murmured frightenedly. "I live in here—I will go in at once."

She turned toward the door when, to her horror, she discovered that she was on the stoop of a strange house in a street she had never seen before.

"Oh, Heaven!" she cried bitterly. "What is this? I never saw this house before."

"I guess you had better be movin' on," the officer observed heartlessly. "Guess you're not in condition to know your house when you see it. You've lost your hat, too!"

Unhappy Lillian Day realized what while she lay in that death-like faint, Mateo Blanco had caused her to be carried from the stoop of his house into another street. She knew only too well what it meant. He would never forgive her, he would never take her back, and she was alone—alone in the cruel world.

But she could not stand there, she must obey the officer's commands and move on.

"Where? where?" she moaned wretchedly, as she staggered blindly down the street.

Where could she hide her head? Where could she go for protection?

She thought once of her parents, those good, simple, honest, ignorant souls, but she only shuddered at the recollection of them and ran on. She could never return to them now.

Like every other wretch driven to the verge of madness, poor Lillian Day thought of the river. It would be better to bury her disgrace beneath the cold waters, better for her, and better for those poor souls who had loved her. Maybe when she was dragged from the water, dead and pale, they could forgive her then, and pity her.

Alas! How her bruised heart longed for sympathy, for a friendly face, a kindly voice!

Not until she was breathless did Lillian Day pause in her wild flight. Often she thought she heard the policeman's heavy tread behind her, and, unmindful of the jeering remarks of the few pedestrians, she ran on, on, on!

Bewildered and exhausted, she stopped at last and leaned up against a little, begrimed building, when a light from its window caught her eye.

In the window hung countless dirty and worn garments, and as Lillian gazed upon them in silent wonder, a bearded man, as dirty and repulsive as his garments, came out, and, in a whining voice, said:

"Does the pretty lady wish to buy a dress? I can give her something better than this to wear on the streets. Will the pretty lady step inside and examine my garments?"

Still frightened and amazed, Lillian followed the man, and watched him as he took down dress after dress for her inspection, explaining and describing their desirable points.

"You can step back in this room and change to one of these dresses, and I'll give you many pretty dollars, good, lovely money, besides," he added coaxingly.

Like one in a dream, Lillian followed his instructions, and soon came forth, transformed from a princess to a beggar.

"There's your money, my pretty one," whined the old man, rubbing his hands gloatingly. "And a nice, pretty little pile it is. I'm robbing myself to give you a good price, my pretty dear."

Lillian Day knew the old robber was cheating her, but the dress she had bought was more necessary to her than the one she had sold, so she held her peace.

She took the money without a word and started to go, but the man followed her, as if loath to give her up.

"Hard days come to us all, pretty lady," he whined with an envious gleam in his ferrety eyes. "If you ever need money you might get a good, snug pile for that pretty hair of yours. You'll remember that, won't you? and if you want to sell, I'll buy, and I always give tip-top prices, too."

With a shudder, Lillian rushed from his presence and out into the street again.

Before she had gone many blocks she saw a sign of "Rooms to Let" in a miserable, grim, tumble-down old house, and as the hour was getting late, she decided to spend the night there.

Not only was that night spent beneath that poor roof, but many following days and nights. In fact, weeks had crept into months, and still Lillian Day was housed in a little smoky room at the top of the building, where she cooked her own scant meals and slept upon the miserable bed in the corner.

Then came the dark and unhappy day when a little flickering life was added to hers. A little innocent babe with pale, thin face and weak, fitful cries lay in her arms.

His baby, yes, and hers.

She hated it at first, it was so weak and fretful, and it seemed like a reproach sent from Heaven to chastise her for her sin.

After awhile its very weakness appealed to the mother in her heart, and she would clasp it fiercely to her breast and with gentle, tender cooing endeavor to hush its cries.

It seemed as if all the world was dead to her, and she was dead to the world. The little baby was all she had, and even as she had hated it, she grew to love it.

It was a fierce, frantic love she gave it, the love of a half-crazed creature deprived of every other human tie upon this earth. It was her world, her all! She would hold it in her arms, and the very weight of its tiny body made her dead heart live again and grow warm.

In these first, miserable, unhappy days of her young motherhood, Lillian Day had time to think, to remember, to realize all the pain and heartbreak she had caused her dear parents. Never had she loved them as she did when she realized that they were forever dead to her.

That dear, fond old father, with his rough but noble ways, how tender and kind and gentle he had always been with her. Ah! She had not appreciated his sterling qualities in those dear old days.

Yes; dear old days. They no longer seemed poor and barren to her. Even the remembrance of that poverty-stricken old home was precious to her. She had been happier, a thousand times happier, in that shabby old home than she had ever been since. She realized it now, now when it was too late, and she would have given her life could her horrible sin prove but a nightmare from which she would waken to find herself once more the idol of her parents' hearts.

And her mother! Poor, loving, indulgent mother! How many bitter tears and sleepless nights had been caused her by the child she had cherished.

As these memories came surging up, stinging Lillian to the heart with bitter reproach, she would clasp her babe to her breast and burst into a paroxysm of tears.

Terrible had been her sin, and terrible was her punishment. She was paying the bitter cost of vanity and willfulness and disobedience. She knew that every pang she suffered was the result of her own act, and this knowledge only intensified her anguish of soul.

Many times when she looked into the little, wan face of her babe, always contracted with pain, she prayed Heaven to take it sinless from this unhappy world. Again, when she thought death hovered over it, ready any second to make each breath the last, she would clasp it to her in wild despair and beg Heaven not to leave her alone, to spare the baby—her little one.

At last came a time when she had no money. The heartless old hag who rented the rooms was pressing her for the rent and threatening to put her into the streets unless she paid.

Humbly the poor girl pleaded for time, for mercy. Could not the old woman see how ill her baby was? And the medicine and milk had cost so much! If she would only be merciful and wait, baby would soon be better and then its mother would go to work and earn enough to pay all and more than she owed.

The rough hag gave a coarse reply, saying that it was the money or the streets that night.

Left to herself, unhappy Lillian fell prostrate upon her hard bed.

"Oh, Heaven! What can I do?" she moaned piteously. "My poor, helpless little one! Must it die for the want of a few dollars when its heartless father is rolling in wealth? No! It shall not suffer."

Clasping it in her arms, she wept over it until her tears were exhausted; then, faint and dizzy, she got up and, wrapping the baby in a blanket, left her room.

"Poor little one!" she murmured over it as she walked along the streets with her hopeless burden clasped in her arms. "You shall not suffer any longer; you shall have a nurse and fresh air and pure milk, my little one. Your mother is going to part from you, my precious; she will never, never see her little baby again; but you know, little one, she does it so you may live, and she will go back to her lonely room."

Poor Lillian Day! For the sake of her child she determined to return to the house where she had lived in luxury with Mateo Blanco. She would see him once again, and she would demand that he take his child and give it the care it needed.

It was like rending her heart in twain to part from it, but for its sake she had nerved herself to make the sacrifice.

With it held very tightly against her heart, she turned down the street leading to the Spaniard's home, and without glancing to the right or left, she proceeded straight to the door.

She shuddered as she walked up the broad stoop on which she had fallen the night he turned her out into the streets. Nervously she stretched forth her hand to ring the bell, when a notice dangling from its knob caught her eye. With a moan of anguish she started back.

To let! No two words ever brought such pain to a human heart before.

Mateo Blanco was gone, the house was empty, and her baby—

"It must not die! It must not die!" she wept as she hurried back to her lodgings.

On the way she passed the second-hand shop where she had sold her dress that night. The dirty old man stood in the door, and when he saw Lillian he grinned and motioned to his head. She understood him only too well, and with a chill of horror she rushed on to her own bare room.

But she could not forget the horrid old man. She thought of him uneasily, and it seemed that she could feel his dirty, old fingers among her luxurious, golden-red hair.

That beautiful, ravishing hair, its splendor still undimmed by her wretched, starved life.

"My God! Am I still vain?" she wept aloud at last. "Why do I hesitate? What is this long, heavy hair when my baby is hungry? It shall have food."

With new-born courage Lillian rushed from her room to the pawn-shop.

"What will you give for it?" she cried breathlessly, taking out a pin and letting the luxurious mass fall like a cloak around her.

The dirty old man fingered the beautiful tresses with a gloating chuckle.

"Two dollars," he whined, "an' dat's robbin' my wife and own children."

"Two dollars!" echoed the girl with a groan. "It's not enough. I won't sell for that miserable price. Why, see, it sweeps the floor, and the color—only look!"

"T'ree dollar, then!" he groaned. "You break me up, you make me a poor man. Is it a bargain?"

"Give me five dollars. I owe three dollars for my room, and my baby must have some fresh milk!" Lillian gasped in desperation.

"Oh, pretty lady, I'm a fool. I break myself up, my wife and children will go to the poorhouse, but I'll pay you the money, such big money, such good money!" he answered with a well-assumed groan.

He took a big pair of shears and cut the shining tresses as close to the head as he possibly could, and then he counted out to her slowly and regretfully the pitifully few dollars.

"I'm a very liberal man, too liberal, too liberal," he whined as she started to go, "but when you need more money, come back to me."

"I have nothing left to sell," was the sad reply.

"Oh, yes, pretty lady," he chuckled.

And as she looked wonderingly at him, he tapped his black teeth, and then pointed suggestively to Lillian's pearly ones.

With a weak cry of horror she rushed away, leaving the dirty old man chuckling as he watched her.

She was so sparing, so saving, poor girl! She hardly ate a bite herself, but husbanded her little change to buy milk for the baby. But the days were stifling warm, and the milk would sour, and before she realized she was penniless again.

Penniless, ay, and a baby ill and fretting and hungry.

She was bitterly hungry herself, and as she thought of the last words the old pawn-broker said to her, she laughed wildly and asked herself why she should have such beautiful, fine, pearly teeth when she had no use for them.

"It's better to have no teeth and something to eat, than to have teeth and be hungry," she told herself.

So once again she set forth, only to return with a bleeding mouth, minus all the front teeth, but with money in her pocket.

But such a pitiful bit! Teeth did not bring as high a price as hair, and so it was less time until Lillian was again penniless, and truly, this time, with nothing left to sell.

She endured it as long as she could, and then she grew terrified at the strange look upon her baby's face, and the labored way it breathed and the weak way it cried. It seemed to be dying before her eyes, dying for the want of a few pennies with which to purchase milk.

Poor unfortunate Lillian Day! The sight seemed to drive her mad. Wild with grief and hunger, she rushed desperately out into the street and to a dairy. Ah, she knew the place well. She had begged almost upon her knee for a glass of milk for her child.

Now she did not mean to beg. She knew where stood the bottles, filled with the pure, sweet milk. When the man's attention was engaged, she slipped a bottle in the folds of her dress and hurried away.

But hardly had she left the door with her stolen property when a strong hand grasped her by the shoulder and whirled her around.

"You are my prisoner," said the officer who held her in his grasp. "Come along with me. I saw you steal that milk."

With a despairing cry, like that of a lost soul, Lillian fell face downward in a dead faint, the stolen milk spreading over the dirty stones where she lay.

XXXVI

HOMELESS AND FRIENDLESS.

WHEN THE OFFICER CLAIMED LILLIAN as his prisoner, and she fell fainting to the ground, a number of persons heard the despairing cry which parted her white lips, and came hurrying to the spot. They gazed curiously upon the prostrate girl, whose miserable rags made her a fit companion for them.

Some, bolder than the rest, asked the officer what the girl had done, and, as he rapped for assistance, he told them.

"She is a thief," he said. He saw her, as he stood idly by the milk-shop window, steal a bottle of milk. That was the very milk running in little dirty pools between the stones.

The women gazers whispered among themselves. The girl was a bad-looking creature, they thought—hairless and toothless, as those parted lips disclosed.

The men were not of the kind that count much on such attributes; but one said to the other that the girl's complexion was wondrously white, and that she must have been good-looking when she had more flesh on her bones.

Among the crowd that pushed and shoved to get a better look, not one felt the least inkling of pity for the poor unfortunate. They were only curious.

As the second officer came running up, he was accompanied by a tall, handsome man on whose face shone the light of happiness and nobleness of heart.

"What is wrong?" he asked the officer who stood guard over the insensible girl.

"Caught stealing. Saw her do it myself," was the reply, adding sagely:

"She's a slick one, you can take my word for it, Mr. Van Lynn."

"Poor girl!" the man addressed as Mr. Van Lynn said softly, bending over Lillian. "She is very young, and she cannot be an old offender, since she has taken her capture so much to heart. Disperse the crowd and let me see if I can revive her."

While the officers were obeying his commands, Mr. Edgar van Lynn bent over Lillian and, with the deftness of a practiced physician, sought to bring her out of her faint, and to such good purpose did he work that in a few moments she revived and opened her big, velvety eyes, gazing wildly up into his face.

"Don't arrest me," she moaned feebly. "I could not help it; my baby is starving."

"My poor child," said the man in the softest, tenderest voice Lillian had ever heard. "You shall not be arrested. Where is the baby? Tell me, and we shall take it milk at once."

"Bless you—bless you!" sobbed Lillian hysterically. "You know I never would have taken it for myself—it was only for baby, to keep it from dying."

"Officer," he said huskily, "this is a case of starvation. Take this money and pay for the milk, and if you think you must have your prisoner, I'll be responsible for her."

"Well, I guess as there hain't been any charge brought against her, except what I saw myself, I can let her go to oblige you," was the reply.

"Then will you please take this and buy some milk, and bring it over to that house?" pointing out the one indicated by Lillian. "The young woman says she has a baby starving to death there."

"I'll be right along," said the officer; and before Mr. Van Lynn had assisted Lillian into the door, he was at their elbow.

"Garret floor; last room back," Mr. Van Lynn said, and the officer preceded them up the dirty, rickety stairs.

He met them again at the head of the stairs, and his face bore a strange expression, which Mr. Lysle noticed at once. So did Lillian.

"My poor baby!" she gasped, and shaking off Mr. Van Lynn's detaining hand, she burst into the room before they could prevent her.

Her baby was dead. It lay upon the bed, cold and stiff and lifeless.

When Lillian realized this, she became unconscious again, and all efforts to revive her proved fruitless.

"Call a doctor," Mr. Van Lynn said at last. "This is more serious than a mere faint."

Indeed it was. The physician made a hasty examination, and turning quickly to Mr. Van Lynn, with whom they all seemed acquainted, he said:

"This woman has the smallpox. It is either in the house, or she has got it from some of those cursed second-hand shops, the very air of which is filled with pestilence."

"Let everything be done for the poor girl that can be, and I will bear the expense," said Mr. Van Lynn softly. "And if you give me a death certificate, I will have an undertaker called to bury the little baby."

As the months crept on, and Lillian Day unwillingly struggled back from the valley of death, she found she had a friend and protector.

Long and earnestly Mr. Van Lynn had talked to her; and she, in turn, had confided the story of her sin and misdoings to him.

She told him all about her home life, and her dear old parents, and the beautiful, mysterious Amor, and the noble little Christmas. Lillian told him all this, but she could not be persuaded to tell the name of her parents, or to send them word of her welfare.

"I am dead to them forever. That is part of the punishment for my folly," she said, and he ceased to urge.

WHILE LILLIAN DAY WAS BEING nursed back to life, and was receiving the comfort and consolation of confiding talks with a sympathetic listener, little Christmas Cherry was experiencing the bitterness of having a secret to guard, a secret that came between her and her friends.

Mrs. Day had urged and coaxed the girl to give an account of her strange absence; the kind physician spoke of the necessity of giving some explanation; good Peter Day said bluntly that only some shameful wrong could induce a girl to hide where she had been; but to one and all Christmas remained firm.

She would not tell; she had sworn to keep the whole affair secret. Coaxing, pleading, and anger did not succeed in changing her determination.

"I would tell you gladly," she once cried helplessly to Peter Day, "gladly, if I could do so without violating my oath. But I swore solemnly to remain silent, and I mean to keep my vow."

"No good can come of it, gal," the old man muttered, dissatisfied. "Mark my words; people will turn away from ye when they know what a secret you bear."

Poor Christmas! She found Peter Day spoke too truly.

As time went on, she found the doctor, who had been prepared to think the world of her, grow colder and colder in manner, until at last his eyes avoided meeting hers, and when the nurses were dismissed from the care of his patient, he always gave his directions to Mrs. Day, giving Christmas no part or place in the care of the invalid.

Christmas felt this bitterly, and many a burning tear did she weep in seclusion, and sore and troubled grew her gentle, loyal heart.

Even George Chesterland, whose slow progress dated from the time of Christmas' return, felt the bitterness of the secrecy which the girl maintained.

Once in his low, weak voice, he spoke to her on the subject.

"Do you know, little angel," he said sorrowfully, "that everybody is worried because you refuse to tell where you were, and why you absented yourself all those weeks. I am sorry you refuse to give some explanation. It hurts Peter and Mrs. Day, and even the doctor is annoyed at your conduct."

"I am very sorry, George," Christmas replied, the tears filling her big eyes. "I cannot tell—it would only cause more trouble if I did. Surely they don't think I did anything wrong?"

George saw the wistful, troubled eyes, and hastily avoided looking into them.

He sighed wearily, for it seemed very hard that all the world should prove to be unfaithful and unworthy. And what could he think of Christmas, except that she was also false? Had not that other one, whom he had not strength to name, possessed the appearance of an angel?

So fair to look upon; so beautiful, so pure, so refined, and yet—Oh, pitying Heavens! Falser than a demon, a fiend! The knowledge of Amor's wickedness had left little in George Chesterland's heart that believed in womankind. If Amor, the personification of all that was pure and lovely, could be base beyond belief, what could he expect of others?

Naturally these bitter thoughts had an effect on his manner toward one who was devoted to him, body and soul. And she was quick to feel the change, poor Christmas! That George should turn from her and mistrust her was the hardest blow of all, and loyal Christmas staggered under it, feeling bereft of all hope and happiness and courage.

Ah, how different she would have treated him had he been in her position! Nothing could have made her confidence and love and trust swerve for an instant, and the more the world turned from him, the closer she would have clung to him.

Christmas could not talk to George about his lost bride. He never mentioned her name, and no one dared to broach it to him. In fact, he had scarcely anything to say, and what was mainly weariness and despondency on his part, poor Christmas mistook for anger and coldness.

Mrs. Day insisted on doing everything for the invalid, and at the same time refused at all to permit Christmas to assist with the household duties.

As George grew easier to attend to every day, Christmas began to feel her heart chill with a knowledge that she was not needed, and that everybody would be more comfortable with her out of the way.

This thought aroused no anger in her heart. She did not stop to think of what she had done for them, and the more she would have been willing to do for any one of them.

That they were ungrateful and uncharitable, she never supposed. This mistrust only made her sad.

"I cannot stay here depending upon them any longer," she thought one night as she lay awake on a pillow damp with tears. "I am of no use to them, and they cannot forgive me for staying away. I must go away, leave them, and be once more friendless and homeless. No one wants me. I am only in the way."

The next morning she spoke to Mrs. Day about it.

"Since Mr. George needs only your kind attention, it is time for me to be looking for work," she said, with an effort to speak easily. "I have lived too long upon you and Mr. Day, and it is time I looked after myself."

"Work does girls good," was Mrs. Day's only comment. "Father always says, 'idleness leads to wickedness.'"

Christmas' heart contracted with a quick pain. Clearing her voice of all huskiness, she said:

"Will you tell Mr. George good-bye for me? He is sleeping, and I would not like to disturb him. And—Mr. Day—will you tell him I shall never forget his kindness, and yours, to a poor, friendless waif. I was never so happy in my life as I have been beneath your roof."

A great sob rose in her throat and choked her. It was hard to know they cared so little for her going.

"If you'd acted different, things wouldn't be as they are," Mrs. Day said sternly and hastily. "But what can we think of a girl who stays away three weeks, and comes home in a dress as would cost a fortune, and then won't say nothing?"

"You are quite right, I suppose."—huskily. "Good-bye!"

Mrs. Day heard the heart-broken sob that escaped Christmas' lips as she went out, closing the door after her and dropping into a chair, she flung her apron over her head and burst into tears.

XXXVII

"I WANT YOU TO SHARE MY WEALTH WITH ME —TO BE MY WIFE."

CHRISTMAS CHERRY'S DEPARTURE ACTED LIKE a stimulant on George Chesterland's dormant spirits and sluggish blood.

"Christmas gone!" he gasped bewilderingly when Mrs. Day answered his call for the girl by telling him of her departure. "Where has she gone, and why?"

He saw the traces of tears on Mrs. Day's cheeks, and was not prepared to find she had not discouraged the girl's leaving. When he heard the truth, he was angry and provoked.

"You had no right to let her go away!" he declared warmly. "Why, the poor child must think we have no hearts, if we could so soon forget her devotion to us."

"But, Master George, much as I hated to see her go, I thought she didn't deserve much when she wouldn't explain where she was those three weeks and how she got that dress. It doesn't look like the doin's of a good girl," Mrs. Day explained.

"I never doubted her," George exclaimed angrily, forgetting in his dismay the momentary doubts which had assailed him. "I would stake my life on Christmas' honesty! Why, the poor child will starve. It was inhuman to let her go!"

"I'm sure, sir, when she said she was going, I thought it would be better all round, seeing as how none of us trusted her any more," Mrs. Day said, crying softly.

"I trusted her, Mrs. Day—I never failed to trust Christmas," George continued excitedly. "She was as pure as gold, poor little ragged angel!"

"'Twasn't me, sir, as forgot all Christmas had done," returned the sobbing woman. "The doctor wouldn't have anything to say to her, and after his taking such a fancy to her, too. You yourself didn't act pleased, and even father, who'd set such store by the girl, said her being so stubborn didn't look honest."

"We may all have been displeased for the time, and hurt, but I am sure none of us really doubted her in our hearts," declared George.

The doctor, on his arrival, was not less put out by the news than George.

"I was provoked at the girl for refusing to tell where she had been; it didn't look well," he snapped shortly; "but we can't forget that she gave everything she had for you, even her hair, and that she actually saved your life by appealing to Mrs. Neilson, who sent me to you. We can't forget that, George, and I am afraid we were too harsh."

"I know we were," George acquiesced quickly. "Christmas is as true as gold. And she sold her beautiful hair for me? Poor little angel! She would not tell me why she had it cut."

"Do you think she could have gone back to the place she spent those three weeks?" inquired the physician anxiously.

George Chesterland sighed heavily. "I fear she has," he said.

The doctor looked at him quickly, noting something in his voice. "Have you any idea where that can be, George?" he asked quickly.

"Yes."—wearily. "Not the place, but the person. I think she was with the girl I married, and that is why she refused to tell us."

The doctor's face grew sad and thoughtful. "Then it is perfectly useless to search for her," he observed.

"Useless—perfectly useless," George echoed wearily; and thereafter they avoided the subject.

George Chesterland had told his physician and friend something about losing his wife, Amor, but he did not tell how she had deceived him, and the kind old man was too noble-hearted to urge a confidence that was withheld.

And now when George replied to the question, the physician suspected that Christmas' absence was in some way connected to the missing wife, and considerately he dropped the subject and never referred to it again.

But notwithstanding their avoidance of the painful subject, neither of them forgot it, and often they thought of Christmas and prayed for her return.

Her absence awoke a new life in George. He felt a growing desire to be will and up and doing. New life, new energy, new ambitions surged through his veins, stirring his blood to health and strength.

Gradually George's thoughts traveled back to the old days when he had met and loved and won the beautiful Amor.

Naturally this train of thought brought back his old life in the factory, and with that remembrance of that startling truth he had gleaned from his father's old papers the night the fever robbed him of memory.

He was rich! He had forgotten it, forgotten that he had been cheated from his birthright until this moment.

Now he remembered and he burned for revenge. As he had been punished, so would he punish. Joseph Hill, his father's false friend, the oppressor of the poor, should be made to give up the wealth he had stolen.

Thank Heaven! The money would be his at last. He could repay those faithful friends who had done so much for him. Peter Day and his good wife should be provided for the rest of their days; Christmas Cherry should receive a yearly allowance; and so George Chesterland built air-castles until his strength enabled him to drive from his home to the factory.

Weak and spent from his long and serious illness, he walked slowly into the office, where Joseph Hill sat in his father's place.

The millionaire, hardened as he was, started at the sight of the tall young man with the painfully thin frame and ghastly, sunken eyes. But in a moment he rallied and cried boisterously:

"What do you want here, you young upstart? Didn't I put you out for good and all?"

"I have come back to do the same thing with you," George replied coolly.

The millionaire turned a deathly yellow, his hands trembled, but he still tried to present a bold front.

"Get out of here," he thundered, "or I'll call my men to throw you out."

"I don't think they will lay a hand on the owner of this factory," George observed with exasperating calmness.

"On you, I said, you—" began the man stormily.

"So did I," interrupted George. "On me—the owner!"

Joseph Hill started to his feet, pressing his clammy hands against his pallid brow. He looked at George, standing so fearlessly before him, with a dazed expression.

Seeing he was for the moment unable to speak, George Chesterland continued slowly:

"In those old papers, which you flung at me so contemptuously the day you put me out, I found the whole history of your rascality. I know the truth. This factory, the old home on Fifth Avenue, in fact, everything you have owned and claimed, is mine. There is no use for you to deny it; the proofs are too strong against you."

While George was speaking, Joseph Hill sunk into his chair again, where he crouched as if in mortal terror.

"Do you think you can bluff me with such a mad tale?" he tried to say scornfully, but his teeth chattered as if from a heavy chill.

"Look at your trembling hands and ashen face. Do they look as if you thought I was bluffing?" George exclaimed cuttingly.

Joseph Hill tried to cover his tell-tale face as he said, huskily:

"How much money do you want?"

"Every dollar you have stolen and every cent, with interest, that you owed my father," George declared sternly.

The guilty man quailed before the fire in the young man's eyes. "You are certain you have proof of all this?" he inquired huskily.

"If you doubt it, you can go to my lawyers, where you will find all the papers."

The frankness of George's voice convinced the millionaire that he was speaking the truth. There was no guessing or supposition in his clear statements. Besides, the millionaire knew too well his own guilt, and he realized that his course was run, that the vast fortune for which he had sinned so deeply, of which he had cheated the rightful heir, would be taken from him, and after all these years of affluence and honor, he would be reduced to poverty and disgrace.

"Wait a moment," he said unsteadily. "Wait until I get some paper for you to look over."

Poor unsuspecting George did not notice the gleam of hatred and madness which flashed from the guilty man's eyes. He did not know that Joseph Hill had made an excuse to go back to the large safes in the rear to get a revolver which he knew was in a top drawer there. And George Chesterland was far from suspecting the millionaire's designs on his life.

The revolver was not in the drawer where it was usually kept, some one had placed it high on a shelf, high above the guilty man's head. He caught the glint of its shining barrel, and stretched upon his tip-toes to get hold of it.

Pulling it slowly to the edge, he made an extra effort to reach it, when it fell and exploded!

George Chesterland sprung to his feet at the sound of the report and turned in time to see his enemy, Joseph Hill, fall heavily to the floor, pierced by his own bullet.

"Why did you do this?" cried George in dismay, and the frightened bookkeepers, who had also witnessed the accident, came running to the side of the prostrated man.

"I—was going—to shoot—you," he gasped, his life's blood flowing freely at every word.

George told one of the men to run for a doctor, but the dying man interposed.

"It's—no use," he gasped. "Bring me that roll—of papers—marked private—and—sealed. I want—to-destroy—them—"

There was a rattling sound in his throat, the blood gushed forth in a red torrent, and as the clerk, who flew for the papers, returned with them to his employer's side, Joseph Hill gasped and his soul took flight to receive at a higher court the punishment of his misdeeds.

The next day found George Chesterland in full possession of the wealth which had been stolen from him, for the very papers which Joseph Hill, with his dying breath, stated he wished to destroy, furnished additional and conclusive proof of his dishonesty and George's claim.

The morrow found him transformed from a dependent invalid to a courted millionaire. The newspapers were full of his good fortune, and old acquaintances, who had forgotten him in his poverty, suddenly remembered how well they liked the handsome young fellow, and his office was besieged with scheming mamas and gushing men come to congratulate him.

But George turned from them, one and all, with a heavy heart. He knew the worth of their praise and adulation.

"There is to be no more hard work for you, my good friend," he said to Peter Day, whose cheeks were wet with tears of joy at his young master's good fortune. "You shall have that nice little farm that you have always wanted, and dear old Sal, all the rest of her days, shall idly browse in green fields, near enough so she can lift her head occasionally to see her faithful old master as he sits in an easy-chair on his vine-covered veranda."

"And you, Master George, what of you?" Peter Day asked anxiously, his wife weeping for happiness behind her apron.

"I shall sell the factory and leave my other business in the hands of my representatives, and go to Europe. I want a change of scene and thoughts," was the despondent reply.

But George Chesterland had another duty to perform before he went abroad. He wanted to find Christmas.

He did find her, in a way unexpected to him. In walking through his factory with a man who contemplated buying it, he found Christmas in her old place at a machine.

She grew very pale when his eyes rested on her, but her eyes met his fearlessly.

"Christmas," he said reproachfully, crossing to her side, "I never expected to find you here."

Poor child! She misunderstood his meaning and she looked as if she would faint. She thought he still held her unforgiven.

"Do you want me to leave?" she faltered piteously.

"Yes," he answered simply. "Come to my office in half and hour. I wish to speak to you."

How could she face him? She could not bear to hear unkind words from his lips and she would have slipped away had she not thought that such an act would only convince him all the stronger of her wrong-doing. No, she must stay and face him.

Half an hour later, a little, pale girl walked unsteadily to the young millionaire's office and knocked timidly upon the door marked, "Private."

George was smiling when he opened the door and motioned her to a chair near his desk.

Christmas' great, soulful eyes met his wistfully. "I did not run away from you, Mr. Chesterland," she said. It was no longer "George," since he was a millionaire. "It was time for me to earn my own living. I had depended on my friends too long," she added.

"Depended on your friends?" he repeated softly, and touching her short hair, he said: "Do you think I could ever forget what you did for me, little angel? Was there not another reason for your going?"

"Yes!"—frankly—"I could not remain with those who no longer trusted me."

"I trust you, Christmas"—very softly—"you know that I have regained my fortune and am no longer poor. But I am lonely and sad, Christmas. Do you know why—Amor left me? Do you know she was already a wife when she married me?"

"No, no! It cannot be true. She was too good and honorable," Christmas cried, aghast.

"It is true, there is no mistake"—sadly—"I saw her—the man to whom she was married, and before him, she confessed the truth. And now," he continued more rapidly, "I have decided to forget that wretched part of my life and to try to find happiness, if you will help me."

"Help you?"—distressedly. "How can I help you? You are rich and will have plenty of friends."

George took her little trembling hands tenderly in his and, gazing seriously into the great, soulful eyes, fixed so wonderingly upon him, he said gently:

"I can make no false pretences, Christmas, but you know you have always been very dear to me. I want you to share my wealth with me—to be my wife!"

Christmas covered her face with her hands. She thought of all that he had been to her, of the bitter heart-aches she had endured when he loved another; she thought of the long hours she had spent by his bedside, and how she had felt that this world would be a blank to her if he were taken away.

And then another face, noble, handsome, wearing the light of a holy life, came before her mental vision.

She did not know why she thought of him, nor why her heart throbbed with a new sensation, strangely sweet. She only knew that when she remembered him, she felt it impossible to share the future with the man who had been the idol of her heart.

"Have you no answer for me, little angel?" George asked.

"I can only ask you to be true to yourself, George," was the soft answer. "You still love Amor, and you would wrong me and yourself by thinking of another marriage."

"But in time we—"

"No, dear George, say no more. The remembrance of the love Amor bore you would keep us apart without anything else."

With bowed head, George Chesterland listened to Christmas as she told how Amor had confessed to her the deep love she bore her husband.

He could hardly believe it, but still the very thought sweetened his life, which, Heaven knows, had been bitter enough.

He said no more to Christmas about marriage, but he prevailed upon her to accept enough money to keep her until she was educated; and leaving instructions about her and the Days with his lawyers, George Chesterland, a few days later, sailed for Europe.

When, if ever, he would return, none could say. He said—never!

Now more alone than ever, Christmas Cherry turned to better and holier thoughts.

"*He* said I would some day feel the need of religion," she thought. "He was right. I want consolation and help from something All Powerful."

XXXVIII

"I REPEAT THAT, WHILE HIDDEN IN HIS ROOM,
I SAW GENERAL ESCANDON MURDER HIS WIFE
AND BURY HER BODY IN THE WALL."

GEORGE CHESTERLAND LAY IN HIS berth, unable to sleep. Ever and anon he could hear the man in the next cabin groaning, and the sound worried him.

But when it ceased he found himself strangely nervous if the silence was protracted.

At last he heard a voice full of grief and despair cry distinctly:

"Amor! Amor! My darling Amor!"

George was on his feet in an instant, trembling like a leaf.

Some one called Amor!

It must be the girl he loved, and she was near!

Dressing hastily, he went to the stateroom from whence those cries emanated and knocked upon the door.

"Can I be of any assistance? I thought I heard some one calling."

"Please call the physician and my valet; I am very ill," said a voice from within.

After ringing for them, George entered the stateroom and saw a handsome, white-haired man lying helplessly in his berth. His face was very pale and thin, and he seemed to be losing strength rapidly.

Unable to smother the emotions which Amor's name had roused in his heart, he determined to solve the secret of it before the arrival of the ship-doctor.

"Have you any one else you would like called?" he asked. "I thought I heard you mention a name."

"I am all alone," groaned the man.

"And yet I was sure I heard you call the name of one I know—Amor!" persisted George.

The man sprung upright in bed, and then groaning fell back again, grasping George's hand as he did so, and crying in a weak, frightened way:

"Do you know of her? My beautiful Amor, my darling! Where is she? Oh, pity a heartbroken man and tell me where she is!"

"What is she to you?" demanded George.

"My daughter—my child, my only one! Oh, tell me where she is! Is she well, and why did she run away from me?" he pleaded piteously.

Deeply surprised to find that he was really face to face with Amor's father, George was almost at a loss to know what to say.

"The last time I saw your daughter, she was well, Mr. Gray," he replied, with an effort.

"Gray! Gray! My name is Escandon. My wife's name was Gray," was the quick reply.

"I beg your pardon. The young lady I knew was Amor Gray. She had coal-black hair and eyes, and a spotless complexion."

"It is the same—my darling daughter!" he cried gladly, and the arrival of the doctor precluded further conversation.

After making a hasty examination, the doctor returned to his office and for General Escandon's valet. He requested George to kindly wait until he returned. General Escandon begged him to stay with him; he had much to say when they were alone.

Finding that his daughter had given no reason for deserting her friends, and hearing how George had rescued her from the river and afterward given her employment, General Escandon was filled with the bitterest agony.

In his own mind, he knew full well that Amor had fled because she had learned of his crime.

"Was your daughter married, may I ask?" George continued.

"No; nor had she any love affairs, if you think that was her reason for leaving home. She was only a child, and as free as the air."

Then George told how he had saved her one night in the street from a Spaniard, and that the Spaniard had declared she was his wife, and later, had entered the house where she lived, and had compelled her to acknowledge herself his wife.

In eager, excited tones, General Escandon asked minute questions about the man, how he looked and spoke and acted, and when he heard all, he grew ghastly pale.

"It was Mateo Blanco—her bitter enemy and mine," he moaned in agony. "He holds a secret over me, and to save me, he has made her swear that she belonged to him."

"That is true!" exclaimed George, a new light breaking in on him. "He charged her, for her father's sake, to say she was his wife, and I did not see through it, and I would not believe her afterward. But, thank God, she is my wife!"

Even the return of the doctor did not prevent the general from hearing the full story of his daughter's marriage, and his joy knew no bounds, to find his cousin and enemy outwitted and cheated of the prize for which he had played.

"I advise you to talk no more, and to calm yourself," said the physician. "I must tell you that your condition is serious, very serious."

"I know it. I am a dying man," was the quick reply. "My heart is broken, because I could not stand the loss of my daughter with the remembrance of my crime. Before morning I shall be dead, and while I have time I want to make everything clear with this young man, my daughter's husband."

He ordered the doctor to leave them, and then made his valet get all his private papers, and his will, in which he left all his wealth to Amor.

These he gave to George Chesterland, charging him to see that his wishes were carried out.

Knowing his hours were numbered, he confessed his crime to George, and asked him to pray Amor to forgive her sinful father.

Before the day dawned he fell asleep, his hand clasped in George's, Amor's name the last on his lips. George sat there, listening to the roar of the sea as it beat against the side of the ship, until the sun rose and rested upon the face of the dead man, where shone the light of eternal peace and calm.

There was a quiet burial at sea the next day, and all that was earthly of General Escandon was consigned to the waves.

Possessed of a fever of impatience, George Chesterland immediately on landing at Queenstown took a ship sailing for New York, where he landed exactly twelve days after he had left it.

He meant to find his wife, his lost Amor, and he meant to lose no time about it.

He drove directly from the pier to the inspector's office, determined to spare no expense in searching for his lost love, and to have the whole detective force, if necessary, upon her trail.

The inspector was engaged, he was told, and he was requested to step into an adjoining room and wait.

There was one thing which George considered buried with General Escandon, and that was the story of his crime. For Amor's sake, for all their sakes, it should never be revealed.

As he sat there thinking of the hour he would be reunited to his lost bride, he heard a voice, and what it said aroused George from his day-dreams.

"I repeat," said the voice clearly and distinctly, "that while hidden in his room, I saw General Escandon murder his wife and bury her body in the wall. If you bring some officers and come with me, I will show you where the body is hidden."

XXXIX

WHAT THEY FOUND IN THE ESCANDON MANSION.

MAN AS HE WAS, GEORGE Chesterland trembled when he heard those words, for he knew that the terrible story of General Escandon's crime—the story he would have kept for Amor's sake—was being given to the world.

Before he could recover from the shock, a man waited upon him with the information that the inspector would be detained all day and could see no one.

"Please tell the inspector that I shall detain him only for a moment," George explained nervously. "Say that I have some very important information about a case in which he is interested."

This message brought back a new man, who introduced himself as a detective, and said the inspector had appointed him to receive the stranger's communication.

But George was determined that no one but the inspector should hear what he had come to say.

In fact, George Chesterland hardly knew what he wanted to tell. He had come to implore the inspector to search for his missing bride, but the few words he had accidentally overheard had somewhat confused him.

"I can talk to no one except the inspector," he replied determinedly.

And the man, finding all persuasions useless, went back to report to his superior officer.

But that superior officer had gone, and his visitor with him, so there was nothing left for George but to take his departure.

The moment he set foot outside of Police Headquarters a new idea possessed him, and without losing a moment he hurried down to the ferry, reaching the Jersey side just in time to board an outgoing train.

A feverish desire possessed him to know who was on the train, but he did not dare look, for if his intuitions proved correct, he would be seen as well as see.

So, curbing his impatience, he sat quietly behind a newspaper until the train stopped at a station in the suburbs of Philadelphia. And then he was the last to leave it, and the first to get away from the crowd.

An hour afterward he slipped in at the pillared gate of Amor Escandon's home, almost as silently as she had passed through it the night she had deserted home and friends forever, crushed beneath the weight of her father's crime.

George Chesterland glanced around the beautiful park with its rustic benches, gleaming statues and silent fountains. He looked at the palatial mansion, grim and silent, with its tightly closed doors and shaded windows, and sighed.

Even the grand old home seemed decaying beneath its owner's curse. An air of intense desolation hung over everything.

Still George could easily picture what it had been when it was alive with fair guests and mirth, when the beautiful young mistress reigned queen in its stately halls.

How hard it must have been for her to give up all this grandeur for a life of toil and poverty! No wonder the heartbroken girl tried to end her life, and failing this, found nothing to console her for her loss.

Poor Amor! Poor, proud, haughty child! Where was she now?

This thought aroused George from his dreaming and made him hurry toward the silent mansion. Finding the door open, he entered without knocking.

The hasty sounds of rapid work guided his footsteps to the room where General Escandon, in a fit of jealous rage, had given his wife the cup of poison and concealed her body, before it was yet cold, in the walls of his room.

So engrossed were the detectives in their work that they never suspected the presence of an outsider, and hidden by friendly curtains, George watched them.

There were a half dozen men pulling and ripping at the wall. Watching them was the inspector and by his side, the man George now knew to be Mateo Blanco, General Escandon's cousin.

An exclamation of satisfaction announced that the last bit of wall had given way, and the men pressed forward eagerly, trying to gaze into the depths of the dark cavity.

George Chesterland could not repress a shudder, for General Escandon's confession prepared him only too well for the sight these men were about to gaze upon.

"Where's your lantern?" demanded the inspector, and the next instant the ray of a dark-lantern was flashed upon the dark recess.

With a cry of dismay, the men fell back.

The opening within the wall was empty!

Mateo Blanco uttered a fearful oath.

"What is the meaning of this?" demanded the inspector. "Where are no signs of a body here."

"The villain has outwitted me," burst forth Mateo Blanco. "I warned you that he was preparing to leave America and his first work has been to remove the body."

"That is very probable," affirmed the inspector. "I should be surprised if he had left the body here when he knew you possessed his secret. But now, the thing is to find our man and arrest him for murder."

"I shall find him!" Mateo Blanco cried revengefully. "If I have to go to the ends of the earth to do it!"

George Chesterland, at this instant, stepped boldly out before them. Not heeding their exclamations of anger and surprise, he said quietly to the infuriated Spaniard, who recognized him at once:

"You will have to go even farther to find General Escandon."

"What do you mean?" gasped Mateo Blanco, turning white.

"I mean that you will have to go to the bottom of the sea!" was the quiet reply. "General Escandon is dead."

"This is a lie to help the murderer escape," Mateo Blanco cried angrily. "I saw him not two weeks ago in New York."

"Here is my proof to the general's death at sea," George said, taking a paper from his satchel and handing it to the inspector. "You can easily verify the truth of it."

The inspector glanced at the paper and then handed it to Mateo Blanco, who was forced to believe the evidence of his cousin's death.

Drawing a long breath, and flashing a look of hatred at George Chesterland, the Spaniard said authoritatively:

"Then I am the general's only heir."

George smiled disdainfully. "You are mistaken," he said. "General Escandon has a child—a daughter."

He was not prepared for the hatred and venom with which the Spaniard hurled his reply.

"General Escandon's daughter is dead," he hissed, "and no one can stand between me and the Escandon millions."

Poor George Chesterland staggered back, deathly pale. Many times the dreadful suspicion that Amor was dead had crossed his mind, but he had always put it behind him as too horrible to contemplate.

And now to hear in this brutal fashion of his darling's death! It was too much.

"If she is dead," he shouted threateningly, "you shall answer to me for her life!"

"With the Escandon millions to back me, I have no fear of you," was the instant reply.

George saw the Spaniard was trying to torture him to the fullest extent, so, curbing his anger, he answered triumphantly:

"You cannot touch the millions you have always coveted. Amor Escandon has left an heir in the person of myself—*her husband!*"

Mateo Blanco started as if he meant to throw himself upon George and stab him to the heart; but restraining himself by a mighty effort, he laughed insultingly.

"Mr. Inspector, you can see enough of my papers to justify my claim," said George. "I was with General Escandon when he died, before which he knew and recognized me as his daughter's husband."

As the inspector stepped to one side with him, George Chesterland whispered hurriedly:

"I want you to have Mateo Blanco shadowed day and night, for I have reasons to believe that my wife, General Escandon's daughter, if not dead, is his prisoner!"

XL

"AND THE GREATEST OF THESE IS CHARITY."

UNABLE TO BEAR HER LONELINESS, and feeling the need of something greater than earthly guidance, Christmas Cherry had at last gone to church, the church where preached the noble man she had encountered so often, and in such strange ways.

She felt that during the entire service his beautiful eyes singled her out and dwelt upon her, filling her heart with a new sweet thrill, and covering her face with warm blushes.

She meant to go away as soon as he was done, but after the last prayer was said, and the congregation walked slowly forth, Christmas still lingered wistfully.

Her eyes were downcast and her lips trembled when she heard an eager step advancing toward her and that tender, masterful voice, that had haunted her dreams and sounded in her ears for months, once more addressed her.

"You have made me a very happy and thankful man to-day," he said lowly, and then her hand rested in his, and her big soulful eyes were lifted for one sweet instant to his handsome, glowing face.

"I knew you would not go without speaking to me," he continued with a smile of happiness. "I have waited so long for your coming, but I never despaired."

"Your words have come true," Christmas said shyly. "I have learned the need of a greater power."

"And you have found it?"—eagerly.

"I have felt a repentance of all my sins, as I sat here, and a determination to life the pure life of a Christian has entered my heart. You have preached of charity, the charity that makes us slow to anger, that teaches us to forgive our enemies, that makes us give our hand to the wicked; oh, teach this to me, and show me how to go forth to do good among my fellow-creatures."

"You have the secret of true religion—charity! It is the sum and substance of religion. If you possess charity, you can do no wrong. 'And the greatest of these is charity,' says the Bible. Come home with me," added the minister, "I want to talk with you."

So, arm in arm, they left the church together, and walked along the silent streets to his home.

Almost before Christmas realized it she was sitting in a cozy study, and under the intoxicating magic of the minister's eyes and voice and manner, was telling him the story of her life.

She kept nothing back. It seemed as if she was but confiding it to her other self. Her life in the Foundling Asylum, her life in the factory, Amor's beauty, Lillian's disappearance, the Days' goodness, George Chesterland's illness, their poverty, her appeals for help, her following Mateo Blanco thinking to find Amor, her imprisonment and escape, what it cost her to keep the secret of her absence, George's good fortune—were all told to him.

Then, while he held her hands earnestly in his, he told her his name, Edgar van Lynn, and said that he had a story which in some places fit in with hers.

"The lady you appealed to at the Associations was Mrs. Neilson, my sister," he said with a happy smile, "and her greatest sorrow on leaving town was that she must go without making your acquaintance. However, she will be home in two weeks, and then you shall know each other. She will be delighted. And there is some one else who must see you, and that is your friend, Lillian Day."

"Lillian Day!" echoed Christmas with delight. "Then she is no longer with—"

"No!" he replied. "Poor girl, she has suffered bitterly for her sin."

And then he told Christmas, who listened with tears in her eyes, how he had found Lillian, and of all the bitter trials she had endured since she was cast into the street.

"She has refused to send word to her parents, and I did not wish to go against her desires," he added. "But you must see her and try to influence her to go to them. You will find her dreadfully changed, in looks as well as heart. I suppose it is for her own good. As she sinned through her great beauty, Heaven took it away that she might never be tempted again."

Then Edgar van Lynn and Christmas Cherry went out into the night again. They walked slowly to her boarding-house with a great joy in their hearts and a wild tumult coursing through their veins.

They said nothing, because there seemed no need for words. Only when he left her he held her hand and said:

"I will call early for you, and after you have seen Lillian, we will decide how to restore her to her parents."

And Christmas flew up to her room, where she lay awake half the night recalling the glance of his eyes, the tone of his voice, the pressure of his hand.

She had loved George Chesterland once in a mad, worshipful way. He had been her friend, her benefactor, but the love she gave him to the love now filling every pulsation of her being was—

"as water unto wine."

Edgar van Lynn did not call for her in the morning, as he had promised. He sent a carriage and a message, saying he had been called to see a poor woman who was dying; would Christmas go to Lillian (the driver had the address) and meet the writer afterward at his home?

Edgar van Lynn had hardly prepared Christmas for the startling change in Lillian Day. The beauty of her eyes still remained; but her hair, her teeth, and her exquisite complexion were but a memory.

The dainty skin was scarred and lined where the dreadful disease had eaten its way, a little cap covered her shaven head, and an unsightly vacancy told of the missing teeth.

The reunion between Christmas and the erring girl was very touching. Long and tenderly did Christmas talk to her, urging her to see her sorrowing parents. At last her pleading prevailed, and she departed, her face glorified with happiness.

She felt at liberty to use the carriage Edgar van Lynn had placed at her disposal, so she drove to the old home where she had lived with the Days, for George Chesterland had told her that they intended to remain in it until they found and bought the farm they wanted.

Peter Day himself opened the door. "Christmas, gal!" he cried joyously. "Hev you come back at last?"

"I would have come long ago if I had thought you cared to see me," Christmas replied kindly.

By this time Mrs. Day heard the voices and rushed forth. Her greeting was no less cordial, for the good woman had bitterly reproached herself for her conduct towards Christmas.

"Come in and sit down, gal, an' tell us what you're doin'. Bless me! It does my eyes good to see you," Peter Day said.

"And did you know Master George got back his fortune?" chimed in Mrs. Day, unable to keep back the good news.

"I know all about it, for I went back to work in the factory," laughed

Christmas, "and Master George would have told you about me, if I had not begged him not to. I thought you had not forgiven me."

"Let old scores be forgotten, gal," Peter Day said softly. "I've always thought we done you wrong. But we'll make up for it now. Master George bought us a farm—I just this minute got the deed—and we're goin' to it straight off, and you shall come with us and live there all the rest of your days."

"Dear Mr. Day, isn't there some one else whose home should be with you?" Christmas spoke gently.

The old couple dropped their heads.

"Let us forget, gal, let us forget," muttered Peter Day.

"You will never be able to forget her, your wayward child," continued the girl earnestly. "Then can you not soften your hearts, and take her back?"

"Take her back?"—fiercely. "No, by Heaven! Take her back, to have her break our hearts over?"

"But if Heaven had punished her most bitterly, and she was sorry and repentant, and hungry to see your dear faces and hear your loving voices, would you still deny her a place in your home?"

"That can't be!" Peter Day said sternly. "The gal was cursed with a fatal beauty, and no difference how she might try to reform, some one would flatter her to her ruin again."

"Let me tell you the saddest story you ever heard," said Christmas, and she told them the story of Lillian's hardships, and how her fatal beauty was forever gone.

The old couple sobbed as she talked, and when she finished, Peter Day cried huskily:

"Bring our poor child to us. Heaven has punished her!"

Christmas waited for no more. Rushing out, she sprung into the carriage, and, driving to the home where Lillian lived, soon returned with her.

"There is only one request I wish to make, Lillian," Christmas said to the trembling girl. "Some time tell them where I was those three weeks and why I could not tell them the secret of my absence. I cannot bear them to think badly of me."

"I will, Christmas; they shall know how good you were," Lillian wept.

"You need not wait," Christmas said to the driver, when they reached their destination.

She knocked upon the door, holding the plainly but neatly-clad girl by the hand.

The door was thrown open, and Lillian Day, changed and repentant, stood before her father.

He gave a quick glance at her poor, scarred face, and, with a cry of fatherly love and sympathy, drew her into the house and folded her lovingly to his heart.

"Mother!" he cried brokenly, "our little gal's come home!"

And then Christmas gently closed the door, and went away and left them together.

XLI

WHAT A NEWSPAPER DID IN A CONVENT.

IF CHRISTMAS HAD NOT BEEN engaged with other things that day, and had read the morning newspapers, she would have seen the story of General Escandon's crime in type, with an account of how the Escandon mansion was searched and no body found; that Mateo Blanco had put in a claim for the fortune, declaring the only child and daughter dead.

But she had not read the story, and if she had, she would not have known George Chesterland's connection with it; for, strange to say, he had not been mentioned in any way.

Still, the article was destined to make a change in affairs.

A white-robed novice in the House of Good Shepherd, ushering out a visitor, found the newspaper on the floor, and as she stooped to pick it up, the glaring headlines caught her eye.

That was enough.

She read the story through, and then she carried it to the Mother Superior. Softly and calmly they talked it over, and presently the white-robed novice stole away, and, going to a little bare room up-stairs, knocked gently upon the door.

"My child," she said to the occupant, who sat sad and despondent at the end of the tiny room, "our mother wishes to see you at once."

With a sigh of utter weariness, the girl arose and, tossing back her raven tresses from her pallid face, followed the novice down-stairs.

"My dear child," said the Mother Superior when the two entered her presence, "if you are able to bear a shock, I have some news for you."

"I can endure anything, mother," was the weary reply.

"Have you ever thought that some one near to you by the ties of blood might not be in good health?" was the next question.

The black head was raised for an instant, and then the sweet, sad voice said slowly:

"You mean my father? Is he—dead?"

"He is, my child. He died upon the ocean, and his cousin has—"

"I know," interrupted the girl, who was none other than Amor Escandon. "He has told the story of my father's crime. It is like him."

"Not only that, but he says you are dead, and declares himself the heir."

"Let him"—listlessly—"the money has only been a curse. I want none of it."

"Have you no thought of going out in the world again?" asked the Mother Superior.

"I shall never go out now since the world knows my father was a murderer."

"That has not been proven," was the quick reply. "In a way, your father's name has been cleared. A search was made where the body was said to have been buried, and no body was found."

"Are you certain?" exclaimed Amor, with the first evidence of interest.

"There—you can read it for yourself."

She handed the newspaper to Amor, and eagerly the girl read the long, sensational account of the affair. A happy light was on her face when she finished.

"I am going away," she said quickly. "I am going out to claim my fortune and right myself in the eyes of one whom I have bitterly wronged."

"I thought that would be your decision, and have already arranged for Sister Inez to accompany you until you find some friend to bear you company," the Mother Superior said kindly.

"You are very good," Amor replied, and turning to the white-robed novice, she said: "Sister Inez, I shall be most happy to have you with me."

Amor had very few preparations to make, but Sister Inez was ready and waiting when she came down. A black robe replaced the white one, and a strange agitation was in her manner.

A carriage took them to the Fifth Avenue Hotel, where they were met by a tall, grave man with prematurely gray hair. They followed him to the rooms he said had been engaged for them. Once there, he introduced himself to Amor.

"I do not know whether you ever heard of me or not, Miss Escandon," he said gravely, "but I am your mother's second cousin."

"You are Dr. Richard Gray," Amor replied quickly, holding out her hand with charming frankness.

"I am, Amor. May I call you Amor?"—Amor nodded her head. "You do not know the secret of your father's sin, and I want to tell it to you in the presence of this sister, and then I want you to pass judgment upon your mother and myself."

"Is it necessary to tell that story?" asked Amor, shrinking a little.

"Very necessary!"

They sat down, and in a quiet voice Dr. Gray told his story.

"Your mother and I had formed an early attachment for each other," he said; "but we were very young and parental objections overruled our desires, and we were separated; I was sent abroad, and she was forced into a marriage of wealth. She might have learned to love your father dearly had not his mad jealousy and insane love kept her in constant terror. She feared him too much to love him.

"After she had been married some years, I returned to America; we met, and the old love was kindled anew. She was not permitted to meet me openly and naturally; such conditions only served to increase our love. After having been a childless wife for many years, your mother discovered at last that Heaven was sending her a child to comfort and love her. As soon as she realized this, she came to me and told me that we must never meet again. For the sake of the child that was soon to come, she must never do the least thing that would reflect on her; so, yielding to her prayers, I bade her farewell, and once again became a wanderer upon the face of the earth.

"Sixteen years passed and I grew desperate. I was hungry for a sight of her face, for the sound of her voice. If you had ever loved with all the strength of your being and had been forced to live apart from the object of your devotion, you might understand a little how I suffered."

"I may understand better than you know," Amor said with tears of sympathy.

"I was growing old," resumed the doctor, "and in a moment of heart-sick loneliness, I traveled back, reaching your home on Christmas Eve, the night of your ball. I saw your mother, we talked in the conservatory, and she begged me for your sake to go away again, that her heart had not grown cold, and she was not strong enough to see me. Your father overheard our conversation, and afterward while mad with jealousy, compelled your mother to choose between a cup of poison and her daughter's happiness. If she refused to die for your sake, you would be cast forth penniless, homeless, and nameless!"

Amor sighed deeply. She had listened intently to the story and when the doctor paused, she said, in a whisper:

"And she chose the poison?"

"Yes; for your sake she was willing to die," he responded briefly.

"Poor little mother!" wept Amor. "She sacrificed her dear life for nothing. Heaven spare her the knowledge of what her daughter has gone through since then."

"You do not blame us, then?" asked the doctor. "You do not think us guilty of any wrong?"

"I could not live and think evil of my mother"—earnestly—"she is as pure as the angels to me."

"If I were to tell you that a little negro servant had fallen asleep in an adjoining room and overheard the whole affair between your father and Mateo Blanco, and rushed out of the house when your father went to the library with him to draw up some necessary papers, and rushed into my arms—for I was wandering like a lost spirit around the abode of my love—and that I heard his story and compelled him to take me back to the room, where, unmolested, I removed the body of your mother—would you believe me?"

The doctor spoke hastily, and Amor saw the color come and go in his cheeks. He was deeply agitated.

"I would believe you, but why did you not make the crime public?" she said slowly.

"I may have had reasons"—meaningly—"I may have found there was no murder."

Amor's heart almost ceased beating. She understood his meaning, and it made her brain grow dizzy.

"You mean," she whispered frightenedly, "that my mother was not—dead?"

"Yes; and that she is alive and well to-day. Only the thought, until lately, that you were with your father, receiving the benefit of her sacrifice, kept her from disclosing the truth."

With a little cry Amor stretched forth her hands and would have fallen lifeless to the floor, had not the doctor caught her.

When she recovered she was lying on the lounge and Dr. Gray and Sister Inez were bending anxiously over her.

"Where is my mother?" she cried piteously. "Bring her to me."

"She has been with you for many months, Amor," said the doctor solemnly. "Only to-day's events have kept her from becoming a nun."

Amor gave a joyous cry and stretched out her arms with a longing gesture, and throwing aside her novice's hood, Sister Inez, Amor's mother, clasped her long-lost daughter to her heart.

When they had grown calm again, Mrs. Escandon told Amor how she had gone straight to the convent on being restored to life, intending to bury herself there forever.

Many times after her child took refuge within its walls did she long to call out and claim her as her darling daughter, but not know why Amor was there, and remembering her vows, she always restrained herself.

"And she shall never go back now," laughed the doctor happily.

"No," said Amor, glancing roguishly from one to the other, "you must not let her go."

"My child! At such a time!" gently reproved the blushing mother.

"Well, you owe it to yourself and to Dr. Gray," Amor persisted. "Your marriage with my father was a mistake, and I hope we shall forget the name Escandon. The wicked cannot expect those they have injured to mourn their death."

"Never mind, Amor, I do not mean to wait many days," said the doctor. "I have engaged a minister to marry us next week, and then we shall all leave for Europe where we shall stay until our sad stories are forgotten."

"Do not count on me," Amor said, blushing rosily. "I believe in newly married couples being free from the restraints of a third person. I have some friends who need my care. They were good to me, now I intend to find them and show them I was not ungrateful. I am going to begin at once, if you will come with me. I am going to the Days' to see my dear little ragged angel, Christmas Cherry!"

XLI

"RICH MAN—POOR MAN."

AFTER CHRISTMAS CHERRY RESTORED LILLIAN Day to her parents, she hurried along the streets intending to keep her engagement with Edgar van Lynn.

Her mind was filled with happy thoughts of the coming meeting, and she saw and heard nothing until a heavy hand was laid on her shoulder, and an agitated voice said:

"Christmas! I have been waiting for you."

She turned with a smothered cry and faced—Mateo Blanco!

"How dare you address me?" she cried indignantly. "I despise you, and shall not talk to you."

"Christmas, I love you," he said with the energy of a great despair. "I will marry you—anything—only I cannot and will not live without you."

"I have just restored to her parents one whom you should have married," Christmas said sternly. "You are the cause of her child's death, her shattered health, and lost beauty. The memory of her poor scarred face makes me loathe the sight of you."

"Listen to me, Christmas, for I am mad," he cried out fiercely. "What do I care for any other woman? I love you. I want you, and I will have you or die."

"And I would rather die than speak to you," Christmas said cuttingly.

"Do you mean that? For the love of Heaven, you do not mean it?" cried the unhappy man.

"Take it as my last and final word. I mean it. Now please let me pass on."

"God forgive you and pity us both," he said, and flashing out a revolver, he pressed it against Christmas' breast, and then against his own, so quickly that a man who had been watching them had not time to interfere.

Mateo Blanco fell on the ground where Christmas lay senseless. He had barely enough strength to draw her into his arms and press his lips to hers, and then with a sigh he died.

George Chesterland and a detective, who had been shadowing Mateo Blanco in hopes of finding Amor, witnessed the shooting, and immediately took charge of the dead man and his dying victim.

George called for a carriage, and very tenderly raised Christmas in his arms and held her while they were driven rapidly to the Fifth Avenue Hotel, where George was staying.

Messengers were dispatched for physicians and for the Days, for George could not have Christmas there with him alone.

His own kind physician, with two others, were promptly at her bedside, and George was sent from the room.

"Spare no expense, doctor; you must not let her die," he said, and, leaving things in charge of his friend and physician, George went below to consult with his lawyers and the inspector, who had come to say that the death of Mateo Blanco would settle all dispute about the Escandon millions, which George would inherit, in case Amor's death was proven.

While George was out, the Days arrived, and with them Amor, her mother, and Dr. Gray.

Amor insisted on taking her place as Christmas' nurse, and the others, excepting Mrs. Day, waited in an ante-room for the doctor's verdict.

It was a long time before Christmas Cherry opened her eyes, and when she did, her strength seemed to be ebbing very rapidly.

"She cannot last long," said one physician, and George's doctor added huskily:

"We must save her. I have promised not to let her die."

Amor, hearing this terrible news, crept softly to the bed and knelt there, gazing piteously at the pallid face so still upon the pillow.

"Christmas darling!" she whispered tenderly. "Do you hear me, dear? It is I, Amor, who has come to you."

The white lids raised slowly and those luminous eyes, filled with the misty shadows of death, gazed upon Amor. A sweet smile of recognition crossed the white lips, and the faintest voice wafted to them.

"Amor! I am glad. George?"

Amor started, and began to say George was not there, when his physician interrupted with:

"George shall come at once, little angel. Keep up strength; try to be brave and to rally."

"You are not going to die," Amor pleaded brokenly, the tears she could not restrain rolling over her cheeks. "You must live, dearest. I cannot do without you."

Christmas closed her eyes for an instant. "Where is he—Mateo Blanco?" she asked.

"He died by your side," replied Amor, and Christmas closed her eyes again and Amor saw tears stealing from beneath her snowy-white lids. She was weeping for the unhappy fate of the man who had loved her so madly.

She did not look up again until the doctor said that George Chesterland was outside, waiting permission to come in.

Then she asked them all to go away except Amor, and to send George in to them.

Trembling and white, Amor stood waiting the coming of her husband, her heart divided between joy and fear. Was it too late to regain the place she held once in his heart?

"I cannot die happy until I hear you tell George that you love him," Christmas whispered appealingly. "He has suffered so terribly."

And then George came in and walked swiftly toward the bed, his handsome face soft with compassion and grief. But when he saw his lost wife, all his wrongs, all his sufferings flashed back upon him, and he grew cold and stern.

"Christmas," he said without addressing Amor, "you must keep up your courage."

"It is too late, George," was the tremulous answer. "I have only one wish, and then I can die happy."

George turned to ask her what it was, but a trembling hand touched his sleeve and an appealing voice said:

"Let me tell you what her wish is."

He bowed his head, stern and unforgiving. There was no encouragement in his looks, no relenting in his manner.

"Christmas would like for us—to live together—again," faltered Amor.

"There could be no good in that," was the stern and indifferent reply. "When a marriage has proven a mistake, it is better for the couple to live separate. I will give you a divorce if you wish it."

Amor gave a pitiful cry, as if his words had stabbed her, and Christmas watched them with unnaturally bright eyes.

"Oh, you are cruel, you will break my heart," Amor moaned.

"I am sure you are mistaken."—sadly. "You never cared anything for me, and we are better apart."

"I have cared for you!"—desperately. "I learned to love you. Scorn and hate me as you will, but I love you so dearly that I would rather die than give you up."

George Chesterland had grown very pale. He stepped back, as if he could not or would not understand and believe.

"George, my darling, I love you! Forgive me, and take me back!" Amor cried despairingly.

"Are you sure?" he asked, and he gathered her fiercely to his breast. "Are you not deceiving yourself, and me? Do not say it"—hoarsely—"if it is not true. I have endured so much, and I could not stand another disappointment."

"It is true, George, my husband, it is true as Heaven! I went home to tell you that terrible night. I had known it for a long time, but I was afraid to tell you," wept and laughed Amor as she clung to him.

"My darling wife!" he murmured, pressing lips to hers in a long, passionate kiss, and Christmas knew the greatest happiness of this world would be theirs forever.

"You have made me happy," Christmas smiled softly, as their faces, transfigured with love, were turned toward her. "Kiss me, dear Amor and dear George, and do not forget me. Now please send for my minister, Edgar van Lynn. I would like him to be with me when I die."

Kissing her in silence, George Chesterland hastened out to do her bidding; but Lillian Day had been before him, and Edgar van Lynn was already begging permission to see the wounded girl.

Outwardly calm, but with the agony of death tugging at his heart-strings, Edgar van Lynn advanced to the bed. "Christmas!" was all he said, but a man's heart's love was in his voice.

Falling on his knees, he knelt by her bedside, trying to read the story of life or death in her white face. What he saw must have pierced him to the heart, for he cried in agony:

"Christmas, you are not going to leave me?"

"You care so much?" she said wistfully.

"More than I can tell you," he cried. "I have loved you since the first night I saw you, when you defended the poor old woman from the crowd. Christmas, my darling, I cannot give you up. You must live and let me teach you to love me."

"I love you now," she whispered shyly, and he pressed his lips to hers.

A smile of infinite peace stole over her face and her big eyes closed gently.

"Will you do something for me, darling?" he pleaded. "Give me the right to be with you and nurse you?"

Christmas smiled assent, and a half hour later a minister made her the wife of Edgar van Lynn.

It was a long and serious battle; many times they gave up all hope. But love conquered where doctors were powerless, and Christmas lived to spend a life of happiness by her devoted husband's side, doing deeds of charity.

She is idolized not only by her husband, but by her husband's sister, Mrs. Neilson, and George Chesterland often tells his beautiful wife that if he did not love Christmas himself, he could be jealous of the love Amor bears her.

George and his wife are very happy with their young heir, George, Jr., and since his coming they have given up a life of travel and settled down in their luxurious home.

Very frequently Christmas and her husband, with George and Amor, go to see good Peter Day, who lives an ideal life on a farm with his wife and Lillian.

Lillian was never so dear to them as since her waywardness softened her heart and made her the most devoted daughter parents ever had.

Amor's mother, now Dr. Gray's wife, often writes from her home in Italy of the peaceful and happy days that have come to them in the autumn of their lives.

So the heiress, the beauty, and the factory girl learned by bitter experience the respective value of poverty and riches; and may none of you, dear readers, ever be so foolish as to crush the love out of your hearts and merely try to weigh the balance between—

"Rich man—poor man!"

THE END.

AFTER WORD

Of the eleven undiscovered Nellie Bly novels, this was the first one I set out to transcribe, as it was perhaps the least legible (rivaled only by *Pretty Merribelle*), and so the most difficult to prepare for publication.

Perhaps because of this, I developed a deep fondness for this novel. Though it contains so many elements that Bly used again and again in her fiction—the sexless secret marriage, the fickle nature of men's love, the dead infant, and the desperate young woman attempting to end her life by leaping into a river—it was my first encounter with them, and I found them endlessly fascinating.

Reading those watery attempts at self-slaughter in one novel after another, one must pause to wonder why Bly was so drawn to that form of suicide above all others. Was it simply the most romantic? Was it one she had contemplated for herself? Coupled with her depression during this period, it is a question worth considering.

Glaringly obvious here is the theme of men attempting to possess women. Not just the villainous Mateo Blanco, who imprisons Christmas in his home all while having Lillian Day as his plaything. Even the seemingly-noble George Chesterland is obsessed with the notion of possessing Amor. He needs her to be his wife, whether she loves him or no. It is a disturbing recurring theme in Bly's novels, perhaps never so vibrantly displayed as it is here.

Present too is the theme that defined Bly's identity from her first writing to her last breath: being an orphan. The fate of orphans is a constant in Bly's career. She signed her very first newspaper article "Lonely Orphan Girl" (it was only in her next piece that she became "Nellie Bly"). And at the end of her career she upset several adoption agencies by finding homes for orphans herself. Never content with bureaucracies, Bly took delight in circumventing them, to the delight of many childless women and the consternation of professionals who knew how to investigate families for fitness.

Which brings us to the death of the infants. Between this novel, *Little*

Luckie, and *Twins & Rivals*, it became a running joke among my early readers to refer to the author as Baby-Killer Bly. Obviously she is trying to raise the stakes and gain both sympathy and horror on the part of the reader. But with both cases of infant death in this novel, she also dehumanizes the infants by refusing to name them. We don't even know the gender of Lillian's child, let alone its name. It became a warning sign to me whenever I saw Bly introducing an unnamed infant, as it was certain to die.

For all the familiar elements Bly likes to use in her fiction, I feel as if Bly started this one with great energy, then had to finish in a great hurry. Looking at the timeline of her life, I believe I understand why.

The first chapters of *The Love of Three Girls* appeared in the pages of the *London Story Paper* on Saturday, June 3rd, 1893. That day the story took up two whole pages of five columns each (with illustrations on the front page), culminating with George Chesterland's leap into the East River to save Amor.

The tale rolled out in fifteen issues over sixteen weeks—on August 26th, the penultimate week, readers were left in a lurch, and the whole story wrapped up quite suddenly with the final chapter taking up only a single column.

It feels as though, after exploring the relationships deeply, Bly got bored with this story and simply rushed to finish it. There could easily be a version of this story that spreads Lillian's misery out over time while the rest of the action comes to fruition—and a version where we follow Amor's actions after she flees George. It seems as if, having set the pieces, Bly was ready to move on to something else.

One wonders what Bly was up to, until one remembers that it was on August 8, 1893, that she suddenly returned to the pages of the *New York World* as a reporter. Even considering the lag between the editions of the *New York Family Story Paper* and the *London Story Paper*, it is possible that she felt a need to wrap this one up so she could get back to work as a journalist.

While this was far from her last novel (she would pen three more), this was the last written during her hiatus from her life as a reporter. Perhaps she had failed to achieve the fame and recognition she desired as a novelist. Or perhaps she had been living Christmas Cherry's life at Mateo Blanco's, one of bored luxury, with her mother and menagerie of pets, and was eager to do something relevant again. Whatever the cause, this novel comes to an abrupt ending—almost as abrupt as the end of *Pretty Merribelle*, which she wrote the following year.

Nevertheless, I will always carry a fondness for Christmas Cherry and Amor Escandon, my first Nellie Bly heroines.

While striving always for fidelity to Bly's writing, I have made the decision to smooth a few infelicities that came from her churning out these stories so swiftly. Missing punctuation is negligible, and easily fixed. When faced with a period-specific spelling (i.e: "gayly" vs. "gaily"), I've stuck with the period spelling.

There are curious errors in the original text which I have fixed here. The man who cares for Lillian Day after her arrest is called Mr. Lysle in that chapter, only to be called Edgar van Lynn when revealed to be Christmas' ministering benefactor. I have made it Van Lynn throughout.

There are confounding timeline inconsistencies that Bly makes no attempt to address. Lillian's leap from first day of poverty to giving birth to the death of her child all take place within a chapter and a half. Amor is gone for how long? How long was George Chesterland ill? When did Christmas leave to return to the factory? These I have left alone, as any changes would have meant real tampering with Bly's story.

Most notably, I have combined lines into proper paragraphs. More than any other Bly book, she seemed to be using each sentence as filler, padding her column inches to fulfill a requirement. Outside of dialogue, nearly every single line of this book was its own paragraph. I have combined them to make it somewhat less melodramatic.

Somewhat.

As usual, I've attached articles from Bly's reporting career that seem to have inspired pieces of this story. They are presented in chronological order.

The full Blackwell's Island story is covered in Bly's book *Ten Days In A Mad-House*, so I have omitted it here (see my collection of all the Blackwell's Island reporting, *Into The Madhouse*). It is worth pointing out, however, that a Nurse Grady features quite prominently in the story that launched Bly to fame. Seeing as Grady was depicted as cruel and cold-hearted in life, it is no accident that a nurse named Grady is responsible for the death of Christmas Cherry's adopted sister in Chapter One of *The Love Of Three Girls*.

The discovery of Christmas and her subsequent fanciful naming comes straight from Bly's 1889 article "With the Prison Matrons." Christmas and Amor find work in George Chesterland's shoe factory. In 1885, right at the start of her career, Bly went to interview the girls who worked at several factories around Pittsburgh. One of those factories was Schmertz

& Co., a maker of shoes. That article included several drawings of pretty factory girls, and Bly makes a point about how attractive the women are who work there. One can easily imagine these girls as characters in this novel, though, of course, Christmas Cherry is somewhat fashioned after Bly herself, the perpetual orphan.

Readers familiar with Victor Hugo's novel *Les Misérables* will doubtless recognize the selling of hair and teeth from the fall of Fantine. It makes me wonder if Bly had read the novel, written thirty years before this story. I have to admit, reading Lillian's actions here for the first time, I recoiled in horror. In a novel full of melodrama, it was genuinely shocking, far moreso than the death of the two infants or the (attempted) murder of Amor's mother. In literature, as in dreams, the loss of teeth symbolizes death and decay. Here it stands in for the death of Lillian's vanity, which had brought her to ruin.

This story contains a surprising amount of moralizing from Bly. In her writing, both as a novelist and a reporter, she often sides with the plight of the poor girls who are deceived or forced into low behavior. Indeed, in her very first published article, entitled "The Girl Puzzle" (*Pittsburg Dispatch*, 1885), she says this:

> If sin in the form of man comes forward with a sly smile and says, "Fear no more, your debts shall be paid," she can not let her children freeze or starve, and so falls. Well, who shall blame her? Will it be you that have a comfortable home, a loving husband, sturdy, healthy children, fond friends—shall you cast the first stone? It must be so; assuredly it would not be cast by one similarly situated.

Yet here she very clearly blames Lillian Day for her own downfall, and while Mateo Blanco receives his comeuppance, it is not for his role in Lillian's fate.

Fascinating, too, is the prescient story about George Chesterland's factory being stolen by a trusted employee. Twenty years after the writing of this novel this very thing would happen to Bly when, after the death of her millionaire husband, the two men she trusted most at his factory embezzled all her money, forcing her to both flee the country and return to reporting once more.

For those looking for more about Nellie Bly, allow me to direct you to two nonfiction examinations of Bly's life. The first is *Nellie Bly: Daredevil, Reporter, Feminist* by Brooke Kroeger. This is an exhaustive and amazingly researched work, examining every aspect of Ms. Bly's life, making all kinds of connections between the professional and the personal.

The second is Matthew Goodman's *Eighty Days*, an examination of Nellie's trip around the world. It is a wonderfully compelling read, giving much color and detail to Bly's work and world.

Both Ms. Kroeger and Mr. Goodman were of direct help to me as well, graciously sending newspaper clippings that were missing from various library collections, and being generally encouraging about my work.

I hope you've enjoyed this, the eighth volume of "The Lost Novels Of Nellie Bly." Next comes another tale of an orphan wandering the streets of New York. Brace yourself for *Little Penny, Child of the Streets.*

Cheers,
David Blixt

THE GIRL PUZZLE.

What shall we do with our girls?

Not our Madame Neilsons; nor our Mary Andersons; not our Bessie Brambles nor Maggie Mitchells; not our beauty or our heiress; not any of these, but those without talent, without beauty, without money.

What shall we do with them?

The anxious father still wants to know what to do with his five daughters. Well indeed may he inquire and wonder. Girls, since the existence of Eve, have been a source of worriment, to themselves as well as to their parents, as to what shall be done with them. They cannot, or will not, as the case may be, all marry. Few, very few, possess the mighty pen of the late Jane Grey Swisshelm, and even writers, lecturers, doctors, preachers and editors must have money as well as ability to fit them to be such. What is to be done with the poor ones?

The schools are overrun with teachers, the stores with clerks, the factories with employees. There are more cooks, chambermaids and washerwomen than can find employment. In fact, all places that are filled by women are overrun, and still there are idle girls, some that have aged parents depending on them. We cannot let them starve. Can they that have full and plenty of this world's goods realize what it is to be a poor working woman, abiding in one or two bare rooms, without fire enough to keep warm, while her threadbare clothes refuse to protect her from the wind and cold, and denying herself necessary food that her little ones may not go hungry; fearing the landlord's frown and threat to cast her out and sell what little she has, begging for employment of any kind that she may earn enough to pay for the bare rooms she calls home, no one to speak kindly to or encourage her, nothing to make life worth the living? If sin in the form of man comes forward with a sly smile and says, "Fear no more, your debts shall be paid," she can not let her children freeze or starve, and so falls. Well, who shall blame her? Will it be you that have a comfortable home, a loving husband, sturdy, healthy children, fond friends—shall you cast the first stone? It must be so; assuredly it would not be cast by one similarly situated. Not only the widow, but the poor maiden needs employment. Perhaps father is dead and mother helpless, or just the reverse; or maybe both are depending on her exertions, or an orphan entirely, as the case may be.

GIRLS POORLY PAID.

What is she to do? Perhaps she had not the advantage of a good education, consequently cannot teach; or, providing she is capable, the girl that needs it not half as much, but has the influential friends, gets the preference. Let her get a position as clerk. The salary given would not pay for food, without counting rent or clothing. Let her go to the factory; the pay may in some instances be better, but from 7 a.m. until 6 p.m., except for 30 minutes at noon, she is shut up in a noisy, unwholesome place. When duties are over for the day, with tired limbs and aching head, she hastens sadly to a cheerless home. How eagerly she looks forward to pay day, for that little mite means so much at home. Thus day after day, week after week, sick or well, she labors on that she may live. What think you of this, butterflies of fashion, ladies of leisure? This poor girl does not win fame by running off with a coachman; she does not hug or kiss a pug dog nor judge people by their clothes and grammar; and some of them are ladies, perfect ladies, more so than many who have had every advantage.

Some say: "Well, such people are used to such things and do not mind it." Ah, yes, Heaven pity them. They are in most cases used to it. Poor little ones put in factories while yet not in their teens so they can assist a widowed mother, or perhaps father is a drunkard or has run away; well they are used to it, but they mind it. They will very quickly see you draw your dress away that they may not touch it; they will very quickly hear your light remarks and sarcastic laugh about their exquisite taste in dress, and they mind it as much as you would, perhaps more. They soon learn of the vast difference between you and them. They often think of your life and compare it with theirs. They read of what your last pug dog cost and think of what that vast sum would have done for them—paid father's doctor bill, bought mother a new dress, shoes for the little ones—and imagine how nice it would be, could baby have the beef tea that is made for your favorite pug, or the care and kindness that is bestowed upon it.

But what is to be done with the girls? Mr. Quiet Observations says: "In China they kill girl babies. Who knows but that this country may have to resort to this sometime." Would it not be well, as in some cases it would save a life of misery and sin and many a lost soul?

IF GIRLS WERE BOYS quickly it would be said: start them where they will, they can, if ambitious, win a name and fortune. How many wealthy and great men could be pointed out who started in the depths: but where are the many women? Let a youth start as errand boy and he will work his way up until he is one of the firm. Girls are just as smart, a great deal quicker to learn: why, then, can they not do the same? As all occupations for women are filled why not start some new ones. Instead of putting the little girls in factories let them be employed in the capacity of messenger boys or office boys. It would be healthier. They would have a chance to learn: their ideas would become broader and they would make as good, if not better, women in the end. It is asserted by storekeepers that women make the best clerks. Why not send them out as merchant travelers? They can talk as well as men—at least men claim that it is a noted fact that they talk a great deal more and faster. If their ability at home for selling exceeds a man's, why would it not abroad? Their lives would be brighter, their health better, their pocketbooks fuller, unless their employers would do as now—give them half their wages because they are women.

We have in mind an incident that happened in your city. A girl was engaged to fill a position that had always been occupied by men, who, for the same, received $2.00 a day. Her employer stated that he never had anyone in the same position that was as accurate, speedy and gave the same satisfaction; however, as she was "just a girl" he gave her $5.00 a week. Some call this equality?

The position of conductor on the Pullman Palace car is an easy, clean and good paying business. Why not put girls at that? They do many things that are more difficult and more laborious. In the banks, where so many young men are employed,

GIVE THE GIRLS A CHANCE.

They can do the work as well, and, as a gentleman remarked, "It would have a purifying effect on the conversation." Some people claim it would not do to put woman where she will not be protected. In being a merchant traveler or filling similar positions, a true woman will protect herself anywhere— as easily on the road as behind a counter, as easily as a Pullman conductor as in an office or factory. In such positions, receiving men's wages, she would feel independent; she could support herself. No more pinching and starving, no more hard work for little pay; in short, she would be a woman and would not be half as liable to forget the duty she owed her own true womanhood as one pinched by poverty and without means of support. Here would be a good field for believers in women's rights. Let them forego their lecturing and writing and go to work; more work and less talk. Take some girls that have the ability, procure for them situations, start them on their way, and by so doing accomplish more than by years of talking. Instead of gathering up the "real smart young men" gather up the real smart girls, pull them out of the mire, give them a shove up the ladder of life, and be amply repaid both by their success and unforgetfulness of those that held out the helping hand.

However visionary this may sound, those interested in human kind and wondering what to do with the girls might try it. George M. Pullman has tried and succeeded in bettering this poor class. Some of our purse-filled citizens might try it by way of variety, for, as someone says: "Variety is the spice of life." We all like the "spice of life": we long for it, except when it comes in the form of hash on our boarding-house table. We shall talk of amusements for our girls after we find them employment.

LONELY ORPHAN GIRL

OUR WORKSHOP GIRLS.

A CHAPTER ON BOOTS, SHOES, SLIPPERS AND THEIR MANUFACTURE.

TYPES OF FAIR FEMALE WORKERS.

SKETCHED FROM LIFE IN ORDER TO SHOW TO THE WORLD THE FACES OF PRETTY GIRLS AT WORK IN OUR FACTORIES.

Fondly, perhaps, we remember how, in our infantile days, slippers were not bought to be worn alone on the feet, but as a means of punishment. Sentence to Dante's *Inferno* would not be heard with more dread than "I'll use my slipper on you!" which rang in our childish ears as we lay in abject misery across the paternal knee. We wondered why on earth slippers were ever invented. The wonder grew greater, and extended to boots, as the young girl takes off her slippers and quietly slips up the stairs, while the "old man" by the aid of his boot is extinguishing the beau, who feels "they are wonderfully and heavily made." Then we reach the height of bliss when we apply the slipper to our own offspring, and practice Lotta kicking on our oldest daughter's "young man." We reach grandfatherly age as we toddle around in boots four sizes too large and lay claim to being the oldest inhabitant, even remembering when George Washington came with pants stuck to his boots a-courting our ma. During all this time we never stop to ask how are shoes made? Not even when they pinch our toes.

One of the Girls.

A neat shoe is the pride of most every person. Put a new shoe on a man and he feels dressed even if his clothes are shabby. Let him have on a new suit, and work out, crooked shoes, and he will feel like a tramp. Men, in the majority, are more particular in their foot-gear than women. Every day on the streets can be noticed women clad in silks and velvets, with shabby, miserable shoes, heels run over, sides burst out, back ripped, yet they hold their heads as high as if they were wearing the neatest and most expensive shoe in the market. They must fondly imagine people are in blissful ignorance as to how their pedal extremities look. If, like the peafowl, they would glance on past their elegant dresses and see their own feet, they would likewise drop their high heads and go home. Another blessing reserved for me is to be able to have their shoes blackened. Now, when a woman gets her shoes dirty she must clean them herself, if she keeps no one around who will do it. Poor, forlorn creatures, they have not the happiness of making signs of themselves. Of course there is no law to prohibit it, but "you know it is not the fashion." If it only were bootblacks would reap a harvest.

IN A SHOE SHOP

In order to know how shoes are made I visited Schmertz & Co.'s shoe factory, Ohio Street, Allegheny. While looking around "in search of a man," a pretty blonde was asked to designate the proprietor. "There she is," she answered, "over in that part of the room. See? The one leaning against the table."

This was sufficient. "Are you the manageress?" was asked of the lady designated.

"Well, yes; that is, I have the hiring of the girls," she answered looking quite kindly.

"I am not in search of a position today, merely wish to see the owner or manager."

"Very well, I will show you the way to his office." She opened a door leading into another room occupied by men. The manager said, "Certainly you may go through. We have some good-looking girls up-stairs. The only fault is they talk too much. Why, I could put six Yankee girls in there and they would do as much as 25 of those girls. You will want to know what wages they receive. Some of them go as low as $1.50 a week, where I've seen Yankee girls make $3 and $4 a day.

Taken at Her Word.

"Have you any good-looking men on the *Dispatch?*"

"Lots of them."

"Won't you speak a good word for us? Say there is a lot of pretty girls over here who are hunting husbands."

In the course of the gossip the inspectress said: "If the least scratch or blemish is made on the shoe the one who does it must pay for the

pair. Of course she has the privilege of taking them home and selling to her brother, lover or who ever will take them. It is no difference how small the blemish, it is called damaged, consequently must be paid for by the operator. It makes them very careful, but scratches are very easily made. One reason the girls do not make as much as when on ladies' shoes, is because the work does not come in steady. Sometimes we have to wait a half hour. Many such waitings reduce our wages considerably, as we all work by the piece. Last summer when we worked on ladies' shoes, we had 75 girls and were kept busy. Then we made good wages."

SHE CAN MAKE A SHOE

The forelady is well liked by all the girls. Before leaving she said: "I can tell you how to make a shoe complete from beginning to end. My father was a shoemaker, and ever since I was a tiny child I have worked at the trade. I worked with father, and have made shoes often, from the cutting out to polishing heels and soles. I can make a shoe as well as any man in the building. I have not worked at it for a good many years. When I left my father I came here. Since then I have done nothing except oversee, instruct and manage the work. The work we are doing at present is much different from the former, although those who know nothing about it would think it all the same; yet our girls, although experienced on ladies' shoes, have to learn to work on men's. That is one reason they do not make so much as before. This is a trade, you know, and must be learned. You cannot pick it up in a few days. It is hard to teach new ones; they don't know one part of the shoe from another. They sew anything together. It takes the patience of a saint and the eye of an eagle to get along here; but the girls we have understand their business, yet they have to learn to do men's work."

"Be sure and come back again," said most of the girls as we started. "Make good pictures of us;" "Say as nice things about us as you did of the others," were some of the parting words. As Rip would say, "Here's to you and your family; may you live long and prosper." That the world may always appear as bright and cheerful to you as it does to-day is the sincerest wish of

WITH THE PRISON MATRONS.
THEY TELL NELLIE BLY THAT WOMEN NEVER REFORM.

AN INTERESTING VISIT TO THE BIG CITY PRISONS AND TALKS WITH THE FEMALE KEEPERS—MATRON WEBB AND HER FOUNDLINGS—PRISONERS WHO RETURN AGAIN AND AGAIN—A FIELD BEYOND THE REACH OF CHARITY.

NELLIE BLY.

"17 years is a long time for an innocent woman to be in prison."

I answered the speaker with a sympathetic smile. I thought, as I glanced at the kindly face and the neatly dressed hair, which Time has touched with frosty fingers, what love of humanity, what patience she must possess to spend seventeen years in unceasing labor for the ill-fated outcast world. Almost everybody has streaks of charity in them, greater or less, but of all, surely the hard-worked, ill-paid prison matrons represent the truest charity. At least I believed it so, and because of that I decided to visit a few of them. Matron Webb, at Police Headquarters, whose little rooms furnish shelter for every deserted child, waited for me to continue the questioning process.

"Do you not tire of your work?" I asked at length.

"No. There is a variety in it and I have grown so accustomed to it that I should be miserable away from its cares."

"Do you only receive children here?"

"No, indeed. Very often women who are lost or homeless are brought here for a night's shelter." Then, with a smile, she continued: "I used to wonder what disguise you would come in, but I never thought I would see you as Nellie Bly."

"Tell me about yourself. How did you get this position?"

"My husband was appointed janitor when this building was first opened and I was given the position of matron. My husband has since died, but I still retain the place."

"Where are the babies brought from which you take charge of?"

"From all parts of the city. There is a law against children being kept in prison after 9 o'clock at night, so they are all sent here. We receive them at any hour. When the officers find the little deserted babies or lost children they take them to the nearest station-house, where a commitment is made out and they are brought to me. Lost children are always very dirty, and so the first thing we do is to give them a bath and put them in clean clothing, of which I keep a supply. If the foundlings are clean we put them to bed without bathing them. They make very little fuss. The foundlings find the warmth and a bottle of milk so comforting after exposure and hunger that they go to sleep in a very few moments. The lost children are so weary that after I give them food they drop off and do not wake until daylight."

THE CHILDREN TENDERLY CARED FOR.

"Do you ever have any deaths?"

"In seventeen years I have only had one child die while in my charge. Don't you think that a good record?" she asked. "But I was going to tell you about that. Some time in the night an officer brought a baby in. I took it and found that it was sleeping very nicely. It had a bottle with it, and I once determined to take the bottle away; but then, as it was so quiet, I concluded not to disturb it, so I covered it up in the crib. In a few moments another officer came in with another baby. As we were putting it in a crib he remarked that it was one of the smallest he had ever seen. 'It's not so small as the one that came in a little while ago,' I said, and we went over to the crib to see it. I pulled the covers down softly, so as not to awaken the baby, and saw at once that it was in convulsions. We rang for the ambulance, but before the doctor got here the baby was dead. We found that its milk had been poisoned. Since then I am very careful to take bottles away from foundlings the moment they come in and give them everything fresh and clean.

"You would not think," she continued, "to see the condition of the lost children that their parents ever thought of them. Some children are so filthy that we have to take their rags off the first thing and burn them."

"And they look as if they never had a bath in their lives," interposed Mrs. Webb's son.

"They do, indeed," she assented, with a laugh. "You would think their parents did not care for them, yet the dirtier the child the louder their parents wail when they find them. We had a man come in here in search of his lost child. It had not been brought in yet, so he sat here wailing and moaning until the moment it was brought in. Then he doubled down before it and shook his fist in its face and yelled, 'Just wait until I get you home!'

"There is no romance in it. I suppose we get hardened to anything. I recall one time a little girl was found and brought here. She was so filthy that I burned everything she wore. It just happened that I had nothing here which would fit her except a very bright yellow dress. It was very yellow. Evidently it was made for a child's party dress, to be worn under lace, but having nothing else I had to dress her in it. After a while an Italian came in search of a lost child. After looking around at all the children he said his child was not among them. 'How old was she?' I asked, and he replied, 'Four years'. I thought that little girl was about four, so I told him to look again. He looked with the same result.' Isn't this your child?' I asked, pointing to the one in yellow. He shook his head 'No'. Then I told him that I had changed her dress. He went over and knelt before her and only then did he recognize her, and he almost fainted. I don't think he ever saw her washed before, and as it was he only saw the bright yellow dress. Such cases are not rare. Parents often fail to recognize their children because they never saw them clean before."

NAMING THE LITTLE TOTS.

"Do you ever have any foundlings that apparently were born of wealthy parents?"

"No. As I tell you, there is little romance about it. The foundlings are always cheaply clad, with sometimes a show of cheap lace. I never have them here more than twenty-four hours, generally not a third of that time. So I do not become attached to them."

"Do they ever have names pinned to them?"

"No, and you should see how they get their names," said Matron Webb's son. "Some one comes in and says: 'Is it named yet? I'll name it,' and so they give it a name. Other times the place it was found or the time names it, such as in May a baby girl was found in a hallway and we named it 'May Hall.' Last year we had 174 foundlings. When parents abandon a baby they never want to know its fate."

"I can always tell an Italian baby from the peculiar way in which it is dressed," said Matron Webb. "A piece of linen about five inches wide and two yards long is wrapped about them from their arms down to their heels, until their bodies are rigid. I always take it off the moment they come in, for I think it must make them very uncomfortable and cramped."

"What results do you get from your work among women?" I asked of Matron Webb.

"The results are discouraging," she answered, sadly. "But yet, with the hope of some time saving one woman, I am encouraged to persevere. In my seventeen years as a matron I have never known a woman to reform or to have any gratitude for aid extended to her."

Matron Webb has made her rooms in the top floor of Police Headquarters very cozy and homelike. Her mother was a Quaker, so one can know how very neat the house is kept. In the cozy little parlor opening off a pretty little hall are many things of interest. The first thing which impresses one is Mrs. Webb's love of music. In one corner is a fine piano, in another a music-box, and in front of the pier glass, which separates the windows, is an organ-box and table combined. Mrs. Webb does not pay any rent for her rooms, as they are meant for a place for the matron as well as for her charges, who have comfortable cots and cribs and chairs in another part of the flat.

But for all her work, of which one can form but little idea, she is only paid $33 a month. Of that slender amount many a 50 cents goes to help those who have less.

"It is not the deserving poor that one ever hears of," said Matron Webb. "I know of a family who are very much reduced. The mother receives a pension—her husband was in the army during the Mexican war—of some few dollars a year—about thirty, I think. The daughter made an unfortunate marriage, and she and her one child were deserted. Both the mother and daughter are in very poor health. They make hat frames for a living. I have sent missionaries there, but they look about and they see everything clean and well-cared for, so they give no help. If they went into a house where everything was neglected and in a state of filth they would be very anxious to aid the people. Some missionaries cannot understand such things as poverty and cleanliness. I did get one wealthy old maid to visit them, and then because they were not connected with some church—and really it costs too much to go to church for poor people to indulge in it—she would not do anything for them."

THE MATRON OF THE TOMBS.

I went down to the Tombs. The passageway was crowded with people who had come to visit their friends, and I stood aside to watch them. Some had tales of misery in their faces, and some had the misery in their apparel, while their faces were hardened as if it were an old story to them. They formed in a long line. The first, a man, handed a little dirty card in the window to an officer. He looked it over, then slowly open the iron gate. The man entered and the gate was closed but the man was told to stand still. Then, with a rapidity which bespoke long experience, the officer slid his hands into the man's pocket, and in a second he knew everything the man had about him. He found something which looked to me at a distance like a knife. He handed it back to the man and pushed him out of the gate.

While this was going on I attempted to read the long list of rules for prisoners, and then I noticed a smaller black board beside it. This is what was written on it in chalk:

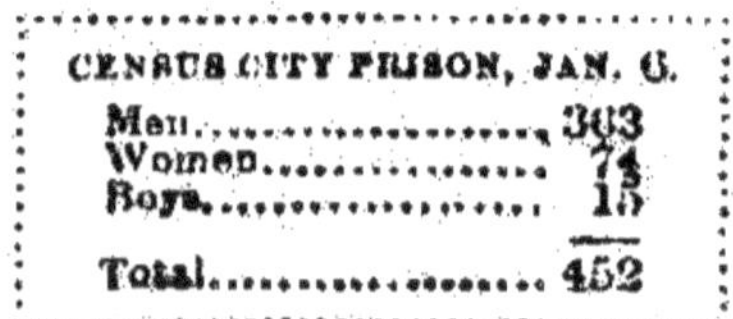

A nice old gentleman in uniform came out then. He was surrounded by a number of eager visitors, so I waited. As he started to enter the prison again, I timidly caught his coat sleeve and said:

"If you please"—

He stopped and looked around. I handed him my card of admission, which he read carefully, and then asked me to follow him. Past the long line we went and to the iron gate. There he said some magic word to the keeper and I was allowed to enter. We came to a second gate.

"Is the young lady with you?" asked the keeper.

"I have her in charge," the Deputy Warden said, smiling at me. At the next door Matron McAuliffe met us, and the old gentleman, after saying a few pleasant words, left us together.

"I have three assistants and a night matron," said Mrs. McAuliffe as she took me into the dining-room, where they have three long tables, at each of which sixteen prisoners eat, "and we change off our work each week. I have been matron twelve years. I was first at the Workhouse on the Island, and then I was transferred here. I like the work; my whole soul is in it. Of course it is very trying, but it does not get monotonous. Our hours are from 7 to 7, and by giving notice in advance we can get a day off every week."

"Are any of the prisoners ever abusive to you?"

"I have very little trouble with them. They are most always obedient to me. We feed the prisoners three times a day. Then, they can also have what their friends send them."

We walked to the door of the prison, where a colored woman and a white woman were talking through the bars to their visitors. We went inside and looked about at the poor, wretched prisoners.

"A number of these are voluntary prisoners," explained Mrs. McAuliffe. "They are unable to work, going to illness, hard times, and oftener laziness, so they come to the police courts and ask to be sent to the Workhouse for shelter."

ADVENTURESS STANTON'S VISITOR.

We had hardly reached the door when some one called out:

"A visitor for Addie Stanton. Addie Stanton."

A slender woman, wearing a light ulster, whose hair was golden on top and brown at the roots, came rushing down from the upper tier.

"Addie, you can step outside," the Matron said to her. She did so, and a handsome man, well clad and with every appearance of respectability, caught her by the hand and pressed a light kiss on her upturned lips.

"How does she conduct herself?" I asked.

"She and Ella Hammond are about the best-behaved prisoners we have. They are quiet and attend chapel every time."

"Please, ma'am, I'd like to bring the children to see their mother," a colored man said who left his wife at the gate to speak to the Matron.

"You cannot do that, because it is against the rules," the Matron answered kindly, but firmly. "The Warden objects to children being brought in here. He thinks the sight of their parents behind the bars is not a desirable thing to impress on their young minds and that the effect is hardening."

The colored man, with many a break in his voice, told his story to the Matron, and she patiently listened, expressing quiet sympathy for his misery.

"These are the same stairs that were used when the old prison was here," said Mrs. McAuliffe, as we went up the winding staircase, which had been scrubbed thoroughly. We entered a small room in which were two altars and a number of benches. "This is the chapel. We have service here on Tuesday, Wednesday, Friday and Saturday. Sunday morning the Sisters of Charity are here, and in the afternoon the chapel is devoted to the Episcopal service. Prisoners can attend or not, just as they wish. Before a prisoner is hanged if he wishes he can come to service here. Poor Danny Lyons came here the day before he was hanged. When a hanging is to take place of prisoners are very sad and quiet. It affects the whole prison. This hall back of the chapel is called 'The Magdalen'. We confine women who have received their first sentence and children to it, to keep them from coming in contact with hardened criminals. You see we have a nice stove fire and comfortable beds in the dormitory alongside. This window, which opens into the chapel, was to enable a crippled woman to hear the service. She could not get up and down stairs, so her chair was always wheeled to this window."

THEY NEVER REFORM.

"Did you ever know of any woman reforming?" I asked.

"No, I never did. I have known of hard drinkers keeping sober for several months at a time; but they can't control themselves, and a wild desire will return which brings them here again."

Out near the gate where the visitors first enter is a small whitewashed room, lighted with a single gas-jet and furnished only with a table and a chair. Here Mrs. McAuliffe introduced me to an assistant matron, Mrs. McLaughlin. She has large brown eyes and short, curly hair, and a very amiable manner.

"I was for some time a matron on Hart's Island and Blackwell's Island, and I read your experience in the Insane Asylum with pleasure," she said to me. "I always say the insane are my people, and I always get along so well with them. I would devote my life to it if I could afford to do so. We know the cruelty to the insane is dreadful, but what else can we expect? They cannot employ educated nurses for $16 a month, and the ignorant are always cruel."

"How do you like searching women?" I asked Mrs. McLaughlin.

"At first I was very much ashamed to do it, but now I don't mind it. They try sometimes to carry in drink and knives and such things. We find them in the funniest places. Sometimes they make a pocket in their stockings; often they suspend a bottle by cords from the waist. They are very new visitors who try to smuggle things in now; others know it is impossible, and they also know that if they send any reasonable thing here it is always given to the prisoners."

UNGRATEFUL FOR CHARITY.

Mrs. Byrnes, the matron at Jefferson Market, is a pretty, slender woman, who looks so girlish that one is astonished to be introduced to her son Edward, a bright, healthy lad of 12, who rushes in at noon and kisses her on the cheek. Mrs. Byrnes was educated in a Montreal convent, and is a French scholar and a musician. She made choice of this work because it is not so public as many things women have to do. Mrs. Byrnes receives the same salary as the matrons at the Tombs—$37 a month. The head matron at the Tombs, Mrs. McAuliffe, receives about $43 a month, and an old lady who was once matron, but is now past work, receives her salary as a pension, which lasts until she dies. I think this very just and considerate in the Commissioners. Mrs. Byrnes once worked at the Tombs, where she had charge of the boys. She liked that very much better than her present position, as she had some hope of good resulting from her work among the young.

"No, I do not find that very many reform," Mrs. Byrnes said. "Indeed, I cannot recall any, but I do find them grateful. Why, one woman was brought in here feverish from long dissipation. I gave her an orange, and many months after when she came back—for they always do—she recalled herself to me and thanked me for the orange. I always find them grateful for a kindness. I am watching a case now of a young woman who began drinking and ended here. She was very young, so I worked hard to get her sent to some home instead of to the Island. After I had everything arranged with the Judge and the authorities of the home she refused to go, preferring the Island. I was so disappointed that it made me sick at heart. Since then I have heard from her, and she regrets that she did not take my advice, so I am waiting until she has served her sentence to see if she reforms or goes back to her old way."

THE CURSE OF CHEAP LIQUOR.

"What is the chief cause of crime among women?" I asked.

"Cheap drink, undoubtedly. These women often tell me that they can get trust for all the drink they want at saloons. If drink was not so cheap the police courts would not have so much to do. It leads to everything else. After these women serve a sentence for being drunk they go out, and probably the next day will find them in again. Why? Well, they say they need something to brace them, and they brace too much. I look on these women as diseased. They really cannot help themselves. The ones I have no patience with are the lazy women who commit themselves in preference to working. I think a young, healthy woman who would rather go to the Island than to work cannot receive too severe a sentence."

Mrs. Stack, who is matron at the Essex Market Prison, has the most uncomfortable place of all. She has only one little corner at the foot of the iron stairs which lead to the upper tiers for herself. The prison is damp, dark and cold. The only heat which comes from the furnace beneath is so filled with gas that the inmates find freezing preferable to it. Mrs. Stack, who has been a helping friend to the unfortunate for eleven years, has some very good ideas of what the weak as well as the wicked need. It was 5 o'clock, the hour they serve supper, when I visited Essex Market Prison. One dim gas jet flickered faintly in the corridor, and a number of wretched women sat on some benches against the whitewashed wall. One woman on the end, who still wore her shabby bonnet and shawl, was sobbing bitterly. She had been arrested while going to her dressmaker's the night before, she said, but the officer had told a different story. She was an old offender, so the officer was believed, and she was sent to jail. A number of the other

women were listening intently to the story of a young girl who alternately stood and kneeled before them. She said that she was not yet sixteen, but she was tall and as slender as a stalk of wheat. Her dress and shoes were cheap, and her bustle had the pointed shape so usual to badly clad women. A strange story she told.

That morning she had left her home to go to the type-foundry where she was employed. On the way she met a "young gent" whom she knew, and he took her in some place and gave her drugged whiskey. How did she know it was drugged? Because as soon as he left her she went into a nearby store and stole a clock.

Two men came in carrying a large boiler, which they placed at the end of the table. Mrs. Stack went down and served the tea from the boiler to the prisoners. Each prisoner had a large tin pan and was given as much bread and tea as she wanted. An old woman came out of a cell way down the corridor. She hobbled to a bench, but made no move to approach the table.

"What is she?" I asked, rather vaguely.

"She is seventy-six years old and bound for the Almshouse," replied to the matron, "the result of a misspent life."

After dinner the women were all appointed to their cells, the young girl marching with them as proudly as if she were a model of goodness. Then they were locked in and Mrs. Stack returned to me.

THE SYSTEM OF PUNISHMENT OF FAILURE.

"Drink is the root of all evil," she said. "Every crime, every wrong deed is the result of drink. And sending women to the Island does more to promote evil than anything else. No woman who serves time on the Island ever reforms. We have one woman here to-day who left the Island yesterday at 10 o'clock after serving a six months' term. Some of the keepers gave her 20 cents to pay her carfare into town. Instead of that she went into the first saloon, and at 4 o'clock we had her back again. Now she has another term to serve."

"Good night, Mrs. Stack, I am going," said a woman coming from one of the cells. "Won't you wish me luck?"

"I do," replied the matron, "and here is enough money to pay your carfare." And with a few kindly wishes she let the woman out and locked the door.

"Now, you see there is a woman who has served her sentence. She is going out at night, homeless and penniless. What is there for her to do? Who will take her in or trust her? A few days will bring her back, because there is nothing else for her."

"What of those Homes?"

"They are filled already with women who have not served time. If, instead of the Island, they had a place for women where they could, while serving time, be taught to work, and for good work and conduct receive 50 cents a month, when their time was up they would have enough to support them until they could find work, and while there they would have learned to do something. If arrested on the same complaint a second time they should get, instead of a few months, a year. Make the punishment severe for a third failing. The Island makes women worse instead of better, so what is the use of sending them there? It neither punishes them nor reforms them, so it is a failure."

I bade her and the Warden, who has served forty years at this one post, good-by and went out into the night sick at the sight of misery and discouraged at the idea of reform.

NELLIE BLY.

CHARITY GIRL

NEW YORK, NY
SATURDAY, OCTOBER 29, 1887

"I'M GOING TO BE A published author!"

I said this aloud to my empty apartment, so there was no one to hear my exciting news. I had just signed the lease, and had barely a stick of furniture. That didn't trouble me—eager as I was to outfit my new home in New York City, I didn't want to buy anything that was less than perfect. Having pinched pennies since the age of six, I knew better than to play the drunk when flush. *You never know when disaster will strike.*

In fact, disaster had struck almost exactly a month earlier. On the twenty-second of September my bag had been stolen, and it contained nearly one hundred dollars: all the money I had in the world. I couldn't even afford to pay the rent on my shabby little furnished room uptown.

However, the experience made me realize something about myself: crisis brought out the best in me. When pushed to the brink, I could be devilishly resourceful. That night I borrowed enough money to take me downtown to Newspaper Row and marched into the offices of Joseph Pulitzer's *New York World* and pitched them a story.

They didn't buy it.

Yet Pulitzer's prize editor, Colonel Cockerill, was impressed by my pluck and gumption, and he suggested a different story: getting myself incarcerated in the Woman's Lunatic Asylum on Blackwell's Island to expose the goings-on there. At the time, I had no idea it was a repeat of a stunt performed a decade earlier by a man. All I knew was that it was a chance to prove myself—while also peeling back the curtain on misdeeds against women. So I played shatterpated and got myself committed.

I'd emerged three weeks ago—*Was it only three weeks?*—with a story that had made my moniker a household name. Well, not my *actual* moniker. No one knew who Elizabeth Cochrane was. But everyone knew the name

Nellie Bly.

Which was how I ended up with the letter in my hand. It was from the publisher Norman L. Munro, offering me more money than I could have hitherto imagined for the rights to publish my story from the madhouse: a whopping five hundred dollars! Considering that I had started off at five dollars a week, and had made only twenty-five dollars for the madhouse exposé, it was a small fortune.

Hence my new, if empty, apartment on West Seventy-Fourth Street. Compared to the furnished room I'd occupied all summer, it was a palace: six large rooms with a private hall, a bathroom with a tub, and a kitchen with a range. There was a common freight elevator in the building for groceries, and a janitor's service was included. The rooms were outfitted with gas chandeliers, steam heat, and fairly decent woodwork. I even liked the wallpaper. All for twenty-two dollars a month—a steal.

And I wouldn't be alone for long. Even before the book deal, I had sent to Pittsburgh and asked—well, told—my mother to sell her house and come live with me. I did it partly out of duty, partly as repayment for all the trouble I'd caused her over the years, and partly because we had been good companions during my months reporting in Mexico.

There was another, less worthy reason as well: I wanted to show up my brothers.

Of my four siblings, the oldest two were both married and employed. But Charlie had remained at Mother's house even after his wife had produced a bundle of joy. And Albert, the eldest of us all—and Mother's favorite—now lived in a fine house of his own in Pittsburgh, yet he hadn't invited our twice-widowed, once-divorced mother to live with him. No, *I* had done that. In New York, no less. Me, the troublemaker. Me, the heck-raiser. Me, the one Albert considered undignified and incapable.

It was petty of me, but it felt so good to throw my money and success in their faces.

However, if I really wanted to show up my brothers and impress my detractors—of whom I had many—I needed to continue making my name. Knowing enough to strike while the iron was hot, I had been on the lookout for another story just as good as Blackwell's Island. I had to keep producing unique pieces for the *World*. Every Sunday that Nellie Bly had her name in print was a victory.

My male colleagues resented my sudden success, which seemed to have struck from out of the clear sky. Few of them rated a byline, and they all thought I got mine simply because putting a woman's name above a story gave it the level of sensationalism that Colonel Cockerill prized.

While I understood their resentment, I dismissed it. They had enjoyed their exclusive "no girls allowed" clubhouse for long enough. They could open the doors to admit just one lone girl. *If they don't like it, well, they can lump it. Nellie Bly isn't going anywhere but up.*

To do that, however, I had to find another story.

I'd gotten some initial inspiration from a passing comment by the *World's* lawyer. His tip led me to stint of impersonating a woman in search of work to expose the underhanded practices of New York's employment agencies. These swindlers fleeced women by demanding money in exchange for empty promises to find them placement. It wasn't as exciting as my stay in the asylum, but it made for a good story, and it fit all of Cockerill's criteria: it was titillatingly sensational, it had a strong moral component, and—most important—it was exclusive. The piece would run in the *World* tomorrow.

But today, I thought, I need to figure out what to write about next. And it needs to be big.

Fortunately, I got help from the *World's* readers.

I hadn't known what kind of letters to expect after the Blackwell's Island exposé. Praise, I'd hoped. And, yes, there had been laudatory notes from all quarters: doctors, housewives, bricklayers, even a circuit court judge! My favorite was the one that extolled me for giving those madhouse quacks "such a magnificent black eye with such a tiny fist."

On the other hand, there had been many letters condemning me for thinking I knew better than the doctors and nurses, and even some claiming I actually *was* mad and deserved to be locked up for the rest of my life. Though I'd tried to laugh those off, they lingered in my mind far longer than the praise.

However, by a fair distance the majority of the response had consisted of letters telling me where I should investigate next. Within days I'd collected a catalog of outrages that would make a normal girl take to her bed in a faint. Whereas I found them to be full of exciting possibilities. *What does that say about me?* I wondered as I flipped through my stack of recent correspondence.

Amid all the swindles and scandals, one story leapt out to sock me right in the chin. Instantly, I knew what outrage I would be swinging at next.

Babies. Specifically, unwanted babies.

The typewritten letter read:

> *Dear Miss Bly,*
>
> *I have followed your work since the days of your journeys to Mexico, and read with heartfelt sorrow of the plight of the natives of that magnificent but misgoverned country. It was with mingled delight and dismay that I learned of your arrival in New York through your articles on the misdeeds on Blackwell's Island. Delight, that such a smart,*

insightful girl reporter was present in this metropolis; dismay, that you had to undergo such an ordeal. It is my fervent hope that you never again place yourself in such a dangerous predicament. Please count me among your admirers.

I am writing because I would like to know what becomes of unwanted infants in this city. Without giving details which such a talented reporter as yourself could easily use to identify me, allow me to say that I am a well-off man who, through my church, recently became aware of an unmarried girl who was with child. It was my intention, with the aid of our pastor, to assist the fallen female in a Christian way. We discussed with her the various institutions available to assist her and her expected child. But just as she approached her joyful day she disappeared from our church. Not much later I saw her on the street. As she was clearly no longer bearing, I, meaning nothing but well, congratulated her on her deliverance. First she pretended not to know me. Then she pretended she had never been pregnant at all. At last she said she gave her son away and, cursing me, departed from my sight.

I do not want to invade her privacy, so I will not presume to offer up her name, which is likely an alias. Yet since that chance encounter I have been unable to sleep, worrying about that newborn child. Is he still alive? Where could she have taken him? And how many more children like him are given up each day in this massive city? What becomes of them? Where is it best to donate money? I have asked at my church, and they advise me to give to them. But I am moved to give funds where they are put to the best use. After all, as they say, I cannot take it with me.

I also worry of extralegal means. My wife called on a Mrs. Gray who advertises manicures and vapor baths. She was horrified to discover the house full of new mothers and their babes, and she had the worst feeling that the infants were not there to be cared for.

She was too frightened by her experience there to ask any more questions. We discussed it and decided I should write to you. If there is any fearless ferreter of truth in our Gotham, it is Nellie Bly.

Would you consider looking into the plight of unwanted infants in New York? I can think of no one better suited to the task.

Pitying Philanthropist

My initial reaction to the letter was outrage, naturally. My second was suspicion. *Does he have an ulterior motive?* Yet the writer seemed sincere. He wasn't after this particular woman or seeking her child, which had been my first concern. In fact, I was surprised a man had written this letter—which I recognized as a troubling statement on my opinion of the average male.

Whoever it was that had written, they traveled in wealthy circles. Only the best homes and businesses had typewriters. There had been only two at the *Pittsburg Dispatch,* and even at the World there weren't more than a dozen. Mr. Pulitzer claimed he wasn't yet convinced of their longevity, but Cockerill had privately confided the real reason to me: Pulitzer was subject to terrible headaches. It was bad enough when the presses were running, but the clacking keys and ringing returns drove him from his office in an agonized state. So Mr. Pulitzer preferred that his reporters use their Blackwing pencils.

Returning to the letter, I considered the subject matter. I had certainly heard of girls who became pregnant and disappeared, only to return without their child. I wondered how much happier my own sister might be if she were not a mother. Things were not looking well for her marriage. What if their relationship had soured before the birth of Beatrice? Where would Kate have gone?

To Mother, of course. And the family would have seen her through, as we would do if someday she left her louse of a spouse. But what about the girls who couldn't go to their mothers? What about the girls who hadn't married first, but had "fallen" for a man? I certainly knew enough of those. I thought of Ada, probably still toiling away in the smelly cigar factory, letting her hair down at the end of the day to pick up men on the streetcar in order to gain a dinner.

I felt a pang of guilt. I had built the foundations of my career thanks to Ada, and how long had it been since I'd thought about her? Too long. *I am not a good person.*

Whereas the writer of this letter certainly *was* a good person. He seemed genuinely interested in helping—though it did not escape me that it wasn't the women he wanted to help, but rather the children. Because women who gave up their children were abominable, of course. Inhuman. Unnatural. Not worth caring for.

Still, it was a good cause. Better still, it was a good story. And it had a sharp "hook." I had landed a honey with the madhouse, and while I was under no illusion that they would all be such smash sensations, this one felt like it had the potential to build on the legend of Nellie Bly, Crusader for Social Justice. If I did it right, it might just keep my name in the papers and prevent the Colonel and Mr. Pulitzer from thinking my success to be a flash in the pan.

So where do I begin?

CHARITY GIRL
On Sale Now From Sordelet Ink

THE MYSTERY OF CENTRAL PARK

A rejected marriage proposal and the corpse of a dead beauty confound Dick Treadwell's hopes for happiness, until his beloved Penelope sets him a task: she will marry him if he solves— *the Mystery of Central Park!*

EVA, THE ADVENTURESS

Nellie Bly's ripped-from-the-headlines novel of a poor girl determined to revenge herself upon the world, only to find that, in the battle between love and revenge, only one can triumph.

NEW YORK BY NIGHT

Setting out to solve the bold diamond robbery, millionaire detective Lionel Dangerfield finds himself in competition with Ruby Sharpe, daring young reporter for the *New York Planet*. Will "The Danger" solve the case before Ruby can steal the story—and his heart?

ALTA LYNN, M.D.

A prank goes awry and Alta Lynn finds herself wed against her will. Leaving love behind, she throws herself into the study of medicine, only to find that love has other plans for her!

WAYNE'S FAITHFUL SWEETHEART

Beautiful Dorette Lover is rescued from poverty when she finds work as an artist's model. That same day she witnesses a seeming murder. To protect the man accused, she agrees to become his bride—only to fall desperately in love with him!

LITTLE LUCKIE

Luckie Thurlow longs to be accepted by society and gain the heart of the man she loves. But she harbors a dark secret—she is the daughter of the murderous Gypsy Queen, who plans to use Luckie to gain her own revenge!

IN LOVE WITH A STRANGER

Kit Clarendon is in love! Trouble is, she doesn't know her love's name. But she is determined to track him down and force him to love her! A wild pursuit filled with disguises, desperate deeds, and declarations of love as Kit determines to go through fire and water to win him!

THE LOVE OF THREE GIRLS

An heiress in disguise, a factory girl with dreams of wealth, and a sweet child of charity are forced into rivalry when they all fall in love with the same man! Murder, fever, fallen women, and a desperate villain conspire against— *the love of three girls!*

LITTLE PENNY

Little Penny Pendleton, child of the streets, is taken in by a kindly man and given a home. But when he is wrongly accused of murder, Penny must use her wits to clear his name, even if it means betraying the man she loves!

PRETTY MERRIBELLE

Trapped in a burning factory, pretty Merribelle's life is saved—but not her memory! A bizarre tale of amnesia, desperate love, and an even more desperate villain determined to use Merribelle to ruin his rival and achieve an inheritance worth millions!

TWINS AND RIVALS

Dimple and Della may be twins, but they have differing views on love. Dimple sees love as a contract, and marries for wealth to support her family, while Della longs to marry for love. The sisters collide when Dimple falls in love with Della's betrothed, turning them into rivals!

THE LOST NOVELS OF NELLIE BLY

ON SALE NOW FROM

SORDELET INK

WWW.SORDELETINK.COM

INTO THE MADHOUSE

Never before collected! "Who is this insane girl?" asked other papers, completely taken in by Nellie Bly's plan to infiltrate Blackwell's Island. The complete reporting surrounding her daring expose, including details not included in her initial accounts and her scathing rebuttal of the doctors' excuses!

NELLIE BLY'S WORLD - Vol. 1
1887-1888

Bly's complete reporting, collected for the very first time! Starting with the stunt that made hers a household name, Nellie Bly spends her first year at the New York World going undercover to expose frauds, sharpsters and boodlers, interviewing Belva Lockwood and Hangman Joe, and tackling Phelps the Lobbyist!

NELLIE BLY'S WORLD - Vol. 2
1889-1890

Bly's complete reporting, collected for the very first time! Nellie buys a baby, has herself followed by a detective and arrested, interviews Helen Keller, champion boxer John Sullivan, and convicted would-be killer Eva Hamilton, all before setting out on her greatest stunt of all, a race around the world!

COMING SOON:

NELLIE BLY'S WORLD, Vol. 3 & 4
NELLIE BLY'S DISPATCHES, Vol. 1 & 2
NELLIE BLY'S JOURNALS, Vol. 1 & 2

ALL FROM SORDELET INK

ABOUT NELLIE BLY

Nellie Bly was born Elizabeth "Pink" Cochran. Her father, a man of considerable wealth, served for many years as judge of Armstrong County, Pennsylvania. He lived on a large estate called Cochran's Mills, which took its name from him.

Being in reduced circumstances after her father's death, her mother remarried, only to divorce Jack Ford a few years later. The family then moved to Pittsburg, where a twenty-year-old Pink read a column in the *Pittsburg Dispatch* entitled "What Girls Are Good For." Enraged at the sexist and classist tone, she wrote a furious letter to the editor. Impressed, the editor engaged her to do special work for the newspaper as a reporter, writing under the name "Nellie Bly." Her first series of stories, "Our Workshop Girls," brought life and sympathy to working women in Pittsburgh.

A year later she went as a correspondent to Mexico, where she remained six months, sending back weekly articles. After her return she longed for broader fields, and so moved to New York. The story of her attempt to make a place for herself, or to find an opening, was a long one of disappointment, until at last she gained the attention of the *New York World*.

Her first achievement for them was the exposure of the Blackwell's Island Insane Asylum, in which she spent ten days, and two days in the Bellevue Insane Asylum. The story created a great sensation, making "Nellie Bly" a household name.

After three years of doing work as a "stunt girl" at the *World*, Bly conceived the idea of making a trip around the world in less time than had been done by Phileas Fogg, the fictitious hero of Jules Verne's famous novel. In fact, she made it in 72 days. On her return in January 1890 she was greeted by ovations all the way from San Francisco to New York.

She then paused her reporting career to write novels, but returned to the *World* three years later. In 1895 she married millionaire industrialist Robert Seaman, and a couple years later retired from journalism to take an interest in his factories.

She returned to journalism almost twenty years later, reporting on World War I from behind the Austrian lines. Upon returning to New York, she spent the last years of her life doing both reporting and charity work, finding homes for orphans. She died of pneumonia in 1922.

BOOKS BY NELLIE BLY

JOURNALISM

TEN DAYS IN A MAD-HOUSE

SIX MONTHS IN MEXICO

NELLIE BLY'S BOOK: AROUND THE WORLD IN 72 DAYS

NOVELS

THE MYSTERY OF CENTRAL PARK

EVA THE ADVENTURESS

NEW YORK BY NIGHT

ALTA LYNN, M.D.

WAYNE'S FAITHFUL SWEETHEART

LITTLE LUCKIE

DOLLY THE COQUETTE

IN LOVE WITH A STRANGER

THE LOVE OF THREE GIRLS

LITTLE PENNY, CHILD OF THE STREETS

PRETTY MERRIBELLE

TWINS AND RIVALS

ABOUT DAVID BLIXT

David Blixt is an author and actor living in Chicago. An Artistic Associate of the Michigan Shakespeare Festival, where he serves as the resident Fight Director, he is also co-founder of A Crew Of Patches Theatre Company, a Shakespearean repertory based in Chicago. He has acted and done fight work for the Goodman Theatre, Chicago Shakespeare Theatre, Steppenwolf, the Shakespeare Theatre of Washington DC, and First Folio Shakespeare, among many others.

As a writer, his STAR-CROSS'D series of novels place the characters of Shakespeare's Italian plays in their historical setting, drawing in figures such as Dante, Giotto, and Petrarch to create an epic of warfare, ingrigue, and romance. In HER MAJESTY'S WILL, Shakespeare himself becomes a character as Blixt explores Shakespeare's "Lost Years," teaming the young Will with the dark and devious Kit Marlowe to hilarious effect. In the COLOSSUS series, Blixt brings first century Rome and Judea to life as he relates the fall of Jerusalem, the building of the Colosseum, and the coming of Christianity to Rome. And in his bestselling NELLIE BLY series, he explores the amazing life and adventures of America's premier undercover reporter.

David continues to write, act, and travel. He has ridden camels around the pyramids at Giza, been thrown out of the Vatican Museum and been blessed by John-Paul II, scaled the Roman ramp at Masada, crashed a hot-air balloon, leapt from cliffs on small Greek islands, dined with Counts and criminals, climbed to the top of Mount Sinai, and sat in the Prince's chair in Verona's palace. But David is happiest at his desk, weaving tales of brilliant people in dire and dramatic straits. Living with his wife and two children, David describes himself as "actor, author, father, husband - in reverse order."

WWW.DAVIDBLIXT.COM

WHAT GIRLS ARE GOOD FOR
A NOVEL OF NELLIE BLY

Nellie Bly has the story of a lifetime. But will she survive to tell it?

Based on the real-life events of the tiny Pennsylvania spitfire who refused to let the world change her, and changed the world instead.

CHARITY GIRL
A NELLIE BLY NOVELETTE

Fresh from her escape from Blackwell's Island, Nellie Bly investigates the doctors who buy and sell babies in Victorian New York. Based on real events and her own reporting, Nellie Bly asks the devastating question—what becomes of babies?

CLEVER GIRL
A NELLIE BLY NOVELLA

A blizzard has frozen all of New York, and Nellie Bly is going stir-crazy when she and Colonel Cockerill plot out her most daring undercover assignment yet: she's going to trap the most crooked man in politics, Edward R. Phelps, the self-styled "King" of the Albany lobby.

COMING SOON:

STUNT GIRL

A NOVEL OF NELLIE BLY

BY DAVID BLIXT

Books by David Blixt

Nellie Bly
What Girls Are Good For
Charity Girl
Clever Girl

The Star-Cross'd Series
The Master Of Verona
Voice Of The Falconer
Fortune's Fool
The Prince's Doom
Varnish'd Faces: Star-Cross'd Short Stories

Will & Kit
Her Majesty's Will

The Colossus Series
Colossus: Stone & Steel
Colossus: The Four Emperors

Eve of Ides - a play

NON-FICTION
Shakespeare's Secrets: Romeo & Juliet
Tomorrow, and Tomorrow: Essays on Macbeth
Fighting Words

MORE FROM SORDELET INK

PLAYSCRIPTS

ACTION MOVIE - THE PLAY BY JOE FOUST AND RICHARD RAGSDALE

ALL CHILDISH THINGS BY JOSEPH ZETTELMAIER

CAPTAIN BLOOD ADAPTED BY DAVID RICE

THE COUNT OF MONTE CRISTO ADAPTED BY CHRISTOPHER M WALSH

DEAD MAN'S SHOES BY JOSEPH ZETTELMAIER

THE DECADE DANCE BY JOSEPH ZETTELMAIER

EBENEZER: A CHRISTMAS PLAY BY JOSEPH ZETTELMAIER

EVE OF IDES - A PLAY BY DAVID BLIXT

FRANKENSTEIN ADAPTED BY ROBERT KAUZLARIC

THE GRAVEDIGGER: A FRANKENSTEIN PLAY BY JOSEPH ZETTELMAIER

HATFIELD & McCOY BY SHAWN PFAUTSCH

HER MAJESTY'S WILL ADAPTED BY ROBERT KAUZLARIC

IT CAME FROM MARS BY JOSEPH ZETTELMAIER

THE LEAGUE OF AWESOME BY CORRBETTE PASKO AND SARA SEVIGNY

THE MOONSTONE ADAPTED BY ROBERT KAUZLARIC

NORTHERN AGGRESSION BY JOSEPH ZETTELMAIER

ONCE A PONZI TIME BY JOE FOUST

THE RENAISSANCE MAN BY JOSEPH ZETTELMAIER

THE SCULLERY MAID BY JOSEPH ZETTELMAIER

ANTON CHEKHOV'S THE SEAGULL ADAPTED BY JANICE L BLIXT

SEASON ON THE LINE BY SHAWN PFAUTSCH

STAGE FRIGHT: A HORROR ANTHOLOGY BY JOSEPH ZETTELMAIER

A TALE OF TWO CITIES ADAPTED BY CHRISTOPHER M WALSH

WILLIAMSTON ANTHOLOGY: VOLUME 1

WILLIAMSTON ANTHOLOGY: VOLUME 2

WWW.SORDELETINK.COM

Nellie Bly